The

WARS

of the

GREEN BERETS

The
WARS
of the
GREEN BERETS

Amazing Stories from Vietnam to the Present

ROBIN MOORE and MICHAEL LENNON

FOREWORD BY SCOTT NEIL

Skyhorse Publishing

Skyhorse Publishing books may be purchased in bulk at special discounts for
sales promotion, corporate gifts, fund-raising, or educational purposes. Special
editions can also be created to specifications. For details, contact the Special Sales
Department, Skyhorse Publishing, 307 West 36th Street, 11th Floor, New York,
NY 10018 or info@skyhorsepublishing.com.

Skyhorse® and Skyhorse Publishing® are registered trademarks of Skyhorse
Publishing, Inc.®, a Delaware corporation.

Visit our website at www.skyhorsepublishing.com.

10 9 8 7 6 5 4 3 2 1

Library of Congress Cataloging-in-Publication Data is available on file.

Cover design by Laura Klynstra
Cover photo credit: Thinkstock

ISBN: 978-1-63450-416-4
Ebook ISBN: 978-1-5107-0145-8

Printed in the United States of America

The military man learns early to bury his friends, and to move on. Men have traditionally sought danger in the military, and have traditionally found it. Servicemen are always in motion, in the air at more than the speed of sound, underwater at depths whales could only dream of, or on the surface of the water cruising at thirty miles per hour through crashing seas with another ship almost touching theirs, hoses connecting them like weird sex, replenishing their oil supplies. Or they are on the ground, in the dirt, training and testing weapons that may someday kill others but today may deal them that same irony. The smallest margin of error separates a live man from a dead one, even in the boring vacuum of peace. And in war, of course, they are the first and usually the only ones to pay. The president and the congress may suffer bad-news stories and ulcers and hemorrhoids. The military man suffers the death of his friends, early and often.

—James Webb, *A Sense of Honor*

CONTENTS

Foreword

The Wars of the Green Berets captures the essence of the heroism and valor of the small group of men who risk everything for the love of their country and teammates and the pride of being the best of the best—Green Berets. *The Wars of the Green Berets* is a collection of little-known actions deep behind lines and on the edges of war that most Americans have never heard about nor would never know if they weren't told in this collection.

I had the pleasure of meeting Robin Moore in 2002 at a private house party near Clarksville, Tennessee. I had just returned from my first deployment into Afghanistan following the tragic events of 9/11. Green Berets from 5th Special Forces Group, known as the "Legion," were the first responders to this national crisis, and small teams of Green Berets had done in less than ninety days what the Russian Army could not do in twelve years, and what still faces the coalition forces fighting today—depose an oppressive regime that had been harboring Osama Bin Laden and his terrorist organization.

Fifth Special Forces Group and the local community were welcoming home the teams, and everyone was anxious to get back home and share their experiences with each other. Due to security and OPSEC reasons, in case anyone was captured or compromised, each team operated autonomously and had no idea what actions and activities other teams had conducted. Robin sat with all of us and shared his own personal stories of his time in Vietnam with the Green Berets and ultimately the writing of his 1965 book, *The Green Berets*. That book, as well as the movie starring John Wayne it was adapted into, is what had inspired not only me as a young man to join the Regiment but almost every other Green Beret I know. Green Berets felt comfortable telling Robin their stories, as we felt he understood the courage and commitment of the Green Berets and would be conscious of protecting our tactics and most importantly our identities as we continued to operate against our nation's enemies.

The Regiment lost a great friend and lifelong member of 5th Special Forces Group when Robin Moore passed in 2008. I had the honor and privilege of attending his service and watched as all levels of the Special Forces Command down to the newest Green Beret paid tribute to a great man and author. Robin

Moore's legacy and contributions to the Green Berets still inspires the next generation of Green Berets and will continue well into future generations.

The Wars of the Green Berets is a tribute to the legacy of Robin Moore and told in such a way that honors the Regiment and protects the sensitivity of the men and missions. Green Berets are not about talking about ourselves; our stories are about the team and the sacrifices, the cunning and courage, and the mindset that has served the country since our first inception in 1952 and President John F. Kennedy's remarks that, "the Green Beret was a mark of distinction in the fight for freedom!" Green Berets are known as Quiet Professionals and are still fighting on America's frontiers and are deployed in over fifty-five countries and in every combat zone, known and unknown, at any one time. Since 9/11, Green Berets have suffered more casualties than any other Special Operations Unit and they remain America's first responders, often already inserted into trouble spots and working quietly before conventional forces deploy.

Scott Neil
Green Beret (ret.)

Preface

This is a story of the men of the United States Army Special Forces: the "Quiet Professionals." These shadow warriors neither get, nor generally want, a great deal of publicity due to the highly secretive nature of their work. They often operate behind enemy lines, making things happen without a sound. Only when they have spectacular success, as in Afghanistan and Iraq, or mass casualties, as in Somalia, do they receive press coverage. This sometimes works to their disadvantage at budget time. Special Operations Forces (SOF) account for less than 2 percent of the total Department of Defense budget; a single piece of military hardware often costs more than it takes to run a Special Forces Group for years. The difficult, often dangerous work they do usually goes unheralded and the public is rarely cognizant of the enormous debt of gratitude they owe these special warriors for protecting their freedom. Afghanistan brought to the forefront the capabilities of the Special Operations soldier, yet it wasn't without cost. Many Special Operations soldiers were killed and wounded in Afghanistan. There was a high price to pay at home as well, especially among the families of these warriors.

Michael Lennon has been fortunate enough to spend most of his career in Special Operations, almost all of it as a staff officer, although he has very fond memories of his time in the field with the ODAs (Operational Detachment Alpha—the "A" Teams) as a team member and commander. He was also fortunate enough to work at the company, battalion, and group level, as well as assignments at the SOF higher headquarters, and United States Army Special Operations Command (USASOC), and the joint command, and United States Special Operations Command (USSOCOM). As a third generation US Army officer, he aspired to be the best. He remembers sitting in the barracks as a freshman cadet at Pennsylvania Military College (PMC), listening to Douglas MacArthur's "Duty, Honor, Country" speech (Farewell to West Point), and later watching John Wayne in *The Green Berets*. This was pretty heady stuff for an impressionable eighteen-year-old. The story we tell here has been rattling around in our heads for a long time. It is a tribute to the men, especially the noncommissioned officers (NCOs), who *are* the United States Army Special Forces.

Because it is a historical novel, it is based on true events, although in some cases we have altered the names, the details of some incidents, and the units to ensure security and privacy in much the same way as the original version of *The Green Berets*, published in 1965. To describe publicly known events we've used open-source documents and our own recollections, no classified material has been compromised by this work.

—*Robin Moore* and *Mike Lennon*

Prologue

Darkness swirled around the flickering firelight as the men squatted like Bedouins in the dust. The fire was banked against the wall of the roofless mud hut, with a blanket angled down to keep the fire from reflecting off the opposite wall. It was as much for light as to lessen the biting cold that knifed through even the thickest wool. The hut was in the high snowy pass above the valley that was the Hindu Kush. The air was very thin at this altitude, with slightly more than two-thirds of the oxygen available at sea level.

They were big men, bigger than most Central Asians, with fierce eyes and wild, full beards and dirty scarves falling down over their long Afghan coats. Their features were more Occidental than Asian, these descendants of Alexander's Greek warriors who swept across Afghanistan more than two millennia before, leaving their genes to be passed on from generation to generation in this isolated wilderness. They wore thin cotton *shalwar kameez* shirts, pants under their coats, and flat *pakol* hats on their unkempt heads. A couple of them wore comical looking "bear suits"—long fuzzy underwear used by US troops a decade before. Unlike their forefathers who carried *jezails*, the long flintlock rifles favored by Afghan soldiers for centuries, these fighters carried a variety of assault rifles from SKS carbines and AK-47s to newer AK-74, which fired a 5.45 mm bullet with greater accuracy, velocity, and killing power than the 47. A few had the SOPMOD M4, the most advanced weapon found in the American arsenal. They had dark complexions, made more so by exposure to the sun, except for one. The soldier drawing in the dust had a head covered with shocking red hair and beard and piercing blue eyes. He looked up at the biggest and fiercest of the men gathered around the crude sand table drawn in the dust.

"What do you think, captain?" asked Chief Warrant Officer (CW2) Ryan Gallagher in English.

"I'm worried about those mortars. We're really channelized going through the pass; are they sure we can get through before they can open up?"

The chief had memorized the Intel reports. The enemy, mostly Chechen and Arab al-Qaeda, had nothing to lose and nowhere to go. The various courses of action (COA) developed by the Intel weenies were not reassuring. They would run, fighting a rear-guard action, or stay and die, taking as many of the Americans and their Northern Alliance Afghans as they could. With most of the passes into Pakistan cut off by a variety of coalition and conventional US forces, it looked to Gallagher like they would stand and fight. The Intel reports showed that a formidable stockpile of arms and tremendous firepower were awaiting them. And mines. There were mines everywhere. By some estimates there may have been as many as 30 million mines planted in Afghanistan during the last twenty-five years.

Then there was the US Air Force. While it was true that the air force tactical air controllers (TAC-Ps) could call death and destruction down on the enemy in close air support (CAS) with frightening accuracy from the over-flying fast movers and AC-130 gunships, they were also the source of many of the US and Afghan friendly fire casualties. They tried to do everything to prevent this fratricide, from maddeningly slow vetting procedures to reflective tape, VS-17 panels and radio beacons carried by the teams, but it still happened. It was an inevitable consequence in the fog of war, shattering to those responsible, devastating to the comrades and the families of the dead and wounded.

The captain had been reading his mind. "Are all the vehicles marked properly?" he asked Master Sergeant (MSG) Mike Apin.

"Yeah, I personally checked them. Let's hope the Airborne and 10th Mountain troops know who we are," he replied. Apin was the team sergeant and known to the Afghans as "Grey Beard."

The captain looked at one of the others and barked in Pashtun, "Wahid, does everyone understand the plan?"

The big Afghan grinned in a most cruel manner; it was the same grin that haunted the nightmares of so many former Soviet soldiers. "Ready, Captain! We will be victorious."

"*Insh'Allah!*"—if Allah wills it—said Captain Charles Rogers. "Let's saddle up."

As Tiger 501 moved down into the narrow valley, the world suddenly exploded.

BOOK ONE

VIETNAM, 1970

He which hath no stomach to this fight,
Let him depart; his passport shall be made,
And crowns for convoy put into his purse:
We would not die in that man's company
That fears his fellowship to die with us . . .
He that shall live this day, and see old age . . .
We few, we happy few, we band of brothers;
For he to-day that sheds his blood with me
Shall be my brother; be he ne'er so vile . . .

—William Shakespeare, *Henry V*

CHAPTER 1

To pour money, material, and men into the jungles of Indochina without at least
a remote prospect of victory would be dangerously futile and self-destructive.

—John Fitzgerald Kennedy
April 6, 1954 speech

Like most seventeen-year-olds, Mike Apin was consumed with his transition
from the adolescent to the adult world, and in 1968 he paid scant attention
to the growing conflict in Southeast Asia. His world revolved around a neat,
manicured middle-class neighborhood in a suburb of Washington, DC. Football, baseball, basketball, beer (when they could get it), and girls (not necessarily
in that order) commanded much of his attention. Mike drove a blue 1965 Mus-
tang that his father had bought him, and he loved that car. With a 289 high
performance engine and a Holly 4-barrel carburetor, he could really haul ass.

Friday and Saturday nights usually started at a party or the drive-in, and
ended at the McDonald's in Forest Heights, Maryland. In those days, there were
no indoor seats at McDonald's (300,000 hamburgers sold) so you got your food
and ate in your car. The local cop, "One Bullet Barney" as they called him, was
usually around to enforce the no-loitering rule so singles and couples hopped
from car to car to socialize. Mike had a cute girlfriend, one of the junior varsity
cheerleaders, and was a regular with several loose social groups. They had grown
up with the *Mickey Mouse Club, Leave it to Beaver, Father Knows Best,* and Mike's
favorite TV show, *Sea Hunt.*

Mike and his best friend, Dennis, who turned eighteen within a week of
Mike, went down to register for the draft at the county seat in Upper Marlboro
on a cold drizzly February day, and although it should have brought the war a
little closer to home, it didn't.

Mike was your average high school student; average grades, average good
looks. He was five foot-eleven inches tall, a muscular 190 pounds, with sandy
brown hair and green eyes. Although broody at times, like most teenagers, he was
well liked by most of his peers. The dress at Oxon Hill High School in Oxon Hill,
Maryland was still conservative in 1967 and varied only with your social caste,
of which there were three or four. You could tell them by their uniforms: the
"Blocks" (called Greasers elsewhere) wore high-top black Chuck Taylor tennis

shoes, wide Mack work pants, Banlon shirts, and leather letterman jackets. The girls dressed like they were out of *West Side Story*. The Collegiates wore white Levis, button-down shirts, and penny loafers; the girls wore "coulottes," bright dresses, and looked like the girl next door. The Nerds looked pretty much like nerds have throughout the ages; striped ties and short-sleeve plaid shirts with pocket protectors, high-water pants, "fag bags," and uncool shoes. The Jocks sometimes crossed clothing lines, but usually wore the ubiquitous letterman's jacket. Mike was a Jock of the Collegiate variety, having just earned his jacket and varsity letter the previous fall with the football team.

Mike's parents were both immigrants of Eastern European origin who had been forcibly relocated to Germany as slave labor during WWII. His father was Polish and his mother was Lithuanian/Ukrainian. They met, fell in love, and married in a dislocated-civilian camp in Germany after the war, then immigrated to the United States in 1949. Mike was born the following year. His father had wanted to name the new baby Stanislav, after his father, but his mother insisted on an American name. He became Mike Armstrong Apin. His maternal grandparents also immigrated eventually, both of his father's parents having perished at the hands of the Nazis. Mike spent his early years growing up in an Eastern European community on the Jersey shore with his extended family. Mike's parents were fiercely proud of their new American citizenship, and after years of backbreaking work his father landed a comfortable job and a home in suburban, middle-class Maryland.

The antiwar movement, or hippy movement as his dad liked to refer to it, really had not penetrated this small-town, middle-class suburb on the edge of Washington, DC, yet. Drugs were almost unheard of and life was simple and uncomplicated. But the whole fabric of life that seemed so *American* in the 1950s and early 1960s was slowly changing. Mike's father, "Stash" Apin, gradually became consumed with the nightly coverage of the war and the growing divide in the country, and insisted that dinner be either before, or after, the nightly news. He could not seem to interest Mike in the events that he knew would shortly have an impact on his son's life.

Mr. Apin was torn between his hate for communism that had consumed his native Poland and his desire for peace. Those who had witnessed the horrors of the worst war in human history could hardly be expected to embrace the US intervention in Vietnam, but Mike's father had also learned that evil men must be stopped at all costs. He considered Stalin and the communists to be every bit as bad as Hitler. In many ways Stalin had been worse. He had certainly managed to kill more of his own people. Millions of peasants perished at Stalin's hands during the collectivization of the farms in the 1930s, and more than a million died during the Russian–Finnish war in 1939. Untold millions died on the battlefield and in the gulags before, during, and after WWII. Trotsky once called Stalin "Genghis Kahn with a telephone," before Stalin had him assassinated. Stalin himself used to say that if he "killed one person it was murder; if he killed a million it was a statistic." Stash had been too young to go to war in 1939, and now he was too old in 1968, but not Mike. He worried, and at the same time almost wished that Mike would volunteer or be called to serve. His mother was afraid Mike would do something foolish and enlist in the Marines, like the Murphy boy across the street.

She needn't have worried. Politics and international affairs just weren't important to him at this stage in his life. Besides, the slide into the war had been gradual and had been eclipsed by other events in the early 1960s; the Cuban Missile Crisis, the Civil Rights Movement, the assassination of Kennedy, just to mention a few. The average American couldn't even find Vietnam on a map and only the most politically astute could see the coming danger in the mid-1960s. Mike's father sensed it; his son did not.

It was only after the great battles during Tet that he became aware that a real war was going on. The possibility that he might have to go seemed negligible. He had no real anxiety about it; he was going to college and would be draft-exempt. Mike certainly had no interest in enlisting. It wasn't that he was unpatriotic; Mike just wasn't particularly interested in the military or world affairs. He had been accepted to the University of Maryland and he and his friend Dennis were to be roommates in the fall. He planned to study to be an engineer, like his dad wanted, and to make the most out of college life. Mike's father considered education to be of the utmost importance. He had studied nights for five long years to become an electrical engineer when they first immigrated to America. He worked two jobs to make ends meet but it had been well worth it. Education had been the salvation of the Apin family in America, the ticket of poor immigrants to the middle class. Yes, education was everything. He constantly hounded Mike to get better grades. Work, work, work was all he seemed to think about. What Mike couldn't understand, what children *never* understand, is that parents, especially parents with a lifetime of hardship and sorrow, live vicariously through their children. It is inevitable. They want the absolute best for their offspring.

Mike always felt vaguely embarrassed around his father. It wasn't just that he didn't feel he was living up to his father's high expectations; it was his inability to talk to him. He loved his father, but just did not know how to relate to him. He always considered his father to be a cold, unemotional, humorless man.

Then one night during his sophomore year, he had found his father sitting in the back yard at the picnic table. Mike was just about to ask him what he was doing when he suddenly realized he was wringing his hands and weeping silently. Mike retreated, confused and upset. He never saw his father show any emotion before except anger. He was profoundly disturbed by the incident, but it took him weeks to mention the subject with his mother.

It had turned out to be a letter from a long-lost cousin, an officer in the Polish army, one of the few that survived the slaughter perpetrated by the Russians when they "liberated" Poland from the Nazis at the end of the war. The relative, just released from a gulag, had returned to Poland only to discover that the entire Apin family had died. Mike wanted to ask his father about it, but he could never get up the nerve . . . maybe someday.

Mike graduated high school as the last man in the top quarter of his class in ceremonies at Cole Field House at the University of Maryland, got his college draft deferment, and went on to have the best summer of his life down at Ocean City, Maryland. He and Dennis, both lifeguards, shared an apartment with two other guards and got all the sun and girls they could handle. Life was good! War, what war?

CHAPTER 2

In the final analysis, it is their war. They are the ones who have to win it or lose it. We can help them, we can give them equipment, we can send our men out there as advisers, but they have to win it—the people of Vietnam.

—President John Fitzgerald Kennedy
September 3, 1963

Mike's mom yelled at him as he rushed in the door, late for a date as usual. "Mike, there's a letter for you on the kitchen table. It looks important."

He stayed home for the summer for about three weeks and was working at a local pool as a lifeguard. He and Dennis had taken Senior Life Saving down at the YMCA on 14th Street near the White House in DC and they spent that first summer at the beach, but this summer he decided to stay closer to home. The beach had been fun, but they blew all their wages, and their parents wanted them to save some money this summer. They went back to the YMCA during the spring of that year and took scuba-diving classes; they became Water Safety Instructors as well. Now they taught swimming lessons, while lifeguarding. They partied hard and were, in general, having a great time. It was merely a long continuation of the fun they had experienced at school that year.

He made himself a sandwich as he tore open the letter, without looking at the return address. He hoped it was his grades or a letter from the dean taking him off suspension. He and Dennis had shared a room their first year with a kid named Giovanni in Dorm 14, one of the new high-rise dorms on the campus of the University of Maryland. All they did was party their first semester, and the University of Maryland was the place to do it, seeing as it rated in the top ten of the nation's party schools that year. If they weren't going to frat parties, they were down to the Campus Club or the "Vous," where they could drink vast quantities of cheap beer, or they just pitched in and bought a keg. There was a girl's dorm next door and it always seemed as if there was a floor party somewhere. Their resident assistant (RA), a young graduate student, didn't really care *what* they did, just as long drugs were not involved.

Mike tried out for the freshman football team as a walk-on. Even though he had grown two inches and added twenty pounds of muscle, he was still small compared to most of the scholarship students. He was amazed by the size, speed, and strength of the competition. This was definitely not high school ball. He made it to the last cuts before he was told, "Coach wants to see you, bring your playbook." The head coach, always very nice, told him that he'd like to have him in the program; all he had to do was get "a little bigger, a little quicker, and a little faster." Mike wasn't as upset as he thought he'd be. He'd made a lot of friends and just trying out for the team seemed a good way to meet girls. The football team always had groupies hanging around.

The whole fabric of American life was changing around them; sex, drugs, and rock and roll. The Civil Rights Movement was in full swing, as was the antiwar movement. It was a time of idealism and change. The nation seemed to be polarizing into diametrically different camps: hawk versus dove, conservative verses radical, old versus young, white versus black. Mike wasn't sure whether the war was justified or not. He respected the sincere protesters like Joan Baez, but he found Jane Fonda to be abhorrent. He wasn't even really sure where Vietnam was. He confused French Indochina with Dutch Indonesia (something the United States Post Office also seemed to have some problem with). Most of what he knew about Vietnam concerned the debacle of the French following WWII, the assassination of Diem and the Nhus, and the immolation of Buddhist monks. Ho Chi Minh, "Uncle Ho," was alternatively painted as a social nationalist or a vicious communist despot like Stalin. Mike's opinion of the war swayed depending on who was on the soapbox.

His father periodically railed against the Republicans and the right wing in America, the Joseph McCarthys, for eliminating some of the best minds in the state department after the "loss" of China to the communists. As a result of the purges, America went into Indochina largely blind, and without the years of experience of the so-called "old Oriental hands." We gave the French back their colonies and then compounded the error by supporting them in their suppression of Vietnamese nationalism. To compound the error we then took the whole mess over from them. It represented nothing but continued French imperialism by American proxy. It was too bad Kennedy was killed on the eve of his decision on what to do with Vietnam. Mike's father was sure Kennedy would never have committed large numbers of conventional troops, as Johnson did later. Now they were in it, for better or for worse. It was the domino theory; they had to prevent communism from sweeping over Indochina and, subsequently, the rest of the world. It was really just an extension of the Cold War, a fight against the Soviets for world domination.

All the debate on the war and civil rights was fine, but it was also the era of free love. Mike and Dennis took full advantage of that. While they were largely ambivalent to the antiwar message, the protests added to the climate of reckless excitement that many college freshmen feel when first freed of the constraints of their parents. Mike and Dennis attended all of them. During one rally, the crowd blocked Route 1 and the Maryland State Police (the Free State Porkers as they were dubbed) were called in. Both Dennis and Mike got clubbed and sprayed with tear gas, but all in all, it was just plain fun. Drugs were also plentiful, but except for the occasional puff of marijuana at a party, they pretty much stuck to beer and Boone's Farm (apple wine), or "Purple Jesus," a concoction of grain alcohol and grape juice served at the fraternity parties. The only time Mike smoked grass he was already pretty drunk and didn't like the feeling it gave him, the loss of control. As for LSD and the rest of it he had no real use for it. Mike just liked beer.

College, which Mike first approached as he had high school (by never taking a book home) was a lot harder than he expected and he failed miserably his first semester. His father was furious and only relented a little when Mike told him engineering proved too hard for him. He had not taken the right courses in high school to deal with the calculus and physics. Mike changed his major to political science, perhaps to become a lawyer. Although he tried hard that next semester, his heart wasn't in it. There was too much else going on around him. While his midterm grades were passable, finals proved to be a nightmare. Mike was deathly afraid he was in danger of flunking out. He had no idea what he would do if he flunked out. As it was, he didn't have to worry; that little problem had been solved for him.

After opening the envelope, he sat down hard as he read the "Greetings from Your Uncle Sam" letter. Mike was to report to the draft board induction center for a physical the following week. He guessed he flunked out after all.

CHAPTER 3

If you ain't Airborne, you ain't shit.

—Airborne proverb

Mike passed his physical and two weeks later boarded a bus for Ft. Dix, New Jersey, close to where he had grown up. Except for the first few days, Mike found he actually enjoyed basic training. He was in excellent shape, a lot better than almost anyone in his company, and received the highest score on the initial physical training (PT) test. His DI (drill sergeant) found him to be a natural leader and he worked hard to master all of the soldier skills thrown at them. He also had a better attitude than most of his fellow soldiers, three quarters of whom were draftees. Mike took the training very seriously and was made acting corporal, graduating as the Honor Graduate of his platoon. He scored high enough on the army's IQ test to qualify for any of the army's many specialties and decided to become an electronic-intelligence warfare specialist. As a kid, Mike had a neighbor who happened to be a ham radio operator and Mike had been fascinated by the radios and spent many childhood hours with the old man talking to far off lands.

After basic training, Mike went to Fort Devens, Massachusetts, for AIT (advanced individual training) at the Army's school for electronic intelligence and surveillance. There he learned basic communications and radio procedures, as well as RDF (radio direction finding) procedures, signal intercept, counter measures, jamming procedures, and other classified techniques. He trained as a signals-intelligence analyst, MOS (military occupational specialty) 98C. He was a model student and consistently scored at the top of his class. The only real problem he had was getting his top secret security clearance because of his family's background. After an exhaustive background investigation, to make sure he wasn't a Soviet "mole," it was finally granted. Toward the end of the course one of his instructors asked if he would like to attend Airborne School next and become a qualified parachutist. He jumped at the chance, figuring he would wind up with the 82nd Airborne Division, since the 101st Airborne, now in Vietnam, had gone Airmobile. He wasn't really thrilled about going to Vietnam. Anyway, he knew the 82nd, as America's strategic reserve, was still at Fort Bragg, North Carolina, and were unlikely to go anywhere anytime soon, although the 3rd Brigade had just been deployed to Vietnam in 1969 for six months on an "emergency" basis.

Airborne School was a blast compared to the mind-numbing code and intel/ intercept work. It was a mixture of physical training, fear, and adrenalin-charged excitement. He had shown up at Fort Benning, Georgia for "zero" week (mostly physical conditioning and harassment) in the best shape of his life. There were significantly fewer soldiers present for "ground" week that next Monday. Ground week consisted of various torture apparati such as the lateral drift apparatus, swing-landing trainer, and suspended harness. The PT was intense, especially the Friday runs up "Cardiac Hill." If you dropped back in formation, you were out of the course. One soldier complained to the "Black Hats," as the Airborne instructors were called, about having diarrhea, asking to drop out of a Friday run to go to the latrine. His request was refused and the man finished the run with shit running down his leg. That took guts.

The physical training (PT) was even more intense for Mike because he had some wise-guy Navy BUDS (Seal) students in his stick (squad) who all thought Army PT was a joke. As a result, the whole stick went to the proverbial "gig pit" on a daily basis for extra PT, while the rest of the students were smoking and joking. It didn't really matter to Mike; he was young and strong and he reveled in Airborne's *espirit de corps*. The troops at the school were completely different than those in basic and AIT; they were really motivated, all volunteers.

By the time the third, or "tower" week had rolled around, only half the students remained. The thirty-four-foot towers weren't bad but the two-hundred-foot towers were really scary. It was like the Coney Island parachute ride he rode as a kid, but here, you were on your own. You didn't ride down on cables and it was the only part of the course Mike found really terrifying. When they raised him to the top and he got that jolt, and then swung suspended, he was so petrified he almost couldn't respond to the commands of the Black Hats on the ground. It didn't help that before they went up the Black Hats had dropped a dummy from one of the towers with a "malfunction." They watched in horror while the parachute fluttered ineffectually as it screamed into the ground right in front of them. It took several moments before they realized it was just to get their attention. Then one of the first guys on the first tower run steered—or was blown—into the tower and left in an ambulance. Mike had plenty of company in his apprehension.

After that "jump" week was almost anticlimatic. On their first real jump Mike sat right next to the door, first in his stick. His stomach tightened in a knot, just like before a high school football game, until they opened the door and that rush of cool air came in. Mike could see the countryside flying by through the other door. Man, they seemed low! The jumpmaster stood up, hooked up his static line, did a door check, and turned to the jumpers:

"Inboard personnel, stand *up!*"

"Outboard personnel, stand *up!*"

"*Hook* up!"

"Check *static* lines!"

"Check *equipment!*"

"*Sound off* for equipment check!"

"OK, OK, OK," The last man slapped Mike on the butt and he gave the jumpmaster the thumbs up. "*All* okay jumpmaster!"

"*Stand in the door!*" Mike handed his static line to the jumpmaster and stood in the door with his hands on the outside skin of the door as the world hurtled by. Look straight out; don't look down. He could see the orange flanker panel coming up far out on the grassy field.

"*Go!*"

The jumpmaster slapped him on the butt and Mike automatically and involuntary jumped up and out of the C-130 in the tight-body position, his feet and knees locked to the rear, head tucked on chest, and hands over his reserve parachute, just as he was taught, adrenalin screaming through his body. The world went spinning below, his breath gone. He caught sight of the tail of the airplane as he went into freefall and was on "three-one-thousand" of his four count as his T-10 parachute opened with a jolt causing him to grunt, his helmet strap snapping against his chin. Suddenly, he was floating high above the grassy calm. The only sound was the drone of the aircraft moving off in the distance. *What a rush!* The wind fluttered the edges of his canopy and he could see for miles. *What a sight!* His reverie was shortly broken by a Black Hat on the drop zone screaming at him through a bullhorn.

"Get control of your parachute. Slip right."

A smoke grenade on the drop zone indicated the direction of the wind and he reached up, grabbed the right riser and pulled it down to his chest. The ground came rushing up. *Don't look at the ground; don't reach for it, balls of feet, calf, butt, push-up muscle. Bone jarring impact, roll, jump up, run around the canopy and collapse it before you get dragged. And it was over. Hot damn!*

They made all five jumps at Fryar Drop Zone, in nearby Alabama. They conducted the last jump wearing rucksacks and weapons cases containing two-by-fours. Once they landed they received the coveted "silver wings" on the Drop Zone in a ceremony featuring Airborne generals from WWII. "Blood wings" were punched into their chests so the pins drew blood, a right of passage that nobody minded. That night they went into Phoenix City, Alabama and tied one on. They wound up in a tattoo parlor in the early hours of the morning. His two buddies got their tattoos first. Mike picked out a skull and crossbones superimposed on parachute wings with the words "Death from Above," but he sobered up before it was his turn.

In the morning, with splitting headaches, they fell out to the company bulletin board to look at their unit assignments. Next to Mike's name was a unit designation with no address, the 403rd Radio Research Detachment.

"What is it and where is it?" Mike wondered out loud.

The Black Hat First Sergeant was standing next to the board getting some kind of sadistic pleasure out of watching the soldiers sweat over their assignments, many of them heading off to Vietnam. He wore a CIB (combat infantry badge), Master Parachute Wings, and a Special Forces Combat patch. He laughed when he heard Mike.

"What's-a-matter, Airborne? You don't know? You *must* have asked for it!"

"What do you mean?"

"It's a hot-shit classified commo unit attached to the 5th Special Forces Group and MACVSOG."

"What?" stammered Mike.

"Vietnam, stupid; you're going to the 'Nam!'"

CHAPTER 4

At last there is light at the end of the tunnel.

—Joseph Alsop,
syndicated column, September 13, 1965

On a rainy monsoon day in February 1970, PFC Mike Apin landed at Tan Son Nhut Airport, Republic of Vietnam. He had traveled via commercial airline to Travis AFB in California. Travis was a flurry of activity. He had to spend two days in an old open-bay WWII barracks before boarding a "Freedom Bird," a Boeing 707 charter that flew them to Hawaii. After RON'ing (remain over night) at Hickam Field on Oahu, he caught another military charter to Vietnam. It broke down in Okinawa for two days. On the last leg of the flight he sat next to a Marine Corps lieutenant colonel. Seated behind them were two soldiers going back to Vietnam after two weeks of R & R in Hawaii. They were drunk and one was crying the whole trip about having to go back to Vietnam. The Marine Corps officer sat stony face the whole trip, trying to ignore them. It was a long uncomfortable flight for Mike.

At least it had been a commercial flight. There were stewardesses (although they were a lot older than on regular flights), a movie, and food. This was a lot better than in the back of a C-130 or C-141, where you were either too hot or too cold, and you had to eat C-rations and wear earplugs. Looking over the colonel's shoulder, he could see the coast coming up as they approached Vietnam. At thirty-thousand feet all he could see was blue water, a silver ribbon of beach, and green lush tropical land. He wondered if there would be time to go scuba diving. He knew they had good diving in Thailand. His mind drifted back to that last trip they had taken to Key Largo over spring break. They had camped out and enjoyed some of the greatest diving they had ever done. Then there had been those three hippy chicks . . .

"Take your seats and fasten your seat belts! We're beginning our descent," the pilot blared over the PA.

Mike stepped out on the tarmac of Tan Son Nhut Airport on the outskirts of Saigon. It had been cool in the plane, but when they opened the door a blast of warm heavy air greeted them, redolent with an almost visual smell of the East. *So, this was the country that had been fighting invaders for two thousand years; the*

Chinese, Japanese, French, and now us, he thought. There were men on the tarmac in sweat-wilted, starched khakis carrying duffle bags waiting to board the aircraft Jack had just left. So that's why it's called the Freedom Bird; they were going back to the world. Most of them ignored the newcomers; a few called good-natured insults.

"Good luck . . . you're going to need it."

"New meat for Charlie!"

"You'll be sorreee!"

Their days in purgatory were done. Their individual levels of hell determined by their MOS, unit, and circumstance.

Mike was struck by a déjà vu so strong that it made him dizzy.

"What?"

"I said 'get on the bus private!'"

"Yes, sergeant," Mike stammered. As quickly as the feeling came over him, it was gone.

They boarded a bus with screened windows.

"To keep out grenades," a fat-bellied NCO explained to them. They rode down the airfield, past what looked like flag-draped coffins being loaded onto a C-141. Long lines, hurry up and wait, and confusion were the order of the day.

"Everyone get out four copies of your orders," a clerk yelled.

Sweat was already staining Mike's uniform. After processing they exchanged their money for military scrip, MPC (or Military Payment Certificates); ostensibly to cut down on black marketing, and then sat through a myriad of briefings. Because he had traveled alone, not as part of a group as most soldiers did, there was no one to greet and escort him when he landed. After wandering around and collecting his gear, he checked in at the Repo Depo (replacement depot) Barracks. The barrack was a large open bay (just like basic), with a row of double bunks along both walls, and a large latrine with open shitters and showers. It was stifling in the barrack, two large fans working ineffectually trying to cool it. While not very successful, they were very noisy. Even if it hadn't been so hot and he hadn't been so keyed up, he still wouldn't have been able to sleep. Several world-class snorers saw to that. Mike couldn't see how anyone could sleep through that.

After a morning formation and more in-processing and a series of additional briefings (including a sickening VD lecture, showing both male and female genitalia in various states of disrepair), he was sent to draw a mountain of field gear. When they looked at his orders and they found out he was going to the 5th Special Forces Group (Airborne). They made him get back into line and turn all the stuff in.

"SF has its own stuff, stupid! Why didn't you say where you were going?" snarled an overweight supply sergeant.

Mike was bewildered; especially when they told him he had to find his own transportation to the Special Forces operating base at Nha Trang. Mike went back to the Repo Depo and they let him spend the night and in the morning a surly SP4 (specialist forth class) took him over to an SF liaison office. There he was told they had a ride for him on a chopper in a couple of days.

Mike liked riding in the helicopter. It was a large double-bladed CH-46 and it was cool, the wind rusting through the open gun doors to the back ramp with a gunner sitting on the down tail. The loud "whup, whup, whup" of the rotor made talking impossible, and Mike had a good view out the back, watching the mosaic of rice paddies and the occasional village flash underneath. They were flying at about three thousand feet, just higher than his highest parachute jump, and from this altitude, the peasants working in the fields and the water buffaloes were mere specks. Gradually the ground changed from patties into a series of hills and forests. It had become cold in the chopper by the time they landed.

After grabbing his gear, he hitched a ride in a Jeep to the 5th Special Forces Group (Airborne) headquarters, Nha Trang.

"Where the hell you been?" asked the clerk in the S1 (personnel) shop when Mike reported into the 5th Special Forces Group headquarters.

"The sergeant major was about to report you AWOL; you were supposed to be here three days ago."

"Got stuck at the Repo Depo."

"Repo Depo? You weren't supposed to go there, dummy. You were supposed to check in with the Special Operations liaison and come straight here. Let me tell the sergeant major you're here . . . be careful, he's in a bad mood today! Let me see a copy of your orders."

Mike handed his orders, his medical file, and his 201 personnel file to the clerk.

"Oh, shit!" muttered the clerk.

"What's wrong?" asked Mike, his anxiety level climbing.

"Where's your *S*? You're supposed to have an *S*, this says you're only a *P*!"

"I don't know what you're talking about."

"*S* stupid . . . Special Forces qualified . . . you're supposed to be SF qualified . . . you're only parachute qualified. You didn't go to the Q-course?"

"No, I came here straight from AIT and airborne school."

"Holy Mother and Joseph! When the sergeant major sees this he's going to shit a brick. You wait here!"

Mike could here low murmuring and then . . . "YOU"VE GOT TO BE SHITTING ME! I told them to send me a SF-qualified RTO for a change. Send the little peckerwood in . . . babies, they keep sending me babies!"

The clerk came out with a nervous tic and whispered, "the sergeant major will see you now."

By the time Mike was ushered into the CSM's office he was sweating profusely.

"Get lost?" asked the CSM.

"No sergeant, I . . ."

The command sergeant major jumped up from behind his desk and cut him off, "Sergeant? I was a sergeant fifteen years ago. I'm a *COMMAND SERGEANT MAJOR*, and don't you forget it, troop! Now where the hell have you been?"

Mike stammered through an explanation of his travels and the sergeant major softened a bit.

"Yeah, they're always fucking with us SF guys. OK kid, we're real busy here. It looks like Victor Charlie and his buddies from the north are getting ready to hit some of our camps with everything they've got. I talked to your CO at the C team in Pleiku and he wants you down at the B team at Kontum; they're short-handed.

"One more thing. You can drink beer when we got it but we don't do grass or any other drugs . . . we got no potheads here. You get caught doing drugs and your ass is grass! Also don't be putting peace signs or any other crap on your helmet or other gear or you'll be burning shit your whole tour. Got it?"

"Yes, sergeant major!"

The sergeant major looked thoughtful for a moment. "We're going to lose this war! My job is to see how much damage we can inflict on the enemy and to make sure you go home alive."

The sergeant major stood up and unexpectedly put his hand out for Mike to shake.

"Good luck kid," he waved Mike out of his office. "Kennedy! Get in here!"

The clerk rushed in from the orderly room.

"Get Apin signed up for the Special Forces extension course. Then go down to the library and draw a bunch of subcourses so he can get started. After he finishes his box-top course we'll get him on an FTX and put him in for his *S*."

"Roger that, sergeant major."

The CSM was the first person who had shown any kindness to Mike since arriving in Vietnam. Everyone seemed in such a bad humor. This was primarily because things were not going well by the winter of 1970. No one believed that there was "Light at the End of the Tunnel" anymore. The early years of the American experience in Vietnam centered on the work of the "Lawrence of Indochina," General Edward Lansdale. He was a CIA man, a new-old Asia hand. He knew how to fight a war the modern Asian way, and was the antithesis of the "Ugly American." He had helped quell the Huk Rebellion in the Philippines in the 1950s. He was an expert in the new field of counterinsurgency warfare. The American version of the Vietnam War started out with American advisors and Army Special Forces training and assisting the ARVNs (Army of the Republic of Vietnam) to fight the Viet Cong guerrillas. It was an excellent system, but it was not to last. Slowly and surely Secretary of Defense Robert McNamara and his boys commandeered it. They then escalated it into a mass-production war with a half-million American servicemen pitted against the army of North Vietnam.

After Tet in 1968 it all seemed to unravel. Ho Chi Minh and General Vo Nguyen Giap gambled big on that one. They threw the whole National Liberation Front into costly suicide attacks against almost every American installation in Vietnam on the 30th and 31st of January, and the Vietnamese New Year. Despite warnings of impending trouble, the ARVN and American military were largely caught unaware and many soldiers were on leave. Sappers even succeeded in breaching the American Embassy defenses and were only dislodged after a fierce firefight with American Military Police (MPs). While Tet resulted in a military disaster for the Viet Cong, and largely eliminated them as a fighting force, it was a public relations victory for the communists. For many Americans sitting at home watching the fight for the American Embassy on TV, the war appeared to be lost. Their faith in the military and the politicians who supported the war was now in jeopardy. The communists lost the battle, but won the war, at least the media war. Ho Chi Minh's prediction proved correct; for every American death, ten Vietnamese would die, but in the end they would be victorious. They had the will to win regardless of the cost. America did not.

Now America was getting out of Vietnam—"Peace with Honor" and "Vietnamization" were the new slogans, and it was not going well. It was *especially* not a good environment for Special Forces. In August of 1969, Colonel Robert B. Rhealt, the new commander of the 5th Special Forces was relieved of command after some operators in the GAMMA Project eliminated (with extreme prejudice) a Vietnamese double agent. Col. Rhealt, who had only taken command a couple of months earlier, gave General Abrams the same cover story that he received, not realizing that one of the soldiers had spilled the true story of the assassination. Abrams was furious and arrested the colonel and several others. The whole case came to naught when the CIA (it was really their operation) refused to testify, but the damage was done. It ruined the career of one of Special Forces' finest soldiers, and SF lost a great deal of credibility. It was one of the unfortunate legacies of the war that many of the Army's best officers like COL Rhealt and LTC John Vann were lost to the system, while lesser men rose to the forefront because they punched the right tickets and didn't make waves.

GEN Abrams was going to put Special Forces in its place and to add insult to injury, the general assigned a non-SF, leg (non-airborne) colonel to take command, vowing to kick SF out of Vietnam, presumably so the war could be fought *properly*. The general, like most conventional army commanders, did not believe in elite troops and had never liked Special Forces. They always went "native," they "lacked discipline." This was his chance to put them in line or even eliminate them.

The military situation in the area of the Central Highlands was also very dangerous and it began to deteriorate in the winter/spring of 1970. The Central Highlands, II Corps, was tactically and strategically a key area. A series of A Camps (Operational Detachment Alpha) sat aside the east-west route between the Ho Chi Minh Trail in Cambodia and Laos to the west and Binh Dinh Province to the east. Dak To lay at the entrance to the Tu Mrong Valley, and Ban Het controlled access to the Dak Poko and Plei Trap Valleys running down into South Vietnam. Dak Seang and Dak Pek lay to the north against the Cambodian and Laotian borders. Whoever wanted to control the Central Highlands needed to control this area, and whoever controlled the Central Highlands controlled South Vietnam. The A Camps had been a thorn in the side of the Viet Cong and the North Vietnam Army (NVA) for years and now they were committed to wiping out the camps. At this point in the war there were fewer than half the camps that once existed a few years earlier.

A Special Forces Group consisted of approximately one thousand Special Forces qualified personnel and many hundreds of support personnel (logistics, aviation, medical, communications, etc.). The Group Headquarters was called the SFOB (Special Forces Operating Base) and was at Nha Trang. It, in turn, controlled three battalions who's HQs were known as FOBs (Forward Operating Bases) or C teams. Each C team controlled approximately three Companies or B teams and each of them controlled and supported five to six of the A camps.

The camps usually had strong fortifications and housed a twelve-man Special Forces ODA (Operational Detachment Alpha), often times augmented by additional personnel. They lived with and trained indigenous forces, in this case Montagnards or Yards, into the CIDG (Civilian Irregular Defense Group), sometimes up to battalion strength. They usually had a detachment of Vietnamese

Special Forces as well, the LLDB (Luc-Luong Dac-Biet), and occasionally other forces such as MACV-SOG (Special Observation and Studies Group), a classified group of SF soldiers that did all types of "Black" operations.

The LLDB were nominally in charge of the camps, often to the disgust of the American counterparts. Although patterned after the American Special Forces, their ranks were often filled with political hacks and were rife with corruption. They were often times more interested in embezzling funds, getting kickbacks, padding payrolls, and selling American equipment on the black market (usually to the Viet Cong) than they were in fighting the communists. It was almost impossible to get them to fight at night (when the VC reigned) and they rarely stuck their necks out. There were exceptions, of course, and occasionally good soldiers came from their ranks. To make matters worse, Yards and the LLDB hated each other; the LLDB referred to the Yards as *mois*, meaning "dirty savage." The camps sent out regular patrols and ambushes, usually having a company-sized element out in the field at all times. They were extremely effective against the Viet Cong, but less effective against main-force NVA.

Pressure on the A camps, and even the B camps, escalated in 1969. Communist forces had overrun Kham Duc, just north of Dak Pek, the previous year. In May 1969, they laid siege to Ban Het. The NVA were raising the stakes and began to bring in armor, PT-76 tanks, as at Lang Vei (the camp overrun during the siege at Khe Sahn). Only air support had prevented Ban Het from falling. In October of 1969 two Americans were killed at Dak Pek and another soldier from the B team (ODB-24) at Kontum was killed in December.

It was the 503rd Radio Research Detachment (ABN), using radio intercept that identified the vast army arrayed against the camps in early 1970: the 66th NVA Infantry Division, the 28th NVA Infantry Division, and the 40th NVA Artillery Regiment. It was no longer small units of guerrillas, the Viet Cong, that they had to worry about, but large, elite units of the North Vietnamese Army. The Viet Cong, known as VC, Victor Charlie, or simply Charlie, largely ceased to exist as a military force after Tet and North Vietnam had stepped up the infiltration of hard-core NVA regular units.

Morale was at an all-time low among SF soldiers and it was obvious that many of them considered the war lost. Most just wanted out before they got their butts shot off. They were handing things off to the ARVN (Army of the Republic of Vietnam) as fast as they could. Such was the environment that Mike found himself in late February 1970.

CHAPTER 5

We Americans know, although others appear to forget, the risks of spreading conflict. We still seek no wider war.

—President Lyndon Baines Johnson,
Gulf of Tonkin Resolution Speech,
August 4, 1964

On the day that Mike arrived in Kontum, a baby boy was born in a suburb, a village really, of Baghdad, Iraq. His proud father, Abdul Mahdi Shibah, was a minor functionary in the new Ba'ath government. He owed his position to his friendship and clan affiliation with Saddam Hussein. They had grown up together in al-Auja, the small dirt-poor village in central Iraq on the banks of the Tigris River near Tikrit, far removed from the cosmopolitan Baghdad. It was simply a collection of huts made of mud and straw with no electricity, indoor plumbing, or running water. They burned dung cakes for fuel, just as their ancestors had for centuries. It was the birthplace of the Islamic hero Saladin, the nemesis of Christian crusaders during the Middle Ages, and Hussein identified with him.

Saddam was unloved and was not well treated by his parents, especially his stepfather, who abused the boy. His mother would often tell him that she had considered aborting him and had made a mistake in not doing so. Everyone in the village hated Saddam's stepfather, who was known as "Hassan the Liar," and the other boys frequently picked on Saddam. So much so that he took to carrying an iron rod to beat the other children of the village when they taunted him. His stepfather taught him how to steal and called him a "Son of a Whore," and beat the child on a regular basis. Because of his home life, Saddam often sought refuge in the Shibah house. Abdul's mother was a kind and generous person and often fed and cared for young Saddam. Even though he was several years older than Abdul, Saddam, nonetheless proved kind to him and looked after him as a big brother might. Even in those days Saddam was one to be feared and it was good to have him as an ally. Abdul doubted the rumor that Saddam had killed a man at the age of ten, but it *could* have been true. Saddam was a ruthless and dangerous person to those he felt had wronged him.

Abdul and Saddam went off to the same school in the Takriti district of al-Karka and stuck together with other clan members, the Tikriti mafia. Saddam graduated to trouble while Abdul was still in school. Saddam had joined the radical Ba'ath party and was accused in a plot to murder Brigadier General Abdul Karim Qassim, who had taken the title "Ruler of all Iraq" in a military coup shortly after the British had left. Saddam escaped to Egypt and returned only when the Ba'ath party finally took power in 1963. Abdul had also joined the party and went to work for Saddam.

In those days, the Ba'ath party had not yet built a large popular base and numbered only a few thousand. Because of this, they didn't remain in power long. However, by 1968 Saddam had already become the assistant secretary-general of the Ba'ath party and chairman of the Revolution Command Council in charge of internal security; the soon-to-be-hated and feared secret police. Abdul continued to work for Saddam as an underling in the organization. However, Abdul was too poorly educated, a man without vision. He was a rather dull man of limited capabilities; even he recognized this. This was also evident to Saddam, but he was a friend and one of the first party members. Like the original members of the Nazi party in pre-war Germany, he was taken care of when the party finally came back to power in 1969.

The Ba'ath party itself had been the creation of two visionaries who had attended the Sorbonne together in the late 1920s. The Ba'ath party, meaning *renaissance* in Arabic, was modeled after the Nazi model, nationalism cloaked in secrecy. Also like the Nazi party, the Ba'ath party had its storm troopers, the National Guard, later to become the elite Republican Guard. The party was built on an organization of terror and intimidation. In such a system, only the most ruthless rise to the top and Saddam Hussein was well qualified. Those who opposed Saddam seemed to have fatal auto accidents or other mishaps. He became an interrogator and torturer in the "Palace of the End." By the late 1970s Saddam had reached the top. Although he possessed no military experience, he had himself appointed a lieutenant general and delighted in wearing uniforms. Saddam's goal was to see that the party controlled the country while he controlled the party. In addition to eliminating Ba'athist opponents he also targeted groups such as Iraqi Jews, Shiite Moslems, and the Kurds. He also supported the most radical factions of the PLO and dedicated himself to the destruction of Israel. Many may be surprised that he had a law degree, but as the London *Observer* noted, "He added a law degree to his other honors by the simple expedient of turning up in the examination hall with a pistol in his belt and accompanied by four armed bodyguards. The examiner got the point."

He envisioned Iraq as the dominant power in the Arab world and himself as a modern-day Nebuchadnezzar II, the sixth-century Babylonian who conquered

Jerusalem and enslaved the Hebrews. His many opulent palaces were a metaphor for the Biblical walls of Babylon.

He eventually issued the "Pan Arab Charter," also dubbed the "Hussein Doctrine," which called for the collective defense of all Arab states and the elimination of all foreign presence in the Middle East. The doctrine also prohibited any Arab state from resorting to armed force against another Arab state, something he would violate on an impressive scale in the coming years.

Saddam had become a force to be reckoned with and Abdul Mahdi Shibah and his new son, Kemal Mohammed, would ride his coattails into the grand new history Iraq would write.

CHAPTER 6

*We are not about to send American boys nine or 10,000 miles away from home
to do what Asian boys ought to be doing for themselves.*

—President Lyndon Banes Johnson,
Speech, Akron University,
October 21, 1964

The 403rd Radio Research Detachment was part of the 509th Radio Research Group. The name was a cover, in part to disguise Army Security Agency (ASA) presence. The real designator was 403rd (Radio Research) Special Operations Detachment (Airborne). They were attached to the 5th Special Forces Group (ABN) and controlled cells within all levels within the group. Their function was signals intercept (SIGNET); communications security (COMSEC); electronic warfare (EW) operations, to provide communications countermeasures; and electronic intelligence (ELINT) at the tactical and strategic level. The EW part largely involved screwing with enemy communications. They gathered, sorted, and scanned intercepted messages and maintained a signal order of battle (SIGOB) and electronic order of battle (EOB). The order of battle told them exactly what units they were fighting as well as the enemy's strengths and capabilities.

Mike was sent to the B team at Kontum (Operational Detachment Bravo-24), built along the lines of the A camps, but larger and with a lot more personnel. One B team usually controlled and provided support for five to six A camps. They were extremely glad to see Mike, as they had been understaffed for several months. In spite of his training, Mike was a little overwhelmed by all of it. In addition to all their top-secret intercept and electronic-warfare equipment, they also monitored the frequencies used by SOG, the ANGRC-74s, PRC-25s, and Collins Single Side Bands (CSSB) radios at the A camps. They possessed a truly impressive array of antennas outside of the commo bunker. The system used five operators, including a couple of Nung interpreters for decoding NVA and Viet Cong radio traffic. All the stuff they collected went immediately up to ASA headquarters in Saigon for analysis. Most of the stuff was Greek to them but they soon became very adept at identifying trends, units, and even individual enemy radio operators.

Occasionally, the Special Forces medics made rounds of the villages doing "sick call" and Mike would go along as commo support. This was one of the best ways of building support with the locals. The SF medics worked closely with the local shaman, a mixture of modern medicine and good old-fashioned witch doctoring. Working with traditional healers helped to ensure cooperation and to make friends. The local shamans weren't stupid; they knew the value of modern medicine and received much of the credit when they "assisted" the Americans. Once, several years prior, one of the SF medics had saved the life of the daughter of a local village chief. She had stepped on a *punji* stick (a sharpened bamboo stick dipped in human excrement) on a trail left by the VC and contracted blood poisoning. She became septic and was just a few hours from death when the SF medic arrived. Intravenous antibiotics and careful debridement of the infected tissue resulted in a happy, running child in just a few days. The village, and even the whole tribe, had been eternally thankful and subsequently loyal to the Americans.

They also sometimes stopped at the local "factory" in one of the villages to pick up and barter items. Here the mamasans and old papasans were busy making Viet Cong and NVA flags (complete with a little pig blood), yard crossbows, and other "captured" war souvenirs that could be traded to the REMFs (Rear Echelon Motherfuckers) in Saigon for anything from booze to needed equipment for the camp.

On Mike's first trip, they stopped by a village celebrating one of the elders. The mountain people revered old people and their ancestors. After running the clinic, treating everything from boils, malaria, and "brain pain" (headaches), Mike and the medic were invited to the feast. After a ceremony summoning the spirits to bless the intoxicating rice beer, the feast commenced. Mike, sipping the powerful brew through a bamboo straw, had gagged as they set a boar's head and other identifiable dishes on the floor mats in front of them.

"Man, I thought that Bah Me Bah beer was bad!" exclaimed Jack.

"You mean ol' 33 Tiger piss? You know what they use as a preservative?"

"No what?"

"Formaldehyde, you know, the stuff used to pickle frogs in high school biology."

"No wonder it gives me such a headache!"

"Maybe this stuff *isn't* so bad, just don't tell me what's in it. I think I'll just have a little of that rice," he told the medic.

Mike started on the rice when he noticed an eye looking up at him through the sticky concoction. "What kind of rice is this?"

"It's *fish heads* and rice, my favorite. Put some of the *nuoc mam* sauce on it. Gives it some flavor."

Mike recoiled sharply from the smell. "Hey Doc, what the hell is that stuff?"

"They make it by burying dead fish in the ground until they putrefy. The oil runs off, they collect it and make the sauce out of it. Fish oil is highly nutritious and it's real tasty, but it's an acquired taste."

"I think I'm going to throw up!"

"Don't do that; it would be bad for rapport. Just be glad they didn't serve monkey heads; brains are considered a delicacy."

After that, Mike tried to avoid local village celebrations.

The A teams would also sometimes take non–Special Forces qualified soldiers in the camp out on combat patrols. It was a way for them to earn the coveted Combat Infantry Badge (CIB) and for the B team to assess the competence of potential camp defenders, should they ever be attacked. Mike sat in the camp for several weeks watching the patrols coming and going. He was dying to go out with them, and at the same time he was terrified when it came his turn. He received training for these patrols—recon in force, small reconnaissance patrols, trail watching, raids and ambushes—but he was still afraid, not afraid of the danger itself, but afraid he would be a coward, that he would have to endure the scorn of the SF guys who ignored the danger and actually seemed to thrive on it. Mike found himself desperately wanting the approval of these soldiers. He wanted in.

They were the most dedicated individuals Mike had ever met. Almost all of them were on their second or third tour; they didn't have to be there. In spite of the poor morale climate, they threw themselves into the job at hand: winning the war in Vietnam. Even though they felt themselves betrayed by the Army leadership, by the government that had sent them there, and by the American people, they still did their jobs with an unswerving belief in themselves and their mission. *De Opresso Liber*: liberate the oppressed. For their part, the SF guys treated Mike with good-natured disdain.

CHAPTER 7

Americans do not like long, inclusive wars . . . and this is going to be a long, inclusive war. Thus, we are sure to win in the end.

—Premier Pham Van Dong,
North Vietnam, 1962

Finally it was Mike's turn for a mission. Mike was to be the RTO (radioman) for the team executive officer (XO), first lieutenant (1LT) Davis. One other USSF NCO, two of the Viet SF (LLDB), and a full platoon of CIDG (civilian irregular defense) strikers would make up the patrol. It was to be a training mission to an area southeast of the camp. The region had been pretty much cleared of the VC and NVA a couple of years before by the 4th Infantry Division and was now regularly (in theory) patrolled by the Army of South Vietnam (ARVN).

Most of the strikers were relatively new recruits and would be practicing patrolling techniques: actions at danger areas (roads, clearings, streams, etc), immediate action drills (IAD), raids and ambushes, clearing bunkers, and the rest of the craft of counterinsurgency warfare. They spent many hours defusing booby traps such as tripwire-activated grenades in C-ration cans and 105mm artillery shells, as well as mines. It was, of course, best to practice in a relatively safe area with green troops.

The LT had Mike help him plan the patrol. After checking the percentage illumination forecast for the night, they decided to leave at 0100, just before the moon rose. They checked all the strikers and adjusted their equipment to make sure nothing would rattle or shine. Because of their diminutive size, most of the strikers carried the short carbine version of the M16, the CAR 15. They also checked to make sure the little strips of illumination tape (Ranger eyes), was present on the back of each man's cap so the soldier in back of him could follow him in the dark. They moved quietly through the lines, and traveled several klicks (kilometers) from the camp, stopping frequently to listen, each striker facing with his weapon in an alternate direction. At about 0330 they marched into a patrol base for the remainder of the night. They moved into the base on a slight hill in a big circle, the head coming around to cover the tail of the column. A small security element was sent back a hundred meters or so to watch the back trail in case they were being followed.

They left the patrol camp just before first light and marched all day. The Americans wore jungle boots without socks and did not wear underwear. Cotton never dried during the monsoon and could cause tremendous sores and blisters on the march. It was bad enough to have jungle sores without having jock rot or immersion foot. In addition to the PRC-10 radio, Mike carried the full combat load of a Claymore mine, extra ammo, a LAW (Light anti-Tank Weapon), four fragmentation grenades, a flare, smoke grenade, an extra battery, four canteens, and rations. *Damn what a load.* He was glad the LT made him throw out the air mattress, poncho liner, and a bunch of other stuff he had originally packed; *just the essentials . . . beans and bullets.*

Mike had traded his green OG-107 fatigues for the tiger-stripe rip-stop nylon fatigues the strikers and the SF guys wore. Everyone thought of Vietnam as being hot and humid, but in the mountains during the monsoon it could be cold; a light drizzle kept up all day. Even though they were soaked to the skin, it was warm enough while they were on the march. They bivouacked for the night on a hill just short of the operational area. They had used the site numerous times in the past and it took only minimal work to prepare fighting positions for the night.

They settled down to a meal of cold C-rations. One of the SF guys had showed Mike how to break down the boxes, pick through them for the good stuff (like the John Wayne chocolate bars), throw out the bad stuff (like the ham and lima beans, dubbed "ham and motherfuckers" by the troops), and how to stuff them, in order by meals, in the long socks they wore so they would fit easily in his rucksack and not make noise. He also taught Mike how to make an improvised stove out of a C-ration can using a heat tab or insect repellent mixed with peanut butter for fuel. A third option was to burn a small piece of C-4 explosive . . . you just had to make sure not to stomp it out; it would blow off your foot! If you sat carefully over the stove while wearing a poncho, you could eat hot food while maintaining light discipline and warm your balls at the same time. You just had to be careful not to breathe the fumes, as they were toxic.

They were also careful to bring their Halazone water-purification tablets, take their malarial pills, and put on insect repellent. The repellent really worked, but it smelled awful and made your skin so greasy everything stuck to it. It did make it easier to put camouflage on, though. One of the SF sergeants, a full-blooded Cherokee, wouldn't use the stuff because he said he could smell it a hundred yards off and was sure the VC and NVA could, too. All the guys insisted *he* could smell the enemy and whenever things looked hairy he walked the point. They sent out an ambush team on their back trail and put out an LP/OP (listening/observation post). Because they were in fairly safe territory it was decided that a third of the troops would be on watch while the rest slept. Mike got the middle shift and shivered, huddled in his poncho until the LT relieved him at 0200. Before first light everyone was awakened for stand-to, a tradition since the Indian wars; the Indians always attacked at dawn. After another meal of cold C-rations, they sent out two small recon patrols, each under the nominal command of an American advisor. One of the LLDB soldiers accompanied the USSF NCO with the first patrol, Mike and the LT accompanying the other, while the LLDB lieutenant stayed back at the base camp with a small contingent as a guard. After an exhausting wet day, they stumbled back into base camp and rotated responsibilities among the strikers. The process was repeated the next day.

The training had gone off without a hitch. Following an axiom of the hero of the French and Indian War, Major Rogers of "Rogers' Rangers," they returned to camp by a different route than they had come. They were moving down a trail, something they would have rarely done in true Indian country, when the compass and point men of the security element stopped at a trail junction. This area, unlike much of Vietnam, was more forest than jungle. The XO and Mike came up from their position in the middle of the patrol to confer.

"Well, that was a pretty good training mission, although I don't like going out with such large numbers," the LT said to Mike.

"Why's that LT?"

"Too much of a large signature, too much noise. We like to go in light and fast . . . then it's Charlie who has to watch out. You're a lot better off patrolling with us than the Marines or the grunts; they plod around in company-sized units on search-and-destroy missions and Charlie melts before them, sets up booby traps, or ambushes them."

It was raining hard, creating a steady hum of noise in the forest. They were only a few klicks (kilometers) from camp and were relaxed, too relaxed, as were the four NVA who, for a better description, came bee-bopping down the trail, conversing in an animated fashion, their approach covered by the noise of the rain. The NVA had their weapons slung over their shoulders. They wore pith helmets and new khaki-green uniforms, not the black pajamas of the VC. Coming around a bend in the trail, scarcely paying attention, they ran right into the Americans and the two strikers.

For a split disbelieving second, an eternity for Mike, they all just stared at one another, no one moving, not twenty meters apart. Unconscious of definitive action, Mike's M16 came up as his finger slid into the trigger guard and his thumb slipped the safety to single fire. The LT was also bringing his weapon to bear as the NVA struggled to get their AK-47s off their shoulders. It was a race against time. Even as he pulled the trigger, firing before he had acquired a site picture, he was conscious of the LT firing as well, the hot brass bouncing off his face. A scene from the movie *Butch Cassidy and the Sundance Kid* flashed through Mike's mind. He was going for the guys on the left and Sundance, the LT, *the real gunfighter*, was going for the guys on the right, dead center. A thought flashed through his mind, *I've never shot anyone before*. These were not the banditos that had robbed the mine payroll, but boys, soldiers, not unlike their strikers.

Mike's first round went high, catching the first NVA around the collarbone. He could see the dimple appear in the enemy soldier's uniform. The second round struck higher and to the right, taking the top of his head off. He brought the muzzle down as he traversed to the next target, pulling the trigger repeatedly, not really aiming but walking the rounds into their target. One of his rounds caught the next soldier in the center of the chest at the same time as the LT, traversing to the left put one square in his face. The LT had already put both of his targets down but the one who had been the furthest away scrambled up and was around the bend in the trail before they could react. The strikers hadn't moved but stood with mouths agape.

Badly wanting a prisoner the LT had bolted after him yelling, "Let's go!"

Mike and the rest of the patrol raced after him. They followed the blood trail but stopped about a hundred meters down the trail at a danger area, a small clearing. The LT put out flank security and he and Mike went with a two small security elements in a bounding overwatch maneuver to cross the clearing and clear the other side. Almost immediately the woods, a thicket of brush and pines on the other side of the clearing, erupted in a hasty ambush thrown together by a large NVA force. Like an out of sync Japanese movie, the muzzle flashes and the puffs of smoke did not match with the pops of the firing and the zips and zings of the bullets and the arc of green tracers as they went by and the splats when they hit tree trunks. They raced back to the edge of the clearing as the rest of the patrol, deployed on line, gave them cover. The firing became a constant roar punctuated by the staccato burping of an M60 machine gun and the *plunks* and explosions of M79 grenade launchers.

When they reached the other side, Mike threw himself down and trying to catch his breath started firing. He remembered his training: fire low, just above the ground.

"Mike," screamed the LT.

Mike crawled over and the LT called base camp for a fire mission. They were just at the outer fan of their mortar support but well within artillery range. A registration round landed just on the edge of the woods, right from where the NVA were firing.

"Good shooting, LT," said Mike.

"*Trung-ui*, we must *dee-dee* now," yelled the LLDB lieutenant.

"Fire for effect!" screamed the LT into the handset! "We're disengaging. Move out fast."

The LT directed the patrol back the way it came. They were lucky, only two of the strikers had minor wounds. Without a clear knowledge of how many NVA were out there and with green troops, the LT did not want to get them in over their heads. They did a quick search of the bodies on the trail as the woods exploded behind them. The B team sent out a Mike Force Company to escort them in. In the coming weeks many more patrols were sent out and together with the documents Mike's patrol had brought back, they confirmed the presence of an NVA regiment in the area. As usual, the ARVN were patrolling the area only on paper. They also started to pick up signal intercepts confirming large troop movements.

For his part, Mike had conquered his fear. He had felt clinically detached during the action; it was an out-of-body type of experience. He really did not think about what he was doing, he just reacted. The LT praised Mike's cool and the rest of the SF guys treated him deferentially. Even the B team sergeant major made a point of congratulating him.

"Not bad kid. I see you managed not to shoot yourself. Got your first glimpse of the elephant! Maybe we'll make a soldier out of you yet."

Even so, Mike was not anxious to go out on another patrol any time soon.

CHAPTER 8

The enemy will pass slowly from the offensive to the defensive. The blitzkrieg will transform itself into a war of long duration. Thus, the enemy will be caught in a dilemma: he has to drag out the war in order to win it and does not possess, on the other hand, the psychological and political means to fight a long drawn out war.

—General Vo Nguyen Giap, 1950,
Commander, North Vietnam

Even with his newfound status, Mike, the new guy and the most junior, naturally got most of the shit details, which usually included the nightly radio watch. They kept a twenty-four-hour watch monitoring all the A-team camps and all the possible radio frequencies the enemy might use. During the day, Mike caught up on as much sleep as possible between mandatory tactical training and standing guard. Mike really didn't mind the night shift. It was usually quiet and warm and cozy in the commo bunker, especially since the monsoon had started and the constant dampness chilled the air. His regular partner on the shift, a buck sergeant named Chris, was a wiz with radios and taught Mike a lot. Sometimes they would tune in Hanoi Hanna and listen to her spout commie rhetoric. On this particular night, he had managed to tune in WKBW in Buffalo, New York, on one of the radios due to an ionospheric bounce. They were playing hearts and listening to a Stones marathon when a new series of transmissions started coming in that neither Mike nor Chris could recognize.

"What the fuck, over!"

"What is it Chris?"

"I'm not sure but it ain't good."

Chris sent Mike to wake the NCOIC (noncommissioned officer in charge). After listening for a while, the NCO sent Mike to get one of the Nungs out of bed. The Nungs were Chinese minority hill men from up north who had an intense hate for not only the Viet Cong and the NVA Communists, but didn't care for the lowland Vietnamese either. They were intensely loyal to the Americans and were often used as bodyguards. After whispering in low tones they told Mike to get the C team on the horn in Pleiku and sent a coded message, an Operational Immediate, the second most important type of message. While they had voice communication via the Collins SSB, important messages were sent by encoding letter groups in Morse code and were decrypted using one-time pads. There was no real way to break such a code unless you had one of the pads.

"What is it?" asked Mike.

"It's hard to be sure but it sounds like the NVA are using helicopters somewhere west of Dak Seang. Probably just across the Cambodian border."

"Helicopters?" said Mike. "I didn't know the enemy was using helicopters."

"Neither did anyone else up to this point. Of course they thought the same things about tanks when they overran the Lang Vei camp last year. Anyway, this is way above our pay grades. Go get the CO."

Over the next couple of days, enemy radio traffic picked up steadily until it was obvious that an attack was imminent at Dak Seang. An Ops Immediate was sent to the camp to prepare for such an attack. These types of warnings were fairly common and although steps were taken to get ready, no one was overly concerned. "Wolf" was cried so often no one was about to get their tail feathers ruffled over one more impending attack. A few days later, on the night of April 1, Mike was monitoring the frequencies when the radios suddenly came alive. Mike went for the NCOIC again.

The sergeant was not pleased when Mike woke him up at 0600 since he had just gone off duty at 0400.

"This better not be an Aprils Fool's joke," he growled.

"It's not, there's a major attack going on at Dak Seang."

"Shit, I knew it! Send a Flash message to Pleiku and Nha Trang. I'll be right there."

CHAPTER 9

Their casualties are going up at a rate they cannot sustain . . . I see light at the end of the tunnel.

—Walt Rostow,
Look, Dec. 12, 1967

The attack on Dak Seang (ODA-245) began with mortar and recoilless rifle fire in the early morning hours of April 1. Dak Seang was a large, square-shaped camp with secure bunkers and good fields of fire. Over five hundred rounds of direct and indirect heavy-weapons fire was poured into the camp and left all the buildings destroyed or on fire. The CIDG and USSF team managed to repulse several assaults and a CIDG company from Plateau Gi (A-111) was air assaulted just outside the camp, only to get pinned down. They dug in and repulsed several assaults until they were able to fight their way into the camp during early daylight. This CIDG Strike Force was a highly trained, motivated, and competently led counter-guerrilla force that had been in almost constant combat since the early days of the war.

Air strikes came in at daylight and saved the camp from being overrun. Artillery from 105mm and 155mm guns also helped to repulse the human-wave attacks. Because the commo bunker and antenna systems had been largely destroyed, it was hard to get real-time information back at the B and C teams. The defenders were limited to using their battery-powered, hand-held PRC-25s with whip antennas; direct communication back to the B team was difficult, if not impossible at times. The camps at Ban Het and Dak Pek and gunships relayed messages. The 403rd was able to monitor most of these transmissions.

In the late hours of April 2, the NVA attempted another major assault on the camp, but it was repulsed. They attacked again at about 1900, but were again repulsed with the help of helicopter gunships. Several other attacks and probes were broken up during the night with the help of an AC-130 Spectre. Dak Seang needed reinforcements and the Province Reserve, the 1st and 4th Mobile Strike Force (MIKE) battalions went into the battle. In addition, the Air Force conducted B-52 strikes (arc lights) on April 3. Because the NVA were dug in very close to the camp perimeter (as they had against the French at Dien Bien Phu), the strikes had to be called in "Danger Close," within 750 meters instead of the normal 2-3,000 meters.

These measures seemed to break up the attacks momentarily, but the enemy seemed determined to take the camp at all costs. Enemy casualties were in the hundreds. It was the enemy propensity to risk the wholesale slaughter of their own troops, even the sacrifice of whole regiments and divisions, which made them so dangerous. Often lauded as a military genius, General Giap, the North Vietnamese commander, would never have been allowed to remain in command of any American army, his casualty figures were much too high. At the siege of Khe Sahn the previous year, the ratio of NVA casualties to American was estimated to be 100 to 1. The individual NVA soldier was little more than cannon fodder.

The NVA shot down three helicopters. Dozens of friendly personnel had been killed or wounded. On April 4 they launched another major assault but once again they were unsuccessful. The camp now looked like it might hold out. The enemy laid siege to the camp and used constant direct and indirect fire and probes of the perimeter, hoping the Americans would give up and abandon the camp. The siege would last until May 8.

Because the NVA appeared to have committed its whole force to the defeat of Dak Seang several of the other A camps loaned forces to the Dak Seang. Dak Pek sent some of its SF soldiers and a company from its Strike Force. Starting on April 4, however, the 503rd started picking up increased radio traffic and the signature of large units around Dak Pek (ODA-242), the most northern and vulnerable of all the A camps, being out of supporting artillery range. Mike and the rest of the 503rd became convinced that an attack was imminent at Dak Pek. However, Pleiku and Saigon viewed this as highly unlikely since the enemy was already heavily engaged at Dak Seang and largely dismissed the reports. On the night of April 11, the intercepts were so strong that the 403rd implored the B team to send an Operational Immediate to Dak Pek. The camp was already on 50 percent security and no further steps were taken.

It was Mike's unenviable job to wake up the NCOIC again during the early hours of April 12.

"Top, they're attacking Dak Pek."

"Yeah, so *what*! They've been attacking them for over a week," he said groggily.

"No Top, Dak Pek not Dak Seang."

"Shit! Go wake up the skipper," his sleepy face suddenly came awake.

CHAPTER 10

The US has broken the second rule of war. That is, don't go fighting with your land army on the mainland of Asia. Rule one is don't march on Moscow.

—Field Marshal Lord Montgomery

D ak Pek (A-242) was situated on seven hills. Each hill was a separate defensive area, surrounded by an elaborate trench and bunker system. It was located on the west side of the Dak Poko River in sandy soil populated by widely spaced pine trees, unusual in Vietnam. It was in the middle of the valley floor and almost devoid of cover. It was one of the oldest camps in Vietnam, built in 1962 by Special Forces during the early years of operations in Vietnam. Over the years it had become heavily fortified and was a showplace for visiting dignitaries from Saigon. The camp had its own paved runway, large enough for C-123 cargo planes to land, and had a wide-open command of the valley. Although it was just out of the American artillery fan, they had two of their own 105mm howitzers and a 106mm recoilless rifle located on one of the hills, named Hill 106, for obvious reasons. There was a compound down near the runway for MACV-SOG personnel, as this was one of their jumping-off points for their deep reconnaissance missions into Cambodia and Laos. There was a school and a hospital, and most of the buildings and bunkers were solidly built.

At approximately 0200 hours on April 12 enemy sappers from the NVA K80 Sapper Battalion attacked the American hill and Hill 106 with satchel charges. Amazingly, no Americans were killed, although many of the CIDG on Hills 106 and 203 were killed or wounded. The common bunker and most of the other buildings were largely destroyed. This made communication difficult on the PRC-25s and communications were largely relayed back to the B team from Dak Seang. The Collins and 74s were out of commission, all the antennas and half of the radios being destroyed. Although unable to talk directly to the camp, the 403rd was able to monitor all the radio traffic between the camps and the airships.

The initial sapper attack was followed almost immediately by rocket, artillery, and mortar fire from elements of the 40th Rocket Regiment and an attack by a NVA regiment, the 26th Infantry. While the battle at the camp was raging, elements from the 66th INF Reg were attacking all the Strategic Hamlets (fortified villages) in the valley. Worst of all, the NVA managed to seize Hill 106 and Hill 203, the highest hills in camp, and thus commanded the high ground. The American hill was almost overrun and more than thirty NVA were killed in close-quarter battle, sometimes hand-to-hand. One of the few bright spots during the night was a radio intercept of two NVA units running into each other during the night and engaging in a fierce firefight among themselves before they got things sorted out. Mike thought that type of thing only happened to American forces.

A Stinger gunship, an old C-119 cargo plane with a Bofors 40mm cannon sticking out of the tail (looking like a deranged bumblebee, hence the name), came on station during the night and did much to break up the continuing NVA attack. SOG attack helicopters (Cobras) also raked the camp before slicks (UH-1B choppers), evacuated the SOG personnel. By daybreak over half the camp was in enemy hands and air strikes were called in but it was hard to pinpoint the enemy as they were dug in so close to the USSF. The enemy felt that the closer they got to our troops, the less likely we would be to use airpower. In some engagements NVA cooks and clerks in the rear areas often took worse casualties than the infantry closer to the front.

A Sky Raider put two smoke rockets on Hill 203 and called repeated air strikes against it. It seemed like all the aircraft in Vietnam, Sky Raiders, F4 Phantoms and even B-52s were stacked up in the sky waiting to take a turn. They dropped 500 and 750 pound bombs, napalm, and strafed with 20mm Vulcan cannons. Incredibly, instead of withdrawing under this withering firepower, the enemy actually tried to infiltrate more troops. The battle went on all day and it looked like the NVA were just as determined to take this camp as they had (or perhaps instead of) Dak Seang.

At dusk another Stinger arrived and at midnight the ODA managed a successful radio check by code with the B team on an ANGRC-74 and a jury-rigged antenna. Shortly afterward, another major attack was beaten off with the help of an AC-130 Spectre gunship (nicknamed "Spooky"), outfitted with 20mm Vulcans, 7.62mm mini-guns, and a 105 howitzer. During the night command decided to reinforce Dak Pek, although almost all the available troops had already been committed to the defense of Dak Seang. A coded, *NOFORN* (American eyes only) message went to Dak Pek telling them to expect an air assault with reinforcements at daybreak.

The 1st MIKE Force Reconnaissance Company and a number of the Strike Force from Ple Prong would go in by chopper. Several SF soldiers from the B team also volunteered to go with them, but they were short of radios and communications personnel.

"How about it, Rich?" asked the 403rd NCOIC, talking to one of his junior sergeants.

The soldier did not want to meet his eyes. "Top, I'm short. I only got a couple more weeks in country; give me a break."

"I'll go," newly promoted Specialist 4th Class (SP4) Mike Apin heard his mouth say, to the horror of his brain.

The NCOIC looked at him a long time. "OK kid, grab your gear, a 74, and a 25 with some extra batteries and go out to the chopper pad. Five minutes!"

CHAPTER 11

He saw much that was wrong about the war in Vietnam, but he could never bring himself to conclude that the war itself was wrong and unwinable . . . . He could not abide defeat, defeat for himself or his vision of America. He believed America had staked that vision in Vietnam.

—Neil Sheehan,
A Bright Shining Lie: John Paul Vann
and America in Vietnam

They came in at almost treetop level, preceded by the gunships. The sight was apocalyptic, something out of Dante. Fires burned from all seven hills, dead bodies lying everywhere, all the buildings appeared to be wrecked and the gunships seemed to be firing at everything. Mike didn't know how anyone could tell friend from foe. Plumes of dirt and flames were going all up around the airfield from enemy mortars, and green tracers and rocket trails crisscrossed the landing strip. As the choppers landed they dived for cover. Incredibly, none of them were hit and none of the choppers were shot down.

They made their way up the American hill. The first priority was to take back the 203 hill. The defenders had tried several times since the original attack to retake it, but were driven back each time with heavy casualties. The Yards, who were excellent jungle fighters, seemed to have little stomach for this WWI trench-style warfare. Only with a lot of coaxing and cajoling were they able to get the fresh Strike Force troops to agree to charge it. They had to cover approximately thirty meters of open ground and then charge up the saddle, while the NVA rained lead down upon them. The American Special Forces were going to lead them with about ten volunteers.

Mike stayed behind the berm with a radio to signal their progress to the command bunker. He had grabbed a butt pack loaded with grenades, including some of the small experimental grenades used by SOG. They were about half the size and weight of a regular fragmentation grenade. Back in basic training he won a prize during a sporting contest at a picnic to celebrate their impending graduation. The prize went to the soldier with the longest throw with a regulation weight and size dummy grenade. Mike knew he would win it. In high school he used to be able to stand at home plate and throw a ball over the center-field fence.

He wasn't at all accurate with the long throw, which was why he spent most of his baseball career behind the plate, but he sure could throw high and far. He looked at the top of the hill and felt positive he could reach it, especially with the smaller, lighter SOG grenades.

The attack started off badly with none of the strikers initially following the USSF soldiers. Finally they pitched in too, and the attack began in earnest. It was one of the most heroic things Mike had ever witnessed and he started screaming and throwing the smaller grenades in a high arc, raining them down in the NVA trenches. They were taking their toll on the enemy. The enemy gunners had spotted Mike and started to direct fire against him every time he stood up to throw. One of the strikers left back in support had an M79 40mm grenade launcher and got in the rhythm with Mike and started dropping rounds on the enemy who were trying to target Mike. Between the two of them they were really doing devastating damage to the enemy. At the point at which the USSF and Strikers were about halfway up the saddle, Mike ran out of the smaller grenades and decided to get closer so as to not take a chance on hitting his own men with the larger ones. He had completely forgotten his communications assignment. He rushed closer, throwing grenades, and when he let the last grenade go, one of the NVA machine gunners caught him with a burst of fire from an RPD, stitching him across his body. He was thrown back and dragged to cover by the M79 gunner.

"Medic," screamed the Striker in passable English.

"He dead?"

"Yeah, looks like it," said the SF medic as he surveyed Mike's broken body. There was blood everywhere and his unrecognizable face was covered with blood and a large hole had been punched neatly in the center of his helmet. He seemed to have no pulse or respirations. When his helmet was taken off there was a small hole in the center of his forehead and a large one just behind the ear, the size of a silver dollar.

"Shot in the head. Carry him down and we'll evac him with the wounded."

CHAPTER 12

Soldier, soldier, come from the wars,
I'll up 'an tend to my true love!
'E's lying on the dead with a bullet through 'is 'ead,
An' you'd best go look for a new love.

—Rudyard Kipling
"Soldier, Soldier"

As it turned out, Mike would survive after all. He had been hit by four of the large-caliber Soviet machine-gun rounds; one had grazed a forearm, one went under the arm in the meat of his latissimus dorsi muscle, one went through in the meat of the *trapesius* muscle in the neck and one hit the center of his helmet but at a slight angle. None of the first three rounds hit bone and anyone of them could be categorized as a million-dollar wound, a potential ticket home. The bullet that struck his helmet had been slowed down just enough so that when it entered the front of his forehead at an angle it hit the skull, traveled around the bone, and came out the back behind the ear. It never even entered the cranial vault. The resulting concussion had presumably slowed Mike's heart and respirations (or even temporarily stopped them) so that they were not evident to the medic on the first hurried exam.

Once they had gotten him down the hill it became evident that, although he had lost a lot of blood and was unconscious, he was probably not too severely injured. They started him on IVs, dressed his wounds, and put him on a MED-VAC chopper to the combat support hospital. Because he hadn't regained consciousness within twenty-four hours they shipped him to the Nha Trang US Military Hospital where they had a neurosurgeon on staff, suspecting he might have a subdural hematoma or an intracranial bleed and might need some burr holes, a craniotomy. However, all his vital signs remained normal and cerebral angiography was negative for severe damage, although he remained in a coma.

On the morning of April 18, Mike woke up as a boat coming out of the fog.

"Let me sleep in today," he muttered to the corpsman.

"Hey, you're awake!"

The dream gradually dissolved and his irritation turned to fright as he realized he had no idea where he was. He tried to sit up but a wave of nausea forced him down. "Where am I?"

"You're at the hospital in Nha Trang. Let me go get the doctor."

He was confused, had amnesia, and hurt like hell, but a neurological exam showed that he had probably not received any serious or permanent motor or sensory damage. His amnesia was selective; he remembered everything up to two days before going to Dak Pek but nothing since. No one seemed to know exactly what had happened at the hospital and he couldn't find out how he had been shot.

In fact, the defenders at Dak Pek succeeded in taking Hill 203 and eventually took back control of the whole camp, although the siege would not entirely lift until May 9, a day after the NVA also gave up trying to take Dak Seang. The result was a resounding defeat for the NVA. The total casualties on the US side were: thirty-four CIDG and four civilians killed, twenty-two USSF, one LLDB, ninety-eight CIDG, and nine civilians wounded, seven CIDG missing. The NVA body count was 420 killed, and probably hundreds wounded. Mike found this out from reading a week-old *Stars and Stripes* he found in the hospital.

The sergeant major from the B team stopped by a few days before Mike was to ship out to Tripler Army Medical Center in Hawaii for convalescence.

"Hey kid, how ya doin'?" he asked through a big wad of tobacco. Looking for a place to spit, he put one square in the bedpan at the foot of Mike's bed.

"Hi, sergeant major, boy am I glad to see you. What happened? I can't remember a thing. Did you come all the way to Nha Trang just to see me?"

"A pissant like you? I doubt it. Nah, I had business here. Just thought I'd stop by this butcher shop and see how you're doing. Besides, the CO wanted me to give you something," he said as he pinned two medals on Mike's hospital gown.

"What are they?"

"A Purple Heart and a Bronze Star with a 'V' device for valor. Sorry there ain't no big ceremony."

"Did I earn them?"

"Shit kid. If you'd gotten killed or were an officer they would have given you the medal."

"The Medal?"

"The Congressional Medal of Honor, stupid. As it was, the team put you in for a Distinguished Service Cross (DSC) but Group downgraded it to a Silver Star and Saigon downgraded it to the Bronze. Saigon don't really want a lot of SF heroes right now. It's all in the citation. You really can't remember, huh?"

"Not a thing."

"I've also got a Montagnard bracelet, red shirt, and a loin cloth for you from the Yard chief. He decided to make you a Montagnard warrior *in absentia*." The sergeant major smiled a crocked grin, "He also said to tell you he's got one of his daughters for you to marry if you ever make it back."

"Damn!"

"Well, listen kid, I gotta go; you take it easy. You know, you ought to think about stayin'. You might make a pretty good soldier in a few years. Give it some thought."

Mike did think about it and he was sure he wanted to put as much distance as possible between himself and the Army. Lying in the hospital he had decided that he wanted to go back to the world and make something of himself; go back to school and *study* this time.

He spent quite a few months in Hawaii needing physical therapy and he drove the hospital librarian at Tripler crazy. When he could, he went down to Ft. DeRussy, the military R & R center on Waikiki Beach, and lay in the sun, reading. They had a great luau night on Fridays with a roast pig, native dancers, and usually plenty of girls. He read everything he could find on Vietnam, including the Pentagon Papers. He read the newspapers from cover to cover trying to make sense out of the war. It was all very confusing and he wasn't sure how he felt about war protesters and draft dodgers, or whether we should have ever gotten into the war in the first place. He did, however, come to certain conclusions.

The soldiers in Vietnam, and especially Special Forces, served honorably, proudly, and bravely. They did their duty for their county; they were wounded and many died. They came back home and tried to put their lives back together among an indifferent and sometimes hostile population. It was the politicians who started and then lost the war. They coerced the military leadership into corrupting itself. Everyone wanted to get their ticket punched, but no one wanted to stick their necks out. Those who did, and criticized the handling of the war, like LTC John Paul Vann, did so in protest and chose, or were forced, to leave the military. McNamara and his bunch of "bean counters" skewed objective evaluations of the war with their manipulated statistics of body counts, search and destroy missions, the war of attrition, and all the rest of it. They were arrogant. The PR men put a positive spin on everything. They deceived the public into believing the war could be won, even though they didn't really believe it themselves.

During his reading, Mike came across one passage from *The Best and the Brightest* by David Halberstam. To him it became the essence of the war in Vietnam:

"Lyndon Johnson had lost it all, and so had the rest of them; they had, for all their brilliance and hubris and sense of themselves, been unwilling to look to and learn from the past. And they had been swept forward by their belief in the importance in anti-communism and by the sense of power and glory and omnipotence, an omniscience of America in this century."

BOOK TWO

THE PERSIAN GULF, 1991

Some of the evil of my tale may have been inherent in our circumstances. For years we lived anyhow with one another in the naked desert, under the indifferent heaven. By day the hot sun fermented us; we were dizzied by the beating wind. At night we were sustained by the dew, and shamed into pettiness by the innumerable silence of the stars. We were a self-centered army without parade or gesture, devoted to freedom, the second of man's creeds, a purpose so ravenous it devoured all our strength, a hope so transcendent that our earlier ambitions faded in its glare.

—T. E. Lawrence,
Seven Pillars of Wisdom

CHAPTER 13

We've got the cholera in camp—it's worse than forty fights;
We're dyin' in the wilderness, the same as Isrualites,
It's before us, an' be'ind us, an' we cannot get away,
An' the doctor's just reported we've got twenty more today.

—Rudyard Kipling,
"Cholera Camp"

The sun was a rosy glow breaking just above the desert plain as a man, shivering, squatted in the dust. The bunker was on the southern edge of Tallil Airbase up on the Euphrates River, southeast of Baghdad. He had tried to make it to the slit trench down the wadi, but the urgency had been too much for him. A gut-wrenching cramp seized Kemal's bowels, causing him to groan loudly. An explosion of fetid blood and mucus relieved the excruciating cramp, but left him so weak he fell backwards into the mess.

He contracted dysentery at about the same time their battalion commander had "gone on leave." He never returned. That was over three weeks ago, a week after the men of the 46th Iraqi Infantry Division first started to receive the terrifying and withering punishment delivered by the planes of the US Air Force and the occasional US Army helicopter. Kemal, himself, just narrowly escaped being taken prisoner a week ago when, on a supply run, an attack helicopter strafed the civilian truck they were driving. A troop helicopter, what Kemal recognized as an American Black Hawk, then darted in like a dragonfly and whisked the driver and his lieutenant away. He had escaped by hiding under the burning truck. He wished now he had gone with them. There was a lot of speculation among the troops about the terrible tortures and torments that would be visited on the snatched soldiers. He knew they wouldn't be tortured. In fact, he was sure that by now his friend and the lieutenant were warm, well fed, and were being treated for malnutrition, diarrhea, and respiratory diseases. They had all been told what evil monsters the Americans were. He knew otherwise. Americans were warm and compassionate and America was a wonderful place. He constantly dreamed of being back in the United States.

His father had selected the Pennsylvania college just south of Philadelphia for him because, in spite of its small size, it possessed an excellent engineering school and was reasonably priced. It had once been a military college, Pennsylvania Military College, but was now called Widener University. Kemal had always been fascinated by America as a boy and had *lived* for the American films that his father took him to see at the cinema. His favorite subject in school was English and he studied it precisely so he would not have to read the Arabic subtitles superimposed on the movies. Westerns were his favorites, especially those with John Wayne. However, as Saddam Hussein increased his hold on the country, movies from the West, and especially America, were gradually eliminated.

He was ecstatic to be going to college in America, and it was specifically this promise that encouraged him to be such a good student. His father was a member of the Ba'ath party and a deeply religious, although secular, man. He had mixed feelings about his son going to school so far away from Iraq and wished he would go to school in France. He worried that the United States would corrupt young Kemal, and his fears were realized to some extent. Like many youths suddenly released from the bondage of religious, political, and intellectual oppression, Kemal took a hedonistic path and almost flunked out of school his first year. His dark, swarthy good looks, his rising star as a soccer player, and the allure of his Arab sheik persona were very attractive to similarly free young women. He went on a spree worthy of an F. Scott Fitzgerald character. As electives, he studied comparative religion and began to sense a hypocrisy in religions, in general, and in much of Islam, in particular. He came to the conclusion that Islam in its purist form, like Christianity, was a beautiful religion, but as is often the case, was subverted by men to justify whatever cause suited them. Kemal was not anxious to return to the repression of the Iraqi brand of Sunni Islam, the Ba'ath party, *or* Iraqi society.

He developed a taste for very blonde young ladies, old scotch, and cold beer, and became a regular at McGlone's 10-20 Bar and Walio's Frog Pond Café, both neighborhood establishments that, surprisingly, accepted him as one of their own. It was only when his father threatened to bring him home and make him join the army that he knuckled down. At the time his country was still fighting a meatgrinder, trench-type war with Iran, instigated by Saddam Hussein. It resembled the First World War, on a smaller scale, for the effective slaughter of hundreds of thousands of young men; he wanted no part of that.

He did, however, convince his father to allow him to change majors to biology and pre-med after his first year. His grades improved as he settled down and he showed a much greater affinity for biology and chemistry than he had for calculus and mechanics, and he actually made the dean's list every semester starting his second year. He didn't go home those first two summers, but found a job locally and moved into an apartment with one of the assistant soccer coaches. He worked at a wholesale florist in the summer and during vacations, and although it was back-breaking work, he was well paid and happy.

He hadn't planned to go home that last summer either, but his father was sick and his mother implored him to come home. *It was just bad luck, damn bad luck.* No sooner had he gotten home than that psychopath, Saddam, invaded Kuwait. His father promptly died. Without political protection Kemal found himself impressed into the Iraqi Army as a private; cannon fodder for Saddam's grandiose ambitions. No one thought the West would do anything but wring their hands and complain about the invasion, and so plans were made to sweep down the coast to grab up the oil fields of the rich, but defenseless, countries that lined the Persian Gulf. What Saddam couldn't wrest from Iran he would steal from others!

Saddam had seen his fight against Iran as a kind of jihad. A fight of Arab against Persian, Sunni against Shiite, modern against reactionary, and he was livid that the Egyptians, Saudis, Kuwaitis, and other Arab states had not supported Iraq against the hated Persians. The war against Iran had left Iraq bankrupt and Saddam had been bullying his neighbors, especially Kuwait, to make concessions. He so much as told the world that unless he was paid off he was going to invade Kuwait. No one took him seriously. Only the CIA was convinced that Saddam would actually invade, but they moved too late to influence the outcome.

On August 2, 1990, Iraq invaded Kuwait. Within six hours, one hundred thousand troops had streamed into the country. The "Revolution of August 2nd," spearheaded by the elite Republican Guard, swept aside the small Kuwaiti military, outnumbering them thirty to one. Only the Kuwaiti Air Force put up any real resistance and they largely managed to escape to Saudi Arabia after it became apparent that Kuwait was powerless to stop the invaders. Kuwait was then "annexed" as a province of Iraq.

Saddam had always wanted Kuwait and its rich oil fields. He justified the invasion with ridiculous historical claims that went as far back as the second millennium BC. Over the centuries Iraq had tried to lay claim to Kuwait as a part of the Basra province. Iraq always took exception to the infamous Sykes-Picot agreement, in which the French and British carved up the Middle East with the downfall of the "Sick Man of Europe," the Ottoman Empire, after WWI. They had drawn arbitrary boundaries, many of which would be disputed. The new Iraq then objected to becoming a British "protectorate" after the war, and under their mandate, the British installed King Faisal as a constitutional monarch. It was not until 1932 that the British gave up their mandate and left. Iraqis had always harbored resentment against the rich little country of Kuwait, largely the creation, they felt, of the British and Turks. They claimed Kuwait was constantly stealing Iraqi oil from the shared Rumaila oil fields. When Kuwait rejected Iraqi demands, Saddam gave them an ultimatum; when they refused to comply he did what he said he would and invaded.

As a response the United States deployed the 82nd Airborne Division to Saudi Arabia, right in the way of the Saddam's elite Republican Guard; a "Line in the Sand." Operation Desert Shield had begun. Saddam was angry and surprised; he didn't want to tangle with the United States, at least not yet. The 82nd was considered to be a mere "speed bump." He could have rolled over the division in three days, but decided to be prudent and keep what he had gained. . . . at least for now.

Saddam honestly thought he'd be allowed to keep Kuwait and the Kuwaiti oil fields, everyone did, but he had miscalculated. Like the communist invasion of Korea in 1950, the resolve of the West, and specifically the United States, was grossly underestimated. He never thought the United States would respond in any credible way. After all, Iraq possessed the world's fourth largest standing army, as well as formidable armor and air force. For all the talk of Americans not understanding Arabs, the reverse was equally true. Kemal knew that the Americans would come. This wasn't just some small unimportant country. This was about oil and the balance of power in the Middle East.

Now Kemal was suffering from dysentery, dehydration, and a crippling fear. He knew the American capabilities. They would cut through the Iraqi army like a hot knife through butter. They would kill him. They would kill them all. Another series of cramps racked his abdomen and he did something he hadn't done in years. He prayed to Allah for salvation. The Americans were coming soon.

CHAPTER 14

Seven months ago, Americans and the world drew a line in the sand. We declared that the aggression against Kuwait would not stand, and tonight America and the world has kept their word.

—President George Bush,
Feb 27, 1991

Second Lieutenant (2LT) Chuck Rogers arrived in Dhahran, Saudi Arabia, during the middle of the night after a three-day, mind-numbing trip in a C-141. His military police platoon was being sent over to join the rest of the 82nd Airborne Division for the impending invasion of Kuwait. He had barely gotten to Ft. Bragg when he was ordered to take command. He didn't really know his men at all. They were traveling in four C-141s with eight Humvees and all their equipment. One of the planes had broken down in route somewhere over England, and they spent part of a night in a cold hangar at some tiny Royal Air Force base, and the rest of the night sleeping on the floor of a recreation center. As daylight streamed into his face Chuck awoke to someone playing Eric Clapton's "Cocaine" on a jukebox at maximum volume. It took him several moments of semi-panic to remember where he was. It was the first time he was conscious of being apprehensive about the coming battle.

By the time they landed the air war had been underway for a couple of weeks, and so far they were kicking the snot out of Saddam's forces. As Chuck's platoon was unloading on one runway, British Tornado fighter-bombers, empty of munitions, were landing on a parallel runway and others, fully loaded, were taking off on the other side of them. The tarmac was windy, loud, and scary. He knew right then that this was for real; that they were in a war. The whole thing was surreal. Desert Shield had indeed become Desert Storm.

Chuck had the platoon break out the ammo right there on the tarmac, and issued a basic load (210 rounds) of M16 ammo to everyone. Then they had trouble finding all their pallets containing their equipment on the confusing, mind-deafening airfield. Finally, after what seemed like hours, Chuck managed to get all his troops convoyed over to the Kobar towers area to bed down, it was about daybreak. The vast apartment complex at Kobar had originally been built by the Saudis to house the nomadic Bedouins, who in turn, wanted nothing to do with the "cages" the Saudi's wanted to lock them up in. There were several thousand units, and while there was no furniture there was electricity and running water. They set up their cots and a temporary operations center, and while the rest of the platoon bedded down (getting their first real sleep in three days), Chuck and his platoon sergeant headed down to Dragon Country, the XVIII Airborne Corps headquarters.

They found out the Division had already moved several hundred kilometers west, past Raffa on the Iraqi border. Chuck decided that they would spend a couple of days in Daharan picking up essential supplies and would then organize a convoy to link up with the rest of the 82nd. That first night they came under fire from a Scud rocket attack. Chuck was in the middle of a deep sleep at about 0200 hours when the alarms went off. They were chemical alarms, and since no one had briefed them on the meaning of the alarms, there was more than a momentary confusion among the platoon. Finally the guard on CQ (charge of quarters) burst onto the floor and shouted to them to put on their gas masks and head for the basement. Once all the troops were in the dark, cramped basement, Chuck and his NCO looked at one another and without a word, raced for the roof, seven stories up.

Just as they got there, a bright arc from a Patriot missile battery next to the Kobar complex raced skyward and in a millisecond made contact with a streak of fire coming from the north. The resulting explosion lit the sky like the 4th of July, a bright-red star cluster. Chuck and his NCO agreed that the sooner they got to the front, where it was safe from raining death, the better. Saddam was using his scuds as a terror weapon, much as Hitler had used the buzz bombs and the V2 to terrorize the British. He had also fired missiles at Israel, threatening to destroy the fragile coalition in the event that the Israelis responded.

Ammunition was one of Chuck's primary concerns. Because they were one of the last units out of Bragg, everything was in short supply. They were only able to get enough for one basic load per man. The same was true of the new desert-camouflage uniforms, "chocolate chips." They had left Bragg wearing the woodland battle dress uniforms, or BDUs. The army hadn't planned for a desert campaign involving hundreds of thousands of soldiers and almost all of them had been issued out by the time they were ready to go. Chuck's platoon sergeant had been in Special Forces and he and a couple of the junior noncoms were sent out to see what they could scrounge up. Water was another major concern but Chuck needn't have worried; there were thousand of cases of bottled water from Turkey, the UAE, and Saudi Arabia. The ammo and uniforms were another story.

"So you want the good news or the bad news on the ammo, sir?" SSG Jones asked.

"Give me the good first."

"I got 10,000 rounds of M16A2 5.56."

"That's great! What's the bad?"

"It's all tracer!"

"Holy shit. We get in a firefight it's going to look like the 4th of July. OK, show the guys how to load their magazines in some sort of orderly fashion so they have a good mix of ball and tracer. What about uniforms?"

"Good and bad again. I found uniforms but the supply officer wouldn't give any to me. She said they were to be issued out only by order of the Air Force commanding general. She's a cute little lieutenant . . . maybe you could sweet talk her."

"Fuckin' REMFs! Probably keeping them to issue out to a bunch of pogues who won't get any closer to the war than the balcony of their four-star hotel."

They drove down to warehouses near the docks where SSG Jones had found the uniforms. There was stuff stacked everywhere. Vast quantities of material and supplies were flowing into Saudi Arabia by air and sea. Pallets were stacked everywhere. There was so much stuff that the logistics system couldn't keep up with it. They loaded up their five-ton with tow chains, water and gas cans, rebar for pitching tents, kerosene heaters, and a dozen other items that they thought they might need but they had no luck with the uniforms.

"I'm sorry, lieutenant. If I could give them to you I would. You'll have to get permission from Colonel Bitner."

"And where do we find him?"

"He's at the Hotel California." She laughed when she saw the look on his face. "It's what we call it. It's the officer's club at the airbase. They've converted it into the logistics headquarters."

"OK, thanks. Let's motor, sergeant."

When they arrived at the HQ they were directed out the pool area where desks were set up in the shade.

SSG looked at LT Rogers, "Now this is how you should fight a war."

They found the colonel and explained their predicament.

"I'm sorry, lieutenant, but we only have limited quantities in odd sizes. I doubt we'd have enough to outfit your guys."

SSG Jones coughed, "Sir, I went through that warehouse and there are exactly the quantities and sizes we need."

The colonel sighed, "We've got to start putting guards at those warehouses. OK, who are you guys?"

"Sir, we're the MP unit for the advance party of the 82nd Airborne Division." Chuck looked around. "Don't repeat this but we're going to parachute into the Kuwait Airport the night before the ground war starts. We're providing security for the Division Commander and his staff. Sir, we gotta have those uniforms!"

"How many sets you need?"

Chuck thought they would get a set for everyone in the platoon. "Twenty-eight should do it."

"OK, lieutenant. Go see MAJ Arron inside and tell him what you need. Tell him I said so," he waved them off.

They found the major at a desk under a mound of paper. "Major Arron?"

"Yeah?"

"We need some chocolate chips."

"No fuckin' way, lieutenant, we don't have any."

"Sir, Colonel Bitner said to tell you to give us what we need."

"Shit! The General's going to have my ass. How many sets do you need?"

SSG piped in, "Fifty-six should do it."

The major scribbled a note. "OK, go see LT Mendenhall down at warehouse number nineteen. It's . . ."

"We know where it is. Thanks."

When they got to the warehouse the lieutenant looked at Chuck with a newfound respect. "You must really have some juice! How many sets you want?"

"One hundred and twelve sets should do it," answered Chuck, keeping a straight face. *Four sets per man!*

"I suppose you want some night camouflage suits as well?"

"Sure, why not . . . maybe only twenty-eight sets of those."

After they had loaded the truck, SSG Jones turned and looked at Chuck. "We really jumpin' into Baghdad or was that just a line of bullshit you were feeding that colonel?"

"What do you think?"

"Shit, lieutenant," he laughed, "I think we're going to get along just fine!"

In two days the convoy was ready to go. They marked each side of their sand-colored vehicles with a big upside down "V," the mark of the coalition forces and tied fluorescent VS-17 panels on the roof to make sure the Air Force didn't rain destruction down on *them*. It was several hundred kilometers to Raffa and they went north almost to the Kuwaiti border and then headed west on the infamous Tapline Road. It was named Tapline Road because it ran along the border of Saudi Arabia with Kuwait and Iraq, paralleling the oil pipeline. It was infamous because it was one of the world's most dangerous roads. Almost as many soldiers were to be killed on this road as would die at the hands of the enemy.

They started driving at about midnight to avoid the traffic, the whole coalition army seeming to be headed in that direction. They refueled at about 0200, right after turning onto Tapline Road. It was a bitter cold night. The soldiers at the refueling stop were among the most miserable Chuck had ever seen. They were huddled around a small military stove. They were dirty, unshaven, and looked like they hadn't slept in days. They were very helpful, but they had that shell-shocked thousand-yard stare. He left them a case of soda and a couple of boxes of candy one of his "scroungers" had acquired. He felt sorry for them . . . what a way to spend the war; out here in the middle of nowhere being gas station attendants, while the glorious war machine drove down the road. And it was glorious!

Chuck took over the driving of his Hummer as everyone else slept. He put his short-wave radio headphones on (an illegal act while driving) and listened to, of all things, Armed Forces Radio. He had no idea they were up and broadcasting. They were playing some of his favorite rock music and he drove to the west as the sun climbed in the sky behind him. What a sight! He passed division after division as he drove through the desert, American and British mostly, with coalition forces mixed in, arrayed along both sides of the road. It took hours to pass by them all. Armored divisions, mechanized infantry divisions, armored cavalry regiments, air assault . . . they were all here. There were hundreds of M1-A1 Abrams tanks, Bradley APCs (armored personnel carriers), and over one thousand helicopters. The coalition forces also had brought hundreds of fighters, fighter-bombers, bombers, and CAS (close air support) aircraft, including F-14s, F-15s, F-16s, A-10s, and Harriers. They had AWACs radar aircraft, radar-jamming aircraft, the secret F-117 "invisible" night fighter-bombers and even B-52s from the distant island of Diego Garcia. There were also at least three major aircraft carrier groups in the gulf. It was amazing. He had never been so proud of the United States, the Army, or the 82nd Airborne Division, the latter anchoring the far left flank of the three-hundred-thousand-man army. Two entire Army Corps and several Marine Divisions . . . and he was part of it.

Chuck was particularly excited because, despite the story he had told that colonel, he thought for sure he really would have the possibility of getting a gold star for his parachute jump wings, a combat jump. He *knew* the 82nd would be jumping into Kuwait City to secure it in front of the US armored forces. It was what the airborne did. They had done it repeatedly in WWII, in Granada, and in Panama. This move out west was probably just a diversion, or perhaps they would jump onto Tallil Airbase or Jallil Airbase, deep in Iraq. In any case, there would be a jump. Why else would they be here? They employed little armor and this was, after all, an armor war. Little did Chuck know that the lauded 82nd Airborne Division, the "All-American Division, America's Guard of Honor," was, after all those miserable months of being the three-day-speed-bump in front of Saddam, to become the 82nd "Truckborne" Division and largely left out of the strategic planning. Still, they would guard the left flank of the most powerful American army since Vietnam.

Chuck and his platoon linked up with the Division Provost Marshal and the rest of the MPs in the desert west of Raffa. Here they settled in to await the beginning of the ground war. Chuck went into the town as security for some of the supply guys one day. It reminded him of one of those towns in a Clint Eastwood western. If the locals had been wearing sombreros instead of long white shirts and red headscarves, it would have been complete.

Chuck and his men trained and they waited, trained and waited. They lived like the nomadic Bedouins in tents on the open desert. There was no sand and no vegetation, just rocks and powdery dirt. It looked like the surface of the moon, the dark side of the moon. Chuck woke up one morning to find a herd of hundreds of camels surrounding and moving through their camp. Under different circumstances it could have been pleasant; except for the boredom, the *Shamals*, the fierce desert sandstorms, and the cold. Then there was the dust, and the lack of real latrines or showers, and nothing to eat but army rations: the MRE (Meal Ready to Eat), different, but not much better than the C-ration. Then there was the tension of waiting for the war to start. Everyone was getting edgy.

Chuck did learn one new skill in the desert: how to burn shit. The most sanitary way to limit the spread of waste-borne disease was to burn it. They had a couple of piss tubes sunk deep in the earth for urination, but they had to burn all their garbage and the stuff from the sit-down latrines. They were essentially wooden boxes with benches and holes cut in them and toilet seats fixed to the holes. Cans, fifty-five gallon drums cut in half, caught all the shit. When these were near full they had to be pulled out and burned. It was an extremely scientific process however, as explained by a reserve civil affairs preventive medicine officer. He was a grizzled old Vietnam veteran and gave a block of instruction Chuck wished he could have got on tape. It was a riot! Just the right amount of JP-4, a kerosene-like form of aviation gasoline, had to be added in just the right proportions and stirred, just so. Even lighting it was an art. Everyone took turns burning shit; even the officers. For as far as the eye could see, plumes of smoke rose into the sky. If Saddam didn't know they were out there in force, his spies weren't doing their job.

They did weapons training, searching and handling prisoner techniques, and spent a lot of time on chemical weapons (NBC) and first aid training. Everyone was taught to give IVs and handle trauma. The interpreters gave them several language classes so it would be easier to handle prisoners. Phonetic phrases included such commands as "yella'em'she" (let's go), "dur" (turn around), and Chuck's favorite, "an'a'rack'a'til'ic" . . . "do it or I will shoot you." Finally, after a couple of weeks they got the word: D-day would be on February 21. Then, at the last minute, the Soviets tried to negotiate a truce, but the Iraqis were just stalling. President Bush wanted to give the Iraqis and the rest of the world every chance to prove the United States wasn't just looking for a war. D-day was rescheduled for the 24th. On the night of the 24th they moved out into the desert to their staging area. It was a beautiful evening, the sun setting over a desolate desert as they listened to Arabic music on Chuck's radio. It was not hard to imagine being at Tobruk or el-Alamein with David Sterling, the founder of the British Special Air Service (SAS), waiting for the biggest tank battle in half a century to begin. They waited for H-hour.

CHAPTER 15

The days of delusion are dead in Baghdad. The city has finally discovered the obvious: a contest between a third world semi-power fighting WWII and a first world power fighting WW III is no contest at all.

—Michael Kelly,
The New Republic, Feb 11, 1991

Kemal's new acting commander panicked as soon as he heard the first big guns and deserted his soldiers in the face of the American onslaught. Unlike the American army, the Iraqi Army possessed no professional NCO corps. What were left were mostly ill-trained conscripts and junior officers with rock-bottom morale. Earlier in the war "morale squads" had come around to *insure* good morale. The message was clear: you'd have good morale or else! They heard one story of a soldier being strapped to his Scud missile and fired with it. It seemed that the soldier had heard that as soon as a Scud was fired, enemy planes would immediately descend on the launch site. He was caught sabotaging his own equipment, and paid the price for his treachery. Other malcontents had been removed from units for "re-indoctrination." Now, however, the morale squads came no more. They were probably developing their own bad morale as the "mother of all battles" became imminent.

Some of the soldiers just drifted off. Most of the fifty or so who were left to head for Tallil Airbase on foot, only a few kilometers distant. The airbase was adjacent to the ancient Biblical city of Ur, the birthplace of Abraham, and possibly the oldest city on Earth. The Iraqi Air Force had suffered greatly at the hands of the coalition. Those who had engaged the British and American pilots were immediately shot down. Most fled to Iran where their aircraft were confiscated and they were "interned." They tried parking a number of combat aircraft around the ancient Ziggurat (pyramid) in the hopes the Americans wouldn't bomb them for fear of damaging the archeological site. In this land of Babylon, where civilization began, the Ziggurat was a symbol. It was like the Tower of Babel, where the Bible has the confusion of the world beginning. To Chuck that seemed somehow appropriate. What the Iraqis hadn't counted on were American precision weapons. Almost all the aircraft were destroyed with no collateral damage to the archeological digs.

When Kemal's group got to the airbase, they found that an American armor unit had rolled through and shot up the place, taken a bunch of prisoners, and just kept going. As they came onto the base a fanatical Republican Guard major screamed at them for deserting their posts and pressed them into his makeshift base defense. He told them the Americans would torture and kill all of them and they must defend the place to the last man. In the meantime, the major put them to work packing boxes of museum pieces, jewel encrusted daggers, and the like, looted from Kuwait, into his "staff car," a 700-series BMW with Kuwaiti license plates. One of the men told Kemal that there was also a vast amount of cash in the boxes, also stolen from a bank in Kuwait.

They didn't have to wait long for the battle to come to them. As dusk was approaching that first day (the 27th of February), units outside the front gate became engaged in a tremendous firefight with a US Army scouting party. The Americans then retreated, presumably to regroup, and the base defenders retreated to their fixed positions within the base. The major placed Kemal's men on the north side of the base. Kemal, and the men from his unit, waited all night for the Americans to attack; no attack came. However, in the morning they found themselves alone again. The major, and most of the rest of his garrison, having slipped away in the night.

Kemal had been without food for two days and had not had a drink all night. His diarrhea, however, continued unabated. He was dehydrated and weak, but he decided to try and escape out the back gate. He and about fifty of the remaining soldiers headed for it but as soon as they got to the berm an American attack helicopter roared overhead and they ducked into a building. Another helicopter followed with loud speakers telling them the war was over for them, to surrender, and they would be taken care of. American tanks could be heard in the distance.

"It's a trick, they mean to torture and then kill us," said the one officer, a lieutenant wearing a red airborne beret.

"No, they are Americans, not Iranians. If we surrender they will take good care of us," whispered Kemal, who at this point was so weak he could hardly stand up.

An American vehicle came into sight down the berm toward them and the lieutenant told them to start firing. With a roar in his ears, Kemal passed out.

CHAPTER 16

The Gulf War was like teenage sex . . . we got in too soon and out too soon.

—Tom Harkin
The Independent, 1991

Chuck Rogers could barely stay awake. He had been in the three-deep, packed column of vehicles for three days as they wound up the MSR (main supply route), Texas to the Euphrates River, after breaching the virtually non-existent Iraqi defenses. It was the classic end-around maneuver of warfare. While the Marines, VII Corps, and the coalition forces fixed the Republican Guard in place to the east, the XVIII Airborne Corps swung way out west of Raffa and into the rear of the Iraqi army. It was the same maneuver old Stonewall Jackson had used at Chancellorsville. As a Virginia Military Institute (VMI) graduate, LT Rogers was familiar with his daring campaign. He tried to remember his ancient military history; he was sure he remembered that the maneuver had been used a number of times in other classic campaigns; Hannibal at Cannae . . . Austerlitz?

GEN Norman Schwarzkopf was being compared to Napoleon for this brilliant tactic, which he dubbed his Hail Mary maneuver. In reality, he was using one of several war plans that had been formulated before and during his tenure as CENTCOM (Central Command) commander by the CENTCOM staff. It was to be used in just such an occasion as the United States now found itself. It was also being reported on CNN, being channeled into the Division TOC (tactical operations center) at Raffa, that Schwarzkopf, like a lot of conventional commanders and "heavy metal" officers (GEN Abrams in Vietnam being another), had no trust or use for Special Operations Forces and was badly underutilizing or misusing them.

"Stormin' Norman" as he was dubbed, was very much a media personality, despite his obvious bulk (a sore point among many soldiers who questioned his ability to meet the strict Army weight-control standards). He was photogenic and he liked the limelight. Like his father, who got his media start as the head of the New Jersey State Police investigation of the Lindbergh baby kidnapping during the Great Depression, he played the media like a violin.

Now there was no TV to watch and Chuck had been listening to the BBC, and occasionally Radio Moscow, on his shortwave almost nonstop since the ground war began. It was the only way to find out what was going on. It was the classic paradox of warfare: the soldiers fighting the war only saw their small piece of it; they couldn't see the big picture. This radio actually changed that to some degree. Everyone up and down the column would run up during lulls to find out what was happening, like it was the score of a ball game or something.

They had bypassed the al'Salman Airfield as the French 6th Armor, attached to the 1st Brigade, the 504th PIR (parachute infantry regiment), and the 82nd Airborne Division slugged it out with the heavily armed defenders. The 3rd Brigade, the 505th PIR, instead of setting up a tactical assembly area, TAA Cary, as originally planned, swung around to the right and was racing up to one of the war's main objectives, Objective Silver, Tallil Airbase, south of Nasiriyah. As a military police platoon leader, Chuck was part of Team EPW (Enemy Prisoner of War). It consisted of division and attached military police, some psychological operations (PSYOPS), and civil affairs (CA) reservists with interpreters, a small medical detachment, and the 82nd Airborne Division band. He had never really thought about it; what *was* the band's job in wartime since they didn't go drumming and playing into battle anymore? It was guarding and processing prisoners. He hoped they were trained for it.

The civil affairs interpreters were all from Kuwait. They were civilians who had escaped when the Iraqis invaded. Mustafa, one of the interpreters, had been a student and Hamid was a Mercedes-Benz salesman. They all had US connections and had volunteered to help revenge the invasion. There had been a lot of news coverage of Iraqi atrocities; looting, rapes, executions, and torture. Consequently there was no shortage of Kuwaiti volunteers. After a two-week train up at Ft. Dix, New Jersey, the volunteers had been sent straight to the division. They didn't even have uniforms before they arrived. After scrounging equipment for them from the CA guys, they received some quick training, and now were going off to avenge the rape of their country. The military did not even have complete sets of bio/chem defense suits for the interpreters, and they may have to share. Chuck had read the classified intelligence reports on the Iraqis' chemical and biological capabilities. It was really scary stuff. They had sarin gas and maybe even VX, the most deadly of nerve gases. In addition, it was suspected that Saddam had anthrax, *botulinum* toxin, and perhaps other horrors of biological warfare, which were already weaponized. For the first time in his short military career he had really paid attention during the NBC (nuclear, biologic, and chemical) training at Ft. Bragg.

Chuck ended up doing most of the driving. His own driver had narcolepsy, he thought, and couldn't be trusted to drive more than a few hours a day. He had run them into the back of a five-ton truck once and had several other close calls. The LT's head was still sore where he hit it on the windshield. The rest of his crew couldn't seem to stay awake at night either, so Chuck became the designated driver. Hell, he couldn't sleep. For weeks he had the same nervous insomnia that had worried him when he was growing up. He could go for days and weeks on end with only power-naps when he was keyed up. It used to make him crazy, lying awake all night knowing he *had* to get some sleep.

It proved a great advantage in his cadet days, and during Ranger school when sleep deprivation was a conditioned part of the induced stress. It also helped him with his grades. An indifferent student in high school (he had rarely studied), he found that he might as well make good use of the forced three-hour-a-night study hall as a cadet. While his roommate and "brother rats" day-dreamed and nodded off, he studied. They were allowed no radio or TV and were forced to sit at their desk with the door open, so he figured he might as well make good use of his time. He got a 3.33 GPA at midterms and found he was an instant celebrity in the company, even among the upperclassman. He wasn't sure why a simple B average commanded such attention except that most of the freshman cadets were too tired to study on the five to six hours a night they were allowed to sleep, or they were just plain lazy. His GPA dropped to 3.0 at finals, but it was good enough to wear a large gold star on his uniform, get an extra weekend furlough a term, and the instant respect of the Corps. Even though he was a football player, or perhaps because of it, he was marked for great things in the Corps.

He met his fiance on one of those extra furlough weekends. He had seen her at the school on a couple of occasions; once on the arm of an upperclassman at a cadet mixer and another time in town. He had admired her from afar; she was a local girl, an undergraduate at William and Mary, a real classic Southern belle. He had been invited to spend the weekend at an acquaintance of his father. It was a great relief to be out of the barracks, to relax and do nothing ... no reveille, for-mations, or harassment from upperclassmen. They had gone to a neighborhood barbeque and there she was. He was so taken with her that he was tongue-tied when he tried to talk to her. She seemed amused but gave him her phone number and told him to call her when he became "an old man of the Corps." He didn't see her until the following year. He asked her to a cadet dance and from then on they were inseparable, as much as the Corps and her schedule would allow. They planned to be married in the fall following his graduation from school and the MP Officer Basic Course. Then Saddam had invaded Kuwait.

He daydreamed now, as he sat at the wheel of the Hummer, of his past glory as a cadet at VMI. He had almost not attended that school. His father had taken him down to Lexington, Virginia, on a blustery overcast February day for an interview and they had given him to two freshman "rats" to shadow for the day. They talked nonstop about how they hated the Corps and kept calling him a Yankee, even though he was from Maryland, south of the Mason-Dixon line. The cold, gray day matched the cadet's uniforms and his mood by the time he left. He told his father, an Army colonel, that he wouldn't be going there. He had settled on Norwich, a small military school in Vermont.

One day in late March, while he was in senior math, someone came to the door to summon him to the principal's office. On the way to the office he racked his brain for anything he might have done wrong. He had never been called to the office before. Waiting for him was the VMI head football coach. He talked to Chuck's own football coach at Oxen Hill High School, coach East, and after reviewing some films, offered Chuck a partial scholarship. Since he had not been offered the ROTC scholarship he had applied for, he felt obliged to go to VMI and, at the same time, flattered by the attention since he had not really become a starter until halfway through his senior year. He proved to be a late bloomer, and the 5'11", 165 lb. frame of his senior year in high school, turned into 6'1", 205 lb. by the end of his freshman year at VMI. This was achieved by a growth spurt coupled with weight lifting and a special training diet.

He then went on to a less-than-illustrious football career, but played on a regular basis. He found out that his real loves were military history and lacrosse, and he became co-captain of the lacrosse team his senior year. He would have been first captain of the Corps if he had not been a jock. He had to settle for the second highest rank, but he swept almost all the academic honors and prizes.

Being a lieutenant in the 82nd Airborne Division proved a much harder job than being a cadet. *Everyone* dumped on "butter bars," except the lowest enlisted. He remembered what his father once told him; "keep your mouth shut and listen to your platoon sergeant." When he made his branch choices he picked military intelligence, infantry, and military police in that order. He had been assured that as a DMG (distinguished military graduate) he would get his first choice, but inexplicably, had received his third. At the time he really did not care enough to make a big deal about it, but later on decided that he had made a mistake.

He should have gone infantry. He definitely wasn't going to make a career as a military policeman, but he thought maybe he'd get out and become a big-city homicide detective or join the FBI . . . something like that. But first he had to survive this damned convoy and the war.

CHAPTER 17

The Gulf War would not have occurred even a few years earlier when Iraq was the client of an aggressive Soviet Union that might have come to its defense, and it harks back to the pre-1946 period of combat alliances, mobilizations, field maneuvers and large battles. In doing so it is a harbinger of the future. War is back and the future forty-one years may be much more violent than the last.

—Bruce W. Watson,
Military Lessons of the Gulf War

Chuck was just nodding off at the wheel. They were stopped again, as the first vestiges of false dawn snuck through the desert sky. Then all hell broke loose.

"Incoming, incoming," screamed his driver, who had been fast asleep slumped in the passenger side of the HMMWV.

"No it's outgoing," yelled Rogers, equally as excited.

They were positioned just a couple hundred meters in front of, and to the left of, a 155mm howitzer battery. It was, in effect, firing over their heads. The flash was blinding, the concussion deafening. On the other side of them, and just behind them, a MLRS (multilaunch rocket system) launched its missiles, one after another. The large missiles came out of their tubes slowly and with a gathering rush of flame and noise burst into the sky, setting the predawn sky ablaze. They reminded Chuck of flaming dragons from some movie. Between the two weapons batteries, the ground shook and the noise was deafening. As his heart slowed from the adrenaline surge, Chuck thought how glad he was not to be on the receiving end.

After another fifteen minutes of waiting, a message came down to Team EPW to move up to the lead battalion. There they found a couple hundred very sad-looking Iraqi soldiers being guarded by a squad of soldiers from the 3rd Brigade. Almost all the prisoners carried the surrender leaflets dropped by PSYOPS (psychological operations). The leaflets promised good care if the Iraqis surrendered. Although it was bitter cold (as only the desert can be in winter), many of them were bootless and none had winter coats. They were dirty, hungry, and thirsty; docile . . . just glad to be out of it. The few weapons they recovered were in terrible condition, some of the AK-47s had their bolts rusted shut. A number of them had shrapnel wounds and many looked sick. LT Rogers yelled for the medics and they started the process of searching the prisoners. They were searched and put into a makeshift concertina-wire stockade. While they were processing the prisoners Chuck came across one distinctly unmilitary individual, who it turned out was a doctor. He was small, mousy, and wore thick glasses. He told Chuck, in excellent English, that he had been educated in England and Moscow. He was put to work on the casualties along with the two medics that were attached to Team EPW.

As the rest of the brigade passed and they were putting the EPWs onto double-decker buses (who knows where *they* came from) to be shipped to the rear, Chuck got a call from the provost marshal to grab a couple of interpreters and some of the civil-affairs soldiers and head forward again. The lead battalions were moving fast and didn't want to be slowed down with civilians or enemy prisoners who were coming out of the woodwork to surrender. They also didn't want a bunch of Iraqis wandering around in their rear. In the end, so many wanted to surrender that they simply disarmed them, gave them a bottle of water and a MRE (meal ready to eat), and sent them marching back to the rear to another temporary stockade.

Rogers and his group were sent along with the lead maneuver element. They came to Highway 8 after another brief firefight/artillery exchange. They had reached the biblical Euphrates River! The first thing Chuck saw was a small destroyed shack and a burned-out vehicle with bodies lying all around. They turned right and raced down the four-lane highway toward Tallil Airbase, following a line of burning Soviet T-72 Iraqi tanks. The 24th Mechanized Infantry Division had rolled through the area and had really shot things up, but failed to secure anything because, having flanked the main body of the Iraqi army, they were now in the most enviable of spots for a combat commander. They were a highly mobile mechanized force in the enemy rear and they took full advantage of it. They completely annihilated several of the lauded Republican Guard Divisions and would have done inestimatable damage if the ceasefire hadn't been called on the night of the 28th, right in the middle of their rampage.

The 505th Parachute Infantry Regiment (PIR) halted at a small construction worker camp a few kilometers from the airbase on Highway 8 and sent a five-vehicle scouting party from the scout platoon with LT Rogers, an interpreter, and the civil-affairs sergeant major to recon Tallil Airbase. Conveniently, all the road signs were in both English and Arabic and they had no trouble finding the airbase. Maps, especially the 1:50,000 tactical maps used by the infantry, were in short supply. Coordinates from their GPS (global positioning system) units were worthless without maps. It had never really been envisioned that the 505th PIR would be up on the Euphrates, they were supposed to set up a blocking position out in the desert, but because of the rapid exploitation of the enemy weaknesses CONPLAN (contingency plan) MOSEBY was being put into effect. The 505th rushed up to secure Tallil Airbase and guard the 24th Mech rear.

Chuck used a hand-traced strip map from the S-3 to follow their progress to the airbase. The bomb-cratered four-lane road to the airbase was littered with destroyed tanks, trucks, armored cars, and civilian vehicles. Every overpass was destroyed and the vehicles had to carefully pick their way over the littered roadway. One of the things that struck Chuck along the route was that almost everywhere you looked, except in the heart of the desert, there were bigger-than-life posters, busts, or paintings of Saddam. What an ego!

As they were coming up to the main gate they came under heavy fire. One of their HMMWVs, firing a TOW missile, vaporized a truck loaded with soldiers that unexpectedly charged them. Colonel Hale, the brigade commander withdrew them as night was quickly approaching. The plan was to mount an all-out assault in the morning. An operations meeting was held and halfway through the meeting they got word that a ceasefire had been called. Objective Silver, Tallil Airbase and its supply depot, was one of the war's main objectives. *How the hell were they going to take it without shooting the crap out of it and violating the ceasefire?*

CHAPTER 18

Wars with limited military aims do not necessarily solve the root political problems that brought them about.

—Bruce Watson
Military Lessons of the Gulf War

The brigade commander and his staff set up a command post in a walled compound next to a destroyed gas station near Tallil. Although only a couple of kilometers from the Euphrates River, the area was arid and barren with little sign of vegetation. Chuck and half his platoon had been OPCON'd (operational control) to the brigade to provide security. During the day it was warm but the sky was almost orange from the burning oil wells that the Iraqi forces set ablaze during their retreat, as well as the *shamal* they experienced the day before. The nights were cold and starless, even the moon obliterated by the detritus of the burning hydrocarbons and suspended dust. That night was the blackest Chuck could ever remember. They were short of night-vision goggles (NVGs) and the few Chuck had were given to the guards pulling security on the perimeter. Although his hole in the mud that was his perimeter defense position was not more than a hundred meters from the Brigade TOC, Chuck got seriously lost on his way to the staff meeting that evening. They were observing strict sound-and-light discipline and Chuck almost despaired of finding the TOC when he suddenly stumbled into it.

The staff was planning to take the airbase. This was one of those times in warfare when all the right people were in the right place. The brigade commander was a Special Forces officer—rare in the 82nd—and had been commander of the 2nd Ranger Battalion and was well versed in unconventional operations. The Civil Affairs Commander LTC King, who had moved up with the 505th PIR, was a former Recon Marine and a Special Forces officer as was his XO (executive officer), MAJ Gallagher. The CA operations officer had been the S-2 (intelligence) of the 2nd Ranger Battalion under the Brigade Commander. Their sergeant major was SF *and* a PSYOPS (psychological operations) expert. MAJ Caldwell, the Brigade S-3, was bright and flexible. The Division PSYOPs officer was called forward, and a scheme hatched to take the airfield without firing a shot.

LT Rogers stayed up all night listening to the planning. He was extremely impressed by the Special Forces/CA lieutenant colonel, a tall man with bulging muscles and an air of confidence that was contagious. He was surprised to find out he was a reservist, a Secret Service agent in real life. Chuck had always had a bad impression of reservists; they were out of shape, poorly trained, and led. It was a common attitude in the "real" Army. The rest of the CA guys were also reservists and equally impressive and he marveled at their can-do attitude. In the by-the-book 82nd, and the Army in general, original thought was not necessarily always an asset. He remembered a comment from the "sea lawyer," Lieutenant Keefer in Herman Wouk's book *The Caine Mutiny*, that the military was a system designed by masterminds to be run by idiots. This was apparently not the case in Special Forces. These guys were going to take the airbase regardless of the ceasefire and, hopefully, without engaging in any combat. If there was firing, they would blame it on the Iraqis. He decided then and there that if he stayed in the army, he would go Special Forces.

Tallil Airbase was an essential target, not only because it was a major operational airfield with numerous combat aircraft still on it, but because intelligence had determined that the attached Kamasyia weapons depot was filled with thousands of weapons, tons of ammunition (including possible chemical and biological weapons), and was a major supply base as well. Unlike the VII Corps, which had failed to secure the vital road junction that linked Baghdad, Basra, and Kuwait City, the 82nd Airborne Division was going to *seize* all its chief objectives.

Their brainchild was named Task Force PSYOPs and consisted of PSYOPs soldiers, Civil Affairs, 1/17th Cavalry Scouts, and LT Roger's small group as the ground element under the command of the SF lieutenant colonel. The Division PSYOPs officer and the Division PSYOPs helicopter with speakers (right out of *Apocalypse Now*), would fly around the airbase playing, not Wagner, but a message in Arabic that went: "the war is over for you, surrender or you will be killed." A company of Sheridan tanks would rumble around the outer-access road, while a squadron of Cobra attack helicopters would buzz the airfield. The division artillery was zeroed in on a number of preregistered sites and two battalions of the 505th PIR were prepared to enter once the airfield was secure, or if the ground element came into heavy contact. Then it could be called self-defense. The Division Commander was briefed and gave the go ahead. Jump-off time was set for 0900.

CHAPTER 19

Will there be hell to pay in the aftermath of a successful campaign against Saddam? No war begets the consequences men expect of it.

—Editorial, *The New Republic,*
February 11, 1991

The operation started off badly with the CA guys arriving at the jump-off site a few minutes late and the PSYOPS bird, not getting the word, had started the operation prematurely. In addition, the CA vehicles, which were to lead with the scouts, were only equipped with one of the older radios so they could not communicate on both the tactical net for the ground elements and the command net for the brigade commander, who would be flying overhead in the C & C (Command and Control) helo. The brigade commander was hopping mad and the operation was only allowed to continue after grabbing one of the Division HMMWVs with the civil affairs S-3 on the radio and a bit of an ass chewing by the colonel. With the scout team leading, they entered through the back gate. They dropped gun jeeps off at each intersection and rolled by the base administration building, a burned out wreck, onto the runway and past several MIG-21s, Mirage fighters, a fully operational HIND-D Soviet attack helicopter, and the ubiquitous images of Saddam.

At the base control tower they placed a loudspeaker and a sniper team. The base appeared deserted. Just as the CA commander was about to get on the horn to give the signal for the line battalions to move in, one of the scout teams called to say they had movement in a building to their west. LTC King dispatched LT Rogers with his four guys and the CA executive officer, MAJ Gallagher, with two of his men to the intersection. As they came into the open on the berm they started taking small-arms fire. A round went through the windshield right between Rogers and his driver and the two MPs in the back. His adrenalin surged as he charged his M16, forgetting he already had a round in the chamber, and took it off safe. They accelerated, swerved right to bring a building between them and the fire and raced down to the intersection. As Rogers was getting out of the vehicle a large dog rushed, snarling at him from the brush. *Shit.* He shot it with an automatic unconscious movement.

The CA guys set up a loud speaker in defilade of the building, and the XO had them broadcast for the Iraqis to surrender. The Iraqis replied with several rounds from their AK-47s. The XO conferred on the radio with his S-3 and it was decided to send the Cobras over the building on a low pass. The Cobra was a deadly looking aircraft and could be a very convincing argument for surrender. An immediate white flag followed and one-by-one the defenders came straggling out of the building and along the berm road with their hands in the air. Just when it looked like everything was going well, LT Rogers saw several armed men running in back of the building across their flank and into the drainage ditch that ran along the outer fence to their position.

"They're trying to flank us," he yelled as he jumped down into the ditch to try and cut off the men. The CA sergeant major had jumped in it with him and they raced down it just in time to see the running group head through the brush away from them and into the desert toward the river. The brigade commander, who had seen them from his C & C bird, told them to let them go. As the rest of the Iraqis came down the berm they were searched, given an MRE (all the pork meals having been taken out), a bottle of water, and placed on one of the mysterious double-decker buses. The mission was a complete success, although the Chuck almost shot one of the Iraqis who was fiddling with something behind his head as he came down the berm. Instead of a grenade, which Chuck had feared, it turned out to be some prayer or "worry" beads, the rosary that so many Muslims carry.

LT Rogers was pleased with himself. Like most young men, he always wondered how he would behave in combat, although this was not exactly a pitched battle. It was something that worried all untested would-be warriors; that they would be paralyzed by fear or, worse yet, be actual cowards. He had read enough to know that only in actual combat would he find out. Like the youth in Stephen Crane's *The Red Badge of Courage*, he had been tested. It was funny, he had not been afraid and he had done all the right things, and he reacted in the proper way to the fire and the danger. He had run to the sound of the guns. However, his mind just went blank, his body hummed and he just reacted. He wondered if this was a typical reaction among soldiers. Now his knees felt weak and he wanted to sit down. He told his men, who were finished processing the prisoners, to refrain from souvenir hunting because of potential booby traps (there turned out to be none) as the combat battalion swept past them to finish securing the airfield. He walked to the front of the building, which had a large glass case with the ubiquitous picture of Saddam in full military regalia and with the butt of his M16 broke the glass. He would present the poster to the CA lieutenant colonel.

As he got back to the gate a second line battalion came sweeping in to secure the airfield.

"Well LT, you can be proud of yourself; something to tell the grandchildren," said the Civil Affairs XO.

"Yeah, I guess, but we could be in Baghdad in two days."

"Well, the decision to stop here was political; we were slaughtering them. War *is* politics!"

"Clausewitz?"

"Yeah, *von* Clausewitz actually; he was one of the greatest military theorists. What he really said was war was just an extension of diplomacy by other means, something like that. That's one of the reasons our founding fathers wanted to keep our military separate from politics; it's too easy for a military government to pick up a gun to settle international problems."

"What was that some said about war being too important to be left to the generals?"

"In this case it may have been a good decision to stop. The early estimates are that over one hundred thousand Iraqi soldiers have been killed so far. We've fulfilled the UN resolutions; we kicked them out of Kuwait. The resolutions don't say anything about overthrowing the government. Besides, if we kept going we would loose a lot of coalition support, not to mention the casualties we'd take."

"That's true, I guess."

"The other thing is that if we defeat them, we'll have to stay and rebuild the country. Believe me, that's the last thing we want to do. We'd be here for years."

"But this isn't a baseball game; we can't just take our ball and go home when it's all over."

"Who says? I don't know about you, but I've seen as much of the fabled land of Babylon as I can stand."

"You got that right, I guess. But don't you think we should stay and consolidate our gains? We don't want to have to come back here."

"Well, I don't think the 'Powers That Be' want to get into another peace-keeping operation right now. Besides, we don't want to completely destroy Iraq. A destabilized Iraq is not in our national interest, there's the Kurds, the Syrians, and the Iranians to worry about, and a big power vacuum in this part of the world could wreak havoc on the balance of power in the Middle East. Anyway, Saddam will never survive this; he'll be gone in six months."

"I'd feel better if we'd killed the son of a bitch!"

"He'll get his, don't worry."

As he was turning around to walk away a figure half stumbled, half crawled out of the building. Chuck almost shot him.

"Please, don't leave me," whispered Kemal in English.

"Medic," yelled Rogers as his guys rushed up. They gently got him on a litter. The XO, a former SF medic, hooked him up to an IV.

"You're going to be all right," he was told by Rogers. "We're going to MEDEVAC you back to one of our hospitals."

Mustafa, one of the interpreters, came up and told him in Arabic that they would take good care of him.

"You are very kind, are you an American?" asked Kemal, as the interpreter tried to make him comfortable. "How is it that you speak such good Arabic?"

"I'm from Kuwait City," replied Mustafa.

Kemal began to cry.

BOOK THREE

SOMALIA, 1993

Me and my clan against the world;
Me and my family against my clan;
Me and my brother against my family;
Me against my brother.

—Somalian proverb

CHAPTER 20

The minstrel boy to the war has gone,
In the ranks of death you'll find him;
His father's sword he has girded on,
And his wild harp behind him.

—Thomas Moore,
Irish Melodies

When Ryan Gallagher volunteered to join the US Army Rangers it was a great surprise to just about everyone who knew him. That he had joined the army at all was a surprise, especially to his father, a reserve Special Forces major. Ryan had been an unruly teenager, "since about age five," as his parents used to say. At eighteen months he had thrown all his nursing bottles out the window of the car; that had been the end of his infancy. He had fiery red hair, freckles, and an Irish temper to go with his name and complexion. He never really got into any *real* trouble, but was periodically what his father thought of as a pain-in-the-ass.

By his senior year in high school he had grown to six foot two, lean and wiry. He was a natural athlete, but disdained the discipline of organized sports, even though as a student of the prestigious Lawrence Academy in Groton, Massachusetts, he was required to participate in a sport each semester. It was an excellent school and Ryan's father felt very fortunate that he was able to send his sons there. He used to say his *own* father, a career army colonel, child of the Great Depression and self-made man, would be rolling over in his grave if he knew *his* grandson was going to one of "those snotty New England prep schools." Ryan's father, having tried unsuccessfully to interest Ryan's older brother into joining ROTC, was not even going to try with Ryan. He would tell people he was sure Ryan would wind up in the brig if he did. His father, teachers, and headmaster butted heads with Ryan on a regular basis throughout his adolescence.

He had developed a quiet self-assuredness, but not yet tempered by maturity. He showed respect only for the individual and not the office, only to those he had personal respect for as a person. He couldn't hide his contempt for what seemed to be most of the world. Once, he got into it with a new dean of students who, as Ryan saw it, greatly overstepped his authority in the personal affairs of his charges. In the headmaster's office he verbally and systematically took the dean apart in front of his amazed parents, faculty advisor, and headmaster. The adults in the room later reflected that none of them would have challenged such authority at that age or with Ryan's deftness. The dean was not invited back to the school the next year.

This was exactly the type of incident that MAJ Gallagher was worried about if his son ever joined the military; senior officers rarely enjoy having their faults pointed out by a disrespectful subordinate. The military is almost never a good place for individualism, brashness, and freethinking, at least not since the days when George Patton and Douglas MacArthur were junior officers. Besides, Ryan had not shown the slightest inkling of interest in *anything* remotely connected with the military. In fact, one of his instructors at Lawrence (whom Ryan's father thought secretly was a left-wing commie) took great delight at what he thought were Ryan's attitudes toward the military and American imperialism.

What none of them guessed was that while on an eighth-grade field trip to Washington, DC, Ryan had been profoundly moved at the Vietnam Memorial while making a stone rubbing of the name of his father's friend and platoon leader, a Marine Corps second lieutenant who was killed during the waning years of the Vietnam War. He was also deeply affected by Arlington Cemetery while standing on the grassy sea of white gravestones flowing so perfectly down to the Washington monument. One stone in particular brought tears to his eyes: *Colonel Eugene F. Gallagher, WWII, Korea, Vietnam. Born 1918, Died 1976*: his grandfather. He could just recall the old man bouncing him on his knee with a "Ryan-me-boy!" He loved the old man in a way all five-year-olds love their grandfathers, the memory of him frozen in time by his death. Then there was the letter his father wrote him on the eve of his leaving for the Gulf War; a letter like all fathers write to their sons as they depart for war, perhaps never to return. It was typical "duty, honor, country" fare with clichés like "freedom isn't free" and "if I should fail to return," but Ryan secretly kept it and would pull it out sometimes to re-read it. The letter would help him through some of the difficult years to come.

And so, while his father was in Iraq, at Tallil Airbase during the Gulf Was as executive officer (XO) of the Civil Affairs battalion for the 82nd Airborne Division, Ryan went down to the local army recruiter on his eighteenth birthday and joined up under the program that delayed his entry until the summer after graduation from prep school. All his college admissions applications were sent out and Ryan didn't tell anyone about his decision.

His father *did* return from Desert Storm just in time to see Ryan graduate and it was over an illegal beer (his father having grown up in the days when those of draft age could *legally* drink) that Ryan told him what he had done. His father was shocked, angry, proud, and dismayed. Not for the least reason of which was that Ryan had been accepted at much better colleges than his father had hoped for. His mother was not to be consoled and felt it was just one more group of gray hairs. His girlfriend, friends, and teachers all thought he was crazy, but he was secretly pleased with himself. He was nothing if not independent, his own man.

He came home on leave after basic training but reported early to Ft. Benning, Georgia, for advanced individual training (AIT) as an infantryman, because he was tired of everyone, except his father, looking at him like he had some undiagnosed psychiatric condition. That was to be the last time in his career he ever reported early, even a second early, to any Army assignment because they had him doing scout details for the next few days. After AIT, he went to the Army Parachute School, also at the "Benning School for Boys" and earned his parachute (airborne or jump) wings. It was about halfway through airborne school that his orders came assigning him, not to a Ranger Battalion or even to the 82nd Airborne Division, but to the reactivated 10th Mountain Division at Ft. Drum, New York.

CHAPTER 21

Few things grab American interest more than pictures of starving children. And so, in the early 1990s when we were shown the terrible famine in the Horn of Africa, we wanted action. President Bush would have it no other way.

—Kent DeLong and Steven Tuckey,
Mogadishu!

Ryan reported to the first sergeant, the "Top Kick," of one of the companies with the 2nd Battalion, 14th Infantry Regiment, 10th Mountain Division on November 1, 1992. The Division was one of the few in the Army not deployed for Desert Storm and instead had deployed to southern Florida in August of 1991 in the wake of Hurricane Andrew. His new battalion was just readying itself now for an exercise at Ft. Pickett, Virginia, when he reported in. Although unhappy about not going to the Rangers, the 82nd or the 101st, Ryan was nevertheless proud to be a part of the 10th MTN Division. He knew of their history during WWII and he had spent a bit of time at their small museum at Ft. Devens, Massachusetts, near where his father's reserve unit was, A Co, 1st Bn, 11th Special Forces Group. His father had also served with the 10th Special Forces Group (Airborne) at Ft. Devens and they had lived on post when Ryan was little. He remembered the museum as one of his earliest memories. Douglas MacArthur, born in the 1880s on a western cavalry post, used to tell people *his* first memory was a bugle call. Ryan was also was fond of rock climbing and skiing and knew that 10th MTN veterans from WWII started most of the ski areas in the United States.

When he went to the first sergeant's office, he was surprised to see two privates in the leaning-rest in front of his desk. He thought this type of discipline became obsolete once he had finished Basic, AIT, and Airborne.

"PFC Gallagher reporting as ordered," he said, coming to attention and saluting.

"Join your buddies down there Gallagher. We don't salute NCOs, even first sergeants, in this army," he barked.

Ryan assumed the push-up position as Top quizzed him on his background. Ryan, seeing the Ranger scroll on Top's right sleeve known as a Shoulder Sleeve Insignia (SSI) or "combat patch" knew it signified that Top had been in combat with a Ranger Battalion. Ryan told the 1st Shirt *he* had signed up for the Rangers.

"Shit. They'd eat a skinny puke like you for breakfast. I'll tell you what though, you do well and when you make E-4 or E-5 maybe we'll send you to Ranger School and you can go to one of the battalions as an NCO," he growled. "Recover!"

"Now you guys get your stuff stowed away and report back here for equipment issue. We've got an exercise starting down at Ft. Pickett, Virginia, in a couple of weeks and we need to get you guys in-processed and assigned to your platoons."

They deployed down to Ft. Pickett for the battalion exercise. It was exciting for the new soldiers, boring for the old enlisted hands, and nerve wracking for the young leaders saddled with the responsibility for their soldiers and the execution of orders. In this "zero defect" army anything could ruin your career; a lost weapon, a severe injury, or one of the other "individual acts of idiocy" soldiers are known for. For the senior leaders it was an opportunity to evaluate their units, correct deficiencies, and fine-tune the unit, to ready it for the call to war. They didn't have long to wait. In December, halfway through the exercise, the battalion commander received a call from the Division G-3.

"Get your unit back here to Drum ASAP. We're going to Somalia!"

CHAPTER 22

The idea used to be that terrible countries were terrible because good, decent, innocent people were being oppressed by evil, thuggish leaders. Somalia changed that.

—Mark Bowden,
Black Hawk Down

The mission had started out as a purely humanitarian mission, albeit one with muscle. Ryan had watched the "forced entry" into Somalia a year before on TV (along with the rest of the world) with a mixture of disbelief and disgust. Navy Seals came across the sands in the glare of video floodlights, caught like "deer in the headlights." Soon the beach was awash with TV anchormen, journalists of every description, Seals, and Marines; the only thing missing were armed Somalis! "What a fucked-up operation," he had thought to himself at the time. "I'm sure glad I'm not going there!" He had not paid much attention to the mission since that inauspicious beginning, being preoccupied with learning the crafts of a soldier.

Now with the call to war, Ryan remembered his father working on area studies for three countries following his return from Desert Storm: Somalia, Yugoslavia, and Haiti. Ryan had asked him, why those three countries? His father had responded that they were the most likely hot spots in the world in the next few years. Ryan called his father and had him send the unclassified version of the Somalia-area study, which he passed around the barracks. It turned out they had plenty of time to study up, much to the disgust of their battalion commander. After returning to Drum they were informed that parts of the Division were deploying to Somalia immediately. Battalion would eventually be going, but not for a while. They had lost a valuable training opportunity for nothing.

Ironically, the worst of the famine in Somalia was burning itself out even as the armed humanitarian mission started, most of those destined to die having already done so. By most accounts over three-hundred thousand had perished. It was hard to ascertain exactly how much the years of drought and the breakdown of law and order contributed to the famine. Ryan remembered once asking his father about his Irish heritage for a school project. Ryan's great-grandfather had fled Ireland in 1916 after the Easter Rebellion with a bullet in his leg and a profound hatred of the English until the day he died. One of his favorite sayings, referring to the Great Potato Blight that caused the mass exodus from Ireland in the nineteenth century, was that "God created the blight, but the English created the famine." Much the same was apparently true in Somalia. Rival clans of gunman disrupted relief efforts, stole food, ambushed convoys, threatened relief workers, and systematically turned Somalia into a lawless *Mad Max* hell on earth.

Initial efforts to relieve the suffering were thwarted by the lawlessness. Operation Provide Hope in early 1992 was hampered when C-130s bringing in food were regularly fired upon; the 5th Special Forces Group (ABN) had to provide security. Humanitarian supply distribution was completely disrupted and the clans stole most of the food. It never went to those who truly needed it. In September, the Pakistanis stood by helplessly while food was stolen directly under their nose and fighting, starvation, disease, and anarchy spread throughout the country. Food was power in Somalia. Finally, under the glare of the media circus, pictures of starving children, and evil gunmen, the UN/US went into action.

A United Nations Task Force (UNITAF), led by the United States, was formed to "Restore Hope" under the direction of Robert Oakley, a former ambassador to Somalia. It consisted of 38,000 troops from twenty nations, 25,000 of them from the US. The Somalis, even the warlords, almost uniformly welcomed them at first. Unfortunately the only policy that could have ensured that the mission would be a long term success, disarmament, was put in the "too hard" box and was applied either selectively or not at all. Even Mohammed Farrah Aidid (the warlord who was to become the *assigned* great villain in the drama) admitted that disarmament would have been successful if done early in the exercise. This gave many of the warlords the feeling that they were untouchable. In the meantime, the *real* villains in the drama to come, President Clinton and Secretary of Defense Aspin, came to power in the US. While the US was initially hailed almost universally as heroes, they now became viewed as the enemy to many Somalis as "mission creep" changed the mission from humanitarian to selective peace enforcement in mid-1993. Now "good" warlords were favored and "bad" warlords marginalized. Ironically, the Somalia intervention violated almost all the tenants of the "Powell Doctrine," so lauded after Desert Storm. It especially violated the first three: "the United States should not commit forces to combat overseas unless the particular engagement or occasion is deemed vital to our national interests," that if we do commit troops "we should do so wholeheartedly, and with the clear intention of winning," and the troops should have "clearly defined political and military objectives." What was most ironic was that the author of this doctrine, General Clayton Powell, was the current Chairman of the Joint Chiefs of Staff and either allowed what was about to happen or was powerless to influence the Clinton administration.

Somalia was saturated with weapons, again irony was prevalent, the United States having supplied many of the millions of weapons available, just as they had to Iraq and Afghanistan in the previous decades. Now these same weapons were being directed against Americans. Clinton turned the mission over to the UN in May of 1993, but with a US commander. Admiral Jonathan Howe was appointed to take the helm. The admiral now became Somalia's *newest* warlord, hunkering down in the vast US embassy compound, armed to the teeth, and with a "bunker mentality." The United States became the victim of the great paradoxes of counterinsurgency warfare; the more force protection you try to achieve, the less secure you are and the more force is used, the less effective it becomes. Eerily reminiscent of the military-media rift of Vietnam, the admiral and his staff would report everything in glowing terms while the media reported impending disaster, also reminiscent of Vietnam. The positive spin put on every negative incident (and there were many) actually seemed to be believed by those in charge.

The head of the Habr Gedir clan, Mohammed Farrah Aidid, whose name, in the vernacular, means "one who tolerates no insult," was summarily declared responsible for Somalia's troubles and the UN forces went after him with a vengeance. A joke around the compound was that he was Jonathan Howe's Great White Whale. He was declared "Public Enemy Number One," with a ridiculously low $25,000 bounty put on his head. Aidid promptly put a $1,000,000 bounty on Howe's head. Howe imported Task Force Ranger—Rangers, Delta Operators (America's not really secret, but never officially acknowledged unit), and the 160th SOAR (Special Operations Aviation Regiment)—to deal with Aidid and other enemies with "surgical precision." Their commander, MG William Garrison, a cigar-smoking Texan, had smuggled himself into Somalia disguised as a lieutenant colonel. At the same time, Defense Secretary Aspin and President Clinton repeatedly denied requests for critically needed US armor and aviation assets for the Quick Reaction Force (QRF). Armor that, undeniably, would have insured mission (the *new* mission) success.

The incident that sparked the coming disaster, the apparently coordinated attack on Pakistani peacekeepers that left scores dead and wounded, was responded to in a massive show of force. Ironically, the person who approved the upcoming raids on Radio Mogadishu, Aidid's compound, and other targets by AC-130 gunships, was April Glaspie, a foreign service officer and second in command in Somalia. She was infamous for making statements to Saddam Hussein before the Gulf War in such a way that he interpreted her behavior as tacit approval to invade Kuwait. The other great proponent for this gunboat diplomacy was Madeline Albright, then US ambassador to the UN and future secretary of state, who fashioned herself in a "tough" Maggie Thatcher mold.

The result was "Bloody Monday," a June 12 attack on a house owned by one of Aidid's lieutenants where (would ironies never cease) clan members were purportedly gathered to discuss peace talks with the UN/US attack helicopters fired 16 TOW missiles and over 2,000 rounds of 20mm cannon into the building. Estimates of the dead and wounded varied greatly; the Somalis claiming over 700 killed while the International Committee of the Red Cross (ICRC) put the number at 54 civilians killed and 250 wounded. The Somalis responded in kind and the blood feud began in earnest.

So the men of the 10th Mountain Division traded their Woodland Camouflage Uniforms (BDUs) for the new Desert uniforms (DCUs) and found themselves in late July of 1993 in Mogadishu, the "City of Death."

CHAPTER 23

Said the lama, "what profit to kill men?"
"Very little . . . as I know; but if evil men were not now and then slain,
it would not be a good world for weaponless dreamers," said the old soldier.

—Rudyard Kipling,
Kim

They had kept Kemal in the EPW hospital near Raffa, Saudi Arabia, until almost the end. He was one of the last prisoners sent back to Iraq. The doctors at the prison camp discovered that he had contracted an invasive type of amoebic dysentery, a form that invaded into both the walls of his intestine and set up a large abscess in his liver. The abscess was repeatedly drained, and finally he was sent to an American combat support hospital (CSH) near Dhahran for surgery. He pleaded not to be sent back to Iraq and early on had been promised he would receive political asylum, but in the end they sent him back anyway with a bunch of other sick prisoners. No one wanted them; no country would agree to take him.

When they had been repatriated they were treated with suspicion, almost as traitors. It reminded Kemal of a song, a haunting Russian melody he had liked by Al Stewart called "Road to Moscow." It was about a Russian patriot who fought the whole war against the Germans in WWII, only to be sent to a gulag in Siberia at the war's end because he had once been taken prisoner. That's what Kemal was going back to: his own gulag, Iraq.

He was sent to an Iraqi military hospital near Baghdad, a barbaric place, less a hospital than a butcher shop. While he was convalescing he decided to help out in the crude medical lab they had and actually made himself quite useful. The pathologist was glad to have someone with a biology/microbiology background and promised Kemal he would not go back to an army field unit. True to his word, Kemal was made a laboratory technician in early 1993, studied his craft, and within a couple of years was put in charge of the entire microbiology lab; growing cultures, doing bacterial isolates, sensitivity testing, and even some virology. He became so good at it that, unfortunately, he came to the attention of those who were involved in the sinister work of rebuilding Saddam's weapons of mass destruction (WMD) arsenal. The inspections by the UN and the destruction of Iraq's biological warfare labs were merely setbacks but the programs could be reinstated. They had hidden many of their most virulent cultures of anthrax, clostridium (for the production of botulinum toxin), aflotoxin, and several other nasty assorted bugs. They also managed to save a small amount of manufacturing equipment; fermentation vats, incubators, and the like. When the UN WMD inspectors were finally kicked out of the county, Hussein would be free to renew his evil work. Kemal was going to work for them whether he liked it or not.

CHAPTER 24

If you have a yen to see a beautiful land of camels, sand, thorn scrub, endless beaches, and interesting villages completely unspoiled by tourism, Somali is the place to be.

—The Lonely Planet Guide to Africa, 1991

Ryan's first impression of Somalia, getting off the plane on July 29, was not favorable. The heat was almost overpowering. Coming out of the relative cool of the C-130, it struck you like a wall. Then there was the smell of Somalia. It was a mixture of dust, burning garbage, human waste, and the yeasty flavor of starvation. Fecal material was strewn about indiscriminately. Ryan remembered reading a story about the lack of toilet habits of the Somalis. One aid group, so disgusted with this lack of hygiene, imported a number of chemical toilets (that required little or no maintenance) for one of the villages. On a return visit, the health-care worker was surprised when the village elder told him the toilets did not work. Going to see for himself, he found the toilets completely choked with small stones. He finally got the story out of the headman. It seems that Somalis routinely carry two small stones that they roll in their hands and click together while relieving their bowels. When they were finished, for some inexplicable reason, they would drop the stones in the toilet. The aid worker threw up his hands in disgust and gave up.

UNOSOM II replaced UNITAF, Operation Restore Hope became Operation Continue Hope, and the 2nd BN, 14th INF replaced their fellow 10th MTN soldiers, TF 1-22. UNOSOM II was made up of twenty-five thousand troops backed by a United States logistics team and an American Quick Reaction Force (QRF). It was the QRF role that was the 2nd BN's mission under the command of LTC William David. This 625-man task force was stationed at the university compound of Mogadishu, about three-and-a-half kilometers from the airport and TF Ranger, on the other side of the city. By August the climate in Somalia had become very dangerous. There were numerous ambushes and attacks on UN forces in addition to the massacre of the Pakistanis in June. UN forces had retaliated in kind with raids, abductions, and seizure-and-destruction missions. The new blood feud was well underway, orchestrated by Somalia's newest warlord, Admiral Howe and the United States

Army. Casualties mounted on both sides, including the deaths of four US MPs when their vehicle hit a command-detonated mine. It was followed two weeks later with the wounding of seven other American soldiers. Even the local wildlife became the enemy. Soldiers were warned not to swim off the beaches because the Somalis routinely dumped offal in the harbor. In spite of the warnings, one soldier swimming at Black Beach was severely attacked by a shark. Even after the transfusion of dozens of units of blood and emergency surgery he expired at the 46th Combat Support Hospital (CSH).

Many found the Somalis to be contemptible and dehumanized them. It wasn't racial, many of the soldiers were African American, but like most soldiers over the ages they referred to their foes by derogatory names. To the British they were "Wogs" or "Fuzzy-Wuzzys." In Vietnam the VC and NVA were "Gooks." During Desert Storm they were "Ragheads." Here in Somalia they were "Sammys," or more frequently "Skinnys." Of course it worked both ways; "Long Noses," "Hairy Apes," and "Foreign Devils" being applied to the Americans in the same manner. This dehumanization made it easier to kill without remorse. The Somalis all carried guns, but they couldn't hit the broad side of a barn. They rarely carried more than one magazine and usually fired on full automatic, burning up their ammo and adding to their lousy aim. However Ryan found one thing about them to be very disconcerting; they never really seemed to show any fear, even in the face of overwhelming danger. It was as if they had faced death so many times that death didn't seem to matter anymore, and nothing is more dangerous than someone who thinks he has nothing to lose.

It was always a very tense environment on patrols, and certain parts of the city, like the Bakara Market, where an AK-47 could be bought for $75–$150, were pretty much off limits. Whereas the Marines had patrolled aggressively and tolerated no bullshit, the UN troops had almost completely stopped patrolling and sat in their compounds like targets, periodically taking mortars or small-arms fire. It reminded Ryan of his father's stories about when he was with the 10th Special Forces in Lebanon in the early 1980s. The Marines in Lebanon had largely done the same thing. If they weren't able to do anything why were they there? What was their mission?

The warlords even ran their own PSYOPs operation against the UN/US, including leaflets to the effect that the UN was a "peace-killing force" instead of a peacekeeping force. They even staged regular anti-UN/US demonstrations. Aidid had his own clandestine mobile radio transmitter and his PSYOPS campaign was actually more sophisticated than that of the Americans, who tried to wage a campaign without a clear understanding of Somali culture. There were constant riots and lawlessness prevailed. The UN was largely powerless to stop it; unless, it was reasoned, the warlords deemed responsible could be killed or captured. This was the job TF Ranger was going to perform, with the 10th MTN QRF as backup. It was regrettable that the task force and QRF were repeatedly denied the tools that could have proved decisive: armored vehicles and more tactical air support. Still, they were a formidable force. There was also a complicated chain of command for the UN forces and the task force was not in that chain at all. In addition to the Rangers, 160th Aviation, Delta operators, and 10th MTN ground troops they had elements of the 5th Special Forces Group (ABN), who supported the mission with intelligence and sniper teams. SF aerial snipers employed the Barret .50 caliber sniper rifle from Division helicopters, called "eyes over Mogadishu." They were accurate out past a thousand meters and had plenty of targets. It was comforting knowing they were up there.

The rules of engagement (ROE) at least made some sense. Very restrictive ROEs, like unloaded weapons and the ability to fire only granted by commanders, made for very unsafe environments in which to practice peacekeeping operations. Ryan remembered his father saying that SF soldiers uniformly disobeyed theater ROEs when they made no sense: "better to be judged by twelve then carried by six." The army had struggled with these and other issues concerning Operations Other Than War (OOTW), trying to decide what was better—an unruly civilian getting shot or a disaster like the Marines suffered in Lebanon? The ROEs for Somalia, explained by CPT Anderson, their reserve attached JAG, allowed the engagements of crew-served weapons, individuals with scoped weapons, or anyone who was perceived as an "imminent and credible" threat. "Technicals," vehicles mounted with crew-served weapons, were one of the biggest threats and subsequently became targets. They were so named because aid workers would often hire them for security under the guise of "technical support," since their budgets did not allow the hiring of gunmen as bodyguards. Without bodyguards they simply could not do their jobs. These vehicles were also sometimes whimsically called "Klingon ships," because they would usually have riders clinging on to every available site as they rode down Mogadishu's crowed streets. Individuals with assault rifles and other small arms were immune to attack unless they were threatening.

Ryan's platoon leader had made him his radio operator (RTO), even though Ryan was not a communications specialist. The lieutenant was a graduate from Phillips Exeter, an exclusive preparatory school, and had attended Boston College. They had mutual friends, although Ryan was four years his junior. The lieutenant felt more comfortable with Ryan, a yankee and a "preppie," than he did with most of his fellow junior officers, who were almost all southerners. He and Ryan had another thing in common: most of their family and friends thought they were crazy for joining the Army. Ryan became his shadow and friend, closer than junior enlisted and officers are supposed to be. Ryan more than pulled his weight, but he was not saddled with a teacher's pet label by the rest of the troops.

In an incident at the end of August a large crowd of demonstrators gathered outside the Pakistani compound shouting slogans such as "Camp of Murderers," throwing stones and threatening to overrun the camp. The Pakistanis, curiously enough, although brother Muslims, seemed to bear the brunt of the Somalis' hatred and attacks in Somalia. Ryan was among the team sent from the QRF as reinforcements and, coming around a corner, they encountered two technicals out of sight of the Pakistanis. The Somalis were holding back, waiting to see if they could exploit the situation. The surprised gunner on one of the technicals swung a Soviet RPD machine gun around to engage the Americans, but a quick-reacting M2 .50 caliber machine gunner in the turret of the first HMMWV destroyed the vehicle. The second technical could not bring its gun to bear and Ryan, his platoon leader, and the rest of the troops in the second and third vehicles piled out and blasted the second vehicle's crew. Around the block, the Pakistanis, hearing the fire, panicked and fired into the crowd, killing numerous "civilians," many of whom had been carrying small arms. The engagement was over and Ryan and the soldiers of the QRF felt good about their part of the action.

For the most part, however, their work was, hot, dull, and boring. All that was to change in October of 1993.

CHAPTER 25

Witness the birth of the New World Order, the first purely benevolent use of the strongest army on the planet, the military might of the last superpower harnessed to feed people, to save innocent Somalis from the medieval predations of warlords and gunman, to rescue a useless Third World nation in Africa from devouring itself.

—Scott Peterson
Me Against My Brother:
at War in Somalia, Sudan, and Rwanda

"Come on LT, it's Groundhog Day again," whispered Ryan to the sleeping lieutenant under his mosquito net.

"Go away, it's Sunday."

"Hey man, every day is Sunday in this hellhole, get up. We're the QRF Ready Company today."

"What's the date? I think today's my mom's birthday."

"It's October, second, third; I don't know! Come on, get up. We have to be over at the OPCEN in thirty minutes. I've been up for hours."

Ryan had the early-bird guard shift, 0400 to 0600, the best shift of the day as far as he was concerned. It was almost cool at this time of day; by noon the place would be an inferno. Cradling a cup of mocha, two MRE coffee packets with a pack of Coco powder, sugar, and whitener in a canteen cup, he watched as the city and the compound came alive. Up on the roof of the compound he watched the sun come leaping out of the ocean to the east, bathing the dust-colored city in orange as the muezzins in the minarets called for prayers, tinny music coming out of their loudspeakers . . . *Allah-u-Akbar*, repeated over and over in a sing-song chant. You could feel the cool night desert air evaporating as a slight hot breeze came in from the ocean. Mysterious East Africa!

He then went to breakfast and checked the platoon to make sure all was ready in case they were called. They had been spun up a couple of times, ready to assist the Rangers and "D-boys" (Delta Force operators) in case they got in over their heads, but so far had yet to be called out. They were aware that TF Ranger was trying to snatch Aidid and his confederates, but most of their operations had been dry holes. They had some successes but everyone, especially the "Powers that Be" in Washington, were clamoring for results. This prompted the superbly trained and confident TF Ranger to take on riskier and riskier operations.

"Well LT, here we sit while the Rangers get to do all the neat stuff," lamented Ryan. "I had wanted to go to the Rangers but they sent me to the 10th Mountain instead."

"That's *my* plan too, but the Rangers don't take second lieutenants. I figure this operation will make me a little more marketable, especially if we get CIBs (the coveted Combat Infantry Badge) and combat patches out of this."

"Yeah, if we ever see any combat," said Ryan.

"What do you call that little encounter the other day, training?"

"Hey LT, what's Ranger school like?"

"It used to be fifty-eight days of hell but they've added a desert phase. I think it's like seventy-two days now; no sleep, no food, constant movement, shit, I lost twenty pounds! You only get one MRE a day. After RIP."

"RIP?"

"Ranger Indoctrination Program. You do a water test; full fatigues and boots and weapon and you have to swim fifty meters. It's a lot tougher than you think! Then you do the Darby Queen, a kick-ass obstacle course you finish as a team with a variety of torture apparatus. If you have any physical limitations, that will find them."

"Man, I'd waste away on one MRE!"

"They don't let you sleep either. You're always on the go, patrolling, doing raids, and ambushes. You know why they call power naps Ranger naps? 'Cause five minutes is about all you ever get to doze. There are several tactical parachute infills and an air-assault exercise. You see this white thread on my Ranger Tab?"

"Yeah?"

"It's because I went through the winter course. Froze my ass off; frozen Florida swamps, frozen Georgia mountains. In the mountain phase you do a lot of climbing, rapelling, that sort of stuff. It's all about teamwork and leadership. It's a real gut check. You have to push yourself beyond the breaking point. But it's the best small-unit and leadership training in the world. You want to go? When you make Spec 4, we'll get you a waiver and send you."

"Promise?"

"Sure, why not?"

They were in the OPCEN after lunch when the call came in from the Joint Operations Center (JOC) at the airfield. The Rangers and Delta guys were mounting an operation and the Bakara Market area was off-limits. With B company off doing MOUT (military operations in urban terrain) training, they were the QRF element, with A company in support. They were out checking their guys, making sure they were ready, when the Redcon One came in about 1530. At 1630 they were notified to head to the airport. They were mounting a rescue operation; a Black Hawk helicopter had been shot down.

CHAPTER 26

History will record the great success and accomplishments of the US mission and it will be a marvelous story.

—Major General Thomas Montgomery, from
Me Against My Brother: At War in Somalia, Sudan, and Rwanda,
Scott Peterson

The Black Hawk that went down was an MH-60, the special operations version. It had twin 800hp Sikorsky engines, special avionics, twin mini-guns (six barrel M-134 Gatling guns capable of putting four thousand rounds a minute downrange), could carry a squad of soldiers, and do two hundred knots. It had been one of several involved in yet another operation to capture two of Aidid's key lieutenants, Omar Salad and Mohammed Awale. The mission, Operation Gothic Serpent, had initially gone off like clockwork. For once the intelligence was right on. Four Black Hawks carrying Ranger teams had swooped down and the Rangers had fast-roped into the noisy tornado created by the rotor wash to isolate the street in front of the target building. At the same time, Little Birds loaded with Delta operators had fast-roped onto the target building, swept the rooms and captured a bevy of Aidid's staff. The ground recovery convoy, led by LTC Danny McKnight, was waiting to whisk the teams and prisoners away.

The operation went off almost exactly as planned; it was maybe *too* perfect. This type of DA (direct action) mission relied on surprise, speed, violent action, and firepower, but they had done the same operation now six times without changing the mission template; the Somalis knew the modus operandi.

It was clear as soon as the operation started that things were somehow different. The biggest change was that the Somalis were waiting for them. Aidid's intelligence was superb. The Americans never really understood the loyalty of the clan system; loyalty to the clan came before all else. They were not unmindful of security; they had not told the QRF about the operation until an hour before it was to start and they hadn't told their Allied soldiers at all. They simply underestimated the Somali intelligence network. Their spies were everywhere. They knew as soon as the operation kicked off and made a *call to arms*. Burning tires warned the whole city as soon as the TF lifted off. In addition, the Ranger compound was open to surveillance from the higher ground of the city. Requests to stage from a mobile navy platform off the coast, an aircraft carrier, had also been refused.

Barricades were set up on every other street corner, tires were burned and crowds gathered everywhere. Every Somali in "the Mog" was getting his gun. They had stockpiled tons of ammunition, light weapons, and especially rocket-propelled grenades (RPGs). There were a lot more RPGs in Mog than intelligence gave them credit for. In addition, the Somalis had received help. Afghani *mujahideen* were in town, al-Qaeda to be precise, who taught them how to modify their RPGs to shoot up in the air, how to avoid the dangerous back blast, and to aim for the tail rotor. This was a sure way to bring down a Black Hawk. The *muj* had received plenty of practice shooting down Soviet helicopters in Afghanistan. Their dress rehearsal for the coming disaster had been a shoot-down of a Black Hawk on September 25, killing three Americans.

Now the city was mobilized against the Americans with a vengeance, and a storm of fire greeted McKnight and his Rangers as they started their end of the operation. With casualties mounting they fought their way to the target building near the Olympic Hotel, and then to the crash site of Walcott's Super 61 Black Hawk. They were forced to make continuous detours due to blocked streets and to backtrack a frustrating number of times. The combat search and rescue (CSAR) medics were fast-roped in as Rangers and D-boys rushed to secure the site of Walcott's crash. But it was OK, it could be managed.

The 10th MTN QRF was still en route to the airport when the second call came in: another Black Hawk was down.

CHAPTER 27

I will never leave a fallen comrade to fall into the hands of the enemy.

—the Ranger Creed

When the QRF arrived at the airport it was about 1730 hours. Their column consisted of 130 soldiers in six five-ton trucks, four HMMWVs with MK-19 automatic grenade launchers and machine guns, an antitank platoon, and a mobile weapons platoon. LTC David rushed into the JOC to confer with Major General Garrison and when he came out he seemed slightly rattled. At a quick leaders' meeting he sketched out the plan. The QRF was to secure the second crash site where Chief Warrant Officer Mike Durant's Black Hawk had auto-rotated in. At about 1830 they were on the road north. As they passed the K4 Circle and moved into the city they were immediately ambushed.

Ryan was in one of the lead HMMWVs with his lieutenant when the shit hit the proverbial fan. They immediately started taking heavy small-arms and rocket fire. Their column was split and they dismounted to form a perimeter. They were taking AK-47 fire from all directions. Ryan looked up and saw gunmen on every roof. It was a prefect vantage point from which to fire down into the open five-ton trucks. One of the Somalis leaned over with his AK-47 outstretched to give him a better angle of fire and Ryan shot him through the chest. He landed almost at Ryan's feet. An RPG skittered across the hood of the HMMWV with a clang, glanced off their driver's helmet and hit the wall behind them, exploding with such noise and concussive force that Ryan was stunned and momentarily deafened. He rushed over to the driver whose head appeared to be turned around by the blast.

"Jamie, you OK?"

The man was shaken and stunned, but OK. The RPG had knocked his helmet sideways accounting for the deformity. There were a couple of other men down and green-and-red tracers mixed with the cries of "medic," "loading," and the singing and whining of bullets as they passed and the smacks, pings, and bangs when they didn't. Skinnys, some with weapons, others appearing to be just observers or cheerleaders, were everywhere. They barricaded most of the side streets and set tires and refuse on fire. The smell and the smoke added to Ryan's sensory overload. It was a cacophony of confusion. Acrid smoke from the burning tires and garbage stained the air and stung the eyes. It had a palpable taste. The smell reminded Ryan of the hot patch kit his father had used to repair bicycle tires when he was little. Damn, he wished his father was here to tell him what to do! It was suffocating in the Kevlar helmet and vest; it was hard to breathe.

"Ryan, get the CO on the horn and find out where the rest of the column is," screamed the LT above the din.

"Tiger 64, this is Tiger 24, over. I got the captain, LT," he said as he passed the hand mike to the LT. The lieutenant was giving the captain his situation report when LTC David broke in.

"Tiger 24 this is Dragon 6, actual." He told them they were to turn around, join back up with the rest of the column, and return to the airport for reinforcements.

The lieutenant ran down the split column.

"You drivers get these vehicles turned around, we'll give cover!" They carried, half dragged, the wounded and dumped them unceremoniously in the back of the HMMWVs.

When the vehicles were turned around they moved to them in the "bounding overwatch" method they had been taught during MOUT training. They had practiced these immediate action drills (IADs) many times, but this one was for real. One fire team gave cover as the second one moved to safety. Ryan and the lieutenant were among the last to move. Since the vehicles had turned around they were now on the other side of the street. It was the longest run of Ryan's life. He felt like he weighed three hundred pounds and his feet were made of lead. He remembered a poem he had written in junior high about running to the goal line during a Pop Warner football game: *Run, Dodge, Got a Block, Keep Going, Keep Going, Almost There* . . . He chanted what he could remember of the poem over and over in his head. He was running in a nightmare. Bullets puffed the dirt all around him as he ran the hundred miles to his vehicle. His vision was blurry, he heard a roar in his ears, he was sobbing to catch his breath, and when he tried to fling himself back in the HMMWV he found a wounded soldier. He couldn't catch his breath. He felt like he was over-breathing his regulator, like he had that first time his father had taken him on that deep scuba dive to the U-boat in 130 feet of cold, dark New England water off Block Island. *Calm down, relax, control your breathing . . . like underwater.*

Ryan and a bunch of the other soldiers ran alongside the vehicles, giving cover as they raced out of the kill zone. It was actually easier to shoot this way, from outside the vehicles, until they were clear of the hot zone.

"GO! GO! GO!" screamed the lieutenant and the vehicles careened back to the circle firing all the way. Most of them were down to their last of five hundred rounds of ammunition. At the circle they all loaded up and returned to the airport.

It was obvious that they were going to need armor if they planned to go back into the "City of Death." It was the armor, stupid, the armor that had been refused them by Secretary Aspin, who wanted to create a "low profile" and avoid "incidents." Now they had no choice, they had to enlist the help of the UN. They were all summoned to meet at New Port, south of the city. LTC David now had a daunting task; to shape a combined arms task force involving forces from three different countries: 10th MTN Raven attack helicopters, a composite company of Rangers, two companies of infantry from the 10th MTN, two companies of Malaysian APCs, and a platoon of Pakistani tanks. Predictably, it was a cluster-fuck. It took until 2330 hours before they were ready to move out. American troops replaced Malay forces, who were visibly relieved, in the "Dumpsters on wheels" or "mechanized coffins" as many of the soldiers referred to them. The Malay drivers stayed.

Ryan's vehicle was to be in the lead element. He had loaded a bunch of obsolete twenty-round magazines scrounged by the armorer into M16 bandoleers. They could be hung in vehicles or slung around the neck and greatly increased the amount of ammo one could carry. It was a trick he had learned from his father, who in turn had learned it from his commander, a former Secret Service agent, during Desert Storm. He was going to throw a bunch of them in their APC when he saw the lieutenant holding on to the doorframe of their HMMWV, staring into the vehicle.

"What's wrong LT?" he asked glancing in the cab of their shot-up HMMWV. The vehicle was full of holes. Every window was spidery with multiple bullet holes. How the hell had any of them escaped being wounded? The back of the vehicle was littered with shell casings and blood. Large globs of black blood had congealed on the platform between the seats. There was a strong odor of cordite, hot metal, burning oil, the coppery smell of blood, and an almost intangible odor of sweaty terror, the smell of fear and death.

"Ryan, I don't think we can go back there; *I* can't lead these men back there to die!"

"LT, we *got* to go. *You've* got to lead them, they trust you, you've *got* to lead them!"

The lieutenant stood there shaking his head, his eyes shadowed by the headlights.

"LT, you know what a defining moment is? Well this is ours. This will determine our whole future. If we die, we're dead. If we don't go we'll die a thousand deaths. We've *got* to go."

The lieutenant looked up at him.

"You remember what you told me about being a good military leader? You've got to be technically proficient, morally and physical brave, and you take care of the troops. Three out of three here, LT!"

The internal struggle the lieutenant was experiencing was really no struggle at all; *he* knew he had to go to rescue his brothers in arms.

"OK, you stay close. Saddle up, you guys!"

They moved to one of the lead APCs and got into the claustrophobic box. Just as they were moving out a Special Forces officer, a lieutenant colonel, banged on the door and got in.

They started to move out. The whole plan hinged on the tanks leading and breaking through the barricades, but at the last minute the Pakistanis backed down and said they would not lead. The tanks *had* to lead! LTC David undiplomatically harangued the Pakistani commander but to no avail.

CHAPTER 28

Operation Restore Hope and the Somalia intervention of 1992–95 will probably fade to a footnote in American military history. It's easy to understand why; the Somalia intervention was a failure. Not a heroic battle-against-the-odds failure, such as Bataan in WWII, nor a spectacular nation rendering failure, such as Vietnam. No, Somalia was a squalid and puzzling little failure.

—Martin Stanton,
Somalia on $5 a Day: A Soldier's Story

The 106-vehicle convoy finally moved out after a shuffling of the order of march. They headed north and east to National Street and then took a left into Indian Country, where they immediately took fire. At the first checkpoint there was confusion and some of the lead vehicles headed south toward Durant's crash site by accident instead of north as planned. In a blaze of gunfire Ryan's group fought north, through the conflagration of destruction to their first stop; the beleaguered Rangers under CPT Steel's command and the first crash site. *There were so many wounded!* They *all* seemed wounded. They loaded them up, medics working feverishly, and fought their way to crash site two.

When they off-loaded at the second crash site, the 10th MTN Company commander grabbed the lieutenant as the SF lieutenant colonel strode over to the crashed chopper through a diminishing hail of bullets.

"Ryan, stay with him in case he needs commo," yelled the LT.

Ryan scrambled after the LTC, firing as he ran. He had to keep flipping his NVGs up and down to acquire targets in the dark. He fired single-fire aimed shots, as his father had taught him, and avoided full automatic, or "rock and roll," because it was hard to aim and used up ammunition at an alarming rate. His training had been good; he saw his shots strike home time and again. As they got to the helicopter one of the Delta medics grabbed his arm and told Ryan to follow him. Ryan looked at the LTC and he just nodded. The Delta operators were easy to recognize; they wore black flak vests and black Proteck helmets. This one had an aidbag on his back and an MP5 submachine gun around his neck.

"I'm not a medic," Ryan protested.

"Doesn't matter, I need brawn not brains."

For the next hour or so Ryan, holding a flash light in his teeth and IVs in both hands, assisted the Delta medic in treating and carrying the wounded to the HMMWVs. He was amazed at the skill of the medic and thought he must be a physician. Ryan had gone through the Combat Lifesaver course and knew how hard it was to put an IV in even under ideal conditions. The Delta medic was getting IVs started where there appeared to be no veins, in poor lighting, and while bullets and rockets flew all around. Finally the convoy was ready to go. They loaded up and headed to the stadium. Ryan, holding IVs, listened to the ping and whine as bullets bounce off the APC as they raced to safety with the rising sun.

When they arrived at the stadium, a casualty collection point (CCP) was already set up and triage and stabilization of the wounded was begun before choppering them to the Combat Support Hospital where a team of three surgeons awaited them. The Delta medic jumped right in and without a word to the 160th Surgeon, who was running the CCP, started triage on the more than forty seriously wounded, some with wounds twelve to fourteen hours old. There were a lot more minor wounds and in the Army triage system they were classified as *minimal*; a Band Aid, two aspirin, and "call me in the morning." Other wounds were in the *delayed* category, meaning they were not immediately life-threatening, and the Delta medic directed other medics to treat them and make them comfortable while he worked on the others. The most seriously wounded, the *immediate* category, were the ones the Delta medic passed off to the surgeon if he wasn't too busy. These men would need immediate resuscitative care or they would not survive the trip to the hospital. A few died in spite of their best efforts; they were just too badly injured. The last category was the worst; the *expectant*. These were the ones who had no chance of survival and were put aside to die quietly, while those worth saving were afforded the time and supplies. One of the expectant was a Delta operator who had a good part of his lower body taken off by an RPG. Ryan's mentor, the Delta medic, could not bring himself to ignore his friend and worked feverishly on him. In spite of their best efforts he died shortly afterward. With tears in their eyes they continued to work until almost noon when the last of the most seriously wounded were evacuated. Ryan never did find out the Delta medic's name, but he knew now what he was going to be in the Army.

Ryan's lieutenant, who waited for him, looked at his blood- and sweat-streaked face.

"Hey, Ryan, I just remembered, it's Mefloquine Monday. You wouldn't want to do something dangerous and forget to take your anti-malarial pill," giggled the lieutenant. He was just so glad to be alive. Ryan just looked at him.

"Ryan, you OK?"

"LT, what are we doing here? I mean, what's our mission? I don't know what we're doing here." He looked bewildered.

"Ryan, we're soldiers. We go where they tell us and we do the best we can with what we've got; like we've been trained. You know, 'Ours is not to reason why . . .'"

"Yeah, 'Ours is but to do and die.' Well it's not fair!"

Shortly afterward, the politicians in Washington, appalled by the loss of life in Somalia on *Maatinti Rangers* (the Day of the Rangers), as the Somalis called the battle, sued for peace and the return of pilot Mike Durant, the Black Hawk pilot taken hostage. They vowed to leave Somalia. As a final insult to the brave men of the United States Army who fought, were wounded, and died in this most embarrassing of political debacles, Aidid was later flown to peace talks in Ethiopia a few months later in an American C-130. A total of forty-four Americans died in the Somalia intervention and 175 were wounded. Estimates of Somalis killed at the hands of the UN/US varied greatly but was undoubtedly in the thousands. MG Garrison, as a good soldier should, took the bullet for the Clinton administration's political and military failure. In a handwritten letter to President Clinton, shortly after the Battle for the Black Sea, as the Americans called it, MG Garrison wrote in part:

"The authority, responsibility, and accountability for the Operation rests here in MOG with the TF Ranger commander, not in Washington. For this particular target, President Clinton and Secretary Aspin need be taken off the blame line."

This was not the consensus among most of those valiant and courageous soldiers who fought that day; they would blame the politicians. Afterward, there would be some criticism of Garrison; that he was reckless and sent men needlessly to their death. To those that knew him they knew he would have been in the lead vehicle in the thick of things if it had been his place. As it was, he was the commander and was forced to watch the drama from the images provided on the monitors in the JOC by the Orion spy plane circling high above. No more agonizing punishment could ever have been meted out to this warrior than to watch his men die in combat. While MG Garrison took the blame and quietly retired, the Clinton administration and the rest of the politicians were free, at least for the next few years, to continue to ineptly wield the most powerful military in the world. To Ryan it confirmed what all professional soldiers have always believed: that no one should ever serve in that capacity who has not worn the uniform and seen men die.

BOOK FOUR

AFGHANISTAN, 2001

They have looked each other between the
    eyes, and there have found no fault,
They have taken the Oath of the Brother-in-
    Blood on leavened bread and salt,
They have taken the Oath of the Brother-in-
    Blood on fine and fresh cut sod,
On the hilt and shaft of the Khyber knife, and
    the Wondrous Names of God.

                    —Rudyard Kipling,
                "Ballad of East and West"

CHAPTER 29

Those who persecute the Believers, men and women,
And do not turn in repentance, will have the Chastisement of Hell.
Verily, We have warned you of a chastisement near,
The Day when man will see (the Deeds) which his hands have set forth,
And the Unbeliever will say, "Woe unto me! Would that I were mere dust."
And they were destroyed by a terrible storm of thunder and lightning.

—The Holy Qur'an

The team members were almost all combat veterans, depending on whose definitions you used. Their predecessors from WWII, or even Vietnam, might have scoffed at the requirements authorizing the coveted combat infantry badge (CIB) and combat medical badge (CMB) these men wore, but nonetheless, they were the best and most experienced of *their* army. They had been in Grenada, Panama, Somalia, El Salvador, and/or Iraq. The old men wearing the badges of the Mekong Delta and Central Highlands that had been so common in the Army only a few years ago, were almost completely gone from this army; it *was* almost thirty years after the combat troops began pulling out of the Republic of Vietnam. There was one exception to this, the only one in the whole battalion, MSG Mike Apin.

He had left the army in 1973 as a buck sergeant (E5) after recovering from his wounds. He had bummed around for a while and tried to settle down at something but had that restlessness that men always feel after returning from war. Fitzgerald, Hemingway, and others of the "lost generation" had tried to put it in words. He didn't suffer from post-traumatic stress syndrome or anything like that; he just missed the excitement, the adrenaline rush of being in a war zone. He worked at a series of jobs, gas station attendant and wild-catter on an oilrig in the Texas Gulf, and used his GI bill to go to commercial diving school. He worked at that for a few years doing crummy, dangerous work in the Gulf and North Atlantic in sweat-soaked drysuits, in mind-numbing cold and zero visibility. It was a difficult way to make a living but it paid well.

He also took up freefall parachuting and became a scuba diving instructor. He spent a couple of years in the islands and drank too much. He married a girl who was down on holiday and decided to go back to the States and college but found it as boring as the rest. He read the classics, he particularly liked the authors of the late nineteenth and early twentieth century; Faulkner, Kipling, Fitzgerald, and Hemingway, and thought he might major in literature. But he found civilians, in particular, and life, in general, boring. The only time he made a friend was when he met a veteran. Fitzgerald remarked that we make our lifelong friends only in youth and he thought that generally true. A common life-threatening experience like combat seemed to be the exception. Men in the military, and especially those with a common combat experience, became closer than friends; they did, indeed, become the brothers of Shakespeare's *Henry V.*

Mike joined ROTC while in college and returned to the army as a reservist in 1983. He served in a civil affairs battalion, which satisfied him for a time. Then he joined the 11th Special Forces Group (Airborne), one of the Army Reserve SF units. He settled at a small college in Boston, where his new wife was from, and was assigned to A Company, 1st Battalion at Ft. Devens, Massachusetts. It was co-located with an active duty unit, the 10th Special Forces Group (Airborne). It was a great unit, different than most Reserve or National Guard units. After a grueling year on a training team, he went to the Special Forces Qualification Course to become a communications sergeant. Having served with the 5th SF Group in Vietnam and already adept at Morse code and advanced communications procedures, he had an easier time than many of the other prospective Green Beret students. He had never been awarded his Green Beret either because of his early exit from theater or a paperwork glitch . . . he was never sure which. He kept in top shape, despite the drinking. After SFQC they assigned him to the scuba team and they sent him to scuba school at Key West, Florida.

The only thing harder (or worse) than the three-week scuba course was the two-week *prescuba* train up; an exercise in physical abuse and controlled drowning. He was the old man of the group and they naturally picked on him. Even though he was an expert diver, he was sure he was going to flunk out. There were innumerable ways for failure, although officially there was only one . . . failure to train. For example, if you tried to grab the side of the pool as you were blacking out, that qualified as "failure to train." In reality you could get thrown out for a variety of physical deficiencies, the initial physical training test, the initial water test, failure to make the run-or-die early-morning runs in the allotted times (approximately six-minute miles), getting injured on "that bitch of an obstacle course," academic failures in dive physics and math, panicking instead of drowning quietly, etc.

Mike had blacked out doing "cross-overs" and had to be partially revived. Cross-overs consisted of swimming the width of the pool underwater with a single breath, to be repeated on the other side again with only a single breath. The first few were easy but after a dozen or so the carbon dioxide build-up and the hypoxia (lack of oxygen) would inevitably take its toll. But the drown-proofing, for him, was the hardest part. With your feet tied and your hands bound behind your back, you had to lay on the surface for an extended amount of time in the drown-proof mode. On command, you had to "bob" off the bottom (forever it seemed) of the deep-end of the pool, making sure to get a full breath each time, then swim one hundred yards using a dolphin kick, come back, and bob again. You then had to perform a back-and-front flip underwater, and finally retrieve a mask in your teeth and continue bobbing with it. The whole exercise could take thirty minutes and if you missed one breath, you were screwed.

One of the other more difficult "stress" exercises was treading water wearing double scuba tanks and sixteen pounds of weights, while keeping your hands and ears out of the water. To make it worse, the instructors would have you "charge" your mask; fill the mask with water while you struggled to keep your head above water. Accidentally take a breath through your nose and you flunked out in a fit of gagging and coughing for "failure to train." There were also the clump retrieval, ditch-and-don exercise, fifty-meter underwater swim, weight-belt swims (with sixteen pounds of lead), underwater knot tying, long day and night (up to three thousand meter) surface swims, and other assorted tortures. During the open cir-cuit (scuba) phase, instructors were constantly turning off your air or pulling the regulator out of your mouth and hiding it behind you or tying the hose in a knot, stealing your equipment during buddy-breathing equipment exchanges, etc. It was undoubtedly the hardest course in the Army, maybe the military.

The Seals had a higher dropout rate but the BUDS course was an initial entry to Special Operations; they took raw recruits or average soldiers, not sol-diers who had already been through the grueling Special Forces Qualification Course (SFQC). In spite of the demanding pace of it all, Mike had finally found something he loved to do. He felt at home, part of a family.

His revived military career, albeit part-time, did little to help his failing mar-riage. After a series of dead-end, part-time jobs trying to make ends meet while in college, he got a divorce and dropped out of college just a few credits short of graduation. He went back on active duty in 1990. The Army was always short of SF soldiers and always willing to take a reservist and put him back on active duty.

Mike decided he didn't want to teach and he certainly didn't want to work at one of the mundane professions most of his college classmates strove for. He had been in the Army long enough to get staff sergeant (SSG E6) stripes upon active reenlistment. He was in training at Monterey, studying a six-month course in Dari, when the Gulf War broke out. It was infuriating to sit in the rear with the REMFs while almost all the rest of Special Operations were in the biggest ground war since Korea and Vietnam. Assured it would last long enough for him to get in, the ground combat phase was over almost before it began. The "100-hour war" left him by.

He went to back to the Special Forces Underwater Operations School on Fleming Key in Key West, Florida and took the dive supervisor course. He received a slot as a commo sergeant with a scuba team with the 2nd Battalion, 10th Special Forces Group (Airborne) and went to Fort Devens, Massachusetts, where he had trained more than a decade earlier as an AIT student. It was also where his Reserve unit had been. He loved New England. He went climbing in the White Mountains spring and fall, dove for lobsters in the summer, and skied Vermont in the winter. Deployments were often to Europe and he spent a good deal of time with the 1st Battalion at Flint Kaserne in Bad Toltz, the best-kept secret in the Army. He went to Jumpmaster School, Danish Scout Swim School, and Norwegian Ski School and, in general, had a great time. When the group moved to its new quarters in Colorado, he moved to Ft. Bragg to JFKSWCS (JFK Special Warfare Center and School) as an instructor for Phase II, Officer Committee, Special Forces Qualification Course.

He was promoted to sergeant first class (SFC E7) and, after a stint on a 5th Special Forces Group scuba team, and as an operations sergeant on battalion staff, he made master sergeant (E8) and was made team sergeant of his own scuba team with the 5th Special Forces Group (Airborne) in July of 2001. Although he had just turned fifty he still had a powerful physique and was in superb physical condition. His hair was a little thinner with a streak of gray, his face lined from the years working in the sun and wind. He was a little thicker about the middle but he could still outrun, outruck, and outswim the younger guys.

Most of the team members on ODA (operational detachment alpha) 501 were new. They either came from other teams, tours with recruiting, SWC or Civil Affairs, or just back from scuba school. They represented the backbone of the United States Army Special Forces: twelve men commanded by a senior captain, a warrant officer as the XO, an 18Z master sergeant as the team sergeant and the rest all senior noncommissioned officers, an 18F intelligence sergeant, two 18D medics (the best in *any* army), two 18E communications sergeants, two 18C engineer/demolitions sergeants, and two 18B weapons experts. They were all cross-trained, proficient in a number of languages and could "accomplish any mission, any place, any time." They were all in peak physical condition, expert parachutists and scuba divers. Some were trained in mountain warfare, technical climbing, and winter warfare while others were expert in desert operations. With the exception of their new commander, they had all been in SF for a number of years. Officers came and went, but it was the NCOs that made Special Forces. Even the warrant officers were former SF NCOs. They wore the coveted Green Beret, authorized by President John Kennedy in the early 1960s, who called it, "a symbol of excellence, a mark of distinction, and a badge of courage."

MSG Mike Apin was looking forward to pulling this team, *his team*, together for their first real mission, scuba training with the Egyptian Army in October. They were to conduct a train-up for the mission and they had two weeks scheduled at the Naval Diving and Salvage Training Center (NDSTC) and the Naval Experimental Diving Unit (NEDU) in beautiful Panama City, Florida, for early September. Life didn't get any better than that!

CHAPTER 30

The wind of change is blowing to remove evil from the peninsula of Moham-
med, peace be upon him. As to America, I say to it and its people a few words:
I swear to Allah that America will not live in peace until peace reigns in Pal-
estine, and before all the Army of Infidels depart the land of Mohammed, peace
be upon him. Allah is great and glory be to Islam.

—Osama bin Laden (2001)

Captain Charles Rogers arrived at Ft. Campbell in early August to command his "A" team. He didn't receive the normal transition time with his predecessor as he was supposed to and he was a little nervous about taking command. However, he was very impressed with his team sergeant and the rest of the guys, especially his XO. The tall redhead's name was Gallagher.

"I served in the 82nd with a SF major named Gallagher during Desert Storm, any relation?"

"Yeah, he's my old man," replied the XO.

"You're Mike Gallagher's kid? No shit! You ever meet his boss, LTC King?"

"Once! Great soldier from what my old man said."

"You got that right. Well it's great to have you here!"

There was one other coincidence. Both Chuck and his team sergeant had both gone to the same high school in Oxon Hill, Maryland, although a decade apart. A lot of the same teachers and coaches were still around, including the head football coach, "Bullet Bob" East, so named for his bald head. They spent a lot of time talking about the neighborhood and telling each other funny anecdotes about the school. It really was a small world.

After a few days of evaluating the team, he called his team sergeant and XO together for their opinion.

"So what do you guys think about the team? Anything we need to address or change, Top?"

"Nah, everyone seems pretty solid. A couple of the guys are pretty green."

"Yeah, like me," said Chuck.

"Well, that's why they keep old farts like Top around," grinned Ryan.

"I was going to say a couple of the guys seem like they might be prima donnas, that may go for the XO, too!"

"Yeah, well it takes a pretty big ego to be a Special Forces Combat Diver," replied Chuck.

"Well, I've seen a lot worse scuba teams. The training in Florida should shake things out. I'm not sure what's on tap after the JCET (training mission) to Egypt. The battalion's had a pretty high OPTEMPO the last couple of years. Hopefully, it will be quiet for a while," Mike responded.

"You think so? That's what everyone thought when the Soviet Union went tits-up. Then the Gulf War, Haiti, Somalia, and Bosnia came out of nowhere," said Ryan.

"Yeah, well, I grew up with the Soviet bear ready to wipe us out. We always thought nuclear war could happen at any time, at least *that* threat seems to have vanished. I can remember going to bomb shelters and having nuclear bomb drills at school in the 1950s. I still remember this sign that used to hang in every classroom when I was in first or second grade . . . it must have been 1957 or '58 . . . something like that. It had this long list of things you were supposed to do and someone had added a line at the end about putting your head between your knees and kissing your ass good-bye. I thought it was all over when Kennedy stood up to the Soviets over the missiles in Cuba. My dad was sure it was WWIII."

"And we thought all of our troubles were over when Russia collapsed."

"Well," said Mike, "I think it's going to be quiet for the next few years. After the Egyptian trip we'll probably stand down for a while and relax."

"I hope so," said Chuck. "I need to spend some time with my wife. She wants to have kids and isn't real fond of me being in SF."

Chuck liked the easy camaraderie between NCOs and officers in Special Forces, so different than in Division or the rest of the Army. It was not unusual for officers and NCOs in Special Forces to address each other by their first names, at least in private. This was considered a major breach of discipline in the regular Army. After Desert Storm he went to the MP Officer Advanced Course and after the wedding had taken command of an MP company back at Bragg. That at least made his wife happy, since it was only a two or three hour drive to her home in Lexington. What he didn't tell many people, especially civilians, was that he had enjoyed the small amount of combat he had seen. It had been exciting; it had made him feel alive, to appreciate things back home.

He remembered reading a quote in *Newsweek* just before going over to the Gulf War. It was by Daniel Ellsberg, vilified by the Nixon administration for leaking the Pentagon Papers in the 1970s, but actually a courageous man who had volunteered to go to Vietnam as a Marine Corps Officer. He leaked the Pentagon Papers in the honest belief that the war was unwinable and the administration was leading the country further into the quagmire of Vietnam. The quote went something like this: "Battle can be very interesting, as long as you don't get your legs or your balls shot off." It was true, war could be intoxicating, leading many of the veterans that returned to civilian life to feel a sense of restlessness and a lack of fulfillment, while many of those who remained on active duty looked for a higher-risk MOS like Special Forces.

CHAPTER 31

A hundred men we'll test today, only three win the Green Beret.

—SSG Barry Sadler and Robin Moore,
"Ballad of the Green Beret"

CPT Chuck Rogers was one of those looking for more action and after the Gulf War had applied for Special Forces training. He was lobbied by a number of senior MP officers, especially his battalion commander, about the mistake he was making. It was made clear that whether he was selected or not, his career in the MPs would be over. Most army branches did not really like SF, especially since the Special Forces Qualification Course was a branching course, awarding the 18-series MOS to its graduates. That meant losing some of their best officers from their own branch, never to return.

He had gone back to Ft. Bragg for SFQC Phase I, Special Forces Assessment and Selection (SFAS). Brigadier General Richard Potter borrowed the techniques from the British Special Air Services (SAS). Potter had been a 10th SF Group commander, second in command of Delta Force during its birth, and a former British exchange officer. One of his favorite sayings from Delta, was "we ain't making corn flakes here." He felt that way about training new Special Forces soldiers, and was committed to making sure only the best were awarded the coveted Green Beret.

SFAS was twenty-five days long and designed to eliminate the weak of body, mind, or character from Special Forces training. It was a course without definite standards; you were told to simply do your best. Rucksack marches might be ten to thirty miles. You would get to a truck thinking, *thank God its over*, only to have them tell you to head up the road to the next stop. It combined inhuman physical tests; sleep deprivation, emotional, mental, and psychological stress to assess leadership potential, personality strengths, and survival skills. At the end you were simply told you were selected or you were sent home. Many simply decided that this wasn't for them and quit. Timothy McVeigh, of the Oklahoma bombing infamy, was one of those who quit. Selection greatly cut down the attrition rate during the remaining phases. In the old days Phase I (now termed Phase II) had been the primary weeding out phase.

The change allowed Phase II to teach more than to harass. Yet it was still easy to get thrown out or recycled. It was forty-eight days of long-range navigation, patrolling, survival, and special operational techniques, taught at remote Camp McCall in the Uwharrie State Forest. At one point during the patrolling phase Chuck almost drowned. You had to be a strong swimmer in Special Forces and Chuck was one of the strongest but he still almost drowned . . . in two feet of water. They were on a weeklong patrol and it was night, as black a night as he had ever seen . . . at least as bad as during Desert Storm. He was last in line carrying over eighty pounds of gear in his ruck when the bank of a stream they were crossing collapsed on his right leg. The weight of his ruck pulled him over and with his leg stuck in the mud he couldn't move. His head was underwater and he had just about given up struggling when a strong arm pulled him up.

"Rogers, you OK?"

Sputtering on the ground, he looked at his savior, one the evaluators, "Yeah, why? I was just taking a rest."

"Yeah? That would have been the longest rest you ever took if I hadn't of called a halt and came back to check on you."

After six weeks they came back to Ft. Bragg and split up for several months of training in their respective MOSs, Phase III. This phase lasted several months, over a year in the case of medics. The officers received a smattering of all the specialties (weapons, demolitions, communications, medicine), as well as leadership and intelligence classes. They also learned the tradecraft of the spy and covert operations: dead-letter drops, cutouts, the cellular structure of the "underground," and other clandestine operations. By the time they finished Phase III they were trained in almost all aspects of unconventional warfare and direct-action missions. Then came the time to put all this knowledge into practice.

Chuck got a small apartment and his wife came to stay for the next four months of Phase III. She really didn't like Ft. Bragg *or* the Army but it was reasonably close to home. She was an Army brat, the daughter of a retired infantry colonel, and was tired of being what she thought of as a camp follower. Her father had retired following her junior year in high school, but before that they had moved every two or three years all over the globe. She really had expected Chuck to get out of the Army after his mandatory obligation was up and was very disappointed he had decided to go into Special Forces. All the wives talked about it being a sure road to divorce. She made the best of it.

If Phase I was challenging, and Phases II and III informative and fun, Phase IV was a surreal month-long experience. Known as Robin Sage, it was designed to evaluate technical proficiency, tactical skills, and overall performance. The

SF students parachuted into the mythical country of Pineland deep in the North Carolina wilds. There they were to link up with a guerrilla force (the "Gs") and help overthrow the rogue government and restore the legally elected, US-friendly government. After receiving their mission, they were put into isolation for five days where they were to plan every last detail of the mission with contingencies, backups, and bailout plans. Each of the twelve men planned and executed their portion of the mission just as they would during a real mission.

The Guerrilla, or G chief was also their evaluator and the Gs were a mixture of Marines, support personnel, and who knows whom else. Chuck's Gs had two women with the band. The auxiliary, or the civilian support, for the guerrillas were local civilians who derived a perverse joy from playing this elaborate charade. Aggressors, the 82nd Airborne, scoured the woods for them, as did the local law enforcement as agents of the "bad" government.

From the start it was screwy. First, they dropped them (intentionally) in the wrong drop zone in the middle of the night and after an hour or so of trying to get their bearings, they finally got on a trail for the fifteen-kilometer all-night "death" march to the link-up. They were late for the link-up and after giving them a hard time the G chief abandoned them deep in the woods. They formed a patrol base for the night and in the morning were finally able to establish "rapport" with the Gs by having one of their team medics treat several of the guerrilla band for diarrhea, and an infected finger on one of the females. They were also successful in convincing the G chief that they had something to offer them.

The next step was a Special Forces specialty: train the band to be a fighting unit. They conducted classes in communications, first aid, weapons, intelligence, camouflage, patrolling, raids, ambushes, and air resupply. The G chief made things as difficult as possible. In order to get food they had to conduct ambushes or set up Drop Zones (DZ). If things were not perfect they didn't eat; this made for surly Gs. Chuck knew that if the patrol base security was not up to par the G chief would tip off the aggressors, the 82nd Airborne Division, and they would raid the camp. The camp was deep in a swamp and made up of poncho hooches and improvised shelters. He had them set up escape routes, trip wires, flares, and other early warning devices. He always had his men in charge of the guard details (he didn't trust the Gs). One warm sleepy fall afternoon he went out to check on the back entrance to the camp and found one of his weapons guys asleep. He snuck up on him and mock garroted him. The embarrassed soldier was afraid the captain would report him to the G chief (who probably could have thrown him out of Phase III) but he didn't. It turned out to be a good thing.

A "reporter" from the Cantef government showed up and wanted to take pictures and write a story, for the government in exile, to show how the Americans were helping them. Since the mission was supposed to be classified, Chuck had to do some fancy talking to get the G chief to at least compromise on disguising the place and nature of the mission, and to have the soldiers wear camouflage for the pictures. Later that day, the soldier he had garroted saw the reporter out on the main trail marking their camp. When he reported this to the G chief and after showing him the markings, the Gs decided to execute the spy. Mandated to try and prevent atrocities by the indigenous personnel, Chuck argued vehemently to have the spy exfilled for interrogation, to no avail. Did you abort your mission after your Gs committed atrocities? He later found out that the reporter was, in fact, a *real* reporter for the Ft. Bragg paper, the *Paraglide*, and had done a big article on Robin Sage featuring Chuck's team.

Other strange incidents were arranged to test the team's resourcefulness and mettle. One night the G chief said the head guerrilla leader wanted to meet him. He and the XO, a national guard 1st lieutenant from 19th SF, were blindfolded and tied up, put in the back of a cold wet pickup, covered with a wet canvas tarp, and bounced over bumpy trails and roads for what seemed like hours. Shivering and wet, they were taken into a garage with a picnic table and an overhead light angled down at them, like they were being given the third degree. The better-looking of the two women Gs accompanied them and it turned out she was supposed to be the leader's girlfriend. As they were sitting opposite the leader and his girl on the picnic table, his XO suddenly began to fidget and suddenly stood up and said he had to go to the bathroom. *Probably the trots*, thought Chuck, then while he was in mid-sentence, the girl, who really *was* good looking, suddenly stuck her foot in his crotch under the table and began to wiggle her toes. He never missed a beat, but when his XO came back he excused himself to use the bathroom as well. If he hadn't been so cold he would have broken out in a sweat. He figured he probably would be executed for dallying with the leader's girl. Sometimes it became hard to separate reality from fantasy.

A few days later the same girl (she was becoming a lot of trouble) accused his team sergeant of rape. The Gs insisted on a trial and he was to be executed if found guilty. Chuck was the defense lawyer and after a very tense trial, the sergeant was acquitted. The G chief came to him later in his role as team evaluator and asked Chuck what he would have done if they had convicted the team sergeant. He told the Chief that he had told his team to insert a magazine in their M16s, lock and load, and on his signal to fire up the Gs, gather up their stuff and abandon the mission. Chuck never found out if that was the *right* decision or not. The team sergeant, an old national guard SFC, had acted badly during the trial. He was obviously having trouble with *his* perception of reality. The girl, who turned out to be a SP4 (specialist 4th class) with COSCOM (corps support command), now began to have an affair (real this time) with one of his demo guys. He put a stop to that, at least while they were in the field. Weird!

The final exam was to involve a link-up with another ODA and their guerrilla band, and mount a coordinated attack on a small civilian airfield. They were to link-up at an old farmhouse for a coordination meeting with the other team. Chuck took half his team and put surveillance on the target several hours early. Sure enough, while they were in position, a squad from the 82nd Airborne Division snuck up to set up an ambush. The *ambushers* became the *ambushees*, but the paratroopers had a company-sized element to back them up and Chuck's team had to beat feet. They ended up spending a cold night in a swamp where they got an uncharacteristic six inches of snow.

They subsequently linked up with the other ODA and their guerillas and on a pitch-black night, made a picture-perfect assault on the airfield, completely surprising the defenders. Chuck led a small team right up to the defenders while the rest of the teams and the Gs crawled across a field. He was able to lob several flares right into the enemy camp, confusing and blinding the enemy, and making the assault easy. They were supposed to be exfilled by Black Hawk helicopter back to Bragg the next day, but the chopper was cancelled for unknown reasons. They wound up having to spend the night around a small pond. It was quite pleasant after the rigors of the last month. They went "admin" and the G chief disappeared, reappearing about an hour later with two cases of beer. They built a fire and spent a pleasant evening under the stars. Their evaluator did an informal debrief and told them they were one of the best teams he'd seen. They were "truckborne" the next day for Bragg.

Chuck wound up being the Distinguished Honor Graduate for the officers and was offered his choice of assignments. He really wasn't fond of Ft. Bragg either and would have chosen the 10th SF, newly moved to Colorado, but his wife wanted to stay on the East Coast close to her parents in Virginia. His second choice was the 5th SF, legendary for their actions during the Vietnam War, at Ft. Campbell, Kentucky. But first he wanted to go to either the military freefall (MFF) course, also known as HALO (high altitude-low opening), or to CDQC (Combat Diver Qualification School); scuba school. He attended SERE (survival, evasion, resistance, and escape) training, nineteen days of hell, and then went to Monterey for six months of language training in Farsi and Pashtun. His wife came along and enjoyed California. Right after he reported to Campbell he went to prescuba, a real bitch, and then down to Key West. His wife stayed in the guesthouse awaiting quarters, while he went off to have "fun." After earning his combat-diver badge he returned to Campbell and was assigned as Commander ODA 501.

His wife informed him she didn't like Ft. Campbell any better than Ft. Bragg.

CHAPTER 32

Afghanistan possesses a machinery of agitation singularly well adapted for acting on the seething, fermenting, festering mass of Muslim hostility . . . with such a people as the Afghans, it is necessary to always be on one's guard.

—Sir Henry Rawlinson, 1868, from
*Tournament of Shadows: The Great Game
and the Race for Empire in Central Asia,*
Karl E. Meyer and Shareen Blair Brysac

CW 2 Ryan Gallagher skimmed twenty feet below the surface on the long-underwater three thousand-meter swim back to the navy docks at Alligator Bayou. The Dragger Lar 5 on his chest was the standard oxygen rebreather used for bubble-free clandestine underwater infiltration. This was a navigation swim and his buddy, tethered to him by a buddy-line had the compass board while he tried to keep track of distance. Panama City was a great place to do refresher training. The navy dive school, Naval Diving and Salvage Training Center, and the Naval Experimental Diving Unit (NEDU) supported them. Although he had been diving since he was thirteen, he had never seen anything like NEDU. They had a huge wet tank, big enough to drive a truck in, that could be pressurized to two thousand feet of sea pressure with multiple air locks above. The control panel looked like something out of NASA and they did research on saturation diving, medical problems at depth, mixed gases, and just about every other facet of diving theory and practice.

His mind drifted as he swam. He had decided after Somalia that he wanted to become a Delta operator, a medic. Ranger and Special Forces time were some of the stepping stones to getting there. His lieutenant had been as good as his word, and after Somalia, Ryan had gone to Ranger school. He went to the 18D medic course after SFAS and phase II of SFQC. The SF medic Phase III, 300-F1, was the longest of the specialties, requiring approximately two years to complete. The SF medic is the most highly trained in the world and is often required to act as physician, dentist, and veterinarian in remote areas of the world where better medical care or evacuation may not be available. It is a daunting responsibility. Ryan's initial training was one of the last classes taught at Ft. Sam Houston in San Antonio, Texas, before it was moved up to Ft. Bragg. Ft. Sam was distracting; it was the home of all Army Medical Department training and there were about five women for each male (nurses, lab techs, etc). And they picked on the SF guys; they *knew* SF guys were easy. A lot of guys flunked out because they spent too much time fooling around. The 300-F1 course was very difficult academically, the toughest in SF and possibly the toughest enlisted academic course in the Army; if you didn't study you flunked out.

Ryan partied like the rest and the women were plentiful. Because he was handsome, SF, and wore parachute wings, the Combat Infantry Badge, and a 10th MTN combat patch, he was lusted after by many of the young ladies in training. He found it easy to get a date, even at the last minute. Although he grew up in New England, he liked country music and the Texas dance halls. His favorite watering hole was just outside the loop near the airport, "Denim and Diamonds." He spent a lot of his off time there where he learned to two-step and drink tequila. There was also the River Walk downtown with its great restaurants, shops, and bars. Strolling along the river on a warm Texas evening was one of his favorite pastimes.

There was history here, too. Besides the Alamo, and the other old Spanish missions, there was the bar at the Menger Hotel where Teddy Roosevelt had raised his Rough Riders and the old German section with the grand antebellum mansions. On weekends they'd drive down to Laredo and go across into Mexico, or go down to Corpus Christi or South Padre Island and camp on the beach to go diving or fishing. He would have done a lot better in 300-F1 if it had been at Ft. Bragg. Still, he was at the head of his class and watched several of his classmates get recycled or sent to 18B (weapons) or 18C (engineer and demolitions) training instead. After San Antonio, he went to Madigan Army Medical Center for an "internship" and then spent a month at shock-trauma in Baltimore. He finished up with Robin Sage almost two years after starting.

After SERE and a course in Farsi he was assigned to a 5th SF team. The following year he was promoted to E6, staff sergeant, and went to the jumpmaster course and then attended scuba school. He was assigned to a dive team and almost immediately went back to SFUWO in Key West for DMT (dive medical technician) training and eventually, the Dive Sup (supervisor) course. He spent two more years on the team. He finished his bachelor degree in biology at night between deployments, and was thinking about applying for the physician's assistant course or maybe even medical school, but decided to put in his packet for warrant officer instead. The warrant officer course really sucked, almost like being in basic training again, but he got through it and was promoted to the officer ranks (sort of). In July, they assigned him to be the XO of the scuba team in a different battalion, ODA 501, 5th Special Forces Group (Airborne). This was his first mission with his new team and he was extremely happy, cruising twenty feet below the surface as he entered the bayou.

CHAPTER 33

An act of catastrophic terrorism would be a watershed event in American history. It would involve loss of life and property unprecedented in peacetime and undermine America's fundamental sense of security, as the Soviet atomic bomb test in 1949. Like Pearl Harbor, this event would divide our past and our future into a before and after. The United States might respond with draconian measures, scaling back civil liberties, allowing wider surveillance of citizens, detention of suspects, and use of deadly force. More violence could follow, either further terrorist attacks or US countermeasures.

—Ashton Carter, John Deutch, Philip Zelikow,
"Catastrophic Terrorism: Tackling the New Danger,"
Foreign Affairs, 1998

When Ryan surfaced he immediately knew something was wrong. Everyone was at the docks waiting for them. The captain and team sergeant seemed very agitated.

"What's up?" Ryan asked, coming up on the dock as the sun was casting the long shadows of impending evening. They were at it all day, out of communication with the rest of the world.

"We've been recalled to Campbell, someone has attacked the World Trade Center and the Pentagon," said CPT Rogers. "Thousands are dead!"

"Shit, do we know who? How was it done?"

"Looks like Arab terrorists," replied MSG Apin. "They flew commercial aircraft into them; we'll find out more when we get home."

They got their gear together and went back to their temporary quarters. The news was sickening . . . watching those planes fly into the World Trade Center over and over. Ryan finally turned off the TV since there was nothing else on. In spite of a sleepless night, they left at o'dark thirty the next morning. After an all-day drive, they got to Ft. Campbell well after dark but battalion and group headquarters were ablaze with lights and buzzing with activity. Mobilization orders had also gone out to the US Army Special Operations Command at Ft. Bragg, North Carolina and the 10th Mountain Division at Ft. Drum, New York. Over the next few days, the picture gradually emerged of a well-orchestrated plot by the al-Qaeda terrorist network. They pored over the intelligence reports, up to the top-secret level. While the media was wringing their hands and guessing, the 5th Special Forces Group (Airborne) was quietly preparing for unconventional warfare in Afghanistan.

CHAPTER 34

The leadership of the West in the world is coming to an end, not because west-
ern civilization is materially bankrupt or has lost its economic or military
strength, but because the Western order has played its part, and no longer
possesses the stock of values that gave it predominance. . . . The scientific rev-
olution has finished its role, as have nationalism, and the territorially limited
communities that grew up in its age. . . . The turn of Islam has come.

—Sayyid Qutb,
Ma'alim fi'l-tariq, Cario, 1964

The concept of Joint Special Operations was the recognition that an evolution in the nature of warfare had occurred. That in the future we probably
would *not* be fighting mass tanks battles with the Soviets on the plains of Europe,
as the United States Army and Air Force war plans had prepared for in the last
fifty years. One of the catalysts for this idea was the debacle at Desert One. When
the Iranian Revolution resulted in the assault on the US embassy in Tehran and
the taking of scores of American hostages, the Carter Administration was forced,
by national pride, to do something. It was a bold move in post-Vietnam America.
The country, its leaders, and even the military seemed to have a "Vietnam Syndrome," unable to act.

The rescue plan, under the command of Colonel Charlie Beckwith, the Commander of the new and secret Army Delta Force, was not a bad one but it was
complicated and ambitious. It was doomed to failure for the simple reason that
units from three different services had never worked together, had incompatible
equipment, the wrong machines for the job: and inadequate training, experience,
and rehearsal. They were thrown together at the last minute.

The Sikorsky Sea Stallion helicopters, thrown into the mix to give the Navy
(Marines) part of the pie, had a special intake inside the chopper. When a flak
Mikeet was inadvertently jammed against it the chopper overheated and was
rendered inoperable. The desert, always a harsh climate for equipment, was
responsible for other helicopter problems. Since the radios were incompatible,
the Army, Marines, and Air Force had trouble communicating with one another.
The disaster came when a chopper, believing he was following a ground guide,
collided with a C-130, then the whole operation went to hell. COL Beckwith

(referred to by some as "Chargin' Charlie, I'll Get You Killed Or My Name Ain't, Beckwith"), a man with a somewhat controversial Vietnam reputation, was left to call President Carter to recommend cancellation of the mission.

The resulting crash in the desert left a number of dead Americans, the loss of millions of dollars in aircraft, and resulted in international embarrassment. It became a black eye for the military and the administration. It confirmed the opinion of many in the world that the United States really *was* a paper tiger. Many in the Special Operations community, the government, and the military vowed that a disaster like that would never happen again.

The result was the formation of the United States Special Operations Command with oversight and integration of Army, Navy, and Air Force Special Operations forces. New units were formed like the 160th SOAR (Special Operations Aviation Regiment), under the command of United States Army Special Operations Command (USASOC), along with Army Special Forces, PSYOPs, and Civil Affairs. Units that were trained together and had compatible equipment became standard. It was, indeed, a new era in warfare. The employment of joint forces soon began in earnest, in Grenada, Panama, Iraq, and Somalia. Command structures, techniques, and equipment became more refined and USSOCOM became a force to be reckoned with.

Thus, the commander of the 5th Special Forces Group (Airborne), Colonel John Mulholland, became the Commander of Joint Special Operations Task Force (JSOTF) at a secret base, Stronghold Freedom, in one of the former Soviet Republics that border Afghanistan in October of 2001. He was a student of history and had pride in the regiment. He commissioned an American flag to be adorned with the 5th SF Flash and logo, just as regiments had done in the American Civil War. In his office at the JSOTF, hung a flag with a harp on a shamrock-green background, the famed banner of the New York Irish Brigade from that same war. He coined the motto for the task force, which he named Dagger, simple, but all-inclusive: Strength and Honor. His XO was an Air Force colonel, a man of impeccable special operations credentials, and they worked closely together. His command sergeant major, Mike McIntyre, was of vast experience and capabilities, as was the rest of his staff. The battalion commanders and their respective staffs were the best. The group had been given *carte blanche* to recruit individuals of special talent from elsewhere in the Special Operations community. These recruits included his J3, an operations officer from another SF Group, as well as a reserve Special Forces qualified veterinarian and a mule-pack expert, from USSOCOM; anything that would make the Task Force work. Staff meetings were a patchwork quilt of Army and Air Force Special operators,

PSYOPs and CA, the 160th SOAR, and various civilian liaisons (State, CIA, DEA, etc). All were dedicated to one mission: the overthrow of the Taliban and al-Qaeda, and the capture or death of Osama bin Laden.

That Special Operations was given the lead in the attack on Afghanistan, and the war on terrorism, was largely the decision of General Franks, the commander of CENTCOM (Central Command), which was the same unit that Schwarz-kopf commanded during Desert Storm. GEN Franks was a "heavy metal" warrior, more accustomed to commanding armor battalions and mechanized infantry brigades than he was in working with Special Operations Forces. He was also a student of history and to his to his credit, unlike much of his training, he recognized that Afghanistan was not a place for large numbers of conventional, heavy troops. The Soviets and the British had found that out the hard way. GEN Franks was an easy man to underestimate, with his "aw shucks" persona, but he didn't wear the four stars of a full General for being obtuse. If GEN Franks had any reservations, they were dispelled by a brief he received by a Special Forces lieutenant colonel at his headquarters in Tampa, Florida, shortly after 9/11. USASOC had obviously picked the right man for the job. While the media, the armchair quarterbacks, and "military experts" on TV discussed what a long, dirty, campaign it was going to be, some even voicing their opinions that it couldn't be done, GEN Franks had already unleashed his Special Operators.

It was going to be a risky operation, impossible many thought. Sending teams into the "box," as the operational area was called, without hard intelligence was dangerous. But Special Forces soldiers are trained to be flexible, to throw away the book when required. It *would* be dangerous and there would be a lot of pressure from above. Washington, always bothered by the lack of observable and measurable progress, would not be happy with these "shadow" warriors, these "quiet professionals" with a penchant for secrecy. In an era of instant gratification that had developed since the end of the Cold War, and in the era of "zero casualties," they would want to see results now *and* without anyone getting killed. It was a tall order and the 5th Special Forces Group (Airborne) was going to rise to the call: "Let's Roll" had become the rally cry of a nation.

CHAPTER 35

When you're wounded and left on Afghanistan's plains,
And the women come out to cut up what remains,
Jest roll to your rifle and blow out your brains
And go to your Gawd like a soldier,
So-oldier of the Queen

—Rudyard Kipling,
"The Young British Soldier"

"Fifteen seconds to impact, brace . . . brace . . . brace," screamed the pilot in Ryan's headphones, as the Spec Ops MH-47E Chinook made a controlled crash-landing in the almost zero visibility of the sandstorm-whipped night. It had been a mind numbing, stomach churning six-hour flight from Stronghold Freedom, an old Soviet airbase named Karshi-Kalabad (K2) in Uzbekistan, involving mid-air refueling and NOE (nape of the earth) contour flying. The chopper was the most advanced in the world, a $27 million helicopter with $30 million of special equipment added to it, terrain navigating radar, in-flight refueling capability, forward-looking infrared displays, and countermeasure devices. The Night Stalker pilots, from the 160th Special Operation Aviation Regiment (SOAR), were every bit as good as their equipment.

They approached a small plateau where their "contacts" had set up a small LZ, or landing zone. The smudge pots looked like bright explosions in their night vision goggles and were quickly extinguished by unseen hands as they made their approach, as to not interfere with the night vision of the pilots. There was little snow here, even though it was winter. This was the edge of the great desert where it touched the Hindu Kush. They dumped out their gear and formed a perimeter as the big helo lifted off. The adrenaline rush of being dropped in this wild, dangerous country had stretched their nerves taut. There was no one to be seen until a single turbaned, bearded Afghan stepped from the shadows.

"It's a dark night to venture about on Allah's business," whispered CPT Rogers in broken Dari, his knuckles white on the grip of his weapon.

"All the better to deceive unbelievers of the True Way," replied the man, also in Dari.

"May Allah be merciful on the People of the Book," Rogers finished the bona fides.

"You Rogers?" asked the man in English.

"Yeah, and this is Mike Apin, my team sergeant, and Ryan Gallagher, my XO," he said as they crowded around. The rest of the team had set up a small defensive perimeter. The senior commo man was in touch with the helos and the gunships in case they needed immediate extraction.

"You can call me Al."

"Al what?" Pete asked.

"Al Bundy, if you like," he said, as he suppressed a grin.

"Where are the Afghans?" asked Ryan.

"There're here. I know that most of you can't speak Pashto. Some of you probably speak Russian, and a lot of them do, but wait 'til they speak it first," he said. "They really don't like the Russians."

Al whistled and a small band melted from the shadows. They picked up the loose gear and danced down the rocky trail like mountain goats, while the team struggled with their heavy rucks. The new "MOLLE" ruck was supposed to be an improvement over the old ALCE ruck. It was easier to compartmentalize stuff for easy access, but it seemed to bounce around more. It was also larger, which was no improvement in the mind of MSG Apin. It just meant you could stick more mission non-essential junk in it, thus making it weigh more. His aching knees confirmed this.

After what seemed like hours, they found themselves at the base of the hills, looking out over a wide desert plain. The helos had come down the high valley to screen their approach to this border area northeast of the legendary city of Qandahar. It was a fairy-tale vista that greeted them. A full moon had gradually risen as they made their way down the mountain and revealed a wide plain dotted with mud redoubts that cast deep shadows, small hills fortified by mud castles, and the snow-covered mountains of the Hindu Kush in the background to the north. In the clear, cold air, it was bright enough to read. Camels, horses, and sheep herds were surrounded by a series of low patchwork tents favored by the nomadic Kuchi tribes of the region. It was here on this high desert plain that their journey would begin.

CHAPTER 35

The Afghan will bear poverty, insecurity of life; but he will not tolerate foreign rule. The moment he has a chance he will rebel.

—Sir John Lawrence, Viceroy of India, 1867, from
*Tournament of Shadows: The Great Game
and the Race for Empire in Central Asia,*
Karl E. Meyer and Shareen Blair Brysac

It was just like a Robin Sage exercise from the Q course. After the link up with their Afghan Gs, they were taken to see one of the Afghan warlords of the region. He had made it clear he was not fond of unbelievers in general, and Americans in particular. He was one of the more successful of the *mujahideen* in the fight against the Soviets, but unlike the "Gucci muji," had disdained Western help. The *mujahideen*, meaning "Soldiers of God" in Arabic, had been called to the *jihad* to expel the Soviet infidel invaders from Afghanistan. As he had feared, support from the West went along with the Soviets, leaving Afghanistan to founder in continued civil war. Like the Afghan horse trader/spy of Kipling's *Kim*, he started out almost every discussion with the Americans with the oath, "Allah's curse on all unbelievers."

Afghanistan lies in the middle of what had once been the great empires of the Middle East, Eastern, and Central Asia. As such, it had been at the crossroads of religions, cultures, armies, the Silk Road, and conquest. Alexander the Great had last successfully conquered it in 323 BC. Genghis Kahn, Tamerlane, and Burbur had ravaged it in ancient times. More recently the British in the nineteenth and early twentieth centuries and the Soviets in 1979, had invaded and captured the cities, Qandahar, Balkh, Heart, and Kabul, but had never really been successful in subduing the Afghan tribes. The warrior tribes stood defiantly in the mountains of the Hindu Kush, biding their time. The British found that their influence in the countryside only went as far as a musket ball, and the Soviets, employing airpower, discovered the same thing. A strong central government was practically unknown in Afghan history. This fierce warrior nation was more likely to heed the edicts from their Islamic mullahs or tribal chiefs than from a government in Kabul. Only one thing seemed, periodically, throughout history to be able to mobilize the Afghan people across tribal, ethnic, and economic boundaries to a common cause: invasion by infidels. It was because of these two unifying principals, national self-defense and loyalty to Islam, that resulted in successful jihad against the British, and almost a century later, the Soviets.

One of the things that made the Afghans different than Arab Muslims was the lack of an inferiority complex when dealing with the Americans. They were not particularly fond of *ferengi,* but they did not automatically hate them as many Arabs did. While the Arabs had a tremendously sophisticated civilization in the centuries after Islam swept through the Middle East, Europe was in the Dark Ages, their citizens little more than savages. But their civilization had since declined—or failed to progress—to the point that it was now the Arabs who had to catch up. It was the Americans, for all their success, that now bore the brunt of Arab hatred, because of their hegemony and their support of Israel. But the Afghans, in general, harbored no such feelings for the Americans.

The warlord, Atta Mohammed, had his own reasons for not liking the Americans and would not have tolerated them at all but for the protestations of one of his lieutenants and his CIA advisor (he knew where the dollars were coming from). He was also well aware of the great success General Dostum and his forces had when they were provided these same Special Forces teams at Mazar-i-Sharif and Herat. This invading army would be small; they would only number twelve, could speak several local languages, be respectful of Muslim customs and religion, and would be wearing beards and Afghan garb. The Afghans had an inherent distrust of anyone not wearing a beard. Women, considered good only for domestic chores and child bearing, didn't have beards, nor did homosexuals, known as *foo-foo* (girly) boys, nor the effeminate Bengali. The Soviets hadn't had beards either. A man without a beard would never be considered a warrior in Pashtun Afghan society and would never be entirely trusted.

These *ferengi* would also carry the technology for smart bombs they would need to defeat the Taliban armor and their brothers-in-evil, the despised Arab al-Qaeda. So they would use the tools these *ferengi* provided, but the sooner Afghanistan was rid of *all* foreigners the better. His lieutenant was extremely friendly to the Americans and the team was put in the charge of Commander Wahid Mohammed Wardak.

So they gained rapport, and trained their hundred-plus band in basic tactics, weapons (AK-74s, RPGs, mortars, and other Soviet-style weapons supplied by their CIA contacts), as well as close air support (CAS). But the team had to tread lightly. Every Afghan considered himself an experienced warrior and it was an insult to suggest otherwise. The training had to be couched as an exchange of ideas and techniques. They also provided communications training, foreign communications equipment, satellite phones, and cold-weather gear and clothing.

Besides the money, equipment, and close air support, it was the team's medical capabilities that really endeared them to their "Jungees." The team medics, just as they had been in the Special Forces Qualification Course, were essential to the team's success with the Afghans. In a country where a two-day donkey trip *might* provide you with half-assed medical care, the 18Ds were sent from heaven. The Afghans never had better medical care. In addition to treating severe battle wounds, the medics set up sick call and treated everything from colds to hemorrhoids. They provided medicines and expertise, and the Afghans loved them for it. Soldiers always fight better if they know they will receive good medical care if wounded.

Perhaps the only thing the Jungees liked better than the medical care was the *Sports Illustrated* swimsuit issue that Ryan brought along with him. They were invited to Wahid's tent to share a traditional Afghan meal. They took their shoes off at the door and sat on colorful pillows on the carpeted floor of the tent. Dinner was preceded with *chi*, sweet green tea, and dried mulberries, almonds, and some other type of nut none of them could identify. The Afghans supplied each of the Americans with a spoon, out of deference to US customs, while they ate the rice, beans, and goat meat by scooping it in the naan bread with their right hand. Always with the right (the left being used for a different vital function in the absence of toilet paper). After dinner, Ryan presented the magazine to the leader, who he caught admiring it from afar, and the Jungees went wild. Used to seeing women clad only in burqas, they were enthralled by the scantly clad beauties in the magazine. Rather than offending the puritanical instincts of radical Moslems like the Taliban, the Northern Alliance soldiers seemed to appreciate the female form. After that, the soldiers were constantly bugging the Americans for Western magazines.

The Americans were, in turn, trained on packing animals Afghan-style and riding the sturdy little horse of the high desert plains, as well as *mujihadeen* tactics. Several of the team had some experience with pack animals, having attended courses out west or ones run periodically in the Special Operations community. Several brought along the new Army Field Manual, FM 31-27, *Pack Animals in Support of Army Special Operation Forces,* and a couple had the manual from a course 2nd Bn, 5th SF had run a few years earlier. Pack animals and horse cavalry had been used in Afghanistan since 323 BC, when Alexander the Great conquered it. For the last twenty-five years, they had been the main mode of transport in many areas of Afghanistan, first against the Soviets, then in the civil war that consumed much of the country, and now against the Taliban. Like their Scythian ancestors more than 2,500 years ago, they would sweep down from the high plains and from their mud redoubts to attack on horseback. These early warriors were among the first to discover that skilled riders on horseback could shock foot soldiers. It was a stretch using them against old Soviet armored vehicles, as obsolete as they were, but it worked time and again. They conducted several small exercises, attacking small Taliban outposts and convoys.

One of these training missions was terrifying for CPT Rogers. They mounted their horses with their Northern Alliance soldiers in the dead of night for a fifteen-kilometer movement to attack one of the Taliban police stations. The horse CPT Rogers was given was a cantankerous, ill-mannered beast who knew that Rogers was not at all comfortable in the saddle. He kept reaching around and nipping Rogers on the leg, and periodically tried to dump him. After a particularly difficult ride they dismounted for a break and planned their pre-dawn attack. It was cold and dark as the riders started off and Chuck's beast lagged behind and finally would not move at all. Chuck, afraid to yell, suddenly found himself completely alone in hostile territory. His efforts to get the horse moving were to no avail, and he finally dismounted and tried dragging his charge along in the general direction he thought the party was headed. Just as he was near panic, one of the Afghan soldiers appeared, and chuckling, bade him to get on the horse and he drug it by the bridal to the rest of the team. The attack went off like clockwork with an honest-to-Allah cavalry charge, the first for US soldiers since the Battle for Bataan sixty years before.

Several weeks went by and it was decided by the JSOTF that it was time to eliminate the Taliban and al-Qaeda from this part of southern Afghanistan. The Afghans mounted an attack against the citadel at Gazni, last captured by the British following the massacre of the Kabul garrison in 1842. The warlord, Commander Atta, wanted to mount the attack without American help, attacking the citadel from horseback much as his ancestors did. The attack was foolish and failed with heavy losses to the Northern Alliance Afghan cavalry. The 18Ds got plenty of practice that day.

CPT Rogers had argued, unsuccessfully, that cavalry against T-55 and T-62 Soviet tanks was suicide. He decided to take matters into his own hands. He called in CAS as MSG Apin "lit up" the target, a heavy concentration of armored vehicles below the citadel wall, with a SOFLAM Tactical Laser Designator (TLD), for the "smart" GBU-32 JDAM (Joint Direct Attack Munitions) laser-guided bombs. Unknown to him, Wahid was standing next to Atta and was arguing with him about the Americans. As he pointed to the armored vehicles near the citadel, an F18A Hornet from the USS *Theodore Roosevelt*, circling at twenty thousand feet, released its bomb vaporizing the tanks and armored vehicles before his eyes. Atta was convinced. He got on his INMARSAT satellite phone (supplied by his advisor) and told his men to bring up the Americans. With the fading light, a Spectre AC-130 gun ship was called on station and through the night it fired 25 rounds from its 105 howitzer, 50 rounds of 40mm cannon, and over 5,000 rounds from its mini-guns. The piece de resistance was a BLU-82, a 15,000-pound bomb about the size of a car that was dropped from an MC-130. In the morning, what was left of the Taliban garrison surrendered.

Many of the Taliban then swore allegiance to Atta, Afghans being notorious throughout history for switching sides when a battle appeared to be won. The Afghans treated their errant Taliban brothers surprisingly well . . . not so with the Arab, Pakistani, and Chechen al-Qaeda. The living were treated severely and the dead were left out to rot, unlike their deceased countrymen who were buried under stone sarcophagi before sundown according to Islamic tradition.

As they were collecting stragglers, they came under small-arms fire and one of the weapons men was slightly wounded. Mike Apin wrenched his knee diving for cover. One of the former Taliban told them there were still thirty or forty hardcore al-Qaeda holed-up in the catacombs of the fort. CPT Rogers wanted desperately to get some Arab prisoners but all attempts to talk them out failed. One of the team's engineers, SSG Preston, suggested they divert an irrigation ditch and flood the basement, hoping the cold water would cause hypothermia and convince them to surrender. When this failed after two days, Commander Atta, over the objections of the Americans, ordered hundreds of gallons of fuel oil to be poured into the basement on top of the water. A single Chechen struggled out before the fire was set, roasting the dozens of holdouts. It was a cruel act in a cruel land.

CHAPTER 37

The spheres of heaven revoke uncertainly,
Now blooms the rose, now shapely pricks the thorn,
Glory's the hazard, O man of women born!
The very name Pakhtun, spells honor and glory,
Lacking that honor, what is the Afghan story?
In the sword alone lies our deliverance.

— Khushal Khan, Pashtun warrior poet,
circa 1630

The new communications technology allowed ODA 501 to follow the war, something that would have been unheard of even a scant decade ago during the Gulf War. By hooking up their computer to their PSC-5 radio with its satellite antenna, they could read the daily classified SITREPS (situation reports) and INSUMS (intelligence summaries) from the B team, FOB (forward operating base) and the JSOTF anywhere in Afghanistan. They could follow the progress of the whole war. With their small MBITR radio they could talk secure to over-flying CAS or hooked up to the antenna, go SATCOM. The Taliban and al-Qaeda were collapsing in the north, south, and west. Kabul and Qandahar had both fallen and those who had not fled were killed or hiding in the vast cave complexes on the border with Pakistan. Thermobaric bombs, which sucked all the oxygen out of the air, were very effective against the caves, such as at Tora Bora (meaning black widow in Pashtun), as long as they were dropped near an entrance.

The Taliban and al-Qaeda had seriously underestimated the technology and global reach of the US military. The ineffectual cruise-missile strikes by the Clinton administration after the African embassy bombings should have been a harbinger of what was to come. Like the Japanese after the Pearl Harbor attack, al-Qaeda had awoken, as Admiral Yamamoto had put it, a "sleeping giant." The initial cruise missile and bombing campaign began on October 7, attacking Taliban compounds, command centers, and airfields; the small Taliban Air Force was completely destroyed on the ground. The campaign had quickly run out of targets in this "target poor" environment. One of the news commentators had even talked about bombing Afghanistan *up* to the stone age. The backward nature of the country had been an advantage against the Soviets. The Afghans were so primitive it became a strength; there was little worth destroying.

A lot of criticism started to appear about the ineffectual air campaign, and it soon became obvious that eyes had to be on the ground to direct the bombing. This is where the Army Special Forces and their attached Air Force TAC-Ps came in. The unconventional warfare "exercise" was a complete success, so wildly successful, so quick, that not enough conventional troops had been in position to cut off fleeing enemy.

One important aspect of the victory was the vast amount of intelligence they collected. The team found radios and cryptographic material, which were forwarded to NSA (National Security Agency), the evolution of the old Army ASA, through secure intelligence channels. They also found intercept and other sophisticated electronics, surprising, or perhaps not, considering al-Qaeda's deep pockets. Laptop computers revealed a wealth of information that was put to work elsewhere in the world in the war against terrorism. Army computer experts could extract information that the authors thought they had deleted from hard drives.

ODA (Tiger) 501 moved for hours by convoy to Qandahar Airfield with their Jungees in a variety of vehicles scrounged where they could. They traveled over what had to be the worst roads in the world—worse even than southern Iraq after the air campaign. They were careful to call in their routes and mark the vehicles with orange VS-17 panels and glint tape; they didn't want any trigger-happy pilots firing on them. Ryan sat in the back of the Pakistani SUV with Mike. Mike had given up reading and was staring out the window.

"You reading history again, Top?" quizzed Ryan.

"Was. These mountain passes make me nervous. Historically, they've been the Afghans' major allies against invading armies. During the retreat by the British in 1842 from Kabul to Jalabad, the Afghans sniped at the British from the heights. Their *jezail* rifles had an effective range of up to five hundred meters compared to that of the British Brown Bess. It was a smooth-bore musket and only had an effective range of about 150 meters. The Afghans slaughtered them. Over fifteen thousand Brits and sepoys died during that retreat."

"I read about that, there's a famous painting I saw. I think I've seen it. My dad took me to the Imperial War Museum in London. What was it called . . . ?"

"The *Remnants of an Army?*"

"Yeah, that was it. Only one Brit survived. It was the greatest defeat in British military history."

"Oh, there were a few others. Gordon at Khartoum and Lord Chelmsford at Isandlwana during the Zulu wars to name a couple. You ever see that movie with Michael Caine about the defense of Roark's Drift?"

"*Zulu?* It's one of my favorites."

"For some reason, the British have always seemed to revel in their military disasters. By 1878 when they fought the Second Afghan War, the British had replaced the musket with the Martini-Henry Rifle, accurate to about a thousand meters, and their tactics had improved. They replaced their red uniforms with khaki and pith helmets for their headgear. By 'crowning the heights,' putting flankers of their own on the peaks through the passes, the British managed to avert disaster, but still got their noses bloodied."

"Do you ever think about Vietnam, Top?"

"Every damn day!"

"But it was so long ago."

"When I was a kid I used to listen to my old man tell me about WWII and I used to think he was talking ancient history. But that was in the 1950s. Less than ten years after the war ended. Hell, it's been twenty-five years since Vietnam, but it feels like yesterday to me."

"Yeah, I know what you mean. Desert Storm seems like last week, but it's been over ten years now," Chuck said.

"I read somewhere that war memories never fade in the minds of the living; the war only truly ends when we die."

All along the way to Qandahar there were burned-out Soviet tanks, armored personnel carriers, trucks, and cars. Bombs and/or mines of this war, the previous civil wars, and that against the Soviets had cratered the road. It was sometimes hard to tell in which engagement the damage happened. It was a country populated by the same mud forts that were indistinguishable from the structures razed by the British in the First (1839–42), Second (1878), and Third (1919) British-Afghan wars, not to mention those of more recent vintage. When not fighting foreign invaders, and there had been plenty of those over the centuries, the Afghans engaged in intertribal warfare. Perhaps the most devastating war, except for the Mongol invasion in the thirteenth century, was the recent civil war in which the Taliban was largely, if not completely, victorious. Kabul, spared by most foreign invaders, was turned into rubble.

"You know, Ryan, one of the things that really bothers me is something I was thinking about when we took the citadel at Ghaznavi."

"What was that?"

"Well, when the British marched through Qandahar during the First Afghan War, they had an old king named Shah Shuja with them who they intended to put on the throne as their puppet. They were initially welcomed with open arms by the Afghans. The whole thing, the invasion of Afghanistan, was a paranoid reaction to the Russian incursions into Central Asia, part of the Great Game, and was completely unnecessary. Anyway, the old king had been kicked off the throne for incompetence twenty or so years before and the Brits intended to put him up as 'their man.'"

"Who was running the country?"

"A guy named Dost Mohammed, who only turned to the Ruskies after being double crossed by the British. He really didn't have a choice. The Persians and Sikhs were eating up his territory and all he really wanted was British protection. They refused and because they feared he was courting the Russians they put together this ill-advised invasion. The first real British test came at the supposedly impregnable fortress at Ghaznavi."

"How'd they defeat it? They didn't have smart bombs."

"Well, they did, sort of. One of the Dost's traitorous kinfolk told them that the Kabul Gate wasn't reinforced and a sapper team blew the gate and annihilated the garrison. When the Dost heard about it he fled and the Army marched into Kabul without firing a shot. For a variety of laughable blunders the British garrison, the old shah, and his men were wiped out two years later when the Afghans tired of the *ferengi* army, these foreign unbelievers, on their soil. You see the parallel?"

"Yeah, I think so. You're afraid we're going to bring the old king back from Italy and put him in power while we prop up the government."

"Exactly. The parallels here are frightening. The recent king was also booted out for being completely incompetent. He was off playboying in Europe when the coup happened. We've replaced the British, or the Soviets, take your pick. How long is it going to take the Afghans to get tired of us? The high plains of Afghanistan are littered with the bleached bones of would-be conquerors."

"Well, it's certainly a good reason for keeping large numbers of conventional troops out of the country. Let's hope Washington knows that."

"I gotta tell you though; riding into town on that old Russian T-55 tank was a real rush! I felt like we had just liberated a French town during WWII!"

"Yeah, except instead of pretty girls we got scruffy old men in turbans and a few old crones in burqas looking for a handout. And where were the bottles of vino?"

"Yeah, well it still felt good. The people seemed genuinely glad to see us."

Qandahar Airfield was about fifteen kilometers on the other side of a ridge of hills separating it from the city proper. The Americans built it during the late 1950s in the Cold War rush to match the significant amount of aid the Soviets were also pouring into Afghanistan. It was envisioned as a stopping-off point and refueling base for commercial airliners traveling from Europe and the Middle East to India, but had almost instantly become a white elephant with the advent of commercial jet aircraft. It had, however, proved very useful to the Soviets during their invasion of Afghanistan and would become the major logistical American base for *their* invasion into Afghanistan. By February, the airbase was growing into a sizable American presence. C-17s, C-130s, and helos of various sizes and shapes were constantly taking off and landing, but only at night, and then blacked out. Even so, they routinely took fire. A brigade of the 101st Airborne had just replaced the Marines at the end of January and was turning it into a regular garrison. It was hard to do much patrolling around the airbase because of the ever-present land mines, but the 101st sent out their QRF when needed.

After checking in with the B team, the company command sergeant major came over to see them. "You guys want to get in on the pool? A buck a shot."

"What pool is that, sergeant major?" asked CPT Rogers.

"The rocket pool. See, they shoot these 107mm or 122mm rockets at us all the time and the way the pool works, is if you guess what day and time one hits our compound you win."

"What if you have the right info but you get killed?" asked Mike.

The sergeant major grinned. "Then we have an old-fashioned wake for you when we get back."

"I'm in," said Ryan. "But only if *you* sing 'Danny Boy' at my wake, sergeant major."

One of the best things about arriving at Qandahar was that the SOC-C (the SF liaison) from 5th SF, had acquired three new Toyota trucks from the States with roll bars and mounts for heavy weapons for Tiger 501. Now the twelve-team members and their attached Air Force TAC-P could travel in style.

The team got a shower in a modified chemical decontamination unit, slept on cots in a heated tent, ate pretty decent chow, and would have gotten a good nights' sleep except for the intermittent explosions and constant firing. Qandahar was okay except for the dust. The dust was talcum-powder fine and rose in great clouds from the airfield. In places, it was ankle deep, and it found its way into everything, even sealed waterproof bags. Almost everyone had a hacking cough, deemed the "Qandahar Crud," caused by some virus and was aggravated by the dust. During the first night ODA 501 was there, they came under rocket attack and the perimeter was probed, setting off a huge firefight. In the hour before dawn it also rained, a rare occurrence for this region on the edge of the Mashti-Dago, the "Desert of Death." It turned the whole base from a dust bowl into a mud hole. It flooded their tent and it was like trying to walk on chocolate icing. Even so, it was an improvement from the dust.

The JSOTF at Qandahar also had an impressive array of communications set up by the time Tiger 501 arrived. It was possible to call home and talk to the family via DSN (the military phone system) that was then patched through the military operator at Fort Campbell to their home. It was part of the morale-and-welfare system. The only problem was the half-a-day time zone difference.

It was also a half time zone different than the "Stans" or Pakistan; when it was 0500 in Pakistan it was 0430 in Afghanistan. Chuck had thought someone was pulling his leg when he was told that. Who ever heard of half a time zone? But it was true. The military always tried to work in Greenwich Mean Time, called ZULU, so that operations in Afghanistan, Germany, or Ft. Campbell were always on the same sheet of music, but all of the coordination they did with the Afghans was in local time. Chuck had to wear two watches; it was too hard to keep doing the math.

Chuck hadn't talked to his wife in months. He last talked to her at Stronghold Freedom, just before going into isolation. She sounded upbeat at the time. She was doing her wifely duties as the "team mother," watching for the other wives since neither Ryan nor Mike was married. She lent some of the enlisted wives money when they got overextended, and was afraid one of the others was stepping out on her husband. Other than that everything had been going well. But that had been a while ago. They received no mail in those last two months, but at Qandahar some of it caught up with them. Chuck received several boxes of goodies, but only two slim letters from his wife dated a month apart. She sounded distant and cold and Chuck was worried. They were only allowed fifteen minutes to call, and although Chuck left several messages on the machine he was unable to connect. She was probably visiting her folks. Mike and Ryan had no problem connecting with their girlfriends, and Chuck asked Ryan to have one of his squeezes check on his wife. They also had access to civilian email there, but his wife had never learned to use it. He got up in the middle of every night while they were at Qandahar to call, but was unable to connect.

Their last night together before he had deployed had not gone well.

"Why do you always have to go?" she complained.

He looked down to the long-haired guy sitting on the other side of the bar. "So if I don't go, who's going to . . . him?"

"Well, it doesn't have to be *you*! You've done your bit. I'm so sick of the Army. You never said you were going to make it a career!"

His voice softened. "Look dear, it's what I'm good at . . . I make a difference; this is important. Your father served; he was in Korea and Vietnam. My father served in WWII, Korea, and Vietnam. What do you think would have happened if they had left it to someone else? Them and thousands like them who sacrificed so that America could be free?"

But she was not to be consoled and they both went home angry. He didn't wake her when he left well before daylight. Now he wished he had. He tried one last time, listening to the sound of an empty ring.

CHAPTER 38

When the Afghans have acted in a common cause, their country, though often ravaged, has never been held down by a foreign power. On the other hand, evidence indicates that Afghanistan is only capable of unity when its people respond to a foreign threat. Left to their own devices, Afghans engage in internecine battles, or simply enjoy freedom; not the kind of enforceable by a Magna Carta, Bill of Rights, or Communist Manifesto, but of more ancient divination, unbothered by government at all.

—Steven Tanner,
*Afghanistan: A Military History from
Alexander the Great to the Fall of the Taliban*

The next day Tiger 501 traveled into Qandahar to the C team that had set up, ironically, in the governor's palace. Qandahar had been largely destroyed by the Soviets and was just in the process of being rebuilt by the Taliban when the Americans invaded. Qandahar was the birthplace of the Taliban and had always been a city of Muslim extremism, intolerant of foreigners. The area had converted to Islam during the late seventh century, shortly after the death of the Prophet Mohammed, as Islam swept across the Middle East and Central Asia.

This was Pashtun country, the majority in a country with over seventeen different ethnic minorities; Uzbeks, Tajiks, Turkmen, and Hazars being some of the other major groups. The Pashtuns were the largest, and, traditionally, the most powerful. Almost half of the Pashtuns lived across the border in Pakistan, in areas that were formerly Afghan. The seemingly arbitrary border was an intentional attempt to conquer the area by dividing the Pashtun. It was similar to the way the British carved up the Middle East after the fall of the Ottoman Empire. Both divisions had lent themselves to post-colonial unrest and sometimes conflict. The Pashtuns, further divided into a number of fierce warrior subtribes, were traditionally very independent and did not always get along with their fellow countrymen. They rarely would tolerate *ferengi* of any sort.

ODA 501 moved through Afghanistan's second largest city cautiously, one soldier always in the bed of the truck manning the heavy gun. They mostly saw smiles and waves, although an occasional scowl or black face warned of animosity below the surface. Overall, it seemed that even the people of this radical city were tired of the puritanical, medieval order of the Taliban. The complete subjugation of women, lack of education and entertainment, the public beheadings, the cutting off of ears and hands, and the stonings had all taken their toll. The streets were teeming with throngs of people, men in turbans or skull caps, and women in burqas, the head-to-toe covering women were obliged to wear. Commerce along the route seemed manic all in the roadside stalls and cargo containers converted into shops, selling everything from food to bootleg DVDs and Occidental-style clothing. This was truly the bazaar of Kipling's East.

They traded *salaam aleikums,* the traditional Moslem greeting, with the gate guards at the palace and were ushered into the courtyard for a meal of Kabuli rice, goat kebabs, naan bread, and eggplant. It was a feast after what they had been eating for the last several months. Besides the ubiquitous *chi,* undoubtedly of British influence, they even had Coke in cans with Arabic writing.

While they were eating, one of the teams brought in several flex-cuffed hooded individuals. They were captured in the bazaar buying influence. They were determined to be Iranians and they had a suitcase with the equivalent in Afghanis, the inflated Afghan currency, of several hundred thousand dollars. They had been warned that the Iranians were trying to take advantage of the power vacuum in Herat, even landing Iranian military aircraft there, but Qandahar seemed out of their range. The Persians had coveted the Herat region for centuries and in the 1800s were thwarted by the British at gunpoint. Their goal now was ostensibly to try and destabilize the shaky Karzai government. It was a clumsy attempt. The United States government was not about to let the Iranians muck this up and the perpetrators got an all-expense paid trip to a confinement cage at the airbase, while a formal complaint was filed with this "Axis of Evil" government by the Bush Administration.

The fall of Qandahar was a cooperative venture between Karzai, a former warlord named Sharzai, and US Special Forces. For all practical purposes, this team was running southwest Afghanistan. The lieutenant colonel, a battalion commander in the 5th SF, was the principle advisor for the governor, Sharzai, who was appointed to that post by the interim president, Karzai, his brother. The LTC was badly wounded along with Karzai during the campaign and although in constant pain, had remained at his post for several months. He was one of the true heroes of the victory, directing several A teams that had completely routed the Taliban and al-Qaeda.

After dinner, they went up on the roof of the palace, which was well fortified against attack with several heavy weapons and AT4s. As the sunset crept over a blue-domed mosque and slipped between the mountains, they listened to the call to prayers coming from all over the city. It was a beautiful night. The faint sounds of music could also be heard over the buzzing din of the bazaar and a few kites flew over the city, both of which would have been impossible when the Taliban was in power. Kites, or just about any other form of toy, and especially TV, music, and even whistling were considered blasphemous by the Office to Promote Virtue and Prevent Vice, the Taliban religious police, and punishable by extreme measures. The team got one of the best nights sleep they had in months, inside a real building with working (almost) indoor plumbing.

The next evening, Chuck, Ryan, and Mike stood on the roof taking in the sites, sounds, and smells of Qandahar.

"You think when all this is over, Afghanistan will become a democracy?" asked Chuck.

"Maybe not in the Western mold, but I'm confident they can at least form a government that will keep the country from producing another generation of war orphans and eliminate it as a safe haven for terrorists. I like these people," Mike said.

"Sometimes I think about how the world would be today if we had won in Vietnam, or if we'd taken over Iraq and reconstituted it as a democracy."

"Exporting our vision of government to the rest of the world can be dangerous. I'm not sure certain cultures, religions, or peoples would be able to function like we do, especially in the third world."

"I wonder what the world will be like if we succeed here," questioned Chuck.

"If, if, if . . . if frogs had wings they could fly," mumbled Ryan.

They both turned and looked at Ryan. "Ryan, you look a little green around the gills. You got the scoots or something?" asked Mike.

"I don't know, must have been something I ate. I feel a little dizzy."

Usually it was Chuck that was the team hypochondriac. Doc Murphy, the senior medic on the team had given a medical-threat brief to the team and it scared Chuck half to death; he was always worrying that he had contracted some fatal tropical disease and was constantly admonishing the team against eating local food and drinking untreated water. This was not always possible in an unconventional-warfare environment, where they lived closely with their brothers-in-arms. The Soviet army was decimated by disease while fighting in Afghanistan; suffering over six hundred thousand cases of hepatitis and tens of thousands of cases of typhoid and the other various diseases that ravaged this fourth-world country. The American Army prepared its soldiers with state-of-the-art insect repellents, prophylactic drugs, and vaccines for yellow fever, typhoid, hepatitis A and B, anthrax, Japanese encephalitis, rabies, anthrax, tetanus, etc. However, there was still malaria, cholera, dysentery, plague, leprosy, hydadid cysts, leptospirosis, tuberculosis, brucellosis, amebiasis, leishmaniasis, and a lot of other "-osises" and "-iasises" to worry about. At least this was one place they didn't have to worry about STDs; on this trip, sex was forbidden.

"What are you chewing, Ryan?" asked Chuck. "I thought you ran out of dip."

"I did but one of the Afghans gave me this chew."

"That's your problem," laughed Mike. "That's *naswar*, it's tobacco laced with opium. You better hope we don't have a drug test scheduled anytime soon."

"One of the guys said they just opened a small exchange at the airfield and they have tobacco. We'll go over tomorrow and get you some real stuff before you turn into an addict," laughed Chuck.

By late November the Taliban had largely been routed in almost all areas of the country by A teams, working with local warlords and their Northern Alliance partners. One team, ODA 595, Tiger 03, had been responsible for killing over 1,300 Taliban and al-Qaeda and destroying fifty armored vehicles. Another, ODA 555, the "Triple Nickel" had come down through the Panjshir Valley, taken over the control tower at Baghram Airbase, and had directed strikes against the Taliban defenders of Kabul, finally entering the capital with a victorious force. They found the US embassy untouched, just as it had been left in 1979. An insurrection at Qala-i-Jangi fortress, turned Taliban prison, had been put down and by February 2002 dozens of A teams ruled the country.

September 11 was a good six months ago. By any estimate, Tiger 501 had been wildly successful, but no more than the dozen or so other A teams operating in the country. They had accounted for over a thousand Taliban and al-Qaeda killed or captured, the destruction of over twenty-five tanks and armored vehicles, and the destruction of dozens of trucks, artillery pieces, recoilless rifles, and heavy mortars. They had captured vast quantities of light weapons, mines, and ammunition. But the cold, poor food, constant tension, living on adrenalin and testosterone, all were taking its toll. They were worn out and ready for a rest, hopefully redeployment back home to see their families as the 3rd and 19th Special Forces Groups gradually took over the mission. It looked like they were heading to Baghram Airbase, north of Kabul, and then just one more mission; clearing the cave complexes in the Shah-i-Kot Valley. Maybe they'd be home by June after all.

CHAPTER 39

The course of this conflict is not known yet its outcome is certain. . . . We'll meet violence with patient justice, assured of the rightness of its cause and confident of the victories to come.

—President George W. Bush,
Speech to Congress, Sept. 20, 2001

They arrived in Baghram Airbase in the middle of the night (they never went *anywhere* except in the middle of the night). They rode in the back of a Special Operations Casa-212 (sometimes described as a UPS truck with wings), filled with surveillance and intercept gear with guys working on computers by chemlite in the blacked-out interior. There was almost no room and Ryan found himself sitting on the seat of some kind of four-wheel ATV with Chuck Rogers next to him. The rest of the guys were sprawled on the floor, definitely not a regular US Air Force flight. The take off was almost straight up, and the flight up and down and side-to-side as they zig-zagged through the valleys and mountain passes at low level. Ryan was just starting to feel nauseous when they suddenly dropped like a rock, bounced on the runway, and were dumped on the tarmac. The plane was airborne again in a matter of minutes.

There was nothing more confusing than landing on a runway, in the middle of a war zone, in the middle of the night. It was pitch black and extremely cold except in the back-blast of the plane's turboprops. It was almost impossible to hear and aircraft were constantly taking off and landing. They wandered around in the dark, making sure to stay on the paved surface (the place was lousy with land mines), until they found the air force control tent, where they linked up with a SF liaison from the B team who got them squared away in a tent.

"You guys came at a bad time, we're just about full up here. All our transient tents are full. The only one available is the one we had some wounded Afghani soldiers in. You guys bring cots?"

"Yeah," said Mike. "We don't care where you put us."

"We'll get you squared away with the B team tomorrow. The whole world has shown up here for the big op. Hope you don't mind sharing with some of the Air Force TAC-Ps."

The tent was littered with trash; MRE remnants, bloody bandages, and Afghani blankets. It was so cold they each grabbed a couple of Afghani blankets and—lice and other vermin be damned—put them under and over their sleeping bags for added warmth. It was subzero and the kerosene stoves in the tent were empty. They just about froze to death during the night. Chuck woke early, after sleeping fitfully or not at all, he wasn't sure. As was his custom he went out at daybreak, broke out his small stove and made his mocha coffee; two MRE coffee packs, a pack of creamer, one sugar, and a packet of hot chocolate in a canteen cup. Sipping his mocha, he watched the beautiful sight of the sun rising over the snow-covered peaks of the fabled Hindu Kush.

Baghram stands at the edge of the Hindu Kush, separating northern from southern Afghanistan and is surrounded by a bowl of mountains. It is about forty miles north of Kabul and six thousand feet in elevation and was startlingly cold on this day late in February. There was no snow on the ground, but the 14,000–18,000 foot peaks surrounding it on three sides were completely covered. If it wasn't for the profusion of broken-down armored vehicles, burned aircraft, and ruined buildings, it would truly have been beautiful. The airbase was built by the Soviets in the 1960s and had become that invader's major base of operations. Baghram was also the site of ancient invaders' bases. It was the Persian Afghan military capital, Kapish-Kanish, centuries before Alexander the Great built Alexandria-in-the-Caucasus on the site at about 323 BC.

Mike came out of the tent shivering. "Captain, don't you *ever* sleep?"

"Not much, I guess, at least not when I'm keyed up. Man, what a view! Hey, what's that book you were reading yesterday? You've got more damn books! No wonder your ruck's so heavy."

"It's a military history of Afghanistan. I'll give it to you when I finish. It's mostly ancient stuff, you know, Alexander the Great and all, but there's quite a bit on the Soviets. They really took it in the rear. Baghram was their chief base you know?"

"Yeah?"

"Along with the airbase, dams, schools, and irrigation systems, the Soviets built an impressive kilometers-long tunnel at eleven thousand feet through the Hindu Kush—the Salang tunnel. They also engineered a vast series of roads through northern Afghanistan. Made the invasion a lot easier. You know they invaded on Christmas Day in 1979?"

"Like Washington at Trenton, huh!"

"Yeah. It was the Soviets' turn to learn the age-old lesson that it's *easy* to get into Afghanistan; *ruling* the country's another matter altogether. They set up a puppet communist government, but Barak Karmal, their pick, was deprived of the normal means of getting and keeping power in Afghanistan; blinding or murdering political rivals, and forming political alliances of power based on the tribal system. The British found out the same thing more than once, but the lesson seems lost in history. I hope we don't repeat it."

"That's the truth!"

"The Soviets and the communist troops controlled the urban centers, the 'ring road' linking the major Afghan cities, but were unsuccessful in controlling the countryside. Just like we tried to do in Vietnam. Their answer was a kind of 'migratory genocide,' sort of like our 'strategic hamlet' program except the Soviets forced the peasants to flee the countryside by destroying villages, massacring civilians, killing animals, sowing farmlands with landmines, and other diabolical methods. You know, they say there are over *thirty million* mines in Afghanistan!"

"Yeah, and most of them are here in Baghram. Damn things go off all the time. Look at this," Chuck said as he kicked at a large white object in the dirt.

"What is it?"

"It's a bone, human, I think. They're everywhere; must have been plowed up when they leveled this field for the tents. I don't know if this was a burial ground or a minefield or what. I saw one of those mongrel Afghan dogs sneaking through here this morning with what looked like a human hand in his mouth."

"Pretty grisly!"

"Yeah, see those dogs over there where the blue tent is? I think those are Polish mine-sniffing dogs."

"I think you're right. The mines were a key element in the Soviet depopulation program. It was wildly successful, uprooting an estimated one-third of the rural Afghan population. With no real press coverage there was little world outcry. We were still reeling from Vietnam and who cared about some crummy little piece of real estate in Central Asia anyway? The policy didn't really have the desired strategic affect though, and the Northern Alliance's greatest military commander, Massoud, attacked Baghram repeatedly from his base in the Panjshir Valley. In order to control Afghanistan you have to control Baghram, and the approach to Kabul."

"He was the guy that was assassinated just before the World Trade Center attack, wasn't he?"

"Yeah, he was really pro-West. Bin Laden had him killed as a favor to the Taliban. He was just as big a pain in the ass to them as he was to the Soviets. He'd be president today instead of Karzai if he'd lived. We may be better off with Karzai though, at least he's Pashtun."

Now Baghram was just beginning to become the main US-Afghan operations staging base in late February of 2002. The commanding general of the 10th MTN Division set up his headquarters in a gigantic hangar and almost all the other Special Operations units were using it as well. The Task Force Dagger TOC was set up in a tent pitched on the tarmac of the hangar. COL Mullholland had placed the JSOTF under the two-star flag rank of the 10th Mountain Commander, MG Hagenbach. The media was everywhere and a parade of US dignitaries were marching though the place, nonstop. The JOC at Baghram was incredible. It was a hustle-bustle of people and Chuck, Ryan, and Mike had trouble getting in through the main gate because they were not on the access roster. The center was a marvel of modern technology with TV monitors showing live video feeds from Predators (remote controlled aircraft with a forty-seven-foot wingspan and equipped with Hellfire missiles) as well as a dozen other high-tech computer-generated images, maps, intel, and situational update screens.

Their team would go to the southern providence of Paktia, traditionally a lawless den of competing warlords, drug dealers, smugglers, gunrunners, and other assorted brigands. It was also the site of many Soviet disasters during *their* war. The area bordered Pakistan's lawless northwest frontier area, and was populated with unruly Pashtuns and the nomadic Kuchi tribe. When the British Durand line was drawn in the late 1800s to separate colonial India from Afghanistan, it went right through the Pashtun tribal areas, sometimes right down the middle of villages and pasturelands. The area north of the line was Afghanistan; the area south was destined to become Pakistan. The Pashtun area in Pakistan included the traditional Afghan cities of Quetta and Peshawar, seized by Sikhs in the mid 1800s. The area also included mountains, dangerous passes, and caves built by the *mujahideen* to fight the Soviets. It was sometimes referred to as Pashunistan.

They planned the mission in a modified isolation in a makeshift ISOFAC (isolation facility). They would fly down to the dirt airstrip in Khost with their vehicles, and then convoy to Gardez through the same mountain pass where the Soviet 201st Motorized Rifle Regiment had been destroyed in the mid 1980s. They were up at daybreak and loaded onto a British Spec Ops C-130 for the flight down, but were stood down with no explanation. While the rest of the team dozed on a pallet, the sun warming them in the crystal clear air, Ryan and Mike walked down the runway to look at the squadron of A-10 Thunderbolts (also know as Warthogs, tank busters) that had just arrived from a staging base in Pakistan for the upcoming mission. They had never seen one up close. The air force security policeman, after learning that they were Special Forces, acted like having two bearded, armed, and scruffy civilian-clothed individuals on the flight line was normal. He told them to go and take a close look at the aircraft if they wanted.

"You can even write on one of the bombs, if you want," he said.

It was an impressive, ugly aircraft, much larger than they had imagined. As one of the premier close air support (CAS) aircraft, they had seen them overhead at Ft. Bragg dozens of times doing aerial acrobatics. Its distinctive ugly silhouette belied the power of its tank-busting cannon.

"Anything you want to write, Ryan?"

"Yeah, there is something."

Ryan's father had had a good friend, a retired Air Force colonel, Charles Jones, who was on a trip to California, on September 11, 2001, on American Airlines Flight 11. Instead it had plowed into the World Trade Center. Ryan had been diving with him a couple of times. His father, himself just retired, had asked Ryan to even the score for his friend if he got the chance. Ryan walked over to the bomb rack on the plane, took an indelible marker out of his backpack, and wrote: *Chuck, This One's for You!*

CHAPTER 40

I fired a shot at a Afghan, the beggar 'e fired again,
An' I lay on my bed with a 'ole in my 'ed, an' missed the next campaign; . . .
Ho! Don't you aim at a Afghan, when you stand on the skyline clear;
An' don't you go for a Burman, if none o' your friends is near.

—Rudyard Kipling,
"Private Ortheris's Song"

Since there had been an ambush on the Americans at Khost, they would convoy down to Paktia province from Kabul rather than risk an attack on the dangerous Gardez-Khost road. They would convoy from Baghram down to Kabul to the SF safehouse, ironically one of bin Laden's compounds. One of the B teams had set up there. They took the "new" road to Kabul, built because the Soviets had gotten tired of the constant ambushes on the old road. The new road wasn't on any of their maps. Along the road they could see dozens of hastily marked mine fields, red-and-white painted rocks warning them not to leave the pavement. There were several destroyed tanks and armored vehicles, and a bombed bridge, the work of Triple Nickel. There were also graves marked with rocks flying green flags and an occasional monument to some great martyr in the fight against the Soviets. At the high pass they encountered a checkpoint of Northern Alliance soldiers. It was a few buildings and a scarecrow on the roof manning a 12.7mm Russian machine gun. After giving them a case of bottled water, they moved down to a point just north of the capitol near an old concrete factory and did a commo shout back to the TOC. A mile further and they came to another checkpoint that had a gate and a large ancient sign that read *Welcome to Kabul* in both English and Dari.

They were still dressed in traditional Afghan clothing and by this time all had long unkempt beards. This was essential to their clandestine activities, and to limit recognition from afar, lessening the risk of ambush or snipers. When they got to Kabul, however, they found they had to wear something distinctly American after being stopped at every checkpoint and traffic circle. They even had weapons pointed at them a few times. The Afghan soldiers only saw dangerous-looking armed men, which was exactly what they were. ISAF, the British peacekeepers, also looked at them suspiciously. They all put on their baseball caps, most with NYPD or NYFD, and they wore wrap-around Gargoyle sunglasses. That allowed them instant recognition and they were waved on with smiles. Ryan wore a Boston Red Sox cap, hoping this might reverse the "curse of the Bambino."

They spent the night with the B team in the Kabul safehouse. By some accounts it had belonged to bin Laden. It was a large walled compound with an underground garage and its own generator. It had a large kitchen complete with an Afghan cook and a huge table in the dining room that could easily seat twenty. Even the plumbing worked, with real sit-down porcelain toilets and hot showers! There were a dozen bedrooms and a big-screen TV in the "family room" with dozens of DVDs. Ryan was amazed. *Now this was how to fight a war!* A large communications center filled the basement. The tops of the wall were sand-bagged as was the front entrance. There were fighting positions on the roof and the windows were covered with Kevlar blankets. The street on either side of the compound was blocked off by Northern Alliance guards. The team settled in and, except for pulling guard in one-hour shifts with NVGs on the roof during the night, they spent the most pleasant time they had had since leaving Ft. Campbell.

In the morning they went to the Kabul bazaars to requisition supplies. The bazaars were teeming with the atmosphere of a carnival in the liberated city. Even women were out and about, something the Taliban never allowed, although very few of them had discarded the burqa. Known as the *chadari* in the past, various governments before 1979 had tried to discourage its wear, much as Ataturk had abolished the fez and veil in Turkey. It was an effort to modernize and westernize the country, but to no avail. Their interpreter took them to an outdoor restaurant next to the only functioning movie theater in the country. Mike and Chuck walked over and were amused to see that an Indiana Jones movie was playing. They stopped and talked with some teenagers who spoke passable English and who were very anxious to talk to them. Afghanistan was full of youth, a whole generation, knowing nothing but war. Even with so much goodwill, the team never let their guard down and kept their weapons ready. There had been more than one incident in Kabul and there were bound to be more. This was still a very dangerous country.

The next day Tiger 501 drove five hours south on a terrible road toward Gardez. As they passed through several villages and one large town, they were the object of much curiosity and sometimes hostility. They climbed into the mountains on the Gardez road to a high snow-covered pass bristling with weapons. The road was steep and narrow with overlooking forts and many switch backs. *Good place for an ambush,* thought Ryan. The pass was manned by militia from the Gardez Shura and it was not clearly evident whose side they were really on. There had been an ambush on the American forces the day before, so Tiger 501 radioed the B team at Gardez to pick them up and guide them through the city to the SF safehouses. While waiting, they unloaded some food, water, and sodas for the guards . . . that made them happy and they became more friendly.

When the B team arrived, they convoyed through the busy streets of Gardez. It was overlooked by a huge castle, a Bala Hissar.

Looks like the set from *The Good, the Bad, and the Ugly*, mused Chuck.

They arrived at the pair of mud forts south of Kabul at dusk in a blinding sandstorm. The forts appeared like apparitions out of a khaki mist. It reminded Mike of what the Soviets had called the mujahideen, *dukhi*, or ghosts. The trip had been more than a little nerve wracking, especially through the snow-choked mountain passes, although all along the way most people waved and seemed to be genuinely glad to see them. The mud redoubts on this eight-thousand-foot high desert plain were very spooky. The swirling dust gave the sky an orange hue reminding CPT Rogers of the Iraqi sky during Desert Storm after Saddam set fire to the Kuwaiti oil fields. The sun was a red-orange orb that could barely be seen through the dust, dropping over the mountain range to the west with the forts looming above them. The B team had set up in the bigger of the two forts, with the "agency" guys, D boys, Seals, and coalition forces in the other. It was enormous and reminded CW2 Ryan Gallagher of the French Foreign Legion movie *Beau Geste*.

The walls were at least thirty-feet high and four-feet thick with turrets at each corner. The tents of their Afghan (AMF) soldiers surrounded the forts in concentric circles. Two huge metal double doors, big enough to drive their trucks through, guarded the entrance to the fort. Inside the redoubt, rooms lined interior walls. There were two wells in the middle and animal pens and mud chicken coops at the end. There was also a small orchard. It was at least half an acre square inside.

They were given the "goat room" and it was dark by they time they got their gear unloaded from their new Toyota truck. The room was dark, with a mud floor and walls and smelled of sweet, new-cut hay and goat manure. They set up their cots and sleeping bags and shivered as they closed up the glassless windows with the cardboard from MRE boxes against the savage wind and blowing dust. It was bitter cold by the time they were finished and the small mess room greeted them with a warm and cheery feeling as they stumbled up the steps to eat a meal of rice, red beans, Afghan bread, and some sort of mystery meat (probably goat), supplied by the Afghan cook. They all agreed the food was great after the weeks of MREs and the occasional T rations at Baghram and Qandahar, but it was not as good as at the SF Safehouse.

After dinner they were given the tour. Two of the turrets contained the shitters. There was a hole in the floor where the refuse dropped three stories into a compost pile. An ammo crate was over one of the holes so that you could sit while a cold wind blew up your ass. If you didn't time it right the toilet paper would blow back up the hole in your face. The other shitter had a chair with the bottom removed and a toilet seat secured to it with one-hundred-mile-per-hour tape. CPT Rogers grinned upon seeing it; he had used an almost identical toilet fashioned by one of the CA guys during Desert Storm. This latrine was by far the favorite, but getting up in the middle of the night to go to the bathroom was a real pain in the ass. Shivering, you had to get some clothes on, march across the compound, and climb the two stories up the mud steps. It was easier to piss into the ubiquitous one-liter water bottles and that's what most of them did.

CPT Rogers woke shivering early the next morning, just as the dawn was breaking rosy over the snow-covered mountains, casting deep shadows within the fort. It had snowed during the night and a thin layer of sparkling white covered everything. He climbed the upper wall and could see for miles in all directions, to the mountains in three directions and the Bala Hissar in Gardez. It was a wild and beautiful land. The sky at this altitude was an amazing blue. He heated some water in their extra-large Afghan *chi* pot over a butane heater, acquired in Kabul. He stripped to the waist and took a field bath. The sun provided instant warming as it rose over the wall of the fort. At eight thousand feet the air was thin and the UV rays from the sun strong. MSG Apin stumbled out as Chuck was getting a cup of coffee.

"*East is East and West is West and never the twain shall meet*," quoted Mike.

"I've heard that, where's it from?"

"It's Kipling," said Mike. "When I was in college I took a course on the literature of British Colonial India. If the Russians had read Kipling they would have stayed the hell out of Afghanistan. During the period they called 'The Great Game,' India was the pearl of the British Empire and Afghanistan was the playing field for a kind of cold war played by the English and the Russian bear. The Russians had their own name for it, 'The Tournament of Shadows.' Like the Russian spies in *Kim*, the Soviets went home bloodied and with nothing to show for it. Hell, if *we'd* read Kipling more closely we'd have never sent troops to Vietnam!"

"I thought *Kim* was a children's book."

"It is, sort of, but like a lot of literature it's written on two levels. I've got a copy with me if you want to read it. It was a favorite of Churchill and Adlei

Stevenson. Stevenson carried his copy with him wherever he went; it was on his nightstand the day he died. In the early part of the twentieth century one of the great British experts on Islam, St. John Philby, named his son after the little English spy. Kim Philby became one of the greatest traitors in the history of the British Secret Service. The amount of damage he did to the West spying for the Soviets is hard to estimate."

"I guess everyone's heard of Philby. He was really named after *Kim?*"

"Kimball O'Hara. It really is a great book. It gives a lot of insight into the history of the region. The British fought three wars against the Afghans; they won most of the battles but never the wars. The Soviets got their asses royally kicked. Yeah, it doesn't pay to fight against them; at least not as a conventional force."

"I don't know about the rest of the Afghans but our soldiers are really great. I'd trust my life to them."

"Don't worry. You are brothers-in-arms. I think a lot of the Afghan reputation is probably undeserved, but there are definitely some evil people in Afghanistan and you have to be careful, a smiling face may belie treachery. There is an old Punjabi proverb: 'you can rent an Afghan's loyalty but you can't buy it,' if you get my drift. In *Kim*, Kimball O'Hara tells his Afghan mentor, Mahabu Ali the horse trader: 'trust a Brahmin before a harlot, a harlot before a snake, and a snake before an Afghan.' The name Afghan means 'unruly' in old Persian. But I think most of their neighbors dislike them because they could never best them, and would-be conquerors, like the British and the Russians, have made up a lot of the myth."

"I wonder what makes the Afghans so ornery?"

"Well, theirs is probably one of most difficult lifestyles on Earth as you have seen; it's an uncompromising land with a fierce warrior tradition. Over the centuries they have had to repel invaders from all points of the compass, and when not fighting *ferengi* they keep in practice by fighting each other. Melville would have you believe it's because they are so far from his beloved ocean. He actually makes a reference to the Afghans in *Moby-Dick*. It was published in 1851 and the massacre of thousands of Brits in the First Afghan War only happened in 1842, so it was still fresh in the mind of the world."

Chuck looked at Mike with awe. "Geeze, *professor*, you going to write a book? I tried to wade through *Moby-Dick* once in college and gave up."

"You ought to try it again, it really is a masterpiece. Ever since I read that and Kipling, I've wanted to visit Afghanistan. Best part of the Army; they actually pay you to go to these great, exotic places."

"Yeah, this is exotic all right," yawned Ryan coming out of the goat pen. "I've got goat shit on my boots. Any coffee? They serve anything to eat around here? I don't think I can gag down another MRE." MREs, the standard field ration of the Army, got old fast. Some of the soldiers referred to them as "Meals Rejected by Ethiopians."

"The cooks make fried eggs. If you put some on that flat naan bread the Afghans eat, with a slice of that canned cheese we got in Kabul and some Tabasco you can have an egg McMuffin Afghan style."

"Sounds great," said Mike, "Let's do it. We've got a staff meeting at 0900."

CHAPTER 42

Not in the heaven, not in the midst of the sea, not if you hide yourself away in the clefts of the mountains, will you find a place where you can escape the fruits of your evil actions.

—XXX:63 Dhammapada (The Teacher),
The Teachings of the Lord Buddha

It was hard to tell who was who at the staff meeting as all the men wore beards, some in sterile uniforms (no patches), most in civilian clothes. There were probably a hundred *ferengi* between the two forts; ODAs from 5th and 3rd SF, British SAS, Aussies, intel guys, OGAs (other government agency; CIA, DEA, etc.), Delta, Seals, civil affairs, counter intelligence, etc. There was another new ODA in camp and introductions were made by MAJ Thomas, the B team commander. He was the local "King of Kafiristan" (like Daniel Dravits in Kipling's *The Man Who Would Be King*), at least in *this* part of Afghanistan where power came from the barrel of a gun and in this case, the ability to call in air strikes.

There was an ambush the day before Tiger 501 arrived. Five gunmen jumped out of a drainage pipe on either side of the road to Gardez, just a half-kilometer from the fort, threw hand grenades and fired their weapons. The bullets went through the windshield and into the back of one of the pickup trucks carrying some of their Jungees (Afghan Military Forces or AMF). For some unexplained reason, the ODA vehicles carrying the Americans were first and third rather than second and third, as was the normal SOP. It was the second vehicle that was attacked; and it was obviously meant for the Americans. Rumor had it that one of the local Taliban warlords, Kareem Kahn, put a $10,000 price on any American captured or $6,000 killed, and it was believed that this was an attempt to collect on the bounty. There would be no surrendering by the Americans; they had been briefed on what the al-Qaeda, and especially the Chechens, did to prisoners. If the Afghans wanted to collect a bounty on an American, it would have to be for the "dead" variety.

The attack left two of the AMF soldiers dead and five wounded, which provided the 18Ds with an instant mass-causality exercise. The medics did a hell of a job, undoubtedly saving at least two of the AMF soldiers' lives. Unlike the

Vietnam War, where foreign soldiers were sometimes refused medical care in US hospitals, the AMF soldiers were CASEVAC'd back to the FST (Forward Surgical Team) at Baghram Airfield for treatment and cared for like any American soldier. The AMF and the ODA killed two and captured three. The dead martyrs were promised seventy-two virgins in heaven (Allah being merciful to the True Believers), while the survivors got a one-way ticket to the containment facility at Qandahar and eventually, a spot at Camp X-Ray at Guantanamo Bay.

That morning, as they walked over to the other fort for the staff meeting, they saw a large American flag hanging from one of the ramparts.

"I'm not so sure *that's* a good idea," Mike wondered out loud.

"Yeah, well, it's not like they don't know we're here," said Ryan.

"Not exactly playing it low-key," commented Chuck. They had always tried to downplay the US involvement so as not to offend the Afghans.

"It does send a certain message, though!"

"Yeah, don't fuck with the US of A," laughed Ryan as they had headed up the steep, mud steps to the command center at the top of the fort.

"We have some intelligence that Kareem Kahn is holed up in a nearby village at the head of the Shah-i-Kot valley and we're going to snatch him if at all possible," said MAJ Thomas as the staff meeting started. "This will be a prelude to Operation Anaconda. The S-3 will give you your assignment. We meet at 1500 for a full dress rehearsal; we have to move fast because our sources tell us he's getting ready to flee into Pakistan where his money and contacts will help him disappear. As you know he is high on CENTCOM's 'Most Wanted' list. It would be a real coup if we could take him alive."

The Shah-i-Kot valley was the next in a series of strong points along the Pakistani border that had to be cleared of Taliban and hardcore al-Qaeda. All the intelligence sources had painted a picture of hundreds of foreign fighters in the valley. They would try to eliminate some of the mistakes they had made in the Tora Bora area, letting some of the bad guys, perhaps even bin Laden, escape through the mountains into Pakistan. Operation Anaconda would close the loopholes and was scheduled for next week. They would cut off the bad guys and kill them where they were holed up. The *muj* had beaten the Soviets in this valley, but the Taliban and al-Qaeda would not be able to defeat the Americans, and they could not hide from them. But first they were going to snatch KK, then they were going to clear the valley.

They went over the mission on a vast sand table laid out in the dirt of the fort. They used 550-cord (parachute cord) for the routes (MSRs) and MRE bags representing the blocking positions and objectives. The mission was dubbed

Operation Simpson. KK, the target, was Objective Krusty the Clown. Tiger 501s end of it was to drive at night to the southwest down MSR Marge, around the high hills surrounding the village and seal off escape from the south. The two other ODAs would perform a similar mission on MSRs, Lisa and Bart, to the west and east, respectively. The B team and coalition forces with their AMF would assault the target village, Objective Homer, by different avenues of approach from the north. They were tipped off by a reliable informant that KK and his brother, also wanted for "questioning" would be there for the next two days along with a number of Arab and Chechen al-Qaeda. Tiger 501, along with their twelve AMF soldiers, would move out the day before by a circuitous route, hole up in the mountains overnight, and move down through the pass into position just before dawn.

Intelligence had also revealed that much of the valley villages were taken over by hard-core Taliban and al-Qaeda, and included their families. It was a warning that even women and children were not to be trusted. They had either paid off the inhabitants or evicted them by gunpoint. It looked like the Shah-i-Kot valley was going to be a free-fire zone and this village was at its entrance. The source also warned that the enemy had a concentration of 82mm mortars and anti-aircraft guns deployed around the village. Task Force Dagger had been allocated no less than two fast movers, a B-52, and an AC-130 (Specter) to provide CAS for the operation. The AMF was providing over a hundred soldiers, several T-55 and T-62 tanks, and half a dozen BMPs, armored vehicles.

That night they all gathered in the mess hall to watch a movie on one of the laptops. It was a pirated DVD of *Black Hawk Down* that they picked up at the bazaar in Kabul. The quality was very poor but it was a sobering movie to watch on the eve of battle. Halfway through, Ryan had to leave; he just couldn't watch it. He went back to the "goat room" and put some music on his CD player. One of the British SAS (Special Air Service, the British equivalent of the US Special Forces) soldiers came in, their sergeant major.

"You blokes wouldn't happen to 'ave any spare cold weather boots?"

"What size sergeant major?"

"Size eleven if you got 'em."

"Here, try these; they're ten and a half, but they're big."

"Yeeze mate, they're bloody perfect. You've saved my life, or at least me toes. These 'deserts' weren't cuttin' it at five thousand meters."

"Anything for a comrade in arms."

Half an hour later the SGM came back with a little present. "It ain't much, lad, but if any of you blokes ever get to London, I'll show you a time."

It turned out to be a liter bottle of Russian potato vodka. Ryan gathered up some Cokes and when the team returned they proceeded to break general order #1 (no alcohol) with a toast or two. The liter didn't go very far, certainly not enough to get any one drunk, but it sure tasted good after being dry for several months.

"Wells, here's looking at you," toasted Ryan.

"To bloody campaigns and sickly seasons!"

"What was that sergeant major?"

"Old British toast . . . best way to gain rank in the bleedin' Army," retorted the sergeant major.

A couple of drinks had left Chuck feeling giddy. He couldn't stop laughing.

The next morning the AMF led off with CPT Rogers, MSG Apin and half the team in the second vehicle, CW2 Gallagher and the rest of ODA 501 in the third, and AMF soldiers bringing up the rear. They were loaded for bear with each soldier carrying a double basic load of ammo (420 rounds of 5.56mm) for their M4s, three fragmentation grenades, and one AT-4 (anti-tank rocket) apiece. They traded their bulky LBE (load bearing equipment) harnesses for Afghan AK-47 harnesses, where everything was in front of the body. They were much better suited to vehicle operations and held about the same amount of ordinance *sans* canteens and first-aid pouches. They also had two 7.62mm 240 heavy machine guns, a 50 cal machine gun, a 50 cal Barrett sniper rifle, two Mark 19 automatic 40mm grenade launchers and two 5.56mm SAWs (squad automatic weapons).

Chuck and Mike rode in the front seat of the cab and talked while they drove. Like most operations in dangerous territory, the drive was boring and uneventful, except for the occasional Kuchi (meaning "traveler" in Hindustani) nomads moving with their packed camels and flocks north on the roads and trails from Pakistan toward the spring pastures of northern Afghanistan and Uzbekistan, just as their ancestors had for hundreds of years. They felt they owed allegiance to no government and were sometimes part-time smugglers and spies. They were probably hostile to Americans, or anyone not of their tribe, and were not to be trusted.

"How many years you got in now Top?" asked Chuck, as they climbed along the rocky road.

"Twenty-six this year, but some of it's reserve time."

"You going to stay to thirty?"

"Depends, I think I'm getting too old to hump a ruck. This operation is a little more to my liking, 'truckborne,' but we'll see after all this is over. My brother has been bugging me to go work for him but I think I'd like to go back and get my Master's and teach."

"What subject?"

"Probably history or literature, how about you cap'n?" Mike asked.

"Well, I wouldn't mind going over and working on the 'Black Side,' but I may get out and go to law school. My wife really doesn't like the Army and if I stay in Special Ops I may not stay married."

"Well, you know what they say: you're not really SF until you've been divorced at least once."

"Yeah, that's what I'm afraid of."

"How come you're not married, Top?"

"Tried it, but it didn't work out. Might happen in the future. I met a girl, a woman, last year at the community college night school when I was finishing my bachelors. She's divorced, with two great kids and she decided to go back to school. We've been dating ever since."

"Serious?"

"It was getting to be before we went on *this* adventure."

"I think you and Ryan are the only bachelors on the team. He have any steadies?"

"Don't know, but I hear he had a whole string of beauties at Bragg, including some stripper and some major, physician type, at Womack."

"Well, when he figures out what he wants to do when he grows up maybe he'll settle down."

"Ha! That applies to all of us I'm afraid."

In the next vehicle Ryan was dozing. "Chief, I don't know how you can sleep when we're going through 'Indian Country' like this," commented SFC Colin Donaldson, the team 18F, intelligence sergeant.

"Trouble with you, Colin, is you believe all those Intel reports you put out. I just don't read don't read 'em . . . I sleep better," joked Ryan.

"Seriously," Colin said, "I'm worried. I think this operation may be more than we can chew. There are a lot of bad guys out there and I think higher has seriously underestimated their capabilities. I also think they are going to stand and fight."

"Geeze, you're a worry-wart. By tomorrow evening you'll be warm and snug in the goat room with a belly full of rice and beans. Now let me sleep."

CHAPTER 42

Kabul town's by Kabul river—
Blow the bugle, draw the sword—
There I lef' my mate for ever . . .

Kabul town'll go to hell—
Blow the bugle, draw the sword—
'Fore I see him 'live an' well—

Turn your 'orse from Kabul town—
Blow the buglet, draw the sword—
'Im an' 'arf my troop is down.
    —Rudyard Kipling,
    "Ford O' Kabul River"

"Drop your cocks, and grab your socks. It's o'dark thirty, let's get moving," MSG Apin barked as he went around kicking the soles of the men huddled around the dying fire in the small hut.

At 14,500 feet, the mountain pass was cold and windy with considerably less oxygen than at sea level. Mike had a splitting headache, the first sign of AMS (acute mountain sickness). He had taken a 250mg Diamox tablet, supposed to help with AMS, but it didn't seem to be working. Even though they had acclimatized at six to eight thousand feet for several weeks, half the men would suffer some sort of mountain sickness if they stayed at this altitude for more than forty-eight hours. Usually it would be a mild syndrome: headache, insomnia, breathing abnormalities, cognitive dysfunction and/or loss of appetite. Only a small fraction of climbers to this altitude would develop HAPE (high altitude pulmonary edema) or HACE (high altitude cerebral edema), both fatal without descent. In 1961 during the Sino-Indian War, the Indian Army suffered hundreds of casualties when they suddenly lifted soldiers from sea level to fourteen to sixteen thousand feet. Luckily Tiger 501 would be moving down into the valley within the hour where Mike would feel better.

The half-moon was low on the horizon and it would soon be completely dark, an hour before the faint bluing of the false dawn. Fortunately, it was slightly overcast and the bright stars would be veiled. The night sky in Afghanistan was the most amazing Mike had ever seen. With no ambient light and the crystal clear air at this mountain altitude, the whole heavens seemed on fire. He wanted to be down in the valley, in position before the sun was up. They would set up the blocking position on a road junction that was the only escape by vehicle out of the valley to the west. They were mindful of the Intel reports of a formidable force waiting for them in the Shah-i-Kot and the Soviet experience in that same valley more than a dozen years ago. The Soviets had tried to clean out the valley of its *mujahideen* warriors, suffering the loss of eleven helicopters and 250 casualties. They never did succeed in clearing it.

The Afghan soldiers kneeled on their prayer, or "war" rugs, for the morning prayer ritual. They were called "war" rugs because they were decorated with guns and tanks and symbols of the *muj* defeat of the Soviets. The team had picked up several as gifts while in Kabul. They had enjoyed their day in Kabul, although the capital was the most backward Mike had ever seen, and he had been to some pretty backward areas. Because of the civil war much of the city was in shambles. Large areas of it had been destroyed by the Soviets and even more in the fighting that had raged in the ten years since the Soviets had pulled out. Still it had a certain charm.

Now they moved down the valley road with blacked-out vehicles as the stars shone brightly through the clouds in their night-vision goggles. They dropped AMF soldiers with RPGs all along the route to insure they would not be ambushed from behind and stopped just short of their target road junction to establish an ORP (objective rally point). By now a faint dawn rose in the east. Two of the vehicles carrying CPT Rogers, MSG Apin, one of the medics, and Wahid moved down to do a leaders' recon of the site. Two security teams were placed down each of the roads about four hundred meters to the north and south. They consisted of two Americans and two Afghan soldiers armed with AT-4s, RPGs, and SAWs.

The main blocking force would be arrayed under the cover of a shallow wadi, spanning the road about a hundred meters from the road junction. They would have the MK 19s, 240s, AT-4s, and M2 50 cals, in addition to the RPGs, RPD Soviet machine guns and light weapons the Afghans carried. They would also have dedicated close air support. They could see for a thousand meters in front of them and had excellent fields of fire. They were a formidable force and could handle anything up to, and including, armor.

While the team and the AMF set up in the wadi, the Command vehicle drove up to take a closer look at the crossing. As they moved up to the road junction the world suddenly exploded. The road junction had been bracketed by al-Qaeda 82mm mortars and one of those, a one-in-a-million shot, landed square in the bed of the Toyota pickup carrying the captain, team sergeant, the other medic, one of the weapons men, and Wahid. The flash of light was blinding, the noise deafening, and was quickly followed by others. The rounds all fell short of the wadi but were chewing up the intersection.

"John, help me," Ryan yelled to one of the weapons men as he jumped in their truck and raced to where the destroyed vehicle burned. Dodging mortar rounds they came to a rolling stop and jumped out. Wahid, who was in the backseat, and CPT Rogers, who was sitting beside him, were obviously dead and they were thrown as gently as possible in the back of Ryan's pickup as mortar rounds rained down. Shrapnel had torn through Ryan's clothing and burned his skin like hot pokers. There was no sign of the weapons man who had been in the bed of the vehicle manning the MK-19. The medic, who was driving, and MSG Apin were both seriously injured and were put in the backseat of the pickup.

"Go, go!" John screamed as they drove back to the shelter of the wadi.

While Ryan attended to the two injured men, the other medic came over. A CASEVAC helicopter was on its way. Ryan quickly got two large bore catheters in Mike while the senior medic worked on his junior medic.

"How's Chuck?" whispered Mike. "You're bleeding . . . how am I?"

"Chuck's gone," said Ryan, trying not to cry. "I'm okay and you're going to be fine."

He started his secondary survey and found a large wound in Top's lower back, which he bandaged with one of the large abdominal bandages.

"It doesn't really hurt," said Mike dreamily, "but I'm cold. Can't feel my legs."

"You're going to be okay, the CASEVAC bird is inbound, it should be here any second."

"Ryan?"

"Yeah, Mike?"

"Get them for us?"

"Who?" asked Ryan, tears now streaking down his grime-spattered face.

"Bin Laden, Saddam, the rest of them assholes. I'm going now," Mike whispered.

"Going where? You're just going to the hospital," anguished Ryan.

"No . . . 'now I go far, far into the north to play the Great Game,'" quoting Kipling for the last time, Mike slipped into the featherbed of unconsciousness.

The CASEVAC bird landed and Air Force PJs (parajumper medics) took over the care of the two wounded soldiers. In a plume of dust, MSG Mike Apin disappeared into the high cold air of the Hindu Kush.

BOOK FIVE

IRAQ, 2003

All who serve the Sirkar with weapons in their hands are, as it were, one brotherhood. There is one brotherhood of the caste, but beyond that again the bond of the Regiment.

—Rudyard Kipling, *Kim*

CHAPTER 43

. . . If you can force your heart and nerve and sinew
To serve your turn long after they are gone,
And so hold on when there is nothing in you
Except the Will which says to them: "Hold on!"
If you can fill the unforgiving minute
With sixty-seconds' worth of distance run,
Yours is the Earth and everything that's in it,
And—which is more—you'll be a Man, my son!

—Rudyard Kipling
"If"

He smelled the grass and the red dirt of Rudy Drop Zone near Camp McCall deep in the North Carolina wilds. His face and helmet were screwed into the ground.

"Shit! I'm still alive," murmured Ryan to himself. He did a mental inventory of his body parts starting with his toes and fingers and working inward. *Nothing broken!* He was stunned, possibly knocked out for an indeterminate amount of time but it couldn't have been more than a few seconds. He untangled himself from the spiderweb of his reserve, LBE (load bearing equipment), and his broken rucksack, slid out of the parachute harness and jumped up. He was ecstatic to be in one piece; and then he saw John. He was out cold, hopefully not dead or seriously injured.

"Gallagher, you okay?" asked one of the evaluators as he sprinted over to them.

"I'm fine," he said unconvincingly. His normally pale complexion had turned deathly white, a stark contrast to his carrot-red hair. He looked like a corpse.

"Yeah, well you look like shit. Sit down before you pass out."

Ryan was suddenly weak in the knees and sunk down beside John, SFC John Anderson, his buddy from the 5th Special Forces Group. Ryan's knee was tight and began to swell, but he ignored it. He groaned inwardly, not with pain but with the realization that the accident was, in all probability, his fault. Now he had probably gotten John killed or injured and was undoubtedly going to be kicked out of Selection.

It was just a static line jump and should have been a piece of cake. Both Ryan and John had more than a hundred jumps each to their credit. It should have been especially easy for Ryan who had just graduated from the Military Free Fall, or Halo parachute school. He had been posted back to Bragg after Afghanistan so he could try out for Delta and while he was waiting for Selection to start, he had gone to the MFF course. It was a somewhat dubious reward for being wounded in Afghanistan and having his team blown out from under him, but he had always wanted to do Halo. MFF was the most advanced skydiving course in the world. It taught high-altitude drops using ram-air canopies and practiced jumps from altitudes as high as thirty thousand feet using oxygen, carrying heavy loads, and tracking across the sky for miles as a team. They could hit targets miles away with pinpoint precision. With skill and the right winds, an aircraft could drop a team in Britain and a team could land on the coast of France.

Ryan had been cocky and careless and had violated one of the cardinal "rules of the air"—he had not looked over his shoulder before he pulled down on the toggle line that turned his parachute. This was an unpardonable sin for an experienced jumper and, especially, a veteran jumpmaster. It was drilled into them time and again. It was given in the jumpmaster brief before every jump and all the jumpers had to repeat it, "Look before you turn!" He had been preoccupied with getting the lower tie down on his M4 and had let go of the toggle lines on his MC1 Charlie model parachute while he fiddled with it. He had landed once with his weapon still tied down and it had shoved the rifle butt into his armpit. He had been sore for two weeks. When he finally got the tie unraveled, he was running out of drop zone and was almost over the trees of the DZ, north of Fort Bragg.

He had pulled down his left toggle line and had no sooner started the turn when he ran smack into the top of John's canopy. *Where the hell did he come from?* The last time he looked, John was several-hundred meters away. Ryan went into the spread-eagle position like he had been trained, this technique also being covered in every jumpmaster briefing under "mid-air entanglements." It worked; he bounced off the canopy and everything would have been all right except for two things. One of John's suspension lines had gotten caught in the ripcord handle of Ryan's reserve and as he went to free it his own main canopy collapsed due to the vacuum caused by the lower chute. This caused him to fall past John, pulling the suspension line down and collapsing John's chute. They were now only about five hundred feet from the ground and falling fast. Then they started spinning around one another as the tips of their tangle chutes slowly, and then with ever increasing speed, spun around one another. The world had become a spinning blur as the ground rushed up to meet them.

"John, we've got to throw out our reserve chutes," screamed Ryan.

"Roger," came the muffled reply.

All the jumpmaster instructions that Ryan had ever heard, and had himself given dozens of times, automatically repeated themselves in his brain. He was too busy to be terrified. Hold the ripcord flap down with the left hand, pull the ripcord handle with the right and throw it away, knife edge of the right hand in behind the chute, pull it out and throw it in the direction of the spin. It fluttered ineffectually. The spinning now was severe and the ground and the figures rushing across the drop zone to where they would impact were a blur. He pulled in the reserve chute, gathered it up, and threw it out again. This time it flipped up over his head and he became hopelessly entangled in the suspension lines. His heavy rucksack, which he had been unable to jettison (as John had), hung at his knees, a sure recipe for broken legs.

"John, what's happening?"

"We're coming in and fast!"

That was all Ryan remembered until he did the anatomic checklist on himself. Those watching the accident told him that at the very last second, John's reserve had popped open, probably at 100–150 feet above the DZ, and had slowed the two jumpers just enough so that they figured that one or both of them might still be alive. The main canopies had twisted to the extent that Ryan and John had crashed head to head, back to back, the white reserve canopy falling over them like a shroud.

Ryan was on his knees shaking his partner. "John, you OK?"

He was coming around. "What happened?"

Miraculously, neither of them was seriously injured; beat to hell, but nothing obviously broken. Ryan's knee was swelling fast but it still didn't hurt. Ryan popped an 800mg Ibuprofen (light fighter candy) that was stashed in his cargo pocket of his fatigues and gave one to John with a swig from his canteen. They had to wait until the head rigger and the drop zone malfunction safety officer had examined the tangled mess, then they had to give statements. Afterward, they were told to get into the ambulance for a ride back to Womack Army Hospital at Ft. Bragg.

Ryan and John looked at each other.

"Is that an order or a request?" Ryan asked the evaluator OIC.

"Look, Gallagher, you and Anderson might be seriously injured, internal injuries. I strongly advise you get into the ambulance."

"And if we don't?"

"What? You afraid Selection's over for you? Might be, I don't know. The board will have to determine that, but if you two knuckleheads want to finish the road march be my guest. If you kill yourselves it's no sweat off my ass. I warn you though, if you crap out that *will* be the end."

Unsure of their fate, they gathered their gear, found John's busted rucksack and started the road march. It was to be their last event of the grueling selection process, a forty mile road march with no given time limit. They were just told to do their best. They both vowed they could be nonselected but they wouldn't quit. Ryan was sure the accident was entirely his fault and that John was okay as far as selection went, that he'd be the only one not selected. To his surprise, John thought it might have been *his* own fault. So they marched off with the exultation of surviving a near-death incident and the adrenaline high that comes with it. As the time and miles stretched on, however, the days of sleep deprivation, physical, emotional, and mental stress began to take their toll and they both hobbled along in a dream-like state.

Periodically, Ryan would stop and insert a large bore needle into the large swelling over his kneecap to drain the bloody fluid from the rapidly forming hematoma. If he didn't his pants became too tight to walk.

"Man, I'm already sick, you keep doing that and I'm going to puke," muttered John.

He also bound up John's swollen and painful left foot. They were both hurting badly but they gutted it out. They relied on each other to give them strength; neither of them quitting as long as the other one marched. *March or Die*, the title of an old French Foreign Legion movie repeated itself over and over in Ryan's semiconscious brain. These actions were not lost on the evaluators. At one checkpoint, the OIC of Selection was waiting for them.

"Why don't you two quit?" he asked. "You can join Johnson there," he pointed to the bed of the truck where one of their former classmates rested. "Rest, go back to Bragg, get a hot meal, and hit the rack. There's no sense in punishing yourselves anymore. You're never going to make it."

At that moment he really hated the major. "How far is it? What time is it?"

"It's too far. You guys are finished. Give it up."

"Bullshit! . . . Sir!" Ryan grabbed John and they continued on.

The morning disappeared into afternoon and before they knew it, it was dark, their sweat causing them to shiver. Both of them eventually finished but well after the rest of the candidates; like two old ladies finishing a marathon long after the crowd had gone home. It was probably the fact that they were injured (X-rays later revealed a broken metatarsal bone in John's foot and a cracked kneecap in Ryan's leg) and what the physician at Womack described as "whole body sprains," and the fact that they wouldn't quit that impressed the board the most.

It was mental toughness, not sheer physical expertise that they were looking for, and teamwork, among other attributes. Although they had both done marginally well enough to get selected before the accident, it was their march that won them a spot and a part in the legend that was the United States Army's super-secret Delta Force.

CHAPTER 44

The qualities needed in a serious campaign against terrorists—secrecy, intelligence, political sagacity, quiet ruthlessness, covert actions that remain covert, above all infinite patience—all these are forgotten or overridden in a media-stoked frenzy for immediate results . . .

—Mike Howard
What's in a Name? How to Fight Terrorism

The United States Army's 1st Special Forces Operational Detachment Delta, also known as CAG (Combat Applications Group), Delta Force, or simply "Delta," was the brainchild of Colonel Charles Beckwith. As a Special Forces officer, he participated in an exchange program with the British Special Air Service (SAS) during their successful counterinsurgency operations in Malaysia in the early 1960s. Their unconventional training and tactics in counterterrorism greatly impressed the young Green Beret. This experience convinced him of the need for a similar unit within the United States Army. In 1977, after years of lobbying, Col. Beckwith received permission from the army hierarchy to form Delta along SAS lines.

The first real test of the nascent organization's capabilities came with the aborted Iranian rescue mission and the disaster of Desert One, in which six RH-53D Sea Stallion helicopters and one C-130 were lost in a refueling accident, resulting in a number of deaths and an aborted mission. This military disaster turned into a political failure for the Carter Administration. However, in spite of the failure of the Iran hostage mission, even the former critics of Delta Force now recognized the need for such a unit. In fact, after the debacle in Iran it became intuitively apparent that a larger *joint* organization be formed, one devoted specifically to clandestine special missions. Thus JSOC (Joint Special Operations Command) and the United States Special Operations Command (USSOCOM) were born.

Delta's organization consists of three operational squadrons, a support squadron, a communication or signal squadron, an aviation platoon, and a "special" or "funny" platoon (rumored to even contain female operatives). Squadrons are further broken down into two troops; an assault troop and a sniper/observation troop. Each assault troop consisted of four, four- to five-man teams specializing in unique skills such as scuba, HALO, and a variety of other specialties. The troops can be further broken down into individual four- to six-man fire-teams should the need for a smaller force be necessary. The exact number of soldiers in Delta is still highly confidential, although it is rumored to be somewhere between 1,000 and 2,500 personnel. It was, and still is, the Army's position to never comment on Delta; not even to formally acknowledge that the unit exists.

The unit's mission directive is primarily focused on counterterrorism but Delta is capable of conducting missions that range across the operational continuum. These might include, but are not limited to, Direct Action (DA) missions, counter drug, special reconnaissance (SR), hostage rescue, unconventional warfare (UW), personnel recovery, security assistance, and counter proliferation of weapons of mass destruction (WMD). Since its inception, Delta has performed a number of high-profile missions with attendant media coverage, yet the majority of their operations are very, very low profile.

Even though Ryan had spent a good deal of time at Bragg in Special Forces, and knew some soldiers who went over to Delta, the unit still remained shrouded in mystery. Even those in the Special Operations community were kept in the dark, and like a mushroom, fed shit when they inquired about the existence of the unit. People soon learned to mind their own business; it wasn't healthy to ask too many questions. Ryan knew of one young soldier who had been overly curious about the unit and went all over Bragg asking questions. Then one night the CID (Criminal Investigations Division) grabbed the young man out of the training barracks. He returned the following morning, shaken and reticent. The guys who Ryan knew that went to Delta seemed to drop off the face of the earth. One of his good friends joined Delta and that was basically the end of the friendship. Delta operators didn't even socialize with anyone outside their unit. It was the only way to insure absolute operational security (OPSEC); no one would accidentally talk about classified matters over a beer.

The Delta compound contains, besides several indoor and outdoor shooting ranges, an Olympic-sized swimming pool, dive tank, and three-story climbing wall. In addition, they engaged in regular training with foreign special operators to exchange new operation techniques and equipment. Those units included both the British and Australian Special Air Services (SAS), their sister unit in the US Navy, Seal Team 6, the German GSG-9, and Israel's Sayeret Matkel/Unit 269.

Ryan had heard the rumors that Delta guys had helped shoot down Libyan jets in Chad when Gaddafi needed to be restrained, and that they were involved as advisors for the FBI at Waco. He knew that they had liberated prisoners from the citadel at Ft. Rupert during the Grenada operation, snatched war-crimes prisoners in Bosnia, and chased down Scud missiles during Desert Storm. He knew *exactly* what they had been doing in Somalia; he had barely survived that experience. Yet, there were a lot of their operations that neither he nor anyone else outside the unit was aware of; security was that good. Success could only be guaranteed if they kept operational details and information secret.

Both John and Ryan started their operator training (OTC) even before their injuries healed. Both had survived the grueling selection process designed to eliminate those that really didn't belong, although Ryan really was quite surprised when he was selected. It was similar to Special Forces Selection and Assessment (SFAS) that he went through to get into Special Forces, only harder. The final test was a six-day land navigation hike through unknown terrain. Candidates navigated solo day after day not knowing how far that day's hike would be or how much time they had to finish it. The only thing they did know was that the last day's march would be the infamous forty-miler. Both Ryan and John completed the selection process with enough points to move on the next phase of becoming a Delta operator; others were not so lucky. Only after the selection process was finished did the real training begin.

The six-month Operator Training Course started on the firing range. For the first month the Delta candidates spent eight hours a day on the range getting to know the weapons preferred by Delta, mainly the H&K MP-5 submachine gun, the M4 carbine, M-1911A1 pistol, and a variety of other handguns. They sometimes used AK-47s or other indigenous weapons but their standard assault weapon was the replacement for the M16, the M4 with SOPMOD modification. The M4 was a 5.56mm like the M16, but shorter and had a collapsible stock making it much better suited for shooting in vehicles or in close quarter battle (CQB). It could be equipped with a variety of high-tech accessories including a visible light, a visible red dot aiming sight, an infrared pointer for use at night, and a sound suppressor. An ACOG 4X scope or the M68 reflex site for CQB could be mounted in lieu of iron sights.

Ryan had qualified as an expert marksman with both a rifle and a pistol and considered himself really quite good, but the first few days on the Delta range could only be described as humbling. In Delta you have to hit your target every time without even looking at it. When a hostage has a gun to his head there is no time to think, or to even take aim for that matter. It has to be instinctive.

On the CQB range they began with one shot for one target, a target being a cardboard terrorist. When the candidates mastered that they were given more rounds. They were taught to double tap their targets, to place two shots in the same place either in the head, the throat, or the chest. When they had mastered that skill, the number of targets was increased. Then cardboard hostages were interspersed among the terrorists. For a month they kept this up, slowly increasing the difficulty. They were taught to shoot while running, while crawling, even while jumping. This went on for four more weeks and once the cadre were satisfied the candidates were brought to the "shooting house," where they would spend eight hours a day for the next month.

The "shooting house," as it was appropriately called (others referred to it as "The House of Horrors"), was where the Delta operators honed their room clearing and hostage rescue skills. It consisted of a hallway with three rooms running off it, mock-ups of trains and buses and even the fuselage of a Boeing 727. Here they learned how to enter a room or a plane quickly and violently, to neutralize any and all threats, and to rescue any hostages. At first Ryan found it fun and exciting, but after two weeks it just became work. Yet he was good, very good.

Once the cadre was certain their students could charge into a room and put two bullets into the head of anyone with a gun, the training moved out of the shooting house, and on to other things. The next month was dedicated to demolitions. Anyone with C4 and a blasting cap can make a bang, but here they learned how to shape charges with just the amount of force necessary to blow a door or a window, or any other type of barrier that could possibly get in their way. After that they all learned how to become snipers, even though only a few would be chosen for that actual assignment. Then they learned about tradecraft from the Agency, "spook" stuff. They then learned executive protection from the Secret Service and conducted further training in Scuba, HALO, reconnaissance, climbing, etc. Ryan found it all most enlightening.

After the Operator Training Course there were another few months of unit training. They studied and practiced various hostage scenarios, and conducted missions. The cadre was always keeping the candidates on their toes. After all of this, Selection and their first six months of training, the final review board convened to finally decide if the candidate would become an actual operator. Ryan and John were both selected. After all of the years since his first experience with a Delta operator, he was now one of them, and none too soon.

CHAPTER 45

I feel some misgivings about the political consequences to myself of taking on my shoulders the burden and odium of the Mesopotamian entanglement.

—Winston Churchill (1920)

With the war in Afghanistan virtually won, the Bush administration reset its sites and began considering the next target in the war on terrorism. Yemen, Syria, and the Philippines came to mind. Ryan thought for sure it would be Somalia. During training one day, he and John had speculated on where they would be going after they finished their train-up.

"It's got to be Somalia. We've got an old score to settle there. *I've* got an old score to settle," said Ryan.

"No way, man," answered John.

"Oh yeah, what makes you so sure it's not going to be Somalia?"

"Right after we got back from Afghanistan, Geraldo Rivera, a.k.a. Jerry Rivers, was doing a piece on Somalia. He was in Mogadishu. *He* was sure that was our next target, too."

"I saw one of those reports. He was sitting there like he was waiting for the war, going to get himself a great scoop."

"I have it on good authority that we *were* going to Somalia next, but the whole thing was cancelled just because that douche bag was there." Everyone chuckled.

Because of the USS *Cole* attack, Yemen also appeared a likely next target, but the Yemenis were falling all over themselves trying to appear cooperative. In the Far East, the United States was about to engage Moslem warriors in the Philippines for the third time in a hundred years, but the real action was about to take place in the Middle East. The resting giant had indeed awaked with a vengeance.

Desert Storm, also called the Gulf War, was originally hailed as a great victory, Kuwait successfully liberated, the Iraqi military soundly defeated, and the immediate threat to Iraq's neighbors all but eliminated. But for some it was a pyrrhic victory. Only a few years after the war, the major architects of the victory, Britain's Maggie Thatcher and President Bush, were out of power while Saddam, the great villain, still ruled Iraq with an iron fist and retained his delusions of grandeur. He claimed victory over the United States in the war, and many in the region actually believed that he *had* won. He ignored the terms of the cease-fire and continued reprisals against the Kurds and Shia. He routinely thumbed his nose at the UN and fired anti-aircraft weapons and missiles at coalition aircraft patrolling the mandated No Fly Zones. Sanctions hadn't worked (had they ever worked anywhere?) and Saddam continued to try and rebuild his military power while starving the population of Iraq.

His tyranny had been largely ignored by the world. A true paranoid, he saw plots everywhere and executed ministers at will. In 1979 he thought he saw a plot against him and slaughtered a large number of his Ba'ath party. On just one day, August 8, 1979, he killed twenty-five top officials. One of his quaint maneuvers was to have ministers shoot other ministers, to prove their loyalty. During one unpleasant incident, his Minister of Health urged him on to some action with which Saddam didn't agree. He quietly listened and then had the man taken out and shot. He could best be described as having a Jekyll-and-Hyde personality. His actions earned him the nickname, "The Butcher of Baghdad," but he preferred "Great Uncle."

His favorite movie was *The Godfather* and it would not be hard to imagine him as a Mafioso thug. The chief difference between him and the Mafia is that Saddam routinely wiped out the women, children, and close relatives of those he felt had wronged him. He always made a big show of being religious, claiming lineage to the prophet Mohammed. He donated his blood, one pint at a time, to make a hand lettered copy of the Holy Qur'an, which is in the Baghdad Museum. However, he only used religion when it was to his advantage and he had a fear and distrust of Moslem fundamentalist movements.

Saddam was a particular admirer of Stalin and kept a gold plated statue of him in his bedroom. Like Stalin, he had a rabid fear of poisons and ordered his cooks to prepare him twenty meals a night, whereupon he would select one dinner and had others eat the remaining ones. He had a huge personal bodyguard service numbering 3,600, as well as numerous doubles who stood in for him. He certainly was as ruthless as Stalin, albeit on a smaller scale.

Saddam's obsession with acquiring "the bomb," began in the early 1970s. Although only the vice president at the time, he was nevertheless responsible for the day-to-day business of running the country, and through this consolidated his power. When Saddam became president in 1979, his nuclear-weapons program was already under way.

Yet Saddam was not merely interested in obtaining one or two bombs; he desired the technology and infrastructure to mass-produce them. In order to achieve this, Iraq would have to fool the IAEA (International Atomic Energy

Agency). The first step toward this included an elaborate intelligence gathering operation in which Iraq succeeded in gaining a seat on the IAEA's board. Even Iraqi intelligence officers were working as inspectors for the watchdog agency. These agents sent detailed reports back to Baghdad outlining the inspection process and its limitations. It soon became apparent just how easily the IAEA could be exploited or even bypassed. At the same time, the IAEA was providing valuable technical support, including training for Iraqi nuclear scientists. The IAEA even allowed Iraq to purchase a small research reactor, as well as a large French-built industrial reactor. The Israelis subsequently bombed the latter in 1981. Their intelligence was correct, Iraq was trying to make "the bomb."

As the IAEC (Iraqi Atomic Energy Council) expanded, and as their technical capabilities increased, a large compound known as al-Tuwaitha sprung up approximately twenty miles south of Baghdad. The complex was regularly inspected by the IAEA, but Saddam knew their methods and he also knew how to fool the inspectors. Even if the IAEA had suspected anything, they really didn't have the power to do anything about it.

So the years passed, and with covert assistance from the Soviet Union, the possibility that Iraq would be world's next nuclear power looked inevitable. But as he was getting closer to his goal he made the foolish mistake of invading Kuwait. What followed was a systematic bombing campaign designed not only to destroy the Iraqi infrastructure and military, but also Saddam's WMD facilities.

Following the thirty-nine days of bombing and the three-day ground assault, Saddam was forced to withdraw. The terms of the cease-fire required Saddam to let UNSCOM weapons inspectors into the county to oversee the complete destruction of Iraq's capabilities to design and manufacture WMD. Even with UN weapons inspectors in his midst, many suspected that Hussein was beginning to rebuild the program. Iraq slowly began acquiring all types of machines and tools that could be used for atomic bomb construction through the black-market of former Soviet states, the UK, East Asia, even Africa. The UN weapons inspectors, like the IAEA, could do nothing to stop it. It wasn't until the defections of two high-ranking Iraqis that the full scale of the deception became apparent. Khidhir Hamza, also known as Saddam's "bomb maker," and Hussein Kemal, Saddam's son-in-law, blew the lid off Saddam's deception. These defections, however, were merely a setback. The fears of the United States and much of the international community was that given enough time, Saddam would have his precious device and, in all probability, would use it at some point or threaten his neighbors with its use.

Besides Hussein's attempts to acquire nuclear weapons, his chemical weapons arsenal was far more extensive than anyone ever realized. They had, in fact, produced VX, the deadly chemical nerve agent that requires only a drop the size of a pinhead to kill a human, in addition to many tons of less lethal agents. However, it was in the biological arena in which they had made their greatest and most frightening gains.

CHAPTER 46

The failure to disarm small regional powers of their existing biological war-fare aspirations will add significantly to the apparent impotence of civilized nations to abolish BW as a weapon of mass destruction.

—Tom Mangold and Jeff Goldberg,
Plague Wars: The Terrifying Reality of Biological Warfare

Due to Ryan's status as one of the FNGs (Fucking New Guys), his background as a medic, and the fact that he had attended the military's Biological and Chemical Warfare Causalities Course given at USAMRIID (United States Army Medical Institute for Infectious Diseases), he was assigned the task of developing intelligence on the Iraqi biological warfare program. A secondary mission was to determine a list of BW targets in the event of hostilities. He made several trips in the next few weeks to AFMIC (Armed Forces Medical Intelligence Center), a division of DIA (Defense Intelligence Agency), at Ft. Detrick, and CIA headquarters to gather source material. He knew the Iraqis had biological weapons, but was astounded by the sophistication and magnitude of their suspected programs as he read both the classified and unclassified reports.

Ryan was not particularly thrilled to get the WMD assignment, but he resigned himself to the task, knowing it was important. Other Delta teams had primary responsibility for targeting Ba'ath party members, high value targets (HVTs), terror groups, and hostage rescue. After growing the obligatory "Stalin" mustache they would be able to blend. With his flaming red hair, Ryan might go undercover in Northern Ireland, but not Iraq.

The threat of chemical warfare was real and grim, but the world had survived that. The horrors of mustard gas, phosgene, and chlorine gas were well documented in WWI and the US military was prepared for this terror. The Kurds knew about it too, as did the Iranians. They had both been victims of Saddam's chemical-warfare program. Whole Kurdish villages had been wiped out by nerve gas; thousands had died.

The US war-gamed NBC (nuclear, biological, and chemical) warfare all the time, but the emphasis was always on the "C." It was biological warfare that was the great indefinable; it existed primarily in the dominion of mankind's worst nightmares. Except for several small isolated experiments, conducted by evil madmen, biological warfare was an almost unknown quantity. In one of the most repugnant chapters in the history of civilization, the Japanese had employed biological-warfare experiments and trials against POWs and Chinese cities during WWII from their secret Imperial Unit 731 in Manchuria. Their work made the ghastly experiments of Dr. Mengele and other Germans in Nazi death camps look like child's play. The Iraqis had taken a page from this book.

Biological weapons had generally been considered by most military planners to be of limited value, hard to control, and fraught with difficulties. There was also an inherent repugnance among warriors to use such a weapon. It wasn't what the British called "sporting." BW was considered in these circles to have much greater value as a terror weapon. Ryan had gone to New York after his return from Afghanistan to look up an old girlfriend and was amazed by her preoccupation with the threat of biological terrorism. She had tried to purchase a gas mask (for the exorbitant price of $1,000), but was unsuccessful. She had asked Ryan to get her one, which he reluctantly did.

To be used as a weapon of military significance, biologics first had to be produced in sufficiently large quantities. This is not as hard as it sounds and even small rogue states are capable of producing quantities large enough to be of military importance, hence the sobriquet, "the poor man's atomic weapon." The material also has to be reasonably stable, and put in a form that lends itself to being put into a weapon, or weaponization. Next, a delivery system has to ensure adequate dispersal over enemy troop areas, and avoid collateral damage and infection among your own troops. It seems the Iraqis had solved most of the technical problems with both production on a large scale *and* weaponization.

Prior to the start of the Gulf War American intelligence sources identified approximately eighteen potential biological warfare (BW) sites in Iraq including production and storage facilities. After conferring with various experts about safety and the risk of accidentally dispersing deadly microbes. The US bombed the sites without collateral damage during the opening sorties of Desert Storm. It wasn't until after the war that the true extent of the Iraqi efforts became known. UNSCOM (United Nations Special Commission) had been formed to insure Iraq's compliance of UN resolution 687 ending the Gulf War, mandating that Saddam declare all nuclear, chemical, and biological weapons, reveal their locations, and provide all information dealing with research, production, and storage.

During the next several years of inspections, Iraq took extraordinary steps to protect their covert offensive BW program. It was seven years of lies, deceptions, cheating, false promises, and charges that UNSCOM inspectors were all spies. Some of the Iraqi efforts at deception were laughable; trucks going out the back gate while inspectors entered through the front. There also existed dissent among the inspectors, some feeling that their fellow inspectors were blatantly naive. Some resigned in disgust. In spite of it all, the inspections yielded a vast amount of information. Saddam kicked them out of the country and the UN, as usual, did nothing.

Their UNSCOM efforts were aided by the defection of two top Iraqi officials. The first, in 1994, was a former military general, Wafiq al-Samarrai. His debriefing yielded a wealth of information on Saddam's obsession with WMD, but the mother lode came from Saddam's own son-in-law, General Hussein Kamel. In 1995, he had fled Iraq for the West after a family dinner that ended in an argument, leaving several bodyguards dead. He had been nominally in charge of the Iraqi BW program and yielded up a wealth of information. Irrationally, he returned to Iraq a year later with a promise that all was forgotten. Saddam promptly executed him, and by some accounts, his head came to Saddam on a golden platter.

The Kamel revelations yielded the famous "chicken farm" documents, which were "discovered" by the Iraqis, much to their feigned surprise, and given over to the inspectors. It seems, according to the Iraqis, that Kamel had conducted a vast BW program all on his own, without the knowledge of the Iraqi government. Even the most naive of the inspectors couldn't swallow that one down. The Iraqis had no less than six major production facilities, some of them dual-use and thus hard to identify. Salman Pak, just south of Baghdad, was supposed to be a chicken-feed factory but was really a major technical research facility for BW weapons. The Al-Hakam facility contained huge fermenters, which, in addition to producing veterinary vaccines, was used to produce thousands of gallons of botulinum toxin and anthrax soup. There was also a BW research facility located within the chemical plant at al-Muthana that was used to produce chemical *and* biological weapons.

In all, the Iraqis had experimented with anthrax, botulinum toxin, cholera, plague, salmonella, ricin, staphylococcus enterotoxin, camel pox (similar to smallpox), and aflotoxins. Ironically, the rare materials for their work had been purchased from the American Type Culture Collection (ATCC) in Rockville, Maryland. They had produced 85,000 liters of anthrax, 389,000 liters of botulinum toxin, and 2,200 liters of aflotoxin. All this was enough to kill the world's population four times over! They also weaponized most of these agents, more of a feat of manufacturing than biology, but a very significant one nonetheless. Weaponization changed the material from that of a small-scale terrorist weapon to one of significant military importance.

The inspectors found that at least 157 R-400 bombs were produced with 100 of them filled with botulinum toxin, 50 with anthrax (the same type of anthrax used in the terrorist attacks in the US in 2001–2002), and 7 with aflotoxin. They also discovered that 25 Scud missiles, 16 filled with botox, 5 with anthrax, and 4 with aflotoxin, had been produced. Several 122mm rockets had also been filled with these agents, only for testing purposes according to the Iraqis. Four 155mm artillery shells had been filled with ricin toxin. The Iraqis assured the inspectors that all of these weapons were destroyed. None were ever recovered. The Iraqis had also obtained 50 state-of-the-art sprayers capable of reducing the agents to the 5–15 micron size that rendered them into a deadly mist. These had been fitted on aircraft (MIG-21s and Mirage fighters fitted with vast holding tanks), unmanned drone aircraft, trucks, and even patrol boats, and were capable of spraying over 2000 liters of anthrax at a time. The chief designer of the Iraqi program was Dr. Rihad Taha (trained in the UK), known as 'Doctor Death' or 'Toxic Taha' in the West. One of the more chilling pieces of intelligence that was gleaned by the inspectors was that Saddam had given permission for his field commanders to employ NBC weapons should Baghdad be in danger of being overrun.

Had the inspectors missed anything? The inspectors had, in fact, probably missed a lot; they simply hadn't looked in all the right places. What they had found, according to some intelligence assets, was only the tip of the iceberg. In addition to all the raw intelligence Ryan and his team studied, there was an NIC (Nation Intelligence Council) assessment titled *Iraq: Steadily Pursuing WMD Capabilities.* With the pullout of the inspectors in 1998, the CIA had been all but blind to what Saddam was up to. For years the intelligence community had been relying more and more on technology and less on human assets (HUMINT). The signal intelligence of the NSA (National Security Agency) and other agencies had largely taken the place of agents on the ground. In fact, it was reported that the CIA had as few as four reliable agents in Iraq. Occasional defectors and intelligence agencies of friendly governments often gave intelligence of questionable reliability.

In addition to suspecting that the Iraqis may have had vast stockpiles of chemical and biological agents, some in the national-security community guessed that Iraq could resume and expand its capabilities at any time. They also suspected that Saddam was building dual-use factories: chemical plants capable of making fertilizer or chemical weapons, vaccine plants capable of making veterinary vaccines or germs. That they might use these chemical and biological agents was one of the Bush administration's greatest fears.

The intelligence reports only hinted at some of it, but the Iraqis had been able to freeze-dry the plague organism, *Yersinia pestis*. This organism was the dreaded bubonic plague or "Black Death" that had killed a third of the world's population during the Dark Ages. Worse yet, they had developed a primitive but effective delivery system for this and one other nemesis of mankind . . . smallpox. They had continued to carry on the work, but from small clandestine sites and in mobile labs, and they were importing outside talent, unemployed scientists from the former Soviet Union. British intelligence agents identified several, including a prominent BW expert who had been a high-ranking official of Vector, the massive Soviet biological weapons program.

Ryan's low whistle brought John's head up from the Intel reports *he* was studying.

"What ya got, Ryan?"

"We've got a problem. It looks like Saddam could have smallpox!"

"Now I'm glad they gave us those shots," John said as he lifted his T-shirt and looked at the dime-size blister of pus on his shoulder. "You think he'll use that stuff? He didn't last time."

"That was because Baker had told that asshole Aziz, in no uncertain terms, that we'd nuke them if they did. That bastard Saddam thought he could survive the last time, but this time he's going to know he's a dead man. He's got nothing to lose by using it. He sure doesn't give a rat's ass about the country, or the people, if he can't control them."

"Shit. I hate this NBC stuff. The best part about Special Forces is we never had to wear that damn helmet or gas mask."

"Well, you'd better pay attention to the NBC training next week or you're liable to wind up in a body bag."

"How could the UN have allowed that asshole to go on making that stuff?"

"Same reason they're not going to vote to go back and fix what they didn't do the first time."

"You think we'll go it alone?"

"Naw, the Brits will be with us, but I wouldn't count on the rest of the world."

"Why didn't we do anything before now?"

"Clinton launched operation Desert Fox in 1998 to bomb suspected sites but it was ineffectual in degrading the BW program. Most people think he was just trying to win public opinion and take everyone's mind off his impeachment hearings."

"Ineffectual? You mean like his sending a few cruise missiles over to Afghanistan after the African embassy bombings? Might as well be pissing in the wind. You know, I really hate that guy."

"Who? Saddam, Osama, or Clinton?"

"All three," John laughed.

"If the world knew about all this stuff you'd think they would have been calling for Saddam's head a long time ago."

"Everyone has blinders on; hear no evil, see no evil."

"You need to read this stuff. I think I have some missions for us when this shit finally kicks off."

The reports were voluminous, stocks of NBC items were supposedly hidden under artificial lakes, in dams, mobile factories, and dual-use factories.

"Man, this report is totally whimsical," moaned John.

"Whimsical?"

"W, M, M, S, L; Weapons of Mass Destruction Master Site List. This fucking document says there are 846 sites that we need to consider."

"Yeah, but that list has already been narrowed down to less than a hundred that are credible. We're after the high-value targets, the 75th Exploitation Task Force and other NBC teams will be checking out the other sites," replied Ryan.

"It's still going to take us a year to get through all this."

"Yeah, well there's more; we're not just using the M34 Chemical/Biological Agent Sampling Kit. We've got a bunch of state-of-the-art testing equipment from Ft. Detrick that we need to get up to speed on."

"It looks to me like our first target is going to be the Haditha dam in western Iraq. There is good intelligence from the Kuwaitis and Israelis that there is a large stockpile there. Since the SF guys are going to be running western Iraq; we'll start there."

CHAPTER 47

We must uphold our right to belong to the glorious Qur'an, of historical glories, of the cradle of heavenly religion, prophets and messengers, and the land of the banner and the sword of justice that has honored our nation and humanity at large. Let Zionism be despised along with its aggressive criminal and damned entity of occupation, and let its counterpart in evildoing; American policies and their representatives, be despised.

—Saddam Hussein,
Address to Arab Leaders, 2002

It was obvious that Saddam was not complying with the original UN resolution following Desert Storm, but Europe was either bought off, or simply did not have the heart to do anything about it. Both the Russians and the French had been lobbying the other members of the UN Security Council for years to lift the sanctions on Iraq, hoping to secure lucrative oil contracts from the "Butcher of Baghdad." Both were threatening to veto any resolution to force further concessions from the Iraqis, or even make them comply with the resolutions that were in force.

Ryan's troop had already been deployed to a small, secret compound adjacent to CENTCOM HQ at Camp As Sayliyah, Qatar. They were in the TOC watching the CNN broadcasts with more than passing interest since what happened in the UN would probably be the harbinger of war for their squadron.

"Fuckin' French!" exclaimed John. "They really suck!"

"I'll tell you," fumed Ryan, "The French *have* to be the most worthless people on the face of the earth. Every large war the US has fought in this century has been directly attributed to the ineptitude of the French, WWI, WWII, *and* Vietnam! Hell, we formed NATO just to *protect* the French and who's the first country to pull out of NATO? The Fucking French!"

Jake was sitting at the "morale and welfare" laptop reading email from home. "Yeah, well my email is full of Franco-bashing. Listen to this one by Rumsfeld himself, 'Going to war without the French is like going deer hunting without your accordion.'"

"He didn't really say that?"

"He did. This one isn't Franco-bashing but it's pretty interesting." Ryan was reading over his shoulder.

"What's it say?" asked John.

"Well, basically it's a transcript of a senator questioning Oliver North during the Iran-Contra hearings about why he put a $60,000 security system in his house at government expense. It seems he thought he was being targeted by a terrorist in 1987. Know who the terrorist was?"

"I dunno, who?"

"Osama bin Laden. It gets better, know who the senator was?"

"Who?"

"The junior senator from Tennessee, Al Gore!"

"No shit!"

After September 11, President Bush decided that the United States would not wait for someone like Saddam to enlarge his arsenal of WMD and if the UN wouldn't go along with us, then so be it. Within one day of the terrorist attacks, a number of hawks in the DOD brought up the idea of a preemptive strike against Iraq, some, however, including President Bush decided that the immediate focus would be bin Laden, al-Qaeda, and the governments that harbored them. A year passed while the United States was fully engaged in Afghanistan, during which President Bush gave the "Axis of Evil" speech. Then, on September 12, 2002, a year and a day since the 9/11 attacks, Bush gave a speech to the United Nations General Assembly calling for a new resolution aimed at once again disarming Iraq of its WMD. It was a tough, but firm, speech declaring that the United States would seek international support, but at the same time it challenged the UN to live up to its mandate of 1991. Four days later Iraq agreed to let UN weapons inspectors return to Iraq "without conditions." Two weeks later, Iraq changed the conditions, declaring eight presidential palaces off limits. These conditions infuriated the Bush administration, which consequently began the process of seeking approval from the UN to use force if Iraq failed to cooperate in the slightest way. While this was debated in the UN, the US Congress voted overwhelmingly for a resolution authorizing the use of force against Iraq, 296 to 133 in the house and 71 to 23, including two Democrats with presidential aspirations, Hillary Clinton and John Kerry.

Then on November 8, 2002, the UN Security Council unanimously accepted Resolution 1441, a resolution that laid the groundwork for a thorough and comprehensive disarmament to be conducted by the IAEA. On November 18, weapons inspectors returned to Iraq for the first time since December of 1996. As stipulated in Resolution 1441, Iraq was to give the UN a full report detailing its WMD programs. The resulting twelve-thousand-page document was a joke and offered nothing that the UN did not already know in 1997. On January 16, the weapons inspectors discovered twelve warheads that were designed to carry chemical weapons, and were not mentioned in the report. This should have resulted in an immediate "material breach" of Resolution 1441, yet for some reason the UN weapons inspectors seemed to be playing to both sides of the proverbial fence. They praised Iraq for its cooperation and at the same time deplored it for its harassment and interference. By this time, the Bush administration was through with diplomacy, but once again tried to secure UN support. On March 5, the French, Germans, and Russians announced that they would not permit a UN resolution sanctioning military action against Iraq.

Once again the Untied States, with the support of Britain and Spain, attempted to gain UN support and on March 7, introduced a modified compromise resolution that would give Iraq ten days to completely destroy its WMD program. On March 17, the Bush administration withdrew the resolution from the UN Security Council and advised the weapons inspectors to leave Iraq. That night President Bush addressed the nation, but his intended audience, Saddam was given an ultimatum: leave Iraq within forty-eight hours, or else.

CHAPTER 48

The fire-and-forget policy was torn asunder by the attacks of September 11. Those attacks emanated from the deep structure of Arab life . . . its repressed young people, its mix of belligerence and self-pity, the terrible anti-Americanism blowing like a steady wind in Arab lands . . . and Saddam Hussein's Iraq was the citadel of Arabs and radicalism. One way or the other, the trail that began in Kabul was destined to lead to Baghdad.

—Fouad Ajami,
US News & World Report, March 31, 2003

Kemal had diarrhea again, still, perpetually. This was the sixth time he'd been to the latrine today. It had plagued him for the last eleven years, ever since the Gulf War. *Damn Saddam! Won't that son of a bitch ever die?* thought Kemal in English. *And damn that butcher of a battalion surgeon who has the nerve to call himself a doctor.* Kemal came back from squatting in the dust, wishing he had a Western toilet to sit on and be miserable.

"Why did you take so long?" demanded his section officer.

"I have dysentery!" replied Kemal, a little surlier than he had intended.

"Get back to work or I'll have you shot!"

They were building defensive positions along Highway 8 just south of Baghdad in case the Americans came back. Kemal was put back into a field unit for two reasons: one, they needed the men, and two, his superiors felt he had been directly sabotaging the work on a new, multi-antibiotic resistant strain of anthrax they were developing. In this, his superiors were correct. Kemal had probably single-handedly kept the strain from being mass-produced over the past several years by careful manipulation of the pH for the buffers, the ionic strength of the growth media, infections with bacteria phages from the virology lab and a dozen other clever manipulations. The head of his lab, a Russian who had defected to the Iraqis and had been in charge of a Vektor Soviet BW lab in Kazakhstan, suspected that Kemal was sabotaging the work but could not catch him at it. Kemal had become quite a microbiologist and was horrified by what they were trying to do.

There was a lot of rhetoric in the news in the last few months from the Americans trying to link Iraq to the support of the terrorists and the West's continued search for weapons of mass destruction. Possible UN sanctions and the threat of an American-British invasion put pressure on Saddam to allow weapons inspectors back into Iraq, but it was the same old game of obstruction and delaying tactics. Now it looked as though the Americans had had enough. Western newspapers were illegal in Iraq, but once in a while one would appear. He had also caught several broadcasts from the Arab news channel, *Al Jazeera*, and the BBC. One of the reports quoted the American defense officials referring to "unfinished business with Saddam" and the "return of Desert Storm."

The sun was going down and as punishment for his trips to the latrine Kemal was sent out with another misfit to a LP/OP (listening post/observation post) several hundred meters out in the desert. The post was linked back to the battalion by a field telephone. A fitful night had been punctuated by several trips to his cat-hole latrine and a terrifying visit by a sand viper. The reptile had been seeking warmth in the cold, night desert air and had crawled into the lap of a dozing Kemal. By the time he was aware of the snake it had curled up in his crotch. He had tried to remain absolutely still but in spite of the cold, Kemal began to sweat and tremble. The snake began to stir and, able to endure it no longer, Kemal jumped up and backward out of his hole with a scream. The surprised snake slithered off. Almost immediately, the field telephone sprang to life and the voice on the other end demanded to know what the commotion was all about. Cursing loudly, his officer told him he would spend all week at the post for violating noise discipline and would be shot at the next infraction. Shivering with cold and fear, Kemal was unable to go back to sleep and spent the rest of the night miserably awake.

Kemal climbed out of the hole and was squatted in the faint glow of false dawn, his bowels again in an uproar. Suddenly he was aware of a silent shape hurtled toward him just above the ground. At first he didn't recognize it as a helicopter. It resembled a large bat, a deadly "night-stalker." He stood and waved, even as he knew this was an American helicopter.

Sitting in the jump seat of the Littlebird, CW3 Ryan Gallagher studied the dark through the night-vision scope of his Barrett .50 caliber sniper rifle as they roared deep into Iraq. His Delta squadron was one of the advance parties assigned to eliminate a command and control (C&C) headquarters monitoring southern Iraq. Ryan's own team was targeting a suspected WMD command center just south of Baghdad. He saw the man stand up from the hole at about two o'clock. *The fool*, he thought, as he placed the infrared dot, visible through his night-vision scope, on the target's chest as the chopper screamed toward him. The man suddenly waved and Ryan relaxed his finger in the trigger guard. For some reason he couldn't explain, he waved back. He doubted he would be seen in the low illumination of the almost moonless night, even hanging out of the chopper like he was. This was supposed to be an uninhabited route but they were told to eliminate anyone that might give the alarm. Damn fool probably thought it was one of their own choppers.

Just as the first machine roared by, low enough to kick up a plume of sand, Kemal was doubled up by another of those gut-wrenching spasms and he squatted again, managing to shit on his boots in the process.

Yeah, the Americans were coming all right, and this time they'd finish the job.

CHAPTER 49

What is called "foreknowledge" cannot be elicited from the spirits, nor from the gods, nor by analogy with past events, nor from calculations. It must be obtained from men who know the enemy situation.

—Sun Tzu,
The Art of War

The Americans *were* coming after months of stalling by the Iraqi regime. With most, but not all of their troops in position, they were forced to act early. What preempted their plan and precipitated the first attack, even as the machinations with the UN were still ongoing, was a chance to take out Saddam. US intelligence personnel had infiltrated Baghdad months before and were hiding in the shadows, trying to pinpoint Saddam's whereabouts. Ryan had seen proof of this while watching CNN on the Satcom TV in the Op Center one morning.

"Holy shit! Did you see that?" exclaimed Ryan.

"What?" asked John.

They had been watching a video feed from one of the reporters in Baghdad. The picture was of a ministry building and as they replayed it, a figure could be seen walking in the foreground of the picture and then off the screen.

"That guy, there!" The figure was wearing one of the new black Army cold-weather Mikeets and a baseball hat.

"So, probably a cameraman."

"No! I know that guy. He was in Afghanistan at Gardez. He's CIA."

"No shit! He's got balls."

"There are a bunch of our guys there, too. I hope they keep their heads down!"

The CIA and Delta had tried for years to get an agent inside the Saddam regime, to penetrate the inner circle and to get past the body doubles, and bodyguards. To find out where he would be holed up on any given night. As one intelligence operative put it: "we'll get him when someone rats him out." One of Saddam's primary defenses against assassination was that he never stayed in one place for too long; his movements were always shrouded in a cloak of secrecy. Now, the Americans had been tipped off to where he would be on the night of March 19. Not only had Delta operatives been able to tap the underground presidential phone lines of the dictator in Baghdad, but the CIA had finally developed a source on the inside. Not much was known about him except he was more afraid of the Americans than Saddam, at least at this point.

The intelligence sources had also gotten a fix on Saddam through SIGINT (signals intelligence). The United States had two satellites dedicated to tracking Saddam's whereabouts. The first, code named TRUMPET, intercepted cellphone signals, but Saddam was smart enough not to use them very often. The second, code named MICRON, could intercept landline signals but only if they were relayed by microwave towers. The way they were able to target in on Saddam this time was his use of the Jaguar radio system for secure communications. Only the most trusted of his inner circle used it. The system had been sold to the Iraqis by the British during the Iran-Iraq War and employed both frequency hopping to prevent getting a frequency fix and virtually unbreakable encryption; *virtually*, the Americans *had* broken the code.

The source had told them that Saddam and his sons would be spending the night in a bunker beneath a nondescript residence in Baghdad. SIGINT and the other "eyes on the ground" confirmed the possibility of his being there. The president decided to launch a decapitating strike the night of March 19. Because of the bunker's design, stealth bombers employing bunker-buster bombs would be primary agent of Saddam's demise.

The bunker was much like the one beneath Saddam's main palace in Baghdad but on a smaller scale. The one beneath 305 Guest House at the main presidential palace had been built by German engineers for some 70 million dollars. It was multilevel with enormous layers of concrete, sand, and steel. It was zigzagged with corridors and blast doors and could withstand a Hiroshima-size surface explosion. There were honeycombs of tunnels, shelters, and storage areas that were thought to contain some of Saddam's weapons of mass destruction. They knew what these bunkers were like; the CIA had obtained the plans. In fact, much of underground Baghdad was a rabbit-den of catacombs and secret passages.

Delta operatives from Task Force 20 had eyes on the target. Four operatives in an old French Citroën had arrived at a safe house just across the river from the target building shortly after the tip. They had foreign passports, French ironically, and worked for a real company, a front for the CIA. Their documents weren't "deep cover," but would hold up to anything except intensive investigation. The team made their way to the roof, and after identifying the target building "lit it up" at the designated target window using a British-made Pilkington LF25 laser designator. They sent a DMDG (Digital Message Device Group) message via "burst" transmission to the invisible instrument of doom circling somewhere many thousands of feet overhead, invisible to Iraqi radar. A verbal message, "target illuminated," was also sent to the F-117 and it released two GBU-24B, 2,000-pound "bunker buster" bombs from under its wings. The bombs glided the many miles to the illuminated target. At almost the same time, three-dozen TLAM Tomahawk cruise missiles, each containing a 1,000-pound warhead, were launched from six ships in the Persian Gulf and the Red Sea bound for the target building.

The team watched as the bombs found their target. There was an almost inaudible crash and dust and debris flew up, as the bombs, one after the other, hit the target building and plowed through the ceiling and three floors before burying deep into the eight feet of reinforced concrete of the underground bunker. It was there that they finally detonated. The team was actually "danger close" just over a thousand meters from "ground zero" and they felt the explosion through the ground before they heard it. The roof of the building jumped, then with a crack and roar an expanding fireball mushroomed from the building and it was turned into flaming dust. The team headed for the door as the cruise missiles landed. Nothing could have survived the impending inferno.

Initial reports confirmed that Saddam and at least one of his murderous sons, Qusay or Uday, were either killed or wounded along with a number of high-ranking Ba'ath party officials. Saddam was reportedly removed on a stretcher, but there were no official confirmations. At any rate, "A" day was upon them; Operation Iraqi Freedom had begun.

CHAPTER 50

The statesman who, knowing the instrument to be ready, and seeing war inevitable, hesitates to strike first is guilty of a crime against his country.

—Von der Goltz,
Introduction to *On War* by von Clausewitz

Ryan's teams' first mission since the war had officially begun was a dry hole, just like the one the night before. The special four-man team was organized specifically to search out biochemical weapons. Ryan's team sergeant, MSG Jake McNulty, had been an 18D medic like Ryan, as had John. They all came from Special Forces except SFC Tom Allen. He was from the Ranger Regiment and probably the best sniper in the army. John was also sniper-qualified and they made a good counter-sniper team.

The night the war started, intelligence had pinpointed a target as a biological-warfare control center in a group of farm buildings just off Highway 8 on the Euphrates River south of Baghdad. With two gunships overhead they whisked in on four sides of the small compound in the dead of a moonless night. While a platoon of Rangers secured the perimeter, Ryan's team raced through the buildings looking for documents and anything else they could find. There were a small contingent of Iraqi militia manning the property but they were all asleep. By the time they had responded to the noise of the helicopters they had all been rousted, flex cuffed, and seated in the courtyard, fearing for their lives.

"I don't know what this place is, but there isn't any command center here," said Jake, the team sergeant.

"There's some insecticide here, but it looks like it's strictly for agricultural use."

"Insecticide and nerve agent are basically the same thing."

"Gather up some samples and anything else useful looking and let's get the hell out of here. Grab the most intelligent looking of those sad sacks and we'll take him with us for interrogation."

They were airborne and halfway back to the staging area in Saudi Arabia before the Iraqis fully woke up. The ground was flat and featureless, and on the way back they saw the light from the bombs falling around Baghdad. The coalition aircraft flew over one thousand sorties that first night, four thousand in the first three days. It turned out that Ryan's team hit the wrong complex. Their intelligence was bad. They hit a supply waypoint instead of their intended target. The prisoner told them that a compound a kilometer to the north, closer to Karbala, had some high-ranking officers, communications gear, and a lot of secretive equipment, though he wasn't sure exactly what they did. He was only a captain, commander of a small supply company. Ryan saw to it that a thousand pound bomb hit the site, and imagery the next day showed the Iraqis abandoning it. But the mission had been a failure—they were after intelligence: where bio/chem weapons might be located, what kinds of munitions and delivery vehicles they had, and who was in charge of them. There were bound to be dry holes. Their intelligence now seemed iffy at best. Saddam had years to disguise, destroy, or move his stocks to other countries like Syria.

When they got back to the TOC, they were grabbed by the operations officer. "You guys get some rest. You're linking up with C squadron out at Haditha Dam in the morning. They're deploying from H-5."

"Where?"

"It's out west near the border. There's a secret base in Jordan. They've even got a Warthog squadron out there." They linked up with C squadron at first light, the latter driving Ground Mobility Vehicles, souped up Humvees equipped with MK-19s and 50 cals. Although they did as complete a search as possible at the dam (even doing an underwater search using the Mark 15 rebreathers they had gotten from the navy), and questioned the workers at length, they found nothing. Since aircraft was in short supply, they joined C troop for their ground move to Tikrit, Saddam's power base in the Sunni triangle. They checked out a couple of potential sites along the way, finding nothing. On the way to Tikrit they encountered six Iraqi trucks. They were full of Saddam's irregulars and careened right into the Delta operators. A sharp firefight ensued, in which they destroyed several of the vehicles with Javelin missiles and killed thirty-some and captured seven. After interrogation, they found that they were part of a hundred-strong Fedayeen guerilla group from a local village. An attack with the help of MH-60 helicopter gun ships, F-16s, and A-10s wiped out the unit.

They set up a base, Grizzly, about fifteen miles outside Tikrit and the combined Delta, Rangers, 160th Special Operations Aviation Regiment, intelligence teams, along with Team Tank spent the next several days attacking and harassing forces in Tikrit. Marrying up special operation groups with Abrams A1M1 main battle tanks had proved to be a very effective tactic.

Ryan and the rest of his team got a ride to the TOC. For the next few days his team waited for some good intelligence that would lead them to another mission. The special four-man team was organized specifically to search out bio-chemical weapons. Ryan's team sergeant, MSG Jake McNulty, had been an 18D medic like Ryan, as had John. They all came from Special Forces except SFC Tom Allen.

They were in the JSOTF TOC (Joint Special Operations Task Force Tactical Operations Center) watching the array of TVs that continuously played CNN, Fox, and other news networks. The war, into its first week, was not going exactly how some in the press were expecting and the media seemed to be in a feeding frenzy. In the first Gulf War reporters were largely shut out and only fed the party line. Most of them had been so incensed that they refused to attend the big victory parade in Washington following the war. Now with all the imbedded reporters there was a kind of sensory overload. Individual reporters who were reporting on their little slice of the war were constantly showing satellite feeds. You had to watch for hours to get the big picture.

While conventional forces pushed deep into Iraq, Special Forces teams infiltrated the west, where they seized two vital airfields, H2 and H3. These were capable of firing Scud missiles at Israel and US bases in the west. They were also busy searching for evidence of WMD. Other SF teams secured the Rumula oil fields in the south and teams working with the Kurds attacked Iraqi bases in the north. The Iraqi resistance was surprisingly fierce in the first few days and American casualties began to mount. The 3rd Infantry Division, the 101st Airborne Division, and the 1st Marine Expeditionary units were all engaging in pitched battles on their drive to Baghdad, as were the British around Basra. They were in for a fight this time, not like the one-sided affair during Desert Storm, the first Gulf War.

The Iraqi Army, at least on paper, was still a formidable force. The world's fourth largest standing army was significantly degraded by Desert Storm, but not to the extent that many believed. They still had approximately 285,000 regular troops, 80,000 Republican Guard, 15-30,000 Special Republican Guard fiercely loyal to Saddam, 20-25,000 Fedayeen Saddam (men of sacrifice), a paramilitary organization of thugs and death squads, eight overlapping Secret Police organizations with 15-20,000 members, and the A Qads (Jerusalem) Army, which was a rag-tag bunch of volunteers with little military training.

All along the front US troops were experiencing *Mad Max*–like attacks. Ten pickups would rush out of the sand firing AK-47s and RPGs. These attacks were usually suicidal with the Bradley's 30mm chain gun and machine guns chewing them to pieces. Two Abrams Main Battle Tanks were disabled by a vehicle mounting an antiaircraft gun on the back (reminiscent of the "technicals" in Somalia) that raced around and hit them in their back engine area, the only weak spot on the tank. No one was usually injured and the martyrs were sent to Allah. The 7th Cavalry (General George Armstrong Custer's unit) came under fire from five small boats crossing the Euphrates and they were promptly sunk in the "Gary Owen" tradition.

Many of the reporters and the political pundits were now second-guessing the strategy to go in light and fast with minimal initial air preparation. When the Iraqis didn't immediately throw up their hands as they had during the first conflict, there was talk about flawed assumptions; that the Iraqis would give up without a fight and greet us as liberators. Most of the criticism was centered on GEN Tommy Franks, the CENTCOM (Central Command) Commander and Defense Secretary Donald Rumsfeld for "interfering" with the war plan, for not letting the generals fight the war they planned. Rumsfeld was a proponent for a small, light, fast force integrating new technologically advanced weapons systems and using Special Forces troops as "force multipliers," as they had done in Afghanistan.

The original OPLAN for the invasion of Iraq was crafted under GEN Zinni's watch as CENTCOM Commander, before GEN Franks took command. Plan 100398 called for a force of approximately 350,000 troops with no fewer than five combat divisions racing to Baghdad. The force was also heavy with military police to secure supply lines, enforce the peace in captured areas, and civil affairs to help restore vital services and ensure the peace would be successful. Secretary of Defense Donald Rumsfeld, an ex-navy pilot, thought this was a ridiculous number. It did not adhere to his goal of "transformation," or the principles of a small, lethal force. He thought the war could be won with as few as fifty thousand troops and that he could supplant "boots on the ground" with superior technology. "Shock and Awe," to take out the Iraqi command and control and a rapid dash to Baghdad would be the mantra of his defeat of Saddam. He pressured and cajoled GEN Franks and the rest of the generals into taking less than one third of the troops many thought would be necessary to ensure the peace with virtually no MPs or CA.

His plan for the peace relied on several assumptions. The Iraqi Army would surrender almost en bloc after the "running start" and "shock and awe" campaign, and would be molded into a force that could police the borders and outlying areas of the country. The current Iraqi police forces would be used for the same purpose in the cities. He assumed that vital services would largely remain intact, as would the workers and the people that headed them. He largely dismissed the possibility of a large-scale insurgency, factional fighting, and civil war. There would be no real "nation building" as there had been in the Balkans after the dissolution of Yugoslavia: he referred to this as a "failed operation." The United States would be in and out of Iraq with a small light force, not the ten years and hundreds of thousands of troops that had been used in the Balkans.

Not everyone agreed with him, quite to the contrary. Most US military commanders, including the army chief of staff, calculated that they needed a force between 350,000 and 500,000. Secretary of State Colin Powell, who was the subject military matter expert in Bush's cabinet and the chairman of the joint chiefs during Desert Storm also disagreed. Thought to be too cautious by Rumsfeld and the other hawks, he predicted that Iraq would require up to 40 percent of the nation's military effort and ten years to create a functioning democratic government in Iraq. There were other detractors as well, but Rumsfeld was arrogantly dismissive of his generals' opinions, much like Secretary Robert McNamara had been forty years before. Rumsfeld believed that the top military leaders *were* the problem; he was secure in the knowledge that they were wrong and he was right.

It was starting to look like he was right about a small force beating the Iraqi Army, but that he might be wrong about being able to provide a secure peace. With so few troops, would it be possible to secure the borders, secure vital sites, prevent looting, secure weapons caches, and prevent secular violence or an insurgency? Was the emergence of insurgents, tribal militias, death squads, suicide bombings, and IEDs a harbinger of what was to come? Many military pundits thought so.

John and Ryan stood in front of one of the monitors as a former general discussed the situation. His take on the whole affair was that they hadn't used enough airpower, certainly not the thirty-nine days before the first Gulf War, and they didn't have enough troops, less than a third of what they had during Desert Storm. The supply lines were overextended and would result in more ambushes and more captured Americans (like those from the 507th Maintenance Company at Nasiriyah) and many more American deaths. This unit had lost its way, taken a wrong turn and gone through the city. They had been ambushed and utterly chopped to pieces, thirty-three casualties, eleven killed, and seven captured, including Jessica Lynch. The military analyst was convinced it was going to be a long, drawn-out war with hundreds or even thousands of American casualties requiring many years of combat.

"Was that the same armchair general that was predicting disaster in Afghanistan last year, just two days before the Taliban rolled over and played dead?" Ryan asked John.

"That's what happens when you embed ex-generals in television studios," replied John. "That guy wouldn't know a special operation if you hit him in the face with it."

"Ryan, come here and look at this," said MAJ Hoaglund, Ryan's squadron commander.

Ryan went up to where he was watching another monitor. "Man, if I hear 'Shock and Awe' one more time I'm going to puke!"

They watched while yet another ex-military expert second-guessed the war plan for the hundredth time that day.

"I think I'll be a 'military analyst' when I retire," said John.

"Not unless you're a retired colonel or general you won't. They don't want any know-it-all sergeants on TV," laughed Ryan.

"Ha! There should be some NCOs on these shows. We're the ones that do all the work while you *officers* sit on your backsides drinking coffee," John threw back.

The Squadron S-2 (intelligence officer) came over.

"Chief, I've got a report of an Iraqi EPW who's singing a song about the bio-weapons program the Iraqis were running. He's in a holding facility near Nasiriyah. Seems he wants to defect . . . stole a vehicle and drove down to a 3rd ID checkpoint. Almost got his butt shot off!"

"John, get the guys saddled up. I'm going to go with the captain and get some more details. Have Jake see if he can get us some air. We're going to go down and see this guy."

CHAPTER 51

The regime that once terrorized all of Iraq now controls a small portion of that country. Coalition troops continue their steady advance and are drawing near to Baghdad. We're inflicting severe damage on enemy forces. We are now fighting the most desperate units of the dictator's army. The fierce fighting currently underway will demand further courage and further sacrifice. Yet we know the outcome of this battle. The Iraqi regime will be disarmed. The Iraqi regime will be removed from power. Iraq will be free.

—President George W. Bush,
veterans group speech

They landed the MH-53J Pave Low by the command vehicles of the 2nd Brigade, 3rd Infantry Division near Najah and were taken over to see the brigade commander. They wore semi-sterile uniforms with only their blood grouping and an IR subdued flag on the modified slant pockets on their sleeves; no name, rank, or unit insignia on their body armor. That, in of itself, was significant and spoke volumes for what it didn't say . . . that they were not part of the *regular* Army. In deference to the strait-laced infantry, they replaced their non-regulation baseball caps with standard DCU (desert camouflage uniform) caps and removed their Afghani scarves. The brigade commander had been briefed that they were coming and sent them back to the temporary EPW (enemy prisoner of war) holding area in a Bradley armored vehicle.

The EPWs were in a concertina (razor wire) corral; dirty, tired, and flex-cuffed. A pudgy first lieutenant (1st LT) with thick black Army glasses was questioning one of the prisoners at the back of a Bradley. Sitting on a camp stool, the LT looked remarkably like a bespectacled turtle in the bulky MOPP (chemical protection) over garment. The EPW was still flex-cuffed and on his knees. An interpreter, clearly Arabic, was squatting in front of him just off to the side. A guard stood behind the man with an M-16 loosely trained on him, rapping him occasionally on the back of the head with the flash suppressor.

Ryan walked up to the CI (counterintelligence) officer. "You have an Iraqi here that says he knows something about biological warfare?"

"He's over with the rest of them, but I haven't finished interrogating him yet."

"I need to talk to him."

The CI officer had been warned that someone from higher was coming to question the man and was irked by it. "Let me finish with this one and then we'll talk to him."

"I need to talk to him *now* and in private. I won't need your interpreter."

"You won't need an interpreter at all, he speaks English better than *you* do," the man sneered the comment in a thick southern drawl, a thinly veiled reference to Ryan's clipped New England accent. He got up and walked over to Ryan. He was nearly a head shorter and searched Ryan's uniform for name and distinguishing marks.

"I don't know who you think you are . . ."

"Gallagher," Ryan finished the sentence for him.

"I don't know who you think you are, *Gallagher*, but we've got procedures here that have to be followed. He hasn't been processed yet."

"Lieutenant, we get in a pissing contest here and the only one who's going to get pissed on is *you*. If you want to go see the brigade commander . . ."

"Alright, you can talk to him over there," he pointed to a wide desolate rock-strewn area to the left of the holding area.

"Johnson, go get that raghead for *Mister* Gallagher."

John and Ryan borrowed a couple of the campstools that seemed to be ubiquitous in the combat zone. REI, EMS, and the rest of the camping stores were definitely making a killing out of this war.

SGT Johnson was pulling a dirty flex-cuffed individual over. He had a crude blood-stained bandage on his head and a capture tag that gave the details of his encounter with US troops hanging from the buttonhole of his filthy uniform. He dropped down on his knees. He had heard the encounter between the two officers and for the first time since his attempted surrender, he was afraid. Afraid of the big redheaded stranger. *He had to be the dreaded secret police! Did the Americans have such men?* His brain was still a little fuddled from the accident.

When he had seen the helicopter come over that morning a week (was it only a week?) ago, he knew that he was going to defect at the first opportunity. His chance didn't come for another week. His commander, anticipating the Americans imminent advance, told Kemal to go over to the POL (petroleum, oil, and lubricants) supply point and gas up his staff car. Most of the other soldiers were ignorant conscripts and couldn't drive. The major's regular driver was sick as a dog. On the way back from the point, Kemal pulled over, put on one of the major's uniforms that was hanging in the back of the vehicle and had headed south on Highway 8 toward the advancing Americans. He had trouble getting through the last Iraqi checkpoint, but bullied the guards into letting him pass. He could never have pulled it off except for the uniform. When he was out of sight he got out and hung a white T-shirt to the antenna.

He was racing down the highway, keeping one eye in the rearview mirror when he ran smack into several Bradley scout vehicles. He was taken under fire almost immediately and both front tires and the engine were destroyed in a hail of machine-gun fire. He swerved off the road and the car flipped over and started burning. He was dazed but managed to crawl out just as the car exploded in flames. The Americans came up with their guns drawn and he was sure they were going to kill him. He was not aware that there had been several recent suicide attacks by Iraqis and the Americans were taking no chances. He was cuffed and passed back along the line until he was taken to the EPW holding area. Because he spoke excellent English he was questioned right away. He told them about the biological weapons. Anything to do with WMD was a CEI (critical element of information) and was to be reported to higher intelligence channels immediately. It was this that brought him and this scary looking red-haired man together.

He knelt in front of the man, his eyes downcast.

"Alright, what's your name and what are you doing here?"

He looked up, "My name is Kemal Mahadi Shibah. Who are you?"

"What do you like to be called? Is Kemal okay?"

"Yeah, sure."

"Kemal. Here's how this is going to work. I'm going to ask the questions and you're going to answer them, okay?"

Now Kemal was even more afraid, but as he looked into the man's eyes he saw only quiet self-assuredness with no hint of cruelty or evil. "I'll tell you everything I know about the biological warfare stuff. I want to help the Americans."

Ryan looked at him a long minute and then got up, reached around behind him, and used a switchblade to cut his ties. "You hungry?"

Kemal nodded yes.

"John, bring us another chair and see if you can rustle up some MREs. Make sure they don't have pork or ham in them."

John came back with a couple of bags. "You want 'Chili and Macaroni' or 'Vegetarian Pasta?' Everything else I could find had ham in it."

"Vegetarian pasta I guess. My stomach's been kind of funny."

"John, use the MRE heater to cook that while we have a talk. Tell me your story Kemal and start at the beginning. I want to know where you learned to speak such good English and how you know so much about the bio-war program."

About ten minutes into Kemal's sad tale Ryan interrupted him. "Eat this and then we'll go." He handed Kemal the meal and a bottle of water, both of which were greedily consumed.

He signaled Jake, his team sergeant. "Top, get on the horn and see if we can get the chopper to land here. We're going to take this guy with us and I don't want the brigade commander to get a chance to veto it. Set up a LZ (landing zone) over there," he pointed to a large open area. "There are some VS-17 panels in the kit bag."

"You got it chief!"

When the chopper was inbound, Ryan informed the lieutenant that they were taking the prisoner with them.

"But you can't *do* that," he whined.

Ryan cut him off with a glance. "You want to make captain some day; you'll shut up and release him to me."

"Okay, but you've got to sign for him. I'm going to call the brigade S-2 and make sure it's okay," he muttered as he wandered off. "Fuckin' spooks!"

Jake directed the Pave Low down. They collected the panels and got in, but not before Ryan left a hand written "Memorandum for Record" on the lieutenant's chair. It simply said:

Received from 2nd Bde, 3rd ID. One slightly used Iraqi prisoner.
RYAN C. GALLAGHER
CW3, SF
Commanding

CHAPTER 51

Those skilled in war subdue the enemy's army without battle. They capture his cities without assaulting them and overthrow his state without protracted operations. The worst policy is to attack cities. Attack cities only when there is no alternative.

—Sun Tzu,
The Art of War

They arrived back at their new forward headquarters just as dusk was settling. When they got to their compound one of the operations NCOs came over.

"Hey, did you guys hear? The Seals rescued one of the females from that maintenance company that took the wrong turn in Nasiriyah and got ambushed."

"What I want to know is what the *fuck* were they doing wandering around in the battle area without a strong armored escort?" asked John.

"Supply lines are too long," said Ryan. "What happened?"

"Seal Team 6, the Rangers, some Marines, and the Air Force Spec Ops boys went in and snatched her right out of a military hospital. She was pretty shot up. Combat camera has video of it. It's been all over the news all day."

"Fuckin' Seals. They get all the glory stuff while we run around in the boonies collecting Iraqi prisoners," complained Jake.

Ryan laughed, "You're in the wrong outfit if you're looking for press. You should have gone to squid school."

The operations sergeant major came up. "Chief, the major wants to see you ASAP."

"Okay, I'll be right there. You guys take Kemal and get him some DCUs and boots. Burn those clothes he's wearing; they're a little ripe. And have him checked for lice. I'll be back in five."

It was over an hour before Ryan returned. A lot had happened in the war in the last couple of days. The two American columns had advanced steadily north on either side of the Euphrates advancing on Baghdad, while the Brits secured Basra. In a tactic reminiscent of WWII, they bypassed cities the way we had bypassed Japanese islands in the Pacific. The 4th Infantry Division, refused permission by the Turks to land in Turkey and attack from the north, was still floating around on boats in the Persian Gulf somewhere. The key

Iraqi port city of Um Qasr had been taken and they were expecting to start off loading any day. The political pundits were still criticizing the battle plan—the rush to seize Baghdad and cut off the head of the snake to avoid a battle in every city—but so far it seemed to be working. One day the press would be upbeat, the next predicting doom. They seemed to be suffering from bipolar syndrome, going through "mood swings," according to Secretary Rumsfeld. While there were many fierce isolated pockets of fighting and the population didn't seem to be rising to welcome the invaders as many predicted, there didn't seem to be any coherent plan for an organized resistance; at least from the Iraqi army.

MOUT (military operations in urban terrain), the Army's acronym for urban combat was something the Americans wanted to avoid at all costs. It was supposed to be the Achilles' heel of the Americans, to have to fight in the cities, avoid killing civilians, and destroying the valuable infrastructure of the country that would be required in the rebuilding of the country. Not that the Americans weren't good at urban combat, they were. They had practiced urban warfare for just such an eventuality as now presented itself; fighting house-to-house in Baghdad and the other cities. They just didn't want to do it if it wasn't necessary. It would mean many more casualties and took away many of the technologic advantages of their space-age weapons. Historically, urban engagements resulted in up to 30 percent casualties for an attacking force. Even a low of 10 percent would result in thousands of Americans killed and wounded.

One of the reasons the population was not rising up to throw off Saddam's rule like Rumsfeld had predicted, was the recent memory of the reprisals taken by Saddam after Desert Storm. Many in the south and north revolted following the Iraqi collapse but then the Americans left, leaving only the "no-fly zones" as protection for the rebels. The "no-fly" had not included helicopters, a fatal mistake, for the local populations. Thousands of Iraqis, mostly Shiites and Kurds, were subsequently slaughtered by Qusay Hussein, Saddam's psychopathic son and the heir-apparent to the evil throne. In addition, roving bands of Fedayeen Saddam were kidnapping the children of soldiers to make sure they would fight and committed unspeakable horrors against anyone who showed disaffection with Saddam's Iraq.

Saddam and his sons watched the movie *Black Hawk Down* and borrowed the Somali tactic of putting women and children out in front of gunmen as they attacked the American columns with hit-and-run ambushes. They hanged an old woman from a light post for waving to passing Americans and shot a nine-year-old boy in a town square because his father wouldn't mount a suicide attack against the Americans. Several dozen of the gunmen fired on a thousand or so refugees fleeing Basra as they tried to cross a bridge to British lines, killing hundreds. They cut the tongues out of those whom they thought might be disloyal, and raped the women of men who had run away. They made some drink gasoline, shot them, and set them on fire. But still the Americans advanced.

One of the areas the Americans *were* too light to advance on in great numbers was in the Kurdish north. Using Army Special Forces as "force multipliers" solved this. They joined their Kurdish allies and attacked the Iraqis with precision-guided air munitions, driving them steadily back. The 173rd Airborne Brigade had made the largest combat parachute drop since the Vietnam War, dropping from huge C-17 Globemasters and seizing a vital airfield in the mountain-ringed Harir Valley near the Iranian border. With the oil fields safe and backed up by the airborne troops, the USSF and the Kurds mounted an operation against both the Iraqis and the Ansar al-Islam, a radical group in the mountains thought to contain al-Qaeda and Taliban fighters who fled to this haven from Afghanistan. It was a good mix, the Kurdish warriors were known as *peshmerga*s, meaning "those who face death" or "oppressed people," and the Army Special Forces motto was *De Opresso Liber*, "Freedom for the Oppressed."

It was in this area that the team was going next. They were going to do SSE (sensitive site exploration), searching for evidence of weapons of mass destruction. The troops up in the valley had apparently found evidence that the Islamists were making chemical and biological weapons.

Ryan gave an abbreviated version of the army's standard five-paragraph operations order, known as a WARNORD (warning order). "Get enough gear together for three days. Pack your cold weather gear and bring plenty of WMD sampling equipment. Pack plenty of water and a double basic load of ammo. Bring the Barrett and both radios. Just pack a couple of rations. The SF guys have stuff or we'll eat with the locals."

John groaned, "I'm never going to eat goat meat again when this is all over."

"We're going to leave Kemal with the S-2 for debriefing. Kemal, you look like a new man in that uniform, and you smell a hell of a lot better!"

"I feel better. I got a *hot* shower . . . you know how long it's been since I've had a shower, let alone hot? John gave me some Imodium and Ciprofloxacin for my stomach. Anyway, I feel better than I have felt in months . . . years."

"We're going to put you up in one of the VIP tents. You're to talk to no one but our Intel people; they're going to debrief you. Tell them everything. Don't hold any little detail out. If anyone asks who you are, just tell them you are a new interpreter. You're not a prisoner; you're a defector working for us now. They told me there's some bucks in it for you and possibly a real job when all this is over."

Kemal was not used to people being kind to him and he started to cry. The last time he had cried had been twelve years ago at Tallil Airbase during the Gulf War when another American had been kind to him. It had been Ryan's father.

CHAPTER 52

People say to me, "you are not the Vietnamese. You have no jungles and swamps to hide in." Let our cities be our swamps and our buildings our jungles.

—Tariq Aziz,
Iraqi Deputy Defense Minister

They made the low-level, gut-wrenching flight to the airfield in a C-130 Talon, flying at treetop level. It was below radar detection, and if you were on the ground you couldn't see or hear the dark black shape until to it was upon you, and then it was gone. Ryan remembered sitting on a landing strip during the Special Forces Qualification Course all rigged up with equipment for insertion into the "Robin Sage" exercise. They were rigged with the heavy main parachute on their back over their LBE (load bearing equipment), a small reserve in front, their weapon strapped to the left side and the seventy-pound rucksack hung form the harness at the knees. It was an exquisite kind of torture to stand with the 150 pounds of extra weight and the only *partly* comfortable way to endure it was to sit down while resting your back on the parachute pack tray. He was exhausted and even with the torture apparatus on, he dozed in the sun, waiting for the plane. When he opened his eyes, it came to a stop right in front of him. He never heard a thing. *How could anything so big be so quiet in the approach?*

After landing, they went up to the FOB to talk to the SF battalion commander and then up to the Halabja Valley by Black Hawk. They linked up with the SF Company, and after being introduced to their *peshmerga* allies they went into the village where the suspected biological weapons factory was found. Their Kurdish allies were a hardy, friendly bunch wearing a mish-mash of clothing that resembled uniforms only by their diversity. They reminded Ryan of the Afghans, natural warriors inured to hardship as a long-suffering people in a harsh land. They were very well trained, and the contingent that was to be their bodyguards really knew their business. Whenever they stopped, the men fanned out in their best "executive protection" mode.

The village was about halfway down the valley where Ansar al-Islam made their base. There were approximately six hundred fighters in the valley; approximately 150–200 were believed to be former al-Qaeda or Taliban. They escaped into the valley from Afghanistan, presumably being assisted across Iran by the Iranians, and they had remained there possibly with the tacit approval of Saddam. There was evidence that their terrorist training camps may have received funding from both Iran and Iraq as well as by outside groups. The United States had received intelligence on the area for some time and planned to attack the area from the outset using US Special Forces and Kurds. During the opening bombing campaign, nine precision-guided bombs had slammed into a suspected poison factory near the village of Sargent, one of the places Ryan's team was going to explore.

The Ansar al-Islam was routed out of the valley and into the Shinerwe Mountains bordering Iran. Task Force Viking, as the composite US/Kurdish army was known, was composed of a six-thousand-man-strong Kurdish army broken down into approximately 360-man battalions, each with two SF advisors to call in air strikes. Employing B-52 strikes with mortars, artillery, cruise missiles, Predator unmanned aircraft, and attacking jets, the Americans and Kurds killed more than forty fighters the first day and approximately two hundred were believed killed in the following days of fighting. Many escaped into Iran, where they were supposedly being "detained" by Iranian officials, but many were still fighting a stubborn rear-guard action. The sensitive site exploitations (SSEs) that had been conducted so far had yielded a wealth of raw intelligence, mostly laptops and documents. There were also several terrorist training notebooks, looking every bit like children's composition notebooks except for the chilling tales they told. The information thus far collected was already proving invaluable in linking Islamic terrorist connections around the world.

The team's objective today was a suspected terrorist training camp using an Islamic school for its nefarious work. It was attached to a mosque in the village of Biyara, and was spared much of the damage that was visited on the rest of the village, although the roof containing a machine-gun pit was partially collapsed. In addition to a large cache of weapons and explosives, they found what appeared to be a small lab. They had found a similar lab in Afghanistan, but it turned out to be a drug lab to extract heroin from poppy seeds. This lab was, in fact, set up to do a different extraction, removing the toxin *ricin* from castor-bean seeds. Ricin is an extremely toxic protein, minute quantities of which can kill a human. It was a favorite weapon of Soviet assassins and was responsible for the 1978 murder of Bulgarian dissident Gregori Markov in London. He was poked by a passerby with an umbrella as he crossed a bridge, and scarcely felt the microscopic polycarbonate sphere that was filled with ricin as it imbedded itself in his thigh. He was dead in a matter of hours. The ricin involved in the thwarted terrorist plot in Britain in 2002 was believed to have come from the Ansar al-Islam group, probably from the very lab they were now exploring.

After gathering up as much of the documents and equipment as they could haul they went back to the C Team headquarters for a meal with their bodyguards. It consisted of yogurt, bread, and goat cheese spiced up with some MRE condiments. After the meal they started going through the stash and they made two other rather sobering finds; the group had tried, unsuccessfully, to manufacture botulinum toxin. They also found "glint tape," an infrared-reflective tape that special operators put on their helmets, uniforms, and vehicles so that they could be identified as "friendlies" from the air. It was not good that the bad guys had it. They sent a message to higher with this information and about the ricin lab. Ryan and his team were still sorting through the stuff with one of the CIA interpreters when the SF Company Commander came over.

"Hey chief, I understand your two boys here," he gestured to John and SFC Tom Allen, "are quite a sniper team. One of my NCOs was in sniper school with them and said Allen could knock the eye out of a mosquito at a thousand meters!"

"That's right major, but only if there're those big fellas like we have down on the bayou." Allen was from Louisiana and had a bit of a Cajun drawl.

"We're taking a lot of sniper fire from the ridges right on the border and we could use another good counter-sniper team. Can I borrow them? I've got an extra M-24 system if they'd prefer it over the Barrett."

"I like the M-24, but with these distances I thing I'd rather use the 50 cal," responded Tom. "Besides, like horseshoes and hand grenades sometimes real close is close enough."

Ryan was dubious. It wasn't their mission, but he relented. "Okay. But don't get them killed. I'd have some explaining to do to the boss. Take Jake with you to act as security and run the radio."

Ryan spent the rest of the day going through the caché of intelligence but could find nothing big, nothing linking the small toxin extracting effort to any WMD program by the Iraqis. *Where the hell were they keeping it all?* There were a number of small finds throughout the country. The 101st Airborne had uncovered a compound containing some drums believed to be Tabun and Sarin (two banned nerve agents) and there were a couple of banned missiles found, but no "smoking gun," no evidence of a large Iraqi chemical or biological program. Troops also found a chemical weapons defense training school at the abandoned HQ of the Iraqi Army's 8th Infantry Division and lots of chemical protection equipment, but it was no more than would be found in any modern army.

His thoughts were interrupted by one of the radio operators. "Chief, our CO wants you on the radio."

He reluctantly left his pile of material and went into the commo bunker. "Gallagher here."

"Hey chief, you have any medical gear with you?"

"Yeah, why?"

"We've had a 'Blue on Blue' down at Debecka Pass. I understand you were a medic. I was wondering if you could come down here and give us a hand. We've got a real disaster here."

"Sure. How do I get there?"

"There's an inbound CASEVAC bird going to stop there in five minutes. Get out to the chopper pad and you can get on it."

"What about my guys, sir?"

"They're already here helping. I'll see you in about twenty minutes."

Blue on Blue was the code word for a friendly fire incident. One of the great difficulties in conducting unconventional warfare was that it was sometimes hard to tell friend from foe, especially from the air. Historically in warfare, at least during the last part of the twentieth century, fratricide accounted for around 15 percent of all casualties. During the first Gulf War the percentage was much higher, almost 24 percent, 35 of 146 Americans killed. In Afghanistan it dropped down to about 13 percent. Already in this war, one British Challenger unit fired on another killing two, a US Patriot missile shot down a British Tornado, an A-10 had fired on its own armored vehicles, and one Marine unit near Nasiriyah fired on another, wounding thirty.

Everything was being done to try and keep the numbers low in this war. Measures included opening a dedicated anti-fratricide cell in Saudi Arabia to review targeting decisions, and the development of a new computer system, Blue Force Tracking, that collected GPS coordinates. It projected a real-time fluid image of the battlefield. Units had flashing Phoenix beacons that were visible only with special night-vision goggles, and an encoded radio signal system that responded in milliseconds when interrogated by another friendly radio signal. Then there was glint tape.

For unconventional troops and especially those of foreign allies, these measures were sometimes of little use, and so it was in this case. A pair of F-14 Tomcats, one of which got his cardinal directions mixed up, dropped one of his "smart" bombs near an abandoned T-55 tank where two teams from the 3rd Special Forces Group, their peshmerga allies, and several journalists were. There were sixteen dead, forty wounded, two of whom were SF. The medics and Ryan worked for hours on the survivors, many of them badly burned. Severe burns in a third world environment were almost a death sentence without advanced medical therapy and Ryan wondered if many of them would survive. They were in a somber mood on the way back to base and it dampened the exploits of the counter-sniper team.

They were able to take out three enemy snipers, two of them across a narrow valley, holed up in all but impregnable caves. John was watching through his spotter scope when the enormous .50 cal round had taken the head off one of snipers and blown his broken body twenty feet in the air. It was a shot of almost 1,400 meters.

CHAPTER 53

Men never do evil so cheerfully and completely as when they do so from religious conviction.

—Blaise Pascal

I t was well after midnight when they arrived back at their new TOC at the Baghdad Airport. The rest of the team secured the gear and crashed while Ryan went to the TOC to report in and check on things. Great strides had been made in the war in the two days they were gone. Saddam International Airport was seized and renamed Baghdad International Airport. The American Forces were poised at the gates of Baghdad. Several fast moving reconnaissance patrols raced through the city with no opposition. It was beginning to look like urban warfare might not be inevitable. Rather than go charging immediately into Baghdad, it was decided to consolidate the US gains and convince the population that the issue was no longer in doubt; to demoralize the opposition and get them to give up rather than fight. So much for a repeat of the "Siege of Stalingrad" the pundits were worried about.

One note of comic relief in the drama was Mohammed Saeed al-Sahaf, the Iraqi Minister of Information. Even as the Americans were surrounding Baghdad he was announcing that no American was within two hundred kilometers of Baghdad. After the airport was captured he announced that the pictures shown on CNN and Fox were forgeries. Following the armed recon patrols through Baghdad he announced that the airport was recaptured, hundreds of Americans were killed, and the rest were withdrawing; all except for the hundreds of American troops who "were committing suicide at the gates of Baghdad." Then one morning he didn't show up to work. The "Minister of Misinformation" had vanished. When American troops finally arrived in Baghdad in force, they were met with cheering crowds and helped topple statues of Saddam. A cathartic release of more than twenty-five years of oppression erupted in many neighborhoods. The press lauded the armored advance as a brilliant strategy and compared it to Patton's dash across France in 1944.

There were still several sharp skirmishes in and around the capital and battles still raged in the north and west. The war was far from being over, but the issue no longer seemed in doubt, even to the naysayers. More significantly, the United

States made another strike on Saddam and his loyal following. Bunker-buster bombs leveled a residence in the posh al-Mansur neighborhood of Baghdad. Intercepted cell-phone traffic indicated that if Saddam wasn't dead, at least many in the Ba'ath hierarchy *thought* he was dead.

A strike also hit a residence in Basra thought to be shielding a cousin of Saddam, Ali Hassan al-Majid. Known as "Chemical Ali," he was the mastermind of the Iraqi chemical weapons program who murdered thousands of Kurds with nerve gas. Mosul, a key northern city, had fallen to a joint Kurdish/US force after all the Iraqi army officers deserted the city during the night. The remaining conscripts surrendered. Crowds waved American flags and shouted "thank you, Mr. Bush." The fall of Kirkuk was imminent and only Takrit, Saddam's power base, remained as a major Ba'ath-controlled city.

They still had not found definite evidence of weapons of mass destruction. However, lots of other interesting findings *were* discovered: an elementary school turned into a suicide bomb factory, "death books" chronicling the results of Iraqi death squads, treasures stolen from Kuwait, and opulence beyond description found in the dozens of presidential palaces owned by Saddam. What they did not find was definitive proof of WMD. All of the previous reports of WMD had not proven to be correct. The Karbala find of sarin, tabun, and mustard agent had been incorrect. Like the compound Ryan's team had hit, it turned out to be agricultural insecticide. There were new reports in the media but they were not yet verified. Supposedly twenty BM-21 missiles filled with sarin had been found near Baghdad and caches of atropine and 2-PAM auto-injectors used to treat nerve agent had been found, but they were hardly a smoking gun. A top scientific advisor to Saddam, LTG Amer al-Saadi, one of the fifty-five most wanted of the Saddam regime had surrendered. He was the first of the fifty-five on the "most wanted" list whose faces could be found on the special decks of playing cards distributed to the troops. He was maintaining that Iraq had no WMD.

Wearily, Ryan went to find his cot and sleep like the dead. John awakened him the next morning when he sat on the end of Ryan's cot and handed him a cup of steaming coffee.

"What's up? What time is it?"

"It's 0900, what time did you turn in last night?"

"Don't know, about 0430, I think. What's going on?"

"Jake is getting a mission brief. We decided to let you sleep. Looks like we're going out west to a place called al-Qa'im."

"What's there? I'm getting tired of running all over the place on wild goose chases!"

"I don't know yet but it sounds like it might be hot. I talked to the S-2. He said our boy Kemal is a veritable wealth of information although it's a little dated."

"Oh, yeah? Let me get a shower and I'll meet you over at the S-2 shop."

Thirty minutes later, Ryan walked in as the team was studying a map of western Iraq. "So what's the story?"

The S-2 spoke up. "Kemal has given us a real good picture of the Iraqi biological-weapons program. He was only a small cog in a big wheel, but he knows a hell of a lot."

"Anything we can use?"

"Some. We've got a list of names and places. Our intelligence turned out to be pretty good; we bombed a lot of the sites he knew about, but there's one big problem."

"What's that?"

"When Saddam decided to let the weapons inspectors back in, they destroyed a lot of it, shipped some out of the country, probably Syria, and hid a lot more out in the desert where we'd never find it in a million years. Unless . . ."

"Unless we find the people who buried it."

"Exactly! As a result of his information we've expanded our 'most wanted' list, and get this . . . he thinks he knows where a former Soviet scientist *and* Taha are!"

"Doctor Germ herself?"

"Yeah. Kemal delivered stuff to her on a couple of occasions in Baghdad and he thinks he can pinpoint the house. Supposedly, it has an underground bunker and tunnels beneath it. We've got eyes on it now."

"We want in on any raids to snatch them!"

"Talk to your CO, but Colonel Pete already said he wanted your team in on it."

"Oh boy, a chance to finally kick down some doors," John rubbed his hands together.

"Kemal also gave us details about mobile labs that squares with our previous intelligence. Now we just have to find the stuff. This could take months or even years."

"Man, I hope we find something big. The whole morality of this war depends upon it," worried Ryan.

"The morality of the war? Now there's a contradiction in terms," responded John.

"World opinion is really going to be against us if we don't find something soon!"

"Fuck public opinion. We've worried about it for years and look what it's gotten us. Even the French are calling this a great victory," said Jake.

"Yeah, they just want in on the spoils. I say freeze them out. Same thing for the Turks. They lost five billion dollars *and* a say in the post-war reconstruction of this country by not letting the 4th ID attack from their territory. They're worried about the Kurds? Too fucking bad! And the UN can go to hell, too!"

"Come on John, don't sugar coat it; tell us how you really feel," laughed Jake.

"I think we've entered a new era. The US is no longer afraid to launch a preemptive strike to effect regime change or to protect our overseas interests. We also seem to have a new tolerance for casualties, something that has hamstrung foreign policy since Vietnam. What I'm afraid of is a long, protracted engagement over here that might turn *this* into another Vietnam."

"Yeah, there's tolerance as long as a clear-cut victory is in sight!"

"Your country would now seems to have the will and the might to force change abroad. That will not endear you to the rest of the world, I fear," said Kemal.

"*The world will never love us but they will learn to respect us,*" quoted Ryan.

"That's an easy one, Teddy Roosevelt," came a voice from behind.

"Damn," said Ryan as he tried to turn, only to be seized in a vise-like bear hug by the man who had started the quote game that the team constantly played.

"Hi'ya Carrot Top!"

"Mike, Mike Apin! What the fuck are you doing here? You were all blown up," exclaimed Ryan as he extracted himself from his old team sergeant's grip.

"Working for the 'Company,' what else. Because of my wounds, the Army boarded me out. Since I'm semi-fluent in Arabic the Agency was glad to let me join them. I've got my own little paramilitary army . . . mostly Iraqi ex-pats."

"Man, I'm glad to see you! I tried to find out what happened to you but you just seemed to disappear in the medical system. By the time we got back to Campbell, no one seemed to know what happened to you. I thought you were dead. I might have known you were working with the CIA.

"*Rumors of my death were highly exaggerated.*"

"Hah! Even I know that one," said Tom. "Mark Twain."

"Let me introduce you to the guys."

After introducing them over some German "near beers," they discussed the operation and the war.

"So what's your take on all this?" Ryan asked Pete.

"You don't want to *know* my opinion," quipped Pete.

"What do you mean?"

"Sometime when we have a few hours I'll explain it," replied Pete. "*Cry havoc, and let slip the dogs of war!*"

"Shakespeare! *Julius Caesar!*" shot back Ryan.

"You guys better hit the rack, we've got an early day tomorrow."

CHAPTER 54

You cannot qualify war in harsher terms than I will. War is cruelty, and you cannot refine it.

—General William Tecumseh Sherman,
letter to the mayor of Atlanta, 1864

Kirkuk had fallen and the great battle at Tikrit had never materialized; the Iraqi army had seemed to melt away like ghosts in the night, only a single Iraqi Division surrendering. In one of the greatest triumphs of the war, a vanguard of Marines from the 3rd Light Armored Reconnaissance Company freed seven American POWs—five from the 507th Maintenance Support Company and two Apache helicopter pilots. Surrendering Iraqi soldiers who had been abandoned by their officers tipped them off to the POWs' location at Samarra on the road to Tikrit. Why the fleeing Iraqis did not murder them was a mystery.

One by one other individuals from the "deck of 55" were being captured. The Bush Administration suspected that many had fled to Syria, and gave the Syrians stern warnings. In one instance, Special Forces teams in the west intercepted convoys trying to flee to Syria or Jordan and seized a busload of men of military age carrying over $650,000 in US currency. A search of a presidential palace found a shed containing almost $670 million in US currency, while another search revealed almost $200 million sealed in a dog kennel.

In an action that *could* be termed a "smoking gun," a Delta team made a nighttime raid in Baghdad and captured the infamous terrorist, Abu Abbas. This revealed to the world that the Saddam government *was* harboring terrorists. Abbas, whose real name was Mohammed Abu Abbas was the engineer of the *Achille Lauro* hijacking, He was the head of a splinter group of the Palestine Liberation Front that commandeered the ocean liner, and in the process murdered an American Jew, sixty-nine-year-old Leon Klinghoffer. He was shot in front of his wife and pushed, still in his wheelchair, into the Mediterranean.

Intelligence revealed the destination of the hijackers after the Libyans negotiated a settlement. Originally planned as a snatch mission by Delta, it turned into a mid-air interception of the terrorist aircraft by American warplanes and a forced landing at a joint US/Italian NATO airbase. In an effort to avoid a larger international incident than it already was, he was turned over to the

Italian government who, inexplicably, released him. Under pressure from the United States the Italians tried him and sentenced him to life in prison, but it was too late; he was already gone, living in Palestine, momentarily granted amnesty by the Oslo accords. When the accords fell apart he fled to Iraq. He was now in serious trouble, the United States having an old score to settle with him. He and other terrorists, like al-Qaeda suspect, Abu Musab al-Zarqawi, were known to be in Baghdad.

In addition to setting up roadblocks, searching for WMD and terrorists, and advising the Kurds, Special Forces teams were deployed all over the country, securing the areas that had not yet been secured by armed forces. In an unusual marriage of special operations and armor, they sealed roads and avenues of approach with SF teams with four to five US tanks. There were over six hundred Special Forces soldiers, fifty twelve-man A teams from several Special Forces Groups. They had largely won the invisible war in the country. They had few embedded reporters and conducted most of their work in secret, sometimes with local allies like the Kurds, sometimes alone. They were running whole towns and villages, becoming the *de facto* government in many locales. They were very effective in negotiating the surrender of Iraqi units, as they had at Ramadi and Rutba, and in organizing police forces to try and decrease the looting. They were trained for this sort of thing, unlike the conventional "heavy metal" soldiers. With their organic civil-affairs teams they were trying to restore essential services and social order. They did this largely by getting the Iraqis to do it for themselves. They also mediated between rival groups. In the words of one reporter they made themselves appear "ten feet tall."

In the role of mediating between rival groups they met one of their greatest challenges in the Kurdish north. When the Kurds occupied Kirkuk, the Turks, fearing a rise of Kurdish nationalism that would affect their own Kurdish minority, had declared that they might commit their own forces to fight the Kurds. It was only by supplanting the Kurds with the 173rd Airborne that had kept the Turks out of it. Many felt that the Turkish government forfeited any say in the war by not allowing the 4th ID to open a second front from Turkish soil but the concession was made. Trying to keep the Kurds from exacting reprisals against the Arab population was an even harder task.

In another chapter Saddam borrowed from Stalin, a massed forced expulsion of Kurds was practiced as a tool of the Iraqi government to try and disperse the population and curb nationalist feelings. He conducted a brutal campaign of "Arabization" of the north by ethnic cleansing, massacring thousands, and resettling thousands more to the south. Now armed Kurds were taking back the property seized from them, and in the process were expelling whole villages of Arabs. Tensions were high and gun battles occurred; Arab doctors refused to treat Kurds, and vice versa. It reminded the Americans of Bosnia. They were trying to control the anarchy, but years of ill will and blood feuds could not be eliminated in a matter of weeks, or even months.

After the last mission, the team moved to a safe house in downtown Baghdad, a huge walled compound that previously belonged to the head of one of the Iraqi's overlapping security forces. It was left intact with gourmet delicacies in the pantry and a well-stocked liquor cabinet in the study. Thousands of first editions lined the wall in the library and the wine cellar was superb. Gold-plated weapons hung on the wall, as did intricate antique tapestries and expensive artwork. Inlaid Italian marble was everywhere. There was a movie-sized big screen TV and an assortment of thousands of popular DVDs, and while the power might be out in Baghdad, two powerful underground generators powered *this* castle. Even the plumbing was working! The place had to be worth millions. It was a great place to hang out while waiting for the mission, but Kemal was incensed by its lavishness.

"Those bastards lived like *this* while the average Iraqi starved or died for lack of medicines like my mother did," fumed Kemal.

"Yeah, well it's payback time!"

They then filed into the briefing room containing a walnut table that was at least thirty feet long. The troop commander laid out the plan.

"We have it on good intelligence that Doctor Taha and her husband, General Amer al Rashid are there, along with a former Soviet scientist. Rashid was in charge of the Iraqi missile program and the ex-Soviet was a top scientist at Vektor, the massive Soviet biological warfare program. All three are on CENT-COM's most wanted list."

"Now, there's a marriage made in hell," commented Ryan. "I wonder what they did for fun."

"Okay, listen up, and I'll give you the mission template and your individual assignments. H-hour is 0300."

CHAPTER 55

To win victory is easy; to preserve its fruits, difficult. Those who, when the state is in disorder and the people exhausted, stir up trouble and agitate the multitude, cause insurgent wars.

—Sun Tzu,
The Art of War

With Kemal's revelations and those of a few other captured Iraqis, as well as newlyfound buried material, it was obvious to everyone that the only way they were going to crack the code was by capturing the individuals responsible for the programs. Kemal's defection was a small coup, as was the capture of another Iraqi scientist. They were getting a considerable amount of intelligence from this individual. A team from the Mobile Exploitation Task Force, MET Alpha, had identified the existence of the local scientist through documents and interviews, and one of the Delta teams responsible for the chemical side of the house had grabbed him. With his information and other sources, the DIA's Chemical Biological Support Team identified over 150 new sites to be searched. They were bringing two mobile laboratories equipped with millions of dollars of sensitive equipment into the country now that hostilities were almost over.

While the WMD programs had been highly compartmented, and the scientist had only firsthand knowledge of nerve agent production, he was privy to a lot of secondhand intelligence. He told them what they had suspected: the Iraqis had destroyed a good deal of the chemical and biological arsenal in the weeks before the war began. Some of the material was even taken home with them to disperse it and make it harder to find. Much of what they hadn't destroyed had been sent to Syria, as Kemal had suspected. The Iraqis had been working with the Syrians for almost eight years, sending unconventional weapons and technology to their military. Recent intelligence of Syrian chemical weapons tests bore this out. The scientist also told them that there was a rumor that Saddam was working with al-Qaeda.

Four days before President Bush gave Saddam the forty-eight-hour notice to leave Iraq, the Iraqis had apparently set fire to a huge warehouse where most of their biological research and development (R&D) was conducted. Since Desert Storm the Iraqis had geared their chemical and biological work more toward

R&D instead of stockpiling large quantities of weapons. The plan was to be able to gear-up dual-use facilities to produce vast quantities of the agents in a short period of time. He led the teams to a large store of precursor chemicals required to make banned chemical agents, and gave them descriptions of the mobile chemical labs and the locations where he thought they might be buried.

Now Ryan's team was going after the one individual that would know everything about the biological side of the house, Toxic Taha. The team would be split. Ryan and John would be with the front door breaching team while his team sergeant and Tom would be with the rooftop assault team. They would be numbers five and six on the assault team, responsible for taking charge of prisoners and watching the team's back. They would only be carrying handguns so they could handle the prisoners, while the rest of the team carried sound-suppressed submachine guns.

Ryan preferred the 1911A1 Colt .45 caliber automatic to the standard-issue M9 9mm automatic. The .45 had been the old standby of the army for almost a hundred years. It was developed during the Huk Rebellion in the Philippines to stop the doped-up suicidal charges of the natives. The standard .38 caliber handgun proved ineffective, something with more knock-down power was needed. Ryan's father used to say it was like "shooting doorknobs." Ryan remembered putting three rounds from his M16 in the chest of a Somali and the man kept coming, firing his weapon the whole time. They were fatal wounds, but not immediately. The small, high-velocity, metal-jacketed .556 caliber M16 rounds lost little of their kinetic energy going through soft tissue of the chest. Because of this they didn't have a lot of stopping power, while the big, slow .45 caliber APC rounds transferred almost all their energy to the target; you hit it solid and it went down! While there were other .45 caliber weapons that carried more rounds than the eight in the Colt's magazine, Ryan liked the feel of the big auto and he was consistently more accurate with it than any other handgun.

The first four members of the team would act as the standard room-clearing element. Both of the assault teams were veterans from their own troop; hence they were thoroughly comfortable with each other's skills. Success would depend on speed, surprise, and violence. Kemal would be with the front security element and would be brought in when the all clear was given.

A new tool in their already sophisticated arsenal, infrared imagery, indicated that there were three bodies on the first floor and two on the second. The one in the hall on the first floor was undoubtedly a bodyguard, while the other two, it was hoped, were Taha and her spouse. They knew from Kemal that the main apartment was on the first floor in the back, and that was where the infrared signatures were coming from. Of the two on the top floor, it was hoped that one was the Soviet scientist. A platoon of Rangers was to secure the four corners of the building and another element was to watch the back and side doors. Two sniper teams were to assist, one covering the back from a building a block away and the other from a window in a facing building. They had eyes on the target and were ready to engage targets if things went bad.

They approached the residence in two battered Mercedes, while the Rangers arrived in HMMWVs a few minutes later. The streets were spooky, with no street lights, and as they passed one corner where an armed group of men eyed them warily. There was no telling if they were bandits, vigilantes, or former Iraqi soldiers, and a tense few seconds passed. Ryan could see them walk into the street behind them, but they scattered quickly when they saw the blacked-out HMMWVs following them. They parked around the corner and threw a Kevlar blanket over the glass-studded wall as they scampered over. Their night-vision goggles were set in the passive mode so they would not emit even invisible light. The goggles turned pitch dark into a green twilight. They made their way quickly and quietly over to the main door where a breaching charge of C4 was tamped in such a manner that the door would blow inward. They had practiced this dozens, if not hundreds of times in the shooting house, but this time it was for real!

Static crackled in Ryan's headset.

"Germ Killer 1, all clear." The first sniper team checked in.

"Germ Killer 2, all clear."

"Dragonfly, inbound."

"Get Ready!"

The Black Hawk swept in low over the rooftop and hovered while the fast-rope was dropped and the assault team slid down. It only took a few seconds. As the first man touched down, the front door breaching team went into action.

"Five . . . four . . . three . . . two . . . one . . . EXECUTE! EXECUTE! EXECUTE!"

The door blew inward with a deafening blast and the stacked team went into action. The first man crossed left to the long or "heavy side" of the door, moving down the wall looking for targets to engage in the corner first and then making the turn, clearing out the other corner. The second man crossed to the right side, passing through the "cone of death" (the doorway) in a split second and repeated the corner-clearing maneuver as he moved along one wall and then the other. In the peripheral vision of his night vision goggles, he caught the movement of the surprised guard who had been sleeping in a chair at the foot of the stairway. It took all his training to ignore the man making sure he cleared his corners; the target was the responsibility of the men behind him. The third man moved in the footsteps of the first, but his responsibility was the right center of the room. The noise and movement had surprised the guard, and he was confused by the shadowy figures moving rapidly in opposite directions. He stood and raised his weapon, but two rounds from a silenced Heckler and Koch MP-5 caught him in the forehead before he could aim; the noise from the weapon no louder that the "smack" of the bullets hitting his skull. It all happened in a fraction of a second, the instinctive shooting techniques that Delta hammered into them taking over. The guard just starting to topple over backward when two more rounds from the fourth man, also clearing center to the left, hit him in the chest. It seemed deliberate and slow but was over in a second.

"Clear, Search!"

The guard was dead before he was halfway to the floor. Although it was SOP to clear the rooms in the order they came, they bypassed the meeting room on the left, since the imagery indicated that it was empty, and moved past the kitchen to the apartment. Ryan followed covering the open doorways behind the team while John watched the stairway and their backs. Before entering the apartment, the team leader threw in a flash-bang grenade. It would blind and stun anyone in the room. The room was empty and they moved quickly to the sleeping chamber. Disturbed by the noise, but blind because of the instant hot white light of a second grenade, the two individuals stood like deer caught in headlights as they were thrown to the ground and flex-cuffed.

A similar episode occurred upstairs, the roof door being splintered by a ram. The team spilled through the narrow, winding stairway into a large room just in time to see a second unarmed bodyguard fly down the main stairway.

"Bad guy coming down!"

"Got him," John whispered into the headset on his ballistic helmet just before he pistol-whipped the unsuspecting guard as he reached the foot of the darkened stairs.

They cleared a second upstairs bedroom and Jake cuffed the third suspect. The rest of the house was empty. They brought the suspects and sat them down in the main hallway.

"All clear!"

The support team came in with Kemal and they started a search. A secret panel in the basement study revealed a set of stairs and a cleverly constructed bunker with bunk beds, a refrigerator, tables and chairs, lots of storage space, even a TV, but no evidence of WMD. There was evidence of recent habitation but they couldn't determine how recent. There was a tunnel going into the alley half a block away. None of the security people saw anything and they hoped no one escaped. The study contained several filing cabinets of material and they were taken along with two computers for analysis. They found a barrel safe built into the floor of a closet and called for a team to drill it, not wanting to risk damaging it contents by blowing it with explosives. Unfortunately, none of the suspects turned out to be the three they were searching for, although Kemal recognized one of them as a high-level bureaucrat in the biological-weapons program. They left a team to guard the facility and do a second search. They took all the prisoners for interrogation.

They conducted a debrief and post-mission analysis and concluded that, given the circumstances, it went as well as could be expected. The materials and the one individual looked promising and would hopefully lead them to banned weapons.

CHAPTER 56

If the United States means it about sticking around and helping Iraq become the standard bearer for positive change in a malevolent region, the coming peace will be arduous and time-consuming. It will also be dangerous. The war to dislodge Saddam from Kuwait had little to teach us about what the United States is now undertaking.

—Bill Powell,
Fortune, March 17, 2003

They were pulling the plug on Ryan's Iraq mission. President Bush had made an announcement indicating the end of hostilities. The Second Gulf War seemed to be winding down and dozens of NBC teams were scouring Iraq for banned weapons. As a final task, they sent Ryan's team to provide security and to help search the crowd for potential war criminals at the first of the Iraqi reconstruction meetings going on south of Nasiriyah, at Tallil Airbase, near the ancient city of Ur. Mike's CIA counterinsurgency team was also going to look for feyadeen, committed Ba'athists, and others trying to disrupt or muscle in on the meeting. Ryan's team was also there to coordinate with an exploitation team searching the Khamisiyah weapons depot, a site destroyed by the 82nd Airborne engineers during Desert Storm. The engineers had destroyed the depot with explosives, not realizing chemical weapons were stored there and had inadvertently exposed hundreds of US troops to traces of nerve agent. At least some of the cases of Gulf War Syndrome were attributed to this exposure. Ryan's father and Chuck Rogers, Ryan's captain from Afghanistan, had been among them. He remembered his father's pictures and Chuck telling him about the Tallil Airbase seizure and Ur.

The conference had been largely symbolic and had accomplished little, but it was a start. After a survey of the site, which, like all the other suspected sites, was going to require weeks of searching, they went on what Jack referred to as "armed tourism," to the archeological digs of the ancient city of Ur. By some accounts it was the oldest city on earth, the birthplace of the biblical Abraham. As they were walking around the ruins, an old, white-haired Arab approached them.

"Would you like the tour?" he inquired in a beautifully clipped British accent.

"Sure. Who are you?" asked Ryan.

"My name is Doctor Amer. I am, I was, the curator of this city."

"How long have you been giving these tours?" Ryan remembered Chuck had come for a tour with the SF guys (one being his dad) and some reporters just after the cease-fire in 1991, a ballsy maneuver considering it had been well outside the 82nd Airborne's zone of control.

"Almost thirty years!"

"You recollect taking a bunch of Americans for a tour right after the last war?"

"I could not forget. They were the last Americans I have seen in the past twelve years. One, a major, gave me an American twenty-dollar bill for the tour."

"Well, I'll be damned! That was CPT Rogers and his crew," Ryan responded. "That major was my father. I remembering him telling me the story."

Kemal looked at Ryan with a funny expression on his face. "Your father was here at Tallil in 1991?"

"Yeah, why?"

"He was a Special Forces major with a mustache?"

"He always wore one."

"He saved my life! I can't believe it. You are his son. Allah is truly great!"

"He certainly works in mysterious ways . . . what a coincidence!"

Their guide interrupted. "Let me thank you for getting rid of Saddam. He was a butcher and his only interest in this site or any history was to twist it and resurrect himself and his Ba'ath party as the mythical ruler of Arabia, like the Nazis being Aryan."

They went on the tour. Considering the historical importance of the city, the excavations and restoration seemed amateurish and perfunctory. That was what happened in a seemingly poor country that had largely shut out the West. When the tour was done, Ryan gave the man a hundred-dollar bill which he was thanked solemnly for, and they sat on a stone wall at the entrance to the city. Ryan collected a small piece of brick with hieroglyphics from the city to give to Delta's chaplain.

"Shit, it's getting hot," John said, mopping his brow.

"Yeah, it's good we got the war over with when we did. The next few months would have been a bitch to fight in."

"Being in a MOPP suit in this type of weather is like being in a steam bath, a sure recipe for heat exhaustion."

"It's not even summer yet. I, for one, am glad to be going somewhere else," said John.

"Yeah, to some *other* hellhole to fight terrorists."

"America will never have peace until the Palestinian issue is settled. The Islamic countries look at the US as a great Satan, doing the work of the Zionists," said Kemal. "The Jewish lobby is too strong in your country. The attacks on 9-11 were in direct response to Americas support for Israel! You must force the Israelis to give the Palestinians a homeland."

Ryan looked thoughtful. "It's not that simple, we have to pressure both the Israelis *and* the Palestinians to make an accord that sticks. They are both going to have to make big compromises. After we're done with all this, maybe we can broker a deal. The Palestinians deserve a homeland just like anyone else, but they've got to stop the terrorism."

"One man's terrorist is another man's freedom fighter," Mike quipped. "The Israelis founded their state by using terrorism against the British. Sometimes it seems that they have forgotten that."

"Well, ultimately, international terrorism has to be solved by diplomacy, not military action."

"Kemal, why do you think Saddam never employed his chemical or biological weapons against us? He had nothing to lose! We had intelligence that he was formulating a doomsday scenario. I can't figure out why he didn't use the stuff."

"I think he was killed or wounded in that first strike," said John.

"I think he had destroyed or hidden most of it from the inspectors and just couldn't deploy it in time. Besides, I don't think he really thought that you would come."

"How could he think that?" asked John.

"Same reason he didn't think we'd come during Desert Storm?"

"He didn't *want* to believe it. He thought he could fool the world. He was a megalomaniac and his inner circle always told him what he wanted to hear. If they didn't, they wound up dead. He thought his weapons would eventually make him and Iraq the master of the Arab world and allow him to destroy Israel. He wanted to be a modern day Nebuchadrezzar II! No, he thought if he *willed* it you would not come," responded Mike.

"I still don't understand it. All he had to do was give up the WMD and he could have remained the ruler of Iraq until he died," said Jake.

"Maybe he *did* give it all up," responded Mike. "Maybe we're not going to find anything."

"He would rather die than give into American will," retorted Kemal.

"He's going to get his wish!"

"So Jack, what's your opinion of all this?" Ryan asked.

"I think it was a major mistake to invade Iraq . . . at least when we did it."

"Why do you say that?"

"Because we've left Afghanistan unfinished and we're denying valuable assets from that operation so we can do Iraq. That is a big mistake. We're going to be in Afghanistan for years and now we're stuck in Iraq as well."

"But they say we're going to be out of here in two or three years."

"Bullshit. We'll be here for ten years, and it probably will still go to shit. In the process we'll have spent billions of dollars and lost thousands of our troops. This is looking way too much like a repeat of Vietnam to me. That's the trouble with you young guys . . . you don't remember what Vietnam was like."

"Now you sound like my father," Ryan retorted.

"We came here with way too few troops to control the borders or provide security and rebuild the country and now we're going to pay the price for it. This is going to degenerate into an insurgency against us and probably civil war between the Shiites, Sunnis, and the Kurds. Iran and Syria are going to meddle as much as possible, and a call for jihad will go out across Islamic countries. On top of all this we're somehow not supposed to be an occupying force and we're going to instill our idea of a democratic government on a people that, even under the best of circumstances, probably will not be able to make it work. Arrogance of power!"

"Wow, Top, come up for a breather," Ryan said. "It can't be as bad as all that!"

"I think you're exaggerating," John said. "I mean, we saved these people from a cruel dictator . . . we've given them their freedom."

"Well, I hope I'm wrong, but I guess time will tell. Anyway . . . you asked."

Ryan laughed, "Still giving lectures, professor."

"Kemal, we're going to be heading out as soon as we get back. You said you wanted to go back to the States and finish your schooling. I can fix that up with the State Department, I think. You've been such a big help, I know we can get you some money."

Kemal was silent for a long time. "Come with me Ryan, Mr. Apin, I want to show you something," he said as he headed for the great ziggurat pyramid that loomed over them. At the foot of the steps was a sign in Arabic and English that forbade taking photographs from the top, presumably because of the sprawling Tallil Airbase just to the south. Ryan went back to the vehicle and got his camera. As they climbed to the top of the ancient pyramid, the vast expanse of the desert and the Euphrates River swept before them.

Kemal pointed to the east, "That is the great city of Ur, birthplace of Abraham, revered in Christianity, Islam, and Judaism. We all share the same God, Allah." He pointed to the river, sweeping his arm northward.

"This Ziggurat was part of the ancient Babylonian capital, centuries before Christ. This is the Fertile Crescent of Mesopotamia, between the Tigris and Euphrates Rivers, where civilization began. This is the land of the Old Testament where Eve fed the forbidden fruit to Adam and where men built the Tower of Babel, which so alarmed God that he created languages. It was the home of the Sumerians, Akkadians, and the Assyrians. Writing, the wheel, irrigation, and the laws of man were first developed here. I hope now that Saddam is gone that it can once again be a great country! Do you think the Americans can turn Iraq into a democracy?"

"I don't see why not," said John. "Look what we've done in Afghanistan."

"Afghanistan has a long way to go," Mike warned.

"But we have such divisiveness in the country, Sunni Moslems against Shi'ites, Kurds against Arabs. I don't see how we can ever hold it together without a strong dictator."

"That's true, look what happened to Yugoslavia after Tito or the Soviet Union, when it all came apart," Jake put in. "One thing we've *got* to do is disarm the population. We didn't do it in Somalia and look what happened."

"What, gun control?"

"Where I come from 'gun control' means hitting the target with your first shot," said Tom.

"Listen, Iraq should be easy compared to Afghanistan. We could never have disarmament there. In addition, they have seventeen different ethnic groups, a dozen languages, and Kabul has *never* controlled the countryside. It's always been a loose conglomeration of rival warlords. For the moment, at least, it seems pretty stable."

John laughed. "Yeah, until we pull out. Besides, if Afghanistan goes all to hell it's really no big deal as long as it doesn't become a breeding ground for terrorists again. Iraq is different. It's the key to the Middle East and it has *oil*!"

"Reconstruction is going to be long and difficult," said Mike. "But look what the Marshall Plan did for Europe, post WWII. Look at Germany and Japan today. They're probably better off than if they had *won* the war. Hopefully, we won't screw this up like we did in Haiti."

Kemal added, "History is against us here. Iraq wasn't even a country before WWI. The British just carved up Arabia from the Ottoman Empire and formed Iraq as a protectorate under the leadership of the king, but it wasn't free. The British double-crossed the Arabs; they never meant to give us freedom."

Ryan thought about it for a moment. "Kemal, why have the Arabs never been able to unite? They sometimes seem so self-destructive. Look at all the looting and destruction in Baghdad and Basra. They are ruining their own country. They remind me of the Somalis in a lot of ways."

"I know. Sometimes it's even hard for me to understand. I think some of it is only natural, a response to the years of oppression. They want to destroy everything Saddam and the Ba'ath party stood for, but many of them are just bandits. The people have been so poor since the last war."

"Where do you go from here?" asked Kemal. "Are you going to stay in the army, Ryan?"

"I don't know, I'm getting a little tired of all this. I'm going to finish out my tour with Delta and then I may go back to school. I won't have enough years for retirement for awhile, but I'd like to get my doctorate in history. Maybe teach college."

"Shit. You'd *miss* all this too much," John said, laughing, as he made a sweeping gesture across the horizon.

"*It is well that war is so terrible, least we grow too fond of it,*" murmured Mike.

"What was that?" John asked. "Repeat that, it's on the tip of my tongue."

"Robert E. Lee, right?" asked Kemal.

"How the *hell* did you know *that*?" demanded John.

"I used to read a lot."

"I *would* miss the Army," mused Ryan "but there's a really good National Guard SF unit in Newport, Rhode Island, A Company, 2nd Battalion, 19th Special Forces Group (Airborne). There's also a 20th Group Company in Springfield, Mass. I'm sure they could use an XO on either the scuba or halo team. I went to scuba school with a couple of the guys from the 20th and we worked with some of the 19th Group guys in Afghanistan. They were really squared away. I think that would keep me from missing it too much. Besides, that way I could still get retirement pay someday."

"So what are you going to do, Kemal?" asked Jake. "If you want to come back to the States and go to medical school, I'm sure we can fix it with the State Department and I *know* we can get you some money."

Kemal looked out on the barren vista for a long time before he answered. "This is my home. I can't leave. I'm going to stay and help rebuild Iraq."

"I can understand why you want to stay. A doctor from Johns Hopkins is coming in to be the new interim Minister of Health. I'm sure we can get you a job in his administration."

Kemal looked out to the west past the great Euphrates. The sun was setting, a giant orange orb on a sea of khaki ocean, broken by a ribbon of blue and green, long shadows casting over the sand dunes still shimmering like waves with the day's heat. Two large tears rolled down Kemal's cheeks. For the first time since he was a child, they were tears of joy.

Epilogue

Ryan's troop traveled back to Ft. Bragg, North Carolina, in civilian clothes and carrying nonmilitary bags instead of the aviator kit bags, duffle bags, and rucksacks that soldiers normally carried. Each had two large civilian scuba-diver bags, and the team carried a large locked chest labeled "scuba-diving equipment." The bags contained their field gear and the box was filled with weapons. One of the team personally accompanied the box, with the approval of airport security, to see that it was loaded on the commercial airliner. They had long hair, some had goatees, and they looked distinctly unmilitary; more like the marine salvage divers they were purporting to be.

After several days of leave they reported back to Bragg. Following a week of briefings, isolation planning, and refitting they loaded on the doublewide C-5A Aircraft at the Pope AFB along with two special operations Black Hawk helicopters and four full crews from the 160th SOAR. As they closed the huge nose ramp, an old "Jody" running cadence went through Ryan's head:

C-130 rolling down the strip,
Airborne daddy on a one-way trip,
Mission classified, destination unknown,
Don't know if we're coming home!

They had a new mission in a new place, the next target in the secret war on terrorism.

Taps

O it's Tommy this, an' Tommy that, an' "Tommy, go away";
But it's "Thank you, Mister Atkins," when the band begins to play—
The band begins to play, my boys, the band begins to play,
O it's "Thank you, Mister Atkins," when the band begins to play.

Yes, makin' mock o'uniforms that guard you while you sleep,
Is cheaper than them uniforms, an' they're starvation cheap;
An' hustlin' drunken soldiers when they're goin' large a bit,
Is five times better business than paradin' in full kit.

Then it's Tommy this, an' Tommy that, an' "Tommy, 'ow's yer soul?"
But it's "Thin red line of 'eroes" when the drums begin to roll—
The drums begin to roll, my boys, the drums begin to roll,
O it's "Thin red line of 'eroes" when the drums begin to roll.

You talk o' better food for us, an' schools, an' fires, an' all;
We'll wait for extry rations if you treat us rational,
Don't mess about the cook-room slops, but prove it to our face,
The Widow's Uniform is not the soldier-man's disgrace.

An' it's Tommy this, and Tommy that, an' "Chuck him out the brute,"
But it's "Savior of 'is country" when the guns begin to shoot;

—Rudyard Kipling,
"Tommy"

Military Glossary

ABN	Airborne
AC-130	Armed Version of C-130
AIT	Advanced Individual Training
AK-47	Communist Assault Rifle
AMF	Afghan Military Forces
AMS	Acute Mountain Sickness
ANGRC-74	74 Model Radio
APC	Armored Personnel Carrier
ARVN	Army Republic of Vietnam
ASA	Army Security Agency
AWOL	Absent Without Leave
BDU	Battle Dress Uniform
Bde	Brigade
Bn	Battalion
BUDS	Basic Underwater Demolition/Seal Training
BW	Biologic Warfare
C-130	Hercules 4 Engine Cargo Aircraft
CA	Civil Affairs
CAS	Close Air Support
CASEVAC	Causality Evacuation, MEDEVAC
CAT	Civil Affairs Team
CDQC	Combat Diver Qualification Course
CENTCOM	Central Command
CH-47	Twin Rotor Cargo Helicopter
CI	Counter Intelligence
CIA	Central Intelligence Agency
CIB	Combat Infantry Badge
CIDG	Civilian Irregular Defense Group
CMB	Combat Medical Badge
Co	Company

CO	Commanding Officer
COA	Course of Action
COMSEC	Communications Security
CPT	Captain
CSAR	Combat Search and Rescue
CSM	Command Sergeant Major (E9)
CW2	Chief Warrant Officer-Two
DA	Direct Action
DCU	Desert Uniform
DI	Drill Sergeant
DIA	Defense Intelligence Agency
DOD	Department of Defense
DZ	Drop Zone
ELINT	Electronic Intelligence
EOB	Electronic Order of Battle
EPW	Enemy Prisoner of War
EW	Electronic Warfare
FID	Foreign Internal Defense
FOB	Forward Operating Base
G	Guerrilla
GEN	General, 4 Stars
HALO	High Altitude Low Opening
HQ	Headquarters
IAD	Immediate Action Drill
IAEA	International Atomic Energy Agency
IAEC	Iraqi Atomic Energy Council
ID	(3rd) Infantry Division
ISOFAC	Isolation Facility
IV	Intravenous Fluids
JCET	Joint Training Exercise
JDAM	Joint Direct Attack Munition-Smart Bomb

JSOC	Joint Special Operations Command
JSOTF	Joint Special Operations Task Force
LBE	Load Bearing Equipment
LLBD	South Vietnamese Special Forces
LP/OP	Listening Post/Observation Post
LT	Lieutenant
LTC	Lieutenant Colonel
LZ	Landing Zone
M4	Special Operations M-16
M24	Sniper Weapon System
MACV-SOG	Military Advisory Command Vietnam- Studies and Observation Group
MAJ	Major
MEDEVAC	Medical Evacuation
MFF	Military Freefall
MH-47	Special Operations Version of CH-47
MOPP	Mission Oriented Protective Posture; chemical protection equipment/suit
MOS	Military Occupation Specialty
MOUT	Military Operations Urban Terrain
MP	Military Police
MRE	Meal Ready to Eat, Standard Army Ration
MSG	Master Sergeant (E8)
MSR	Main Supply Route
NBC	Nuclear Biological Chemical Warfare
NCO	Non-Commissioned Officer
NCOIC	Non-Commissioned Officer In Charge
ODA	Operational Detachment Alpha, A Team
ODB	Operational Detachment Bravo, B Team
ODC	Operational Detachment Charlie, C Team
OGA	Other Government Agency
OPCEN	Operations Center
PIR	Parachute Infantry Regiment

PRC-25	25 Model Radio
PSYOPS	Psychological Operations
QRF	Quick Response Force
RDF	Radio Direction Finding
REMF	Rear Echelon Mother Fucker
RON	Remain Over Night
RPG	Rocket Propelled Grenade
R&R	Rest and Recreation
S-1	Personnel
S-2	Intelligence
S-3	Operations
S-4	Logistics
SAS	Special Air Service
SAW	Squad Automatic Weapon
SERE	Survival Evasion Resistance & Escape
SFAS	Special Forces Assessment and Selection
SFC	Sergeant First Class (E7)
SFOB	Special Forces Operating Base
SFQC	Special Force Qualification Course
SGM	Sergeant Major
SIGNET	Signal Intercept
SIGOB	Signal Order of Battle
SOAR (160th)	160th Special Operations Aviation Regiment
SOG	Studies and Observation Group
SOP	Standing Operating Procedure
SSE	Sensitive Site Exploitation
SSG	Staff Sergeant (E7)
SWC	Special Warfare School (JFK)
TAC-P	Tactical Air Controller
TDL	Tactical Laser Designator
TOC	Tactical Operations Center
UH-1B	Utility Helicopter—Bravo, Huey
UNSCOM	United Nations Special Commission on Iraq

USASOC	United States Army Special Operations Command
USSF	United States Special Forces
USSOCOM	United States Special Operations Command
UW	Unconventional Warfare
VC	Viet Cong
WMD	Weapons of Mass Destruction
XO	Executive Officer

Additional Reading

Vietnam

John Stevens Barry, *Those Gallant Men*, Presidio Press, Novato, CA, 1984.

George Dooley, *Battle for the Central Highlands: A Special Forces Story*, Galantine Books, New York, 2000.

David Halberstam, *The Best and the Brightest*, Fawcett Crest, New York, 1969.

Robin Moore, *The Green Berets*, Avon Books, New York, 1965.

Neil Sheehan, *A Bright Shining Lie: John Paul Vann and America in Vietnam*, Random House, New York, 1988.

Shelby L. Stanton, *Green Berets at War: U.S. Army Special Forces in Asia, 1956–1975*, Ivy Books, New York, 1985.

Leigh Wade, *Assault on Dak Pek: A Special Forces A-Team in Combat, 1970*, Ballantine Books, New York, 1998.

The Gulf War

Samir al-Khlil, *Republic of Fear: The Inside Story of Saddam's Iraq*, Pantheon Books, New York, 1989.

Judith Miller and Laurie Mylroie, *Saddam Hussein and the Crisis in the Gulf*, Random House, 1990.

Joel Nadel with J. R. Wright, *Special Men and Special Missions: Inside American Special Forces Operations, 1945 to Present*, Stackpole Books, Pennsylvania, 1994.

Somalia

Mark Bowden, *Black Hawk Down: A Story of Modern War*, Atlantic Monthly Press, New York, 2001.

Kent DeLong and Steven Tuckey, *Mogadishu: Heroism and Tragedy*, Praeger, Westport, CT, 1994.

John Hillen, *Blue Helmets: The Strategy of UN Military Operations*, Brassey's, Washington, DC, 1998.

Scott Peterson, *Me Against My Brother: At War in Somalia, Sudan, and Rwanda*, Routledge, New York, 2000.

Martin Stanton, *Somalia on $5 a Day: A Soldier's Story*, Presidio Press, Novato, CA, 2001.

Afghanistan

John K. Cooley, *Unholy Wars: Afghanistan, America, and International Terrorism*, Pluto Press, London, 1999.

Peter Hopkirk, *The Great Game: The Struggle for Empire in Central Asia*, Kodansha Globe, London, 1990.

Robert D. Kaplan, *Soldiers of God: With Islamic Warriors in Afghanistan and Pakistan*, Random House, New York, 2000.

Rudyard Kipling, *Kim*, Oxford University Press, Oxford, UK, 1987.

Patrick McRory, *Retreat From Kabul: The Catastrophic British Defeat in Afghanistan, 1842*, Lyons Press, CT, 2002.

Karl E. Meyer and Shareen Blair Brysac, *Tournament of Shadows: The Great Game and the Race for Empire in Central Asia*, Counterpoint Press, Washington, DC, 1999.

Robin Moore, *Task Force Dagger: The True Story of the Army Green Berets and the First Six Months in Pursuit of Osama bin Laden*, Random House, New York, 2003.

Stephen Tanner, *Afghanistan: A Military History from Alexander the Great to the Fall of the Taliban*, DaCapo Press, New York, 2002.

Iraq

Laurie Mylroie, *Study of Revenge: The First World Trade Center Attack and Saddam Hussein's War Against America*, AEI Press, Washington, DC, 2001.

Tom Mangold and Jeff Goldberg, *Plague Wars: The Terrifying Reality of Biological Warfare*, St. Martin's Press, New York, 1999.

Michael T. Osterholm, MPH and John Schwartz, *Living Terrors: What America Needs to Know to Survive the Coming Bioterrorist Catastrophe*, Delacort Press, New York, 2000.

Ken Alibek and Stephen Handelmar, *Biohazard: The Chilling Tru Story of the Largest Covert Biological Weapons Program in the World—Told from Inside by the Man Who Ran It*, Random House, New York, 1999.

Bruce W. Watson, *Military Lessons of the Gulf War*, Greenhill Books, CA, 1991.

Eric L. Haney, *Inside Delta Force*, Delacorte Press, New York, 2002.

COL Charles A. Beckwith and Donald Cot, *Delta Force: The Story of America's Elite Counterterrorist Unit*, Avon Books, New York, 1983.

Turi Munthe, *The Saddam Hussein Reader*, Thunder's Mouth Press, New York, 2002.

Acknowledgements

Thanks to the great soldiers and leaders I have had the opportunity to serve with over the years, who taught me what it was to be a soldier and an officer. It is hard to give credit to all of them. Here are but a few: King Davis, Glenn Hale, Charlie Johnson, Al Moloff, Chuck Sellers, Mike McIntyre, Bob Larue, Dick Potter, Ken Getty, Bob Hoaglund, Rich Burmeister, Tim Haake, Mike Hubbard, Pete McDermott, Rocky Farr, Dalton Diamond, Dave Ferris, Tim Sherwood, Mark Rosengard, John Mulholland, Frank Hudson, Dave Fox, John Hillen, Tim Connelly, Chris Carney, Wiley Jones, Preston Pegram, and a bevy of others from the 82nd Airborne Division, the 3rd, 5th, 7th, 10th, 11th, and 19th Special Forces Groups, the 450th CA Bn (ABN), 404th CA Bn (FID/UW), and the 96th CA Bn, all of whom I have had the pleasure to serve with. Thanks to John Vartanian for a memorable "dance in the sky" and the men of CAT-56, Kent, Mark, and Kevin, my "team" in Afghanistan, and my guys from Task Force PSYOPS in Iraq. Special thanks to the guys on the scuba teams with A/1/11 and A/2/19 for letting me be the "junior medic" on the teams for so many years.

I would like to thank Professor Julie Aparin who helped during the early stages of my writing and her husband, Pete; my Special Forces partner on many a mission to exotic, far off places. I would especially like to thank my coauthor Robin Moore, as well as Dr. Will Brownell, two fine authors, who helped me clarify many historical points and put the manuscript in a publishable format, and my son Brad, a budding historian, and my research assistant for the book.

Lastly, I would like to thank my wife of thirty-three years and my other son Ryan, a 1LT with the 3rd Brigade Combat Team, 82nd Airborne Division, Tikrit, Iraq, who put up with my adventurism and absence all these years.

De Opresso Liber.